4/23

PRAISE FOR S

P9-BXX-603
A 2180 267103 0

"A fast-paced tale of piracy among the stars. Featuring a winning cast of misfits who stumble into unexpected kinship, Anderson employs warm humor and pop-culture references to ground the narrative against cosmic-level stakes and underlying commentary about exploitation and the cost of war."

—PUBLISHERS WEEKLY

"*The Mandalorian* meets *Guardians of the Galaxy* in this fast-paced space adventure that will have readers turning the pages as they are pulled into a unique yet strangely familiar world that reflects our own. An ideal pick for middle-grade sci-fi fans."

—ALA *BOOKLIST* (STARRED REVIEW)

"Plentiful references to pop-culture touchstones like Ziggy Stardust and Pokémon give this space opera a lived-in feel. Leo's narration aches with pathos but also provides moments of humor and finally ends on a cliff-hanger. A heartfelt adventure."

—KIRKUS REVIEWS

"Leaves readers eager for a sequel."

—THE HORN BOOK

you can RENEW this item from home by visiting our Website at www.woodbridge.lioninc.org or by calling (203) 389-3433

ALSO BY JOHN DAVID ANDERSON

Riley's Ghost

One Last Shot

Finding Orion

Granted

Posted

Ms. Bixby's Last Day

The Dungeoneers

Minion

Sidekicked

JOHN DAVID ANDERSON

STOWAWAY

BOOK ONE OF
THE *ICARUS* CHRONICLES

WALDEN POND PRESS
An Imprint of HarperCollinsPublishers

Walden Pond Press is an imprint of HarperCollins Publishers.

Stowaway
Copyright © 2021 by John David Anderson
All rights reserved. Printed in the United States of America.
No part of this book may be used or reproduced in any manner whatsoever
without written permission except in the case of brief quotations embodied
in critical articles and reviews. For information address HarperCollins
Children's Books, a division of HarperCollins Publishers, 195 Broadway,
New York, NY 10007.
www.harpercollinschildrens.com

Library of Congress Control Number: 2020952900
ISBN 978-0-06-298595-8

Typography by David DeWitt
22 23 24 25 26   PC/BRR   10 9 8 7 6 5 4 3 2 1
❖
First paperback edition, 2022

To Mom. Miss you.

STOWAWAY

Our posturings, our imagined self-importance, the delusion that we have some privileged position in the Universe, are challenged by this point of pale light. Our planet is a lonely speck in the great enveloping cosmic dark. In our obscurity, in all this vastness, there is no hint that help will come from elsewhere to save us from ourselves.

—*Carl Sagan*, Pale Blue Dot: A Vision of the Human Future in Space, *1994*

Never judge a planet by its crust.

—*Aykarian proverb*

PROLOGUE

CHASING GHOSTS

THEY WERE PLAYING TAG WHEN THE FIRST TORPEDO HIT.

In the narrow hallways of the crew quarters, the clomping of their standard-issue Coalition boots echoing down the corridors. Gareth chasing Leo, gaining, cornering him at a dead end, reaching out to make the tag.

Only to find his hand pass right through his brother's chest. Hologram. Again.

"Cheater!"

The holo flickered, the prerecorded video of a sprinting Leo finally timing out, the illusion dissolving into pixelated bits. Leo laughed, and Gareth turned to see his brother in the flesh, standing right behind him.

A moment's hesitation, muscles tensing, traded smiles. The one saying, *You'll pay for that*. The other: *You'll have to catch me first.* Then Leo turned and bolted back the way he came, Gareth launching himself in pursuit.

Leo knew there was no way he could outrun his older brother; Gareth had been a middle school track star back on Earth, now a tall, wiry seventeen-year-old. It wasn't a matter of winning for Leo. It was a matter of holding out as long as possible. A question of survival. They'd played this game a hundred times before.

He turned a corner, headed toward the commissary, conscious of Gareth's feet pounding on the steel grating. Louder. Closer. Maybe if he could make it to the door he could duck inside, find somewhere to hide, delay the inevitable.

But he wasn't fast enough. Gareth's hand whipped out, grabbing Leo by the shoulder, not so much tagging him as lassoing him, pulling him to a stop.

"Gotcha."

Leo spun around, hands on his knees, sucking in recycled air.

"You okay?"

"Fine," Leo huffed. "Just . . . catching . . . my breath."

"You cheated again. I told you you aren't allowed to use that thing."

That thing was Leo's watch. A gift his parents had given him years ago. A hybrid of human and Aykari technology—like so many things nowadays—it could be used as a data viewer and a communicator. It kept track of his vitals (his heartbeat was currently 142 beats per minute). It could tell you where it parked your car. Almost incidentally, it told time.

But the watch's most advanced feature was its miniaturized holographic generator, capable of creating three-dimensional projections of prerecorded vids. Like the one of Leo running, recorded with the express purpose of fooling his brother in games of tag or hide-and-go-seek. The projections looked real enough until you got up close and could start to make out the digital imperfections. Their parents had given Gareth the same watch, but he'd lost his long ago, left somewhere in the house they grew up in. On the planet they'd left behind.

"Dad says technology is the tool that allows us to overcome our limitations and sets us free," Leo reminded his brother.

"Except you're not free. I still caught you."

"Because your legs are twice as long as mine."

An exaggeration. At one time it might have been true, but a couple of growth spurts since they'd come on board and Leo was no longer the scrawny runt whose head fit underneath Gareth's armpit. Not so easy to boss around, though Gareth could still wrestle him to the ground and rip the watch from his wrist if he wanted. Not that he would. Leo knew Gareth would never hurt him; he just wanted to give Leo a hard time. That's what big brothers were for. . . . That and pretty much everything else. Especially out here, on this ship, where Gareth was the only real friend he had.

Besides, as long as they played nice, their father wouldn't interrupt to badger them about their studies. As important as it was to Calvin Fender that his two sons learn how to balance chemical equations or calculate the masses of nearby stars, it was more important that they got along. And chasing each other around the *Beagle* was always preferable to reading a chapter of galactic history.

Leo's breathing finally evened out. He brushed the brown mop out of his eyes, his bangs hanging like curtains, in sore need of a trim. The *Beagle* didn't have a barbershop, just Leo's father, whose DIY haircuts often resulted in disaster. Cosmetology was one of the few things his father wasn't good at.

"You have to give me at least a ten-second head start," Leo said. "And you have to count loud so I know when you go."

"Fine. Ten seconds. But seriously, no more cheating. If I catch you—"

"You won't," Leo shot back with mock confidence.

"Right."

Leo coiled, ready to sprint down the corridor as soon as his brother started counting. But Gareth never even made it to *one*.

The explosion nearly threw them off their feet as the *Beagle* lurched sideways. The steel beams shuddered. Leo's ears rang. The lights blinked off, on, then off again, triggering the fluorescent yellow emergency lighting that ran along the floor. Leo put a hand on the wall to steady himself. His brother's eyes shone like moons. "What was that?"

The question was answered with a second explosion, the ship quaking again. Every alarm screamed at once. Leo stumbled, falling into his brother's ready arms. From down the corridor he could hear the crew of the *Beagle* shouting to one another, though it was impossible to make out what they were saying. It was impossible to hear anything over the ship's wounded bleating until the captain's voice echoed over the coms.

"Attention crew of the *Beagle*. We are under attack. Security personnel report to the bridge immediately. Engineering to the drive chamber."

Leo looked up at his brother, still holding him tight. "Did she just say we're under attack?"

Gareth nodded, then looked sideways, startled by the sound of boot heels clomping down the hall.

Leo knew the sound. He'd learned to recognize the rhythm of his father's footfalls. Like the sound of his brother's snoring or his mother's pensive sighs. Leo spied his father turning the corner, his eyes falling on him and Gareth, pressed together. Dr. Calvin Fender's face softened, then hardened again. He spoke in a whirlwind. "What are you two doing out here? Didn't you hear what Captain Saito said? You need to hide. Hurry!"

Their father pointed to the nearest door, leading to an empty bunk room barely half the size of the one the Fenders shared. He hustled Gareth and Leo into a corner, his white lab coat flapping on both sides like broken wings. Leo could tell he was scared—he could see it in his father's eyes, even if he couldn't hear it in his voice.

His father was seldom scared.

Dr. Fender tipped over a metal desk, making a barrier,

concealing the boys from anyone passing by the door. "Stay right here. Do not move. Understand?"

"What's going on?" Leo asked. "Are we really under attack? Is it pirates?"

"Worse," their father said.

Worse than pirates? *The Djarik*, Leo thought. And from the look on Gareth's face, he knew it too.

"They've knocked out our engines and navigation systems," Dr. Fender continued. "Communications too. I believe they intend to board us."

"You mean they're coming on the ship?" Leo felt his chest tighten, a coil wrapping tight, working its way up to his throat. He wheezed in a painful breath.

"Dad, I think he's about to have an attack," Gareth said.

Dr. Fender bent over, patting down Leo's pockets. Leo reached for it as well, finding what he needed, fumbling with the cap of his inhaler, squeezing the trigger and hearing the familiar hiss of medicine, the cool sensation as it snaked its way into his lungs, loosening the noose. Leo took a shuddering breath.

"You're okay," his father whispered, hands on Leo's shoulders. "It's okay. Just breathe. I'm right here. We're both right here." Leo closed his eyes and took in his father's voice, the hint of coffee on his father's breath, the feel of his father's hands. And for a moment, he was somewhere safe. He imagined himself back at home. *Home* home.

Until another, smaller blast caused the ship to shiver again, bringing Leo back. In the corridor, even the emergency lights started to flicker. The *Beagle* was wounded, limping, its engines disabled. The Djarik were preparing to board.

Dr. Fender leveled a finger at his sons. "Whatever happens, you two stay here, understand? Gareth, you're in charge. You keep your brother safe. I will be back as soon as I can."

Gareth nodded, but Leo reached out for his father's coat. "Wait—where are you going?"

"To engineering. To see if I can do something to help with the navigation system. Hopefully the security team can hold off the Djarik long enough for us to break free and make a jump. Stay here. Keep yourselves hidden." Dr. Fender gathered his sons in an embrace that lasted all of ten hammering heartbeats.

"I love you both. More than anything."

And then he was up and out the door, letting it whisper closed behind him, leaving Leo and Gareth huddled together, trembling in the dark.

"Gareth?"

"It's okay, Leo. I'm here. And Dad will come back. He's going to get us out of this."

Leo felt his brother's hand smoothing his hair, working his way from front to back. It was something he remembered their mother doing whenever they got sick, running her forked fingers through their sweaty bangs, softly blowing on their foreheads to cool them. *Her* breath always smelled like mint from the gum she chewed. *Everything's all right*, she would say.

Everything's going to be just fine. He always believed her.

But Leo knew it wasn't always true. Of all the things that could happen—of all the things that *had* happened—this was as bad as it could get. The Djarik were sworn enemies of the Coalition, a plague on the universe. Brutal and bloodthirsty, with little care for humanity—or any species other than their own. They had no qualms attacking an unarmed ship, stripping it of its fuel and leaving it to drift, its crew to suffer and starve. Leo had heard all the stories, but he didn't need them to know what the Djarik were capable of. He'd seen it firsthand.

Leo tried to take deep breaths, but they still hitched and sputtered. "What will they do . . . if they find us?"

"They won't find us," Gareth whispered.

"What will they do if they find Dad?"

Gareth didn't answer at first. Their father was one of the highest-ranking science officers in the Coalition. That alone made him valuable. "Dad's smart," Gareth said at last, understating it by a mile. "He'll think of something."

A final explosion drew a whimper from Leo as the alarms abruptly shut off, making it easier to hear the muffled chaos from the other side of the door. Shouting. Gun blasts. The *Beagle*'s limited security forces making their stand against the Djarik boarding party.

It didn't last long.

Leo pressed even closer to his brother as the sounds of battle gave way to silence. The room was bathed in an eerie yellow glow that made the shadows loom large against the wall. He wanted to call out for their father. Why couldn't he have just stayed with them? Why did he have to leave them here, alone? Leo knew the answer, of course: Calvin Fender would do everything he could to save the ship. The crew. As many as possible.

The silence was interrupted by voices from beyond the closed door. They weren't ones Leo recognized. They certainly weren't human.

"Gareth? What's happening?"

His brother clamped a hand over Leo's mouth, but a moment too late.

The door slid open softly and Leo nearly jumped, giving them away, but Gareth held him, both arms knotted around his chest. Leo peeked through a slit in the metal desk that provided their only cover and barely choked down his scream.

It was one of *them*.

He had seen them before—in pictures, vids, but never so close. Close enough to see the skin of diamond-shaped scales stitched together, hard as a sapphire but ashen gray in color. The ridge of spikes running along the jawline, mirroring the rows of serrated white teeth inside. The gill-like slits along their necks, rippling with each breath. Scalies. Lizzies. Gray devils—the nicknames given to them by humans to degrade or diminish them, to make them seem less scary than they were.

It didn't work.

The Djarik's giant, lidless black eyes swept the room. Like a spider's eyes, a glossy black mirror that gave away nothing, showed no sign of pity or fear. The soldier's spindly arms held its rifle at the ready. It was said that the Djarik were somewhat humanoid in shape, with their straight spines and short necks, their splayed, unwebbed fingers, their prominent skulls, but to Leo they looked as far from human as possible.

The creature raised its chin, giving a sniff through two thin slits. Its eyes came to rest on the desk and on the two boys cowering behind it. It made a sound, a clicking from somewhere behind its pointed teeth. A warning. A call to others. Or maybe just some note of satisfaction at having discovered such easy prey.

Tag, you're it.

Leo wondered if they should make a run for it. Try to squeeze past the Djarik marauder, slip into the corridor, make their way to engineering. To Dad. But his limbs were stiff with fear. The Djarik's rifle swept across the room, those black, unblinking eyes reflecting everything in miniature. Leo thought of his mother and a hot anger surged inside him.

The alien's head whipped sideways, the sound of more gunfire from farther down the corridor catching its attention. With another click of its tongue, it slipped back through the entry, leaving the door open, the brothers still bunkered behind the desk.

Leo felt his brother's breath on the back of his neck, the one

Gareth had been holding. "Okay," Gareth whispered. "It's okay. He's gone."

But he wasn't. He was out there somewhere. They were inside the ship. There was no safe place. No matter what Leo's father said.

The brothers huddled in their shadowy corner for five minutes, ten, thirty, their legs cramped, afraid to stand up to even activate the switch on the door, feeling the cold sweat stain their uniforms, twitching at every sound. Until, at last, they heard their names being called.

"Gareth? Leo?"

This voice was familiar, though it wasn't the one Leo had been hoping for. "We're in here," Gareth shouted.

Leo pulled himself to his feet just as Captain Saito appeared in the doorway. She looked different from when he'd seen her earlier that day: her normally tightly buttoned uniform hung loose on her shoulders, one of which supported a makeshift sling for her arm, a spot of crimson soaking through.

"Are you hurt?" she asked.

Leo shook his head. "The Djarik? Are they . . ."

"Gone," she finished. "They took what they wanted and left."

What they wanted. No doubt in Leo's mind what that could be. Ventasium. More fuel for their fleets. The *Beagle* wasn't a military ship. It was a scientific research vessel. They didn't have any weaponry aside from what their small security force carried. Captain Saito was the most valuable officer on the ship. The only other passenger who was even a ranking member of the Coalition was . . .

Leo saw the look in the captain's eyes and felt a chasm instantly open inside him, a black hole forming at his center. He knew without even asking, knew by the twist in his gut, the tightness in his chest.

Captain Saito didn't look away.

"I'm sorry," she said, trying to steady her voice. "We tried to stop them. We did. But it was no use."

Leo reached out for something to hold on to and found his brother's hand as his whole world crumbled.

Again.

Day after day, day after day,
We stuck, ne breath ne motion;
As idle as a painted Ship
Upon a painted Ocean.
—*Samuel Taylor Coleridge*, "The Rime of
the Ancyent Marinere," *1798*

BETTER THAN NOTHING

THE FIRST TIME LEO SAW AN AYKARIAN SPACESHIP up close he peed his pants. Just a little.

It wasn't his fault. He'd warned his parents he needed to go. They'd been driving for two hours already, headed to the California coast—at least one of the stretches that the steadily rising oceans hadn't reclaimed—when the soda cans in the cup holders started to rattle, a low growl creeping up behind them. Leo and his brother looked through the windshield, and that's when they saw it rumbling up behind them: an Aykari transport, gleaming silver, its hull glinting against the light of Earth's modest sun. Bigger than a football stadium, its belly bristled with gun emplacements—even their transports were well armed. It soared directly over their heads, its sleek, sharklike shape casting a giant shadow along the road as it passed, its neon-blue engines too bright to look at for long.

Leo had seen them a hundred times before, of course, but always on a screen or from a great distance. Never right above his head. Just the sight of it—so massive, so *alien*—and the sound of its sublight engines arcing through the sky caused Leo to lose it, a small wet spot blossoming on the front of his shorts.

His dad pulled over and told Leo to just finish in the bushes on the side of the road. Leo didn't even bother to look where he was aiming—his eyes were still turned skyward, taking in the alien vessel disappearing into the horizon.

"Sorry," Leo said.

"Don't worry about it. I almost did the same thing the first time I saw one up close," his father said. "Amazing, aren't they?" Calvin Fender's eyes were trained skyward as well, staring with equal bug-eyed wonder. "As a kid I always imagined *someone* was out there, you know? And now, to see them. To be a part of it. Man . . ." Leo's dad shivered, then he pointed to the back of the ship. "See that bright orange ring back there? That's the FTL drive. That's the game changer. Without that, you and I wouldn't even be having this conversation, because the Aykari would have never been able to find us to begin with."

Leo's six-year-old brain tried to wrap itself around everything his father was saying. "Where's it going?"

"I don't know. It's a transport, so maybe it's dropping off supplies. Or maybe picking up volunteers." Even Leo knew that Aykarian ships spent most of their time hovering high up in the atmosphere or even farther out in orbit. They seldom landed. Except when they had something to give. Or something to take.

"Volunteers for what?"

Dr. Fender watched the ship shrink in the distance. "My guess is they are recruiting colonists. Workers. Miners. Soldiers. Pilots. Anyone willing to help out."

"Help out with what?"

"Building the Coalition," Leo's father said. "The Coalition of Planets? Don't they teach you about this stuff in kindergarten?"

"I learned how to tie my shoes," Leo said.

"Really?"

Leo looked down to see his laces flapping free, but then he glanced over to see his father's shoelaces had come undone as well, so he didn't feel bad. When he looked back up, the Aykarian transport was almost gone, though you could still hear its engines' hum. "Will we ever go on a ship like that?"

"I hope so," his father said. "I think it might be cool, don't you? Go out there. See new stars. New planets. New people. Besides . . . we might not have a choice."

Actually, that all sounded a little frightening to Leo. Especially if it was something he *had* to do.

"You boys almost finished out there? Some of us prefer *not* to pee in the bushes if we don't have to."

Leo smiled at his mother and ran back to the car, gearing himself up for another hour stuck in the back seat with his brother. He looked one last time at the wide expanse of sky

- 17 -

and the Aykarian ship, now just a silver speck on the horizon.

Someday, he thought. Someday he'd go on one, go *out there*, like his father said. Just to see what it's like. But certainly not for forever.

He already knew that he would always want to come back home.

"You'd better eat that."

Gareth pointed to the spongy gray slab with his fork. Leo stared with undisguised disgust at the lump on his plate. He could list the basic ingredients: synthetic protein compound, an injection of vitamins, some kind of emulsifier to hold it together, and a load of preservatives to make it last for three years in deep freeze. It was something cooked up in a government lab to keep spacefarers from starving, and it tasted like it. He and Gareth called it *ficken*.

Admittedly ficken nuggets were better warm, but the ship's power supply had been rerouted to cover only essential functions, and heating up protein chunks was nonessential.

Of course, this was the least of Leo's worries.

It had been four days. Four days since the *Beagle* was attacked by a Djarik warship and left limping, stripped of all its fuel, floating in the middle of nowhere—though to Leo, who'd been on board the ship for nearly three years, everywhere felt like the middle of nowhere. The Djarik had taken everything they deemed valuable, leaving the crew with the ship's crippled and paralyzed remains.

The crew minus one.

There had been Coalition guards on board. Engineers. Navigators. The captain herself, and yet the Djarik had taken only Leo's father. And it wasn't by chance—at least that's what Leo had gathered from the crew who tried to explain, who came to apologize, like Captain Saito, for not being able to stop them. Almost as if the Djarik attacked the *Beagle* for the specific purpose of kidnapping his dad. Except nobody knew why.

Or if they did, they weren't telling the two sons he left behind.

Arguing over their last chunk of ficken.

"I'm serious. Eat it."

"I don't want it," Leo said.

The first two days after the attack, Leo refused to eat anything at all. He barely slept, every sound causing his pulse to quicken, flashes of his father's face in those last minutes, the too brief hug, that broken promise—*be back as soon as I can*—the Djarik standing in the doorway, sniffing them out. The images spun around the carousel of his brain, haunting him and denying him sleep.

Not that he could have slept for long. Not in the same room as his brother, who had woken up every hour thrashing so violently Leo was sure he would throw himself out of the top bunk and break something.

As if they both weren't broken enough already.

Even now, Leo still wasn't sure he could keep this meal

down. But he also knew that what was left of the *Beagle*'s food stores had been rationed, which meant no cold synthetic protein chunk should go to waste.

That still didn't mean Leo had to eat it.

He slid his plate silently over to his brother. Gareth didn't look good. Dark half-moons sagged under his eyes and his hair had taken on a greasy sheen. Somehow he looked thinner to Leo already. And they both smelled ripe, layers of new sweat overlapping the old. Like warm food, warm showers were nonessential, and the cold ones stung, so Leo avoided them. He changed clothes only out of habit. He could feel the fuzz forming along the edges of his gums; he'd brushed his teeth once in four days.

After all, his father wasn't around to tell him to. There didn't seem to be much point.

Gareth considered the metal plate with its one remaining morsel of food for a moment before frowning and sliding it back.

"I told you I don't want it," Leo said.

"Yeah, but what would Dad say if he found out I ate half of your rations?"

What *would* he say? Knowing their father, he would tell them both to keep their strength up. He would tell them to carry on, to use their heads, to not give up hope. Of course if he were here, Leo wouldn't have this second hole inside him. Leo pushed the plate back. "I'm not eating it," he said. "It tastes like Aykari turds."

"How would you know what Aykari turds taste like?" Gareth countered.

"Well, it smells like them."

Truthfully, Leo had never smelled one either. He'd never even seen an Aykari do its personal business, he just assumed it smelled. Just because you've perfected faster-than-light-speed travel doesn't mean your poop doesn't stink. Does it?

"Just eat it. Please. It's good for you. It contains twenty-seven essential vitamins and nutrients," Gareth said, reading off the recyclable container the nuggets came in. Chicken *flavored*, it said. Leo honestly couldn't be sure if it was or not; he couldn't remember what real chicken was supposed to taste like.

"Forget it."

"Eat it. I'm older and you have to do what I say."

"That's not a rule."

They pushed the metal plate back and forth between them, until Leo pushed a little too forcefully, causing it to slide off the table, its chicken-flavored cargo bouncing across the steel floor.

The brothers stared at it guiltily for a moment. Then Gareth recovered it and put it back on the plate, using the edge of his fork to painstakingly saw it in two.

Leo got the bigger half.

The rationing had started the day after the Djarik attack. As soon as all the diagnostics were finished and the captain had a full damage report, she had gathered all ship personnel onto the bridge to give them the news.

"I won't lie to you," Captain Saito began, looking over her bedraggled crew. "The *Beagle* took a serious beating. Our life-support systems are mostly intact—oxygenator, water filtration, gravity generator. We're all still breathing and our feet are on the ground, but that's it for the good news. The ship's propulsion systems are damaged beyond repair, so unless someone can go out there and give us a push, we aren't moving. The jump drive is also not operational. Not that it matters since the Djarik took all of our V. We have no weapons, no defenses, and no coms, which means we are basically sitting ducks."

"What about the shuttle?" a member of the crew asked. The six-passenger Lockheed landing craft that was supposed to be used for planetary surface exploration, but mostly gathered dust in the bigger ship's landing bay. There had been little need to study the surface of planets because, despite being out here for nearly three years, the *Beagle* had found little worth studying. Its primary mission, Dr. Calvin Fender's primary mission—to discover and analyze more potential sources of ventasium—had yielded little in the way of results.

And yet it had somehow attracted the enemy's attention.

"I'm afraid the Djarik sabotaged the shuttle as well. They made sure none of us were getting off this ship," Captain Saito said.

Not none of us, Leo thought, a surge of sour bile burning the back of his throat. *One of us was escorted off at gunpoint.*

"Our best hope is that the Coalition realizes that we haven't checked in and are off the grid and sends a rescue team sooner rather than later. Either that or a friendly ship just happens to pass in range of our emergency beacon, which, given our location, is unlikely, but not impossible. In the meantime we are doing our best to get the long-range communications back up and running. The sooner we do that, the sooner we can get help."

"And what about Dr. Fender?"

Leo traced Lieutenant Berg's voice, spotting her in the crowd. She was the only member of the *Beagle*'s security detail he ever talked to—the rest nodded to Leo in the corridors or gave him a mock salute, but Lieutenant Berg was different. She showed him card tricks and slipped him extra packets of cocoa to mix with his powdered milk. She'd been there when the Djarik took Leo's dad. She'd tried to stop them, as the bandages across her head could attest to, but a handful of Coalition security guards were no match against a squad of Djarik marauders.

Captain Saito's eyes darted to Leo and his brother just for a moment, then focused back on the crew. "We still aren't sure why Dr. Fender was taken, but as soon as communications are back up, we will inform the Coalition of his capture. Until then, we will do what he would expect us to and look after each other. That and pray for his safe return."

In other words, the captain seemed to be saying, there's

nothing we *can* do. They were helpless. Stranded. Lost.

Suddenly Leo felt like he was going to be sick.

"Hey, where are you going?" Gareth hissed, reaching out and grabbing for his brother's shoulder, but Leo brushed him off and bolted from the bridge. For once, Gareth didn't bother to chase him.

Leo wandered the silent corridors, taking in the evidence of the battle—the scars of laser fire scorched along the walls, the hiss of steam from pipes that had yet to be repaired—and made his way down to the engineering level where he could hear the clanging and cursing of someone at work. Someone who, like Leo, was skipping out on Captain Saito's somber status report.

"The devils take you, you bowel-crusted, feces-eating snarf sucker!"

The cursing Leo recognized, even if his translator struggled with some of the words. The nanochip embedded in his skull was remarkable—a piece of Aykarian technology to nearly rival their coveted jump drive—but it wasn't 100 percent accurate or exhaustive. Leo didn't really need to know what a snarf was, though, to get the overall meaning.

Leo moved past the entrance of the engine room and felt the temperature instantly jump. Standing inside with his shirt off, his skin glistening, his coils of long black hair stuck to his back, the ship's chief engineer was busy smashing some contorted hunk of metal with a wrench, mangling it ever further. "Explode your anus a thousand times," he said, tossing the wrench to the ground where it spun nearly to Leo's feet. "Oh. Sorry, Leo," Tex said, wiping his hands on his pants. "I didn't know you were there."

Leo shrugged. He'd heard much worse. Much of it from the alien currently apologizing. Tekzek Zardokus was an Edirin, from a planet orbiting a star not far from the one Leo's house used to circle—relatively speaking. In addition to being a gifted swearer he was also a talented tinkerer; and once Leo got over the fact that he had blue skin, three eyes, and a quick temper, Leo started volunteering to help with simple repairs, learning the ins and outs of ship maintenance from its primary caretaker. Tex—as he reluctantly allowed himself to be called—was the only alien Leo had ever befriended. Or tried to; Leo wasn't sure the alien really had any friends. It couldn't be easy being the only one of his kind on board.

Tex wiped his forehead with a rag that dangled from his tool sash and closed his eyes for a moment. He opened the middle one and fixed it on Leo. "How come you aren't on the bridge with the rest of the crew?"

Leo shrugged again. "I'd heard enough," he muttered.

"So she told you all about our situation."

"She said we were pretty much stuck out here till we get rescued."

"She said 'till,'" Tex said with a snort. "How optimistic."

"You don't think the Coalition will come and rescue us?" Leo asked.

"Oh, I think they'll try. But good luck finding us without

any communications system. Might have a better chance finding a single narp in the hide of a Hoashidian torblat."

Leo's translator struggled with half the sentence, but again, the meaning was clear: the Beagle's chief engineer didn't like their odds of getting rescued.

"Ships get stranded all the time," Tex continued. "I used to be a scavenger, you know. Back before my people were invited into the Coalition. We'd find wrecks littered across the void and break them down for scrap. Some were abandoned. Others . . . not."

"And the people on board?" Leo asked.

"Sometimes you'd find them alive," Tex said.

Others . . . not.

"Of course it's possible I can get this blasted hunk moving again, but I wouldn't bet on it. Not without new parts. The Djarik were thorough in—how do you humans say it? Tearing us a new one?" The Beagle's chief engineer slumped, sliding his broad-shouldered back against the same piece of mangled machinery he'd been beating on before.

Leo went and sat down across from him. He could see the patches of white skin along the Edirin's forearms. Burns. Some steam, some chemical, some ages old, others newly healed. Tex knew things. Had seen things. His people had been attacked by the Djarik as well, their planet bombarded, invaded. The Aykari finding them, inviting them into the Coalition—it had saved them, had saved their world. The engineer had told Leo stories of the battles raged on Edirin soil, the Aykari and Djarik filling the skies with fire, fighting over the most valuable substance in the universe, buried deep below his planet's surface.

Ventasium.

That was humanity's name for it. Even in English it had others: hyperblast, fairy dust, jump juice—but Leo's father had always insisted on calling it by its scientific name, after the Italian scientist who had discovered it on Earth.

Except Enrico Ventasi had no idea what he was really looking at when he pulled that chunk of radioactive rock from deep within Earth's crust, couldn't comprehend the nature of the door he'd just unlocked. He wouldn't know until two years later when the Aykari made first contact, telling the nine billion people of Earth that they were far from alone in the universe, and that because of their ventasium deposits, they were also one of the richest planets in the galaxy.

Which also made them targets.

Just like the planet Edir.

Like Leo, Tex had seen firsthand what the Djarik were capable of, long before two Djarik torpedoes slammed into the *Beagle*'s hull. He had every reason to be pessimistic.

And yet. "He's still alive, you know," the Edirin said, taking in Leo with his three unblinking eyes.

"What?"

"Your father. Dr. Fender. He's still alive. I may be Edirin, but you humans aren't hard to read. I can see it painted on your face. You fear the worst, but it hasn't happened."

"How can you be so sure?" Leo asked.

"Because if they'd wanted him dead," Tex offered, "they would have just left him here with us."

Leo tried to keep that flicker of hope burning as he stared at the half chunk of ficken recently rescued from the floor, doubting it would make it taste any worse. He shoveled the whole thing into his mouth, somehow choking it down. Gareth reached across and ruffled his hair. "That wasn't so bad was it?"

Compared to what? Compared to everything else they'd already been through? No. At least the food he could swallow.

"There's talk of trying to repair the shuttle," Gareth said, eating his half in nibbles as if trying to make it last. "Saito thinks that if they salvage enough parts from the *Beagle* they might make it flight worthy. Then, if they could find a way to power it . . ."

"Then six of us would be able to get off this wreck," Leo said, doing the math. "Leaving the other thirty or so behind."

"Not behind," Gareth corrected. "Whoever takes the shuttle would try and get help."

"Or just get stranded in another part of space."

"It's worth a shot," Gareth snapped. "It's better than sitting around here doing nothing!"

Leo stared at his now empty plate. He hadn't meant to make

his brother mad. Gareth was right. It was better than just sitting here, waiting to see if the food or the power supply ran out first, or if the damaged hull would just split at the seams, sucking all the oxygen out into the void. They were barely staying afloat out here, and Leo knew it. They all knew it.

If only Dad were here, Leo thought. *He would know what to do.*

Gareth put his fork down, leaning across the table to get Leo's attention. "Hey."

Leo lifted his chin, just a little.

"Listen to me. We're going to get out of this. I'm going to find a way to keep you safe. Do you understand?"

Gareth reached into the pocket of his jacket and pulled out a silver foil wrapper. Leo instantly recognized it by the shape. "I thought there wasn't anymore," he said.

"I thought so too," Gareth answered. "But I helped Officer Ridley patch up some ducts this morning and he gave it to me." He slowly peeled back the silver foil, revealing the precious hunk of chocolate underneath, only slightly discolored around the edges. "It will get the taste of ficken out of our mouths at least."

Leo watched Gareth take the chocolate between his fingers, ready to snap it in two when the sound of boots in the corridor outside the mess hall made them both freeze. He followed his brother to the door to see members of the *Beagle*'s crew running toward the bridge.

"What's going on?" Gareth asked.

"A ship," a voice called back. "We've spotted another ship. It's coming our way."

"Djarik?" Leo guessed, hoping he was wrong.

"I don't think so."

"Coalition?" Gareth called out, but he got no response.

Leo looked up at his brother. Gareth's wide eyes were a perfect match for his own. They were both thinking the same thing.

They were saved.

The pirates of today are not so different from the romanticized figures from our own sordid human history, the Blackbeards and Captain Kidds. Yes, they pilot spaceships instead of schooners, fire torpedoes instead of cannonballs, wield energy blasters instead of flintlocks, but they are still misfits and miscreants, resorting to thievery and violence in their quest for fame and fortune—or simply as a way to survive.

—*Dr. Geoffrey Harmon*, Scurvy Dogs in Outer Space: Piracy in the Modern Age, *2053*

2

THE ONES LEFT BEHIND

LIKE EVERY OTHER TEN-YEAR-OLD KID HE'D EVER met, Leo was fascinated by outer space.

Right up until the moment his father told him that's where they were going. Because that's when Leo realized he wasn't coming back.

Back to the house on Briarwood Lane. Redbrick front with a fireplace that still burned actual wood and doors you had to open by hand. An unmotorized swing set in the backyard next to a hydroponic garden that produced plump tomatoes and bloodred strawberries nurtured by a sun that still managed to pierce the polluted haze layered thick by the excavators working around the clock a hundred miles away. The driveway, cracked and colored with chalk. It was the house Leo grew up in. The house where he lost his first tooth, tucking it under his pillow in exchange for a crisp ten-dollar bill. The same house where his mother once burned Thanksgiving dinner so badly it set off the smoke alarm.

It was the only home he'd ever known.

Still, Leo might have gone quietly if it weren't for the cat. A charcoal-colored bundle of fur and mischief named Amos who had more toes than normal. He was still a kitten when Leo had been born, and the two had grown up side by side.

Dr. Fender waited till the last minute to deliver the news, knowing it would break Leo's heart. "I'm sorry, Leo. No pets allowed on board."

"No. No way," Leo said, shaking his head for emphasis. "He can come with. He can sleep in my bunk with me. He can eat my leftovers. He won't be any trouble. I promise."

"There are rules. Besides, how's he going to chase birds on board a star cruiser? He'll be happier here, don't you think?"

"I think we'd *all* be happier here," Leo protested. "I don't see why we even have to go!"

What followed was pouting. Crying. The slamming of a bedroom door. An hour later, ten-year-old Leo, red-faced, defeated, slipped out in search of Amos, finding the cat happily napping in the backyard. He curled up next to it and scratched its scruff, eliciting a satisfied purr.

He knew why. His father had explained it. How his ship had literally come in. How the Aykari recognized his contributions to advancing the practical applications of ventasium and offered him a commission as a science officer aboard a vessel bound for other planets suspected of having significant deposits of the precious stuff. How this was his chance—their chance—to contribute to the Coalition's mission: the promise of peace and stability, not just on Earth but across the entire galaxy.

And Leo understood, sort of. But that didn't mean he had to like it. In fact, he swore not to.

That evening, Amos was deposited into the wrinkled hands of Mrs. Tinsley, the next-door neighbor, who already had two cats of her own and was "too old to be shootin' off into outer space anyhow." Instead, she and Amos would just curl up in that rocking chair and wait for the sky to fall, she said.

Leo told her he'd rather stay and watch the sky fall too.

His father told him to go and pack his suitcase.

They bolted toward the bridge, Leo doing his best to keep stride with his brother, heart hammering, already wheezing from the effort, until he saw Gareth pull up just outside one of the three entrances to the bridge, peering in. Leo squeezed his head in beside his brother's to get a better view.

There stood Captain Saito and most of the crew, each member wielding whatever they could find to use as a weapon: pipes, knives, wrenches. Tex held a blowtorch in his giant blue fists. Lieutenant Berg held a length of chain. They looked like one of those Earth gangs from a hundred years ago, the kind that would rumble in parking lots. The Djarik raiding party had stripped them of their real weapons, taking them along with the ventasium cores. Only Captain Saito still had a gun, an old-fashioned pistol—bullets, not energy bolts. An artifact from another age.

The crew made a wall, shoulder to shoulder with their captain at the fore. Leo was about to join them when Gareth grabbed a fistful of shirt, pulling him back.

"Stay right here. Out of sight."

"But we should—"

"No. Stay put."

That's when it hit him—what his brother already knew: this wasn't a rescue ship. This wasn't his father, somehow escaped from his Djarik captors, returning with help. If so, Captain Saito wouldn't be guarding the bridge with an antique handgun and a wrench-wielding posse of desperate crewmates. "You sure it's not the Djarik?" Leo fretted.

Gareth didn't have an answer, but one came in the form of a booming voice, echoing down the halls. "Look at this. A welcome party."

Definitely not Djarik. The translator chip implanted just behind Leo's ear did a fair job of turning alien speech to English, but you could always tell when it was filtered through the translator. No, the voice Leo heard was a human speaking Leo's own tongue.

What he saw stepping through the main corridor onto the bridge was, in fact, two humans, walking side by side. And just behind them . . .

"What is *that*?" Leo whispered.

Leo had come face-to-face with Aykari and Djariks. Terra-trins, Jorl, and the Edirin. He'd seen holos and vids of dozens of other alien species. But the thing towering behind the two human intruders wasn't part of Leo's year-long unit on alien cultures. He surely would've remembered reading about this: a beast with a short snout on an ox-shaped head with two curled, ram-like horns on either side. A thick neck led to a hulking body, gorillian in bulk and covered in a thick coat of mottled gray and brown fur. The creature walked slightly hunched on massive legs, and had shrewd yellow eyes too small for its face.

At the very least, Leo would have remembered the arms. All four of them.

The creature was covered in a robe, a dingy white, with sleeves for its many appendages. The robe almost made the hulking creature comical, and the way the alien scratched the back of its head with its lower left hand gave the impression that it had little interest in being there.

Leo's eyes darted back to the two humans, dressed much differently from their four-armed companion. The dark-skinned female, who couldn't have been too much older than Gareth, wore a stiff black tunic that stretched up to her chin, brass buttons snapping it together, black trousers, and knee-high boots that clicked along the floor. A holster on her belt held a sleek-looking silver pistol, matching the silver of the cape that came down over only one shoulder, concealing most of her right arm. But it was the girl's left arm that caught Leo's attention. Whereas the creature behind her had limbs to spare, half the girl's left arm was missing, replaced by a titanium prosthesis that started at her elbow and ended in a wicked-looking four-pronged claw, all metal, no skin. Her glossy black hair was pulled into a complicated braid that pendulated as she walked.

She had to be the one in charge. It couldn't possibly be the man standing beside her, wearing raggedy blue jeans with patched knees and a pair of filthy high-top sneakers. He was older—close to Leo's father's age. His burnt-orange hair was cropped short and tight. He wore a light leather jacket over a maroon-colored T-shirt that said *Dr Pepper* in slanted script. The name sounded familiar. Something from an old song maybe? Like the girl next to him, he was packing heat, two pistols riding in holsters on his hips. Only the monster in the bathrobe was unarmed, though Leo realized that wasn't the best choice of words.

Leo knew immediately who they were. Or at least *what* they were.

Carrying weapons but wearing no uniforms or insignias. Clearly not Djarik and definitely not Coalition. Boarding a ship without permission. And sauntering right onto the bridge like they owned the place.

They could only be pirates.

Leo started to say as much to Gareth, got out the "Pi—" before his brother's hand clamped over his mouth.

Captain Saito kept her weapon pointed at the floor, her

finger resting beside the trigger. Against a fully armored Dja-rik marauder, bullets were a distraction at best, but a human in a tattered old T-shirt was a different story. Apparently the three intruders thought so too because they paused just inside the entry, the alien still scratching its head, its fur rippling.

The commander of the *Beagle* got right to the point. "I am Captain Saito of the Coalition Expeditionary Forces; this is my ship and you are intruders. I order you to set down your weapons immediately."

The woman with the shoulder cape grunted. The man made a face as if he was considering the request before shrugging.

"I have a counteroffer, Captain Saito of the Coalition Expe-ditionary Forces. How about *you* put down that fossil of yours before you blow another hole in your hull and we have a friendly conversation like civilized human beings." The man's voice was cool and composed, any threat concealed in the holsters at his sides and the still-bored-looking giant standing behind him. "Well, most of us, anyways," he added.

Leo studied all three of them, trying to gauge who was the most dangerous. Not the sloppily dressed man with the crooked smile. It was either the claw-handed girl with the annoyed look on her face or the hulking apelike bruiser in the bath-robe. Regardless, there were only three of them—against a crew of nearly forty. The *Beagle* had strength in numbers, but pirates were pirates, and if everything Leo had heard was true, they would sooner just take what they wanted rather than ask for it. Just like the Djarik. Leo knew the captain wouldn't want to risk the lives of any more of her crew. She would talk her way out of this if possible.

"Who are you? What are your intentions?" Saito asked, her voice as steady as the hand holding her gun.

The man in the sneakers scratched his chin. "If we're being perfectly honest, I could really go for an ice-cold beer right about now, but I'm guessing by the state of your ship, that you're probably all out, so—"

"We want your V," the girl with the robotic arm interrupted, earning her a dirty look from the man beside her.

"I was getting to that," he hissed.

"No, you weren't. You were trying to be charming and witty and failing."

"I wasn't failing." The man turned and looked at the alien in the robe. "You think I'm charming and witty, don't you?"

The creature shrugged its massive shoulders. It appeared to have only two of them. Two shoulders, four armpits, lots of fur and teeth.

The girl focused her dark eyes on Captain Saito. "Venta-sium," she repeated even more firmly.

"You're too late," Captain Saito replied. "The Djarik attacked us four days ago. Took every core we had. They crippled the ship, injured several members of our crew, took one of us captive, and left the rest stranded."

"See? I told you," the girl hissed at the man.

"Yes, but I didn't listen to you," he retorted. "Because at some point . . . eventually . . . I know you're going to be wrong, and I want to take advantage of it. Besides, she could be lying." He looked back at Captain Saito. "Do you know who I am, Captain?"

"I know *what* you are," Saito spat, her eyes narrowing. "You're pirates. Worse still, human pirates. Parasites feeding off your own kind, though you're obviously not very good ones if you have to pick an already crippled ship to steal from."

"Not very good ones—" The man shook his head and looked at the other two members of his crew. He reached for one of the pockets of his jacket and Captain Saito raised her weapon level with the man's chest. In a flash the girl with one arm had one of her own pistols unholstered, pointed back at the captain.

The man put his hands up. "It's all right. I just want to show you something." He slowly removed a chip from the pocket and pushed a button. Instantly the space between the pirates and the *Beagle*'s crew was filled with a hologram of a man's face. Wry smile. Gaunt, stubbled cheeks. Thinning ginger hair. It was a Coalition bounty notice. Leo had seen them flashed on the news feeds. The text underneath offered a reward of eight thousand pentars for the capture of someone named Bastian Daedalus Black—wanted for piracy and treason. Eight thousand pentars was a freighter full of money.

Captain Saito's eyebrows cinched. She looked at the holo again and then back at the man holding it.

Bastian Black grinned. "I must not be *too* terrible a pirate if my head's worth eight k's. And that's just what your precious Coalition is offering. There are others who would probably pay more." The girl beside him coughed. Bastian Black ignored her. "I don't think you would want to test someone with such a dangerous reputation. So I'm going to ask you one more time: Where's the V?"

Captain Saito returned the pirate's stare. "If we had any ventasium, do you really think we'd be sitting here waiting for some scudlicker like you to waltz in and take it?"

The girl in the black uniform snickered.

"Oh, so *she's* funny?"

The girl holstered her weapon with a sigh. "Are we finished here?"

Bastian Daedalus Black hung his head for a moment, looking like a kid who's just been told he can't have dessert. He looked back at the captain of the *Beagle*, arms spread. "Fine. Obviously you've got a lot you're dealing with already, so we'll just get out of your hair and let you get back to it."

The man from the wanted notice turned his back on Captain Saito and her pistol, his two companions following his lead. Leo shivered with relief. His first ever encounter with pirates and the whole crew had come out unscathed. Maybe all the stories he'd heard about bands of cutthroat brigands from worlds that had rebelled against the Coalition, ravaging its ships and terrorizing their crews, had been exaggerated. These three seemed content to leave empty-handed.

Leave.

It hit Leo suddenly what was happening. It must have hit Captain Saito at the same time because she hollered "Wait!" and stepped quickly after them, her weapon falling to her side. "Wait! Please!"

The three intruders stopped and turned.

"Please," she repeated. "We need your assistance. We've been stranded. We have no engines. No communications. No defenses. We have injured crew. Limited supplies. If you could just take some of us, any of us. To go get help. To arrange for rescue—"

Bastian Black raised his hand, cutting her off.

"You must have missed the part where I introduced myself. I am Bastian Black, wanted pirate. We are not in the rescuing business; we are in the taking whatever we want business. You were just fortunate enough not to have anything worthwhile. Unfortunately."

"But we could find some way to repay you," Captain Saito offered, stepping closer, her voice thick with desperation. "The Coalition would compensate you for our safe passage, I'm certain of it."

Bastian Black laughed. "And *I'm* certain that the moment I dropped you in Coalition hands my own hands would be bound behind my back and I'd be escorted to my own tidy little cell. Don't worry, Captain, if you're really that important to them, they will come find you themselves. And if not, well then . . . welcome to the universe. It mostly sucks."

Captain Saito continued to plead. "Fine. Forget passage.

Fuel. Spare parts. Supplies. If we could just get our communications fixed—"

Bastian Black's head dropped, cutting her off again. And in that moment, Leo thought maybe they were saved. The man was human, after all. Surely he wouldn't turn his back on others from his own planet. Not when their situation was so desperate.

Leo was wrong.

"Sorry, Captain," Bastian Black said, pointing to the patch on her uniform. "You picked your side." He turned his back to her once more.

He made it three steps before Leo heard the click. The hammer cocked on Captain Saito's antique pistol. The one now leveled at the pirate's head. "In that case I demand that you relinquish command of your vessel to me, or I promise to put a bullet straight through your traitorous pirate skull."

It happened so fast, too fast for Leo to scream out a warning or for any of the crew to react. Too fast for Captain Saito, the pistol kicked out of her hand by the long black boot, sending it spinning across the floor of the bridge. In another second the girl with the bionic arm had the *Beagle*'s commander by the throat, lifting her off her feet, legs kicking. Leo felt his brother tense beside him, about to charge.

"That's enough, Kat." Bastian Black nodded and the girl let go. Captain Saito collapsed to her knees, hands to her neck, sucking in ragged breaths. Leo's hand went to his own throat instinctively.

The pirate knelt next to Captain Saito, but he continued to speak loud enough for everyone in the bridge to hear. "That was a mistake," he said, "Don't make another one." He stood up and addressed the entire crew. "I will leave what food I can spare in your hangar. But if you make any more attempts to follow us or prevent us from leaving, I will be forced to do something that will double the price on my head."

Captain Saito, leaning on one hand, motioned for the crew to stay back with the other. She whispered something to Black that Leo couldn't hear, though it might have been more of a hiss.

"I've been called worse," he said.

Leo watched from the side door as the three pirates disappeared through the main bridge door, leaving the captain on the floor, the remaining crew of the *Beagle* surrounding her, helping her to her feet, all of them talking at once. Leo felt like he should join them, to try and help somehow, when he felt a tug on his arm.

"Let's go," Gareth said.

"Go where?" Leo's brother was pulling so hard it seemed he might rip his arm out of his socket. And unlike that furry beast in the bathrobe, Leo didn't have extras.

Gareth flashed him a look. The same look he got when he stood on the starting line back home, waiting for the gun to go off. His race face. Leo knew that whenever his brother got that look, it meant he had a plan for how he was going to win and nothing would stand in his way.

"Gareth, where are we going?" Leo asked again.

"We are getting out of here," his brother said.

How do you pack an entire life, even a short one, into a suitcase half your size? How do you shove ten years into a bag that, as your father constantly reminds you, you will have to carry yourself?

You start by leaving most of it behind.

"You won't need clothes," Dr. Fender said to his two sons. "The Coalition will supply uniforms for the duration. And no soap or toothpaste. All of our necessities are provided. Food. Clothing. Medicine. They will take care of us." Leo wouldn't even need his old inhaler, the one he'd decorated with Spider-Man stickers. They'd give him a new one. A better one. "Just pack the particulars and the peculiars. The things that matter to you but no one else," his father said.

Gareth packed his running shoes and the medal from his first ever cross-country championship, as well as thirty of his most valuable comics, carefully preserved in plastic. They could download any book or vid or game they wanted to their datapads, of course, but there was no way Gareth was leaving his great grandfather's *Avengers* number one, close to a century old and still in near mint condition, behind.

Leo spent hours staring at the inside of his suitcase, imagining everything that might fit. The toys in the plastic bins beside his closet. The wooden trunk full of magic paraphernalia by his bed from back when his wannabe magician of a mother was teaching him sleight of hand. His pillow? They would have pillows on board the ship, obviously, but a head gets used to a certain spot, nestled between familiar lumps formed over time.

In the end, Leo decided to scrap the suitcase and picked a backpack instead—the blue one he'd used for school. In it he threw some trick cards—his mother's favorite Svengali deck—a stuffed rabbit named Houdini, and a picture of Amos. He decided to hold on to his old inhaler, just in case. Then he carefully selected a few of the more unusual seashells that lined his bookshelves and wrapped them carefully in a sock. Most of the rest of the stuff in his room he could leave behind, he decided. Finally he grabbed his watch from his dresser and slapped it to his wrist.

He stood in the doorway of his bedroom, the only one he'd ever known, taking it in one last time. Through the window on the other side he could see the ships, Aykari and human alike, studding the smoggy sky. Used to be they were all only Aykari ships. But that was before. Before the worst day of his life. Before the war came right to their doorstep. Now the factory right outside town spit out starfighters instead of SUVs.

"Trust me. This is for the best," his father told Leo as they got out of the hover car to board the *Beagle*—a hulking, bulbous behemoth that had been designed for reliability over speed and was depressingly devoid of weapons. It looked massive, though Leo's dad told him it would only have a crew of forty or so.

"Isn't she beautiful?" Dr. Fender asked. "Darwin would be proud."

Leo knew who Charles Darwin was. And if Charles Darwin had suddenly found himself staring at a spaceship capable of jumping between star systems, he'd probably have freaked all the way out.

"I think it will be good for you," Dad continued. "I bet the moment we get out there your asthma will start to clear up. Get away from some of this smog. Besides, there's this whole, huge galaxy for us to explore. We are fortunate really. Not everyone gets this opportunity."

Most wouldn't, Leo knew. Like Amos and Mrs. Tinsley. And billions more humans who couldn't afford their own ticket into space. Who weren't famous scientists like Leo's father. Who didn't want to join the Coalition military or volunteer to be a colonist on an industrial mining world. There were many ways off the planet, but few of them were easy.

Staying would be easy, Leo thought. If only his father would let them.

Dr. Fender crouched down and took his son's hands.

"I'm sorry, Leo. We have to do this. We have to think about the future. The Earth isn't going to be around forever. We did too much damage to it early on and tried to make up for it too late. Even the Aykari—as good as they are—won't be able to save it. By the time you're my age it might not even be habitable. Everyone will have to leave eventually."

"Not Mrs. Tinsley."

"No. Probably not Mrs. Tinsley. Though if there were enough ships, I'd tell her that she should go too. I know it doesn't seem like it, but it's better to go now, when we have the choice, when we can pick our destiny, than to be forced out later."

But this wasn't Leo's destiny, it was his father's. He was the one who had been recruited by the Coalition. There were days Leo looked at his prize-winning astrophysicist father with a choking swell of pride. Today wasn't one of those days.

"Trust me. Once we get out there, everything is going to change. You can't even begin to comprehend the kinds of things you'll see. Things that I could only dream about at your age. Things that I *did* dream about at your age."

"But where *are* we going?"

"Wherever it is, I promise to keep you safe," his father assured him.

Leo knew nowhere was completely safe. Not really.

He looked at the gigantic ship—his home for the foreseeable future. One year. Three years. Five. Ten. He had no idea how long he would be on it. It didn't look at all like home. Home had curtained windows. Home had a cement sidewalk and grass that tickled the backs of your knees when you laid out in the sun. Home was finite. Fathomable. It was a space you could fill.

Out there was just emptiness. Cold and black forever and ever.

Dr. Fender held Leo's hand and tried to pull him along, but

Leo dug in. He tried to think of something, anything that could change his father's mind, convince him to let their family stay. There was one.

"What about Mom?"

Dr. Fender closed his eyes for a moment before letting out a long sigh. Leo hoped it was a sigh of defeat, but it was something else. A memory, maybe. Or a promise made.

He opened his eyes again and fixed them on his son. "This is what she would have wanted, Leo. She would have wanted us to take care of each other. And that's just what we are going to do. For her."

His father stood and Leo knew it was over. He had no more magic tricks left. He reluctantly shuffled his feet along the path to the boarding ramp and stared at the opening of the *Beagle*, looking like the mouth of a giant whale, a ramp for its tongue. He took one last look behind him at the only home he'd ever known, past the landing zone and over the rows of buildings to the swatch of trees gleaming emerald green in the distance.

He felt a hand slip into his own.

"Don't worry," Gareth whispered. "I've got your back." He gave Leo's hand a squeeze. "It won't be so bad."

But Leo could hear the same doubt in his brother's voice. Gareth knew, just like Leo. He knew from experience.

Nothing good ever comes from leaving the ones you love.

The threats presented by the Djarik and their allies to our country, our planet, our entire civilization are unlike any we have ever seen before. At no point in human history has our fate hung so precipitously in the balance. But at no point in human history have we come together as a species the way we have in this moment. We will fight back. Together. United by a single purpose: to protect our planet and ensure the survival of humanity, taking our rightful place among the peace-loving races of the galaxy.

—*Gabriella Jackson-Hale, president of the United States of America, State of the Union Address, 2051*

THE WORST PIRATE
IN THE UNIVERSE

LEO'S WORLD HAD ALWAYS BEEN A LITTLE ALIEN.

He was only two when the Aykari made first contact. He had no memory of being huddled around the television watching their arrival like his brother did. He had no recollection of a world without spaceships and jump drives and translator chips. He had no idea what coal was used for or how paper was made, but by age eight he knew how an artificial gravity generator worked (sort of) and could list the steps required to terraform a hostile planet. He couldn't imagine a world without aliens because his world had always been filled with them.

He could remember his father reading his favorite picture book, *Hello, Humans!* over and over though. A pop-up book that told about the day the Aykari first came to Earth, the cardboard pictures of New York and Beijing high-rises snapping to life tickled Leo almost as much as pulling the tab and watching the glittering Aykarian cruiser whip across the page like a silver bullet. The comical-looking alien at the end, spindly arms extended for a welcoming embrace, was a little startling, but the smile on its face suggested everything would be just fine.

Of course the real Aykari didn't smile. Their mouths didn't work that way. They were tiny circles that opened and closed like irises, letting out words the way our eyes let in more light. The only way to know if an Aykari was pleased was if its diamond-shaped eyes turned blue. If they turned orange—well, that was a different story.

In the year 2044, the book began, *someone came knocking on Earth's door.*

It was one of three years every school-aged kid had memorized, counting their birthday. Everything before that was BC, before contact. Before Earth's polluted sky filled with ships of radiant silver. There had been hints of their arrival, Leo would learn in galactic history class. SETI had been issuing reports of increased feedback, potential messages they didn't have the technology to translate. Hubble Five had caught glimpses of strange objects entering the solar system. But nothing was conclusive. Nothing that could prepare them for what—or who—was about to come knocking.

And then, on the one-year anniversary of the first Mars landing—with humans still marveling at their own ingenuity and their baby steps into a larger world—they appeared. A hundred ships hovering over a hundred cities. Leo had seen the vids a thousand times, had heard his father recount the day in excruciating detail. The military response. The scream of sirens. The flooded streets. The panic fed by too many movies where flying saucers fried national monuments with blasts of nuclear energy and bug-like xenomorphs fed on the brains of fleeing Earthlings.

But it was nothing like that. The Aykari broadcast their message in every Earthly language so that no one would misunderstand.

Do not fear, they said. *We are friends.*

That was it, at first. Those two proclamations, though many more followed in the days and weeks to come. Revelations to a shocked and anxious planet.

That we humans were only one of hundreds of civilized species in the galaxy.

That all our wildest dreams about interstellar travel were about to come true overnight.

And that our planet, the lovely blue-and-green marble called Earth, contained a treasure more precious than we ever dreamed of.

Ventasium. Loads of it. Heaps of it. Deep in the planet's crust. And they, the Aykari, would show us how to use it.

And with it all came the stark realization that humans were once again Neanderthals, fashioning axes out of flint. With their ships capable of traveling from star to star and weapons that seemed lifted straight out of pulp paperbacks and summer blockbusters, the Aykari were technologically superior in every way. The one thing the people of Earth had to offer them, that the planet itself had to offer, the visitors could have easily taken by force.

But they didn't. They asked nicely. Share your ventasium, they said, and we will be your personal escorts into this great big universe.

And humanity did the only thing it could do in that situation.

It said, Okay.

Only later did the people of Earth realize that the Aykari weren't the only ones interested in its resources. That ventasium was the hottest commodity in the galaxy. Some, like the Djarik, started wars over it. Others simply stole it and traded it on the black market.

Those others were called pirates.

Leo had heard stories of pirates growing up. Not Captain Kidd and Jack Sparrow, though he'd heard of them too, but *actual* pirates. A disorganized mob of criminals from every corner and crevice of the galaxy who trolled through trading routes, disabling freighters with ion cannons and blasting their way through airlocks, brandishing pistols in both hands as they made their demands. They never said "argh" or flew the skull and bones, but they lived by the same basic code as the pirates from the books: take what you can get wherever you can get it—the devil take the rest.

The Aykari mostly considered pirates to be a nuisance, Leo knew. Outcasts and outlaws who, for one reason or another, refused to be a part of the Aykari-led Coalition of Planets. Occasionally the Aykari would report on the execution of a band of buccaneers who had been caught attempting to raid one of their supply ships, but in comparison to the war with the Djarik, the occasional rogue swiping a few cores of ventasium was little more than a pest. Why bother swatting mosquitoes when you're dealing with a hornet's nest?

Except the mosquitoes were multiplying. If the stories Leo heard were to be trusted, more and more creatures of every stripe were turning to piracy. For some, the cost of ventasium was too dear to acquire it through honest means. For others, it was a chance to make a tidy profit, playing one side against the other and selling the universe's most precious commodity to the highest bidder. Some, Leo suspected, just wanted to watch the universe burn.

Whatever the reason, Leo knew that pirates were not to be trusted. At best they were outsiders, turning their back on the Coalition and everything it stood for: peace and order and cooperation. At worst they were thugs, thieves, and murderers.

Either way, they weren't the kind of people Leo ever wanted to meet.

Leo skidded to a stop just inside one of the hangar doors, his sweaty hand still clutching his brother's. His eyeballs popped.

"What the heck is *that* thing?"

Leo had encountered many different starships over the years.

Hulking cruisers. Sleek skiffs. Solar yachts. The massive box-shaped barges that the Aykari used to transport its shipments of excavated ventasium from Earth. He'd seen military fighters and civilian pleasure boats, but he'd never seen anything quite like the ship sitting in front of him.

It was shaped funny, for starters, like a giant eggplant, or maybe a pear, tapered at the front but spreading out in the rear, perhaps to make room for more cargo. Twin foils jutted from either side and extended past the center cockpit like walrus tusks, an unusual modification for what appeared to be a freighter, and a small freighter at that.

But not a helpless one. Unlike the *Beagle*, this pirate ship carried plenty of firepower. Torpedo bays, front-mounted cannons, a turret in its belly. It also sported three standard propulsion engines in addition to an FTL drive ring, which meant it could probably *move* when it needed to. The ship looked like it had been through some tight scrapes judging by the scorch marks etched along its hull. It was easily four times the size of the damaged shuttle and filled up half the *Beagle*'s hangar.

"It's so . . ."

"Yellow," Gareth finished for him.

True, Leo had never seen a yellow ship before, though the paint was stripped in places, revealing dingy grays and rusted reds underneath. Of course Leo had never seen a pirate ship before either. Not up close. Maybe this is what they all looked like. Leo's initial impression of pirates came from the official

Coalition information vids he saw growing up. The message was always delivered in the same monotone, mechanical voice: *Piracy is a crime. The Coalition is dedicated to the safety and security of all of its member planets. Any pirate caught attacking a Coalition ship will be prosecuted to the full extent of Aykari law.*

Those public service announcements only hinted at the horrors pirates committed. Worse were the tales Leo heard, traded among the *Beagle*'s crew: that pirates took no prisoners. That they were blood-hungry murderers who forced captured crew out of airlocks to suffocate in the cold grip of space or sold them to work as slaves on distant mining planets. That they were all criminals of one kind or another before they even became pirates and therefore accustomed to working on the wrong side of the law. Tex said they were actually worse than the enemy because at least the Djarik were committed to the Djarik empire. Pirates had no such allegiances. They were outlaws. With ships.

Oddly shaped, mustard-yellow ships.

"Gareth, what are we doing?" Leo asked, but his brother's attention was drawn to the sound of voices coming through the main hangar door. He grabbed Leo by the back of his shirt and pulled him behind a set of empty drums that once contained fuel for the *Beagle*'s sublight engines—the same engines that had been decimated by Djarik torpedoes four days ago. Leo was dragged down just as Bastian Black entered, followed immediately by the girl who had nearly choked Captain Saito to death with her clawed hand.

She was the one talking, though it sounded more like lecturing.

"I just wonder sometimes if you have your head screwed on is all. What made you think this wreck was a good target, that they would have anything at all that we would give a Farq's fart about?"

"It was a sitting duck. No weapons. No shields. It was worth the risk," the wanted pirate replied.

"But a Coalition ship? Seriously, Baz. We need to be careful. What if the crew had been armed with more than just pipes and wrenches? And that captain could have blown your brains out. What little of them there are."

"Good thing you were there to stop her."

"Yeah, well, one day maybe I won't be around to save your hide."

"If only that were true," Bastian Black quipped.

The girl shook her head. "You know what I think? I think you might just be the worst pirate in history. And I don't mean human history. I mean the history of the entire universe."

"Tell me that when *your* head is worth eight thousand pentars."

"You're only worth that much because you go around telling everyone how notorious you are."

"Pirates are supposed to be notorious. You can't be notorious if nobody knows you."

"Pirates are also supposed to *take* things," the girl said. "That's the definition of piracy. And what, exactly, are we leaving here with? Oh, wait. Nothing. In fact, you told them you would *give* them food. That's the *reverse* of piracy."

"She has a point," the four-armed creature lumbering just behind the humans said. It was the first time Leo had heard it speak. It had a surprisingly gentle voice, almost like a cat's purr.

Leo crouched beside his brother, watching as the man and the girl stopped to argue by the boarding ramp while the beast began messing with a panel on the ship's belly. Gareth's eyes were fixed on the alien, but Leo couldn't take his off the other two, right up in each other's faces.

"I'd like to remind you that I'm technically the captain of this ship," the man said. He didn't sound angry so much as exasperated.

"Then act like it. Our shipment's already overdue. We don't have time to board every bombed-out, derelict piece of scrap that we happen to pick up on the scanners, especially if we're not going to get anything out of it."

"What's the code for this compartment again?" the creature in the robe called out, interrupting.

"Two-six-E-four-U," the man said before turning back to the girl. "It's one container of food. Besides, it will help ease my conscience."

"Since when do you have a conscience?" she snapped back.

"Good point," he said.

There was a loud clatter as the giant creature pulled not one but two large containers free from the underbelly of the *Icarus*, dropping them to the floor. He and Bastian Black exchanged nods, then the pirate captain spoke into the communicator fixed to his jacket. "Skits? You there? Fire up the engines. We're leaving. This one's a bust."

"Which some of us already knew," the girl added.

A flurry of static hissed through the device followed by what sounded a little like crying, though from where he was hiding, it was tough for Leo to make out. It sounded distorted. Mechanical. Like the high-pitched whine of grinding gears.

"Wonder what that's all about?" the girl asked.

"Who knows. Could be another power surge. Or maybe one of us looked at her funny before we left. Boo—batten down the hatches. We're out of here."

The creature shut the compartment door and followed the two humans up the ramp as it closed. The pirates were leaving, thank the stars.

Gareth muttered something under his breath, then turned to Leo. "You have your inhaler, yeah?"

Leo patted the pocket of his khaki Coalition pants and nodded. He never went anywhere without his inhaler or his watch, both necessities in their own way. "Why?"

Gareth didn't answer. He didn't need to. Leo figured it out soon enough. He knew the way his brother's mind worked. He glanced at the *Icarus* and then back at Gareth, realizing what was meant by *getting out of here*.

"No. No way. Nuh-uh," Leo said. "We are *not* getting on that ship." He looked at the battered freighter, its ramp already shut. Stow away? Aboard a *pirate ship*?

"You heard Captain Saito," Gareth said. "The *Beagle*'s not going to make it much longer. And we can't count on a rescue. These guys found us by accident. And right now, their ship is our best chance of going to get help. It's worth the risk."

Leo shook his head vehemently. It didn't make any sense. Even in its crippled state, stuck out here in the void, running out of food, the *Beagle* was still safer than sneaking aboard a pirate freighter. Captain Saito and the crew were like Leo's second family. He knew every turn of the ship, could tell you who slept in which bunk. He'd seen the faces of a hundred different planets from the *Beagle*'s starboard observation deck. As much as he'd hated getting on it in the first place, as much as he dreaded leaving Earth, staying on board this limping, paralyzed ship was easily preferable to stowing away with a band of outlaws.

"It's too dangerous," Leo said. "You saw what that girl did to the captain."

Gareth put his hands on Leo's shoulders. "I did. But if we do this right, they will never even know we're there. We just hide in that cargo bin and wait till they dock at their next stop, then we sneak away and go get help. Simple as that."

Anytime anyone ever said "simple as that," it was to hide just how complicated things *could* be. "But what about all our stuff?" Leo thought about Houdini the rabbit, tucked under his thin Coalition-issued pillow. Thought about his backpack hanging in the locker that he used for a closet stuffed full of the comics that his brother said he'd grown out of. Thought about the pictures taped to the wall by his bunk, including the only one he had of his whole family, all five of them, Amos included.

"Forget about your stuff. We'll get it when we come back. Now come on!"

With both hands, Leo's older brother dragged him to his feet, pushing him toward the underside of the ship, careful to stay clear of the view of the cockpit. Leo glanced back at the hangar door, expecting—or maybe just *wanting*—to see Captain Saito there. She would order them to stop, override his brother's foolishness. But the hangar doorway was empty.

"Too sexy for you," Gareth muttered, typing in the code he'd overheard. The latch slid open. From inside the ship Leo heard a kind of clanking and then felt a hum of energy, the ship's engines powering up. He looked into the cargo space. A thin strip of light showed it to be half full of metal containers and crates.

And a lot smaller than he expected. How long would they have to hide away in there? Hours? Days? This was a terrible idea.

Gareth frowned when he saw the size of the cargo bin, but then he set his race face again. He reached for Leo to boost him up, but Leo pushed his brother's hands away. "No. No way. Why can't we just wait here?"

"Wait for what?" Gareth said sharply. "For the Djarik to come back and finish us off? For the life-support systems to give out? To starve to death? We can't stay here and just hope for a rescue. We have to do this. We have to go get help."

"But Dad . . ."

"What about him? We have no idea where Dad is or what happened to him. Face it, Leo, we're on our own."

Leo winced, his brother's words biting deep. His eyes stung. He shook his head again. "You don't know that. You can't know that. He's out there. He's still alive, and he's going to come looking for us."

Gareth spoke more calmly. "Okay. Okay. You're right. He's out there. And once we get help we can go find him. But for now I've got to do what's best for you, understand? I promised him. He said I was in charge."

Leo looked at the cramped cargo hold, back at his brother. "I'm not going. You can't make me."

Leo felt his brother's hand, fingers wrapped around his own. Felt the squeeze. Gareth pressed his forehead to Leo's, locking eyes. "Do you trust me?"

Leo felt himself go slack. So many times Gareth had been the only one around. After Mom was gone, with Dad spending all his time at the lab, leaving only one Fender who knew how to cook. Only one Fender around to read stories and tuck Leo in. To make sure he finished his homework and took a bath. To teach him how to whistle with his fingers and to ride his hoverboard. Gareth was there when nobody else could be.

"He'll find us. Or we'll find him," Leo said.

"We'll find each other," Gareth replied. "I promise."

Leo nodded, placing one foot in his brother's hands for a

boost, pulling himself into the belly of the ship. The compartment was dusty and dry and even more cramped than Leo first thought. He wasn't sure how the two of them were ever going to fit. The sound of the engines reverberated in Leo's ears. He lay beside the hatch and put his hand out to help pull Gareth up.

His brother didn't take it. Gareth's face looked pained, but determined.

"What are you waiting for? Get in!"

"There's no room," Gareth called up, talking louder over the sound of the freighter's engines. "Remember the plan. As soon as the ship lands you get out of there and go find help. Be careful who you talk to. Coalition only. Show them your patch. Let them know who you are. Tell them what happened. Send them to come find us. The coordinates should be logged in your watch."

"What?" Leo yelled, seized with a sudden panic. "What are you talking about?" His brother was reaching out now, but not for Leo's hand; he was typing numbers into the keypad that controlled the compartment hatch.

"At least this way I'll know you got out."

"Gareth, what are you doing?" Leo shouted. "You have to come with me! We have to stay together! I can't do this by myself! Gareth!" Leo got to his knees, ready to jump down, but it was too late.

"Be brave, Leo," Gareth said, holding up one hand as the hatch slid closed.

What do you call an exceptionally hairy alien?
An extra-fur-estrial.
—*Stan Fustman*, 101 Jokes That Are Out of This World, *2048*

THE TURTLE AND
THE EXILE

WHEN HE WAS SEVEN, LEO FOUND HIMSELF LOCKED inside the janitor's closet at school.

The closet was set back in the maintenance area by one of those ancient gas furnaces that stank of burned oil and clanged like a marching band, so it took nearly an hour for anyone to hear little Leo screaming and pounding on the door. There was no light in the closet—only the dead bulb that the janitor never bothered to change—and Leo was sure the space was crawling with spiders and roaches, which made him itch and squirm. Even with a hit from his inhaler he struggled to breathe as he kicked and cursed the three boys that had locked him in there. There had been no cause other than Leo was short and shy and an easy target. The three boys had just been horsing around.

The very next day, Gareth Fender was suspended for three

days for fighting, though admittedly it hadn't really been much of a fight. Leo's brother cornered the kid who had orchestrated the prank in the hallway, pulled his shirt over his head, and punched him once in the gut, doubling him over and turning him into a crumpled heap on the floor. Then Gareth bent down and whispered that if he or his friends ever messed with his little brother again he would make the kid choke down his own teeth.

Leo wasn't picked on for the rest of the year.

But he never forgot about the closet, or how it made him feel. It wasn't claustrophobia exactly. He could spend hours in a tent or a cubbyhole, provided he had crawled in there himself, so long as he was certain he could get out whenever he wanted. It was the *knowing* that made the difference. Leo wasn't afraid of tight spaces. He was afraid of being trapped.

It was probably the biggest reason he hated space travel: because no matter how vast and open it seemed, all it had ever done for Leo was close him in, confine him, force him to live on a ship with its tunneled corridors and windowless compartments. It couldn't compare to the tree-studded fields or stretches of sand back on Earth. Even in the places where you could look out, all you could often see was emptiness, like a solid thing, like a dark wall closing in.

Taking your breath away.

Leo screamed until his throat was raw. He screamed for his brother to get him out even though he knew his brother was long gone. And when his voice grew hoarse, he just whispered his brother's name.

"Gareth. What did you do?"

Leo had always been the sly one. The jokester. Good with card tricks. Sleight of hand. But Gareth had fooled him this time. *Trust me*, he'd said. And Leo had fallen for it. *At least this way I'll know you got out.*

Except Leo wasn't out of anything. He was trapped.

And now he was alone.

He could feel the thrum of the ship's engines all around him. He couldn't tell how fast they were going, but he knew they hadn't engaged their FTL drive. You could tell when a ship jumped: time seemed to slow down—or maybe it actually did slow down, Leo had never understood the physics no matter how many lectures his father gave—every part of your body felt like it was stretching, the particles pulling away from each other as if you would literally split into a trillion pieces, fragmenting in every direction. And then there was the blinding pain, right behind your eyes and the overwhelming urge to vomit that first timers—and some twentieth timers—never managed to suppress, only a split second of torture before everything evened itself out for the duration. At least until you came back to sublight speed and it happened all over again: two upchucks for the price of one.

Leo hadn't gotten that feeling—the sinking, sickening stomach drop, the dizzying head spin—which meant the ship was still using its conventional thrusters, saving its ventasium.

Which meant that he couldn't be *that* far from the *Beagle* and his brother.

When I see him again, Leo thought to himself, *I'm going to let him have it.*

When, he told himself. *When. When. When.*

We'll find each other.

Leo stopped pounding uselessly on the hatch door and began searching for a keypad or an emergency release in the darkness, something that would unlock it, though once he felt the ship moving he realized that opening the hatch to the *outside* would be the absolute worst thing he could do—no sense blowing *yourself* out of the airlock. He just wanted to know that there *was* a way out, that he wouldn't be stuck in here forever. At least the cargo holds were hooked up to the ship's life-support systems, gravity and oxygen. At least he could breathe.

Until he couldn't.

Until the space around him constricted even further—the darkness wrapping its fingers around his neck, leaning against his chest. Leo's breaths grew shallower, more hurried, until he couldn't swallow. Until his throat felt like it was the size of a pinhole.

You are alone, the darkness said. *You are alone and you are trapped, and there is no way out.*

Leo choked. Gasped. He fumbled for his inhaler in the darkness, dropped it, scrambled, down on his knees, banging his head against the compartment's metal side, finding his medicine, flipping the cap, wrapping his lips around it.

Taking a breath.

The instant chemical rush. Like being on the highway and opening the car window to stick your head out. He took a second deep breath, then curled into a tight ball on the floor of the compartment, barely fitting between the containers, head pressed back against the steel siding. He conjured his father's words, the reassurances he gave whenever Leo had a panic attack: *Deep breaths, Leo. In. Out. Imagine your chest filling like a hot-air balloon, lifting high into the clouds. Nothing else around. Just clouds and blue sky.* Ever since he was little it was the same image. Always the balloon. Always the clouds. Leo felt the rattle in his chest calm, the grip around his throat ease. Yes. He could breathe. Just breathe.

But he could still barely see. Blinking at the thin strip of dull white light by his feet, barely enough to illuminate his boots, he felt like he was out there already in the vacuum of space. Cold and dark. He rubbed at his arms and his right hand stopped at his wrist. At his watch. The gift from his parents.

In the meager glow of the light strip, Leo turned the dial to twelve—the hologram he played the most—and pressed the button.

Suddenly the space before him was filled with the soft glimmer of the projection. It was the only holo that wasn't of Leo, the one he'd kept in the watch's memory from the very first year he got it.

It was a recording of his mother.

In the holo she is sitting on the porch of the house where Leo grew up, holding a thin blade of grass that she'd just pulled from the cracks between the steps as if it were a delicate flower, looking at it intensely, biting her lip, as if trying to solve the puzzle of it being there, how it managed to grow where nothing else could, living in the most impossible of places. After a moment she turns and says:

I see you, my little lion.

That's what she called him. Often right before she would pounce on him and tickle him furiously, until he roared in laughter. But not this time. This time he'd caught her just sitting there, twisting the bit of grass back and forth, looking thoughtful and just a little sad.

It was the last recording anyone had of her and Leo kept it on his wrist and played it every day, just so he'd never forget—her hair streaked with threads of auburn, her butterscotch eyes. Her calming voice tinged with melancholy. *I see you.*

Leo watched the holo three times until his nerves somewhat settled, his breathing evening out. In normal light the holos appeared lifelike, but here in the darkness the projection gave off a faint glow, enough that Leo could get a better look at his surroundings. Enough for him to realize that there simply wasn't enough room for two in the compartment, not with the four large containers still housed there.

Though that didn't make him any less angry at Gareth. So they both couldn't have fit; that just meant neither of them should have tried.

Leo stood up as well as he was able and looked around for something useful—a release mechanism, an emergency latch. Gareth had said to wait until the ship landed and then make his escape, but what if he couldn't get out? What if he really was stuck in here forever? Leo cursed his brother's name again and pounded on the metal panel above him in frustration.

Moments later there came a pounding from the other side.

Leo froze, breath held, listening. The response was followed by another sound—a bolt sliding, a latch undone.

There was a sudden crack of light, and then a flood of it.

Leo shielded his eyes and curled back into a ball as the panel above him slid away. He blinked through the sudden brightness to see something huge and metal leaning over the edge of the compartment looking at him. The thing was covered in colorful stickers, at least three appendages of various sizes jutting from its torso. It was clearly a robot of some kind.

Leo screamed.

The robot screamed.

The compartment door slammed closed again.

Leo crouched there, back in the shadows, his inhaler clutched in his right fist. Had that been his one chance at escape? If so, he'd missed it. What, exactly, *was* that thing? Leo had some experience with mechanicals—there were two maintenance bots aboard the *Beagle*—but he'd never heard one shriek like that before. And what were all those stickers plastered across it? All those logos and advertisements. Like a billboard on treads.

Leo didn't have long to consider his next move before he heard muffled voices coming from above. The hatch slid open again, revealing a slightly more familiar but no less frightening face framed with two horns.

The alien looked down at him with his large ox eyes. Still dressed in his robe, his horns looked less deadly up close, but the rest of him seemed just as dangerous if not more so. Next to him, the steel contraption Leo had gotten only a glimpse of moments before was poking the beast with one of its metal arms, which didn't seem like a good idea. Leo would never poke something like that with anything.

"See. And *you* thought I was making it up!"

It was definitely a robot. But where most bots Leo'd seen were sleek and polished, carefully manufactured so as not to show their seams, this thing was a wild conglomeration of spare parts seemingly stacked together at random: a set of three tracks at its base, all different sizes, causing the machine to tilt awkwardly to the left, a round metal drum that served as its body with a dozen compartments, and a head with sensors for eyes and a hole the size of a dime where the scream had originated. It looked to Leo like a clunky metal snowman, an oversized science fair project cobbled together by a ten-year-old in his parents' garage, each of its parts a slightly different color, sloppily welded together. Now that he wasn't being screamed at, Leo could read some of the stickers that had been plastered to the robot's frame: *Gone Fishin', Just Do It, Schwarz 4 Prez, My Zombie Ate Your Honors Student*, plus a giant rainbow peace symbol above its center tread. Someone had slapped on a huge black-and-white grin full of painted-on teeth just below the robot's external speaker. Looking at it made Leo shudder.

"*This* is what you were screaming about?" the alien said, pointing at Leo pressed into a corner. "You said there was a vicious monster hiding in here."

"Well, it's not like I had time to run a *scan* on him or anything," the robot protested, its voice tinny and grating. "And how do you know he's not vicious? *Look* at him!"

Leo struggled to find his voice. *I'm not vicious*, he wanted to say, but it only came out as a cough and a wheeze.

Two of the alien's four hands began to tug on the ends of its curved horns. "Human," it said. "Must have snuck on board back at that cruiser."

"A stowaway. Let's just lock it back in there and pretend we didn't see it," the robot suggested, its yellow-bulbed eyes blinking, its hideous smile never changing. "It will die of hunger eventually and then we can just jettison the body."

"How's he going to die of hunger? He's in there with the rest of our food. Sometimes you don't make any sense."

"I said *eventually*."

The robot started to close the door.

"No!" Leo yelled, finally finding his voice. "No. Please. Don't leave me in here. I'm not dangerous. I promise." He stumbled, trying to think of what to say next. The plan—Gareth's plan—had been to wait until the ship landed and then sneak away without the pirates ever knowing he was on board.

Obviously Leo needed a new plan.

He ransacked his brain for everything he knew about pirates, both the space-faring and sea-faring kind. "I demand . . ." he began, but then corrected himself. "No. Sorry. I *request* to be taken to see your captain." After all, wasn't there some rule about that? A pirate's code? Honor among thieves? Leo was sure he'd seen it in a movie once.

The robot and the alien looked at each other. The alien named Boo reached over and touched a button on the bot, activating some kind of ship intercom. "Kat? Can you come to the aft storage compartments, please. We have a minor situation," he said in his soft, purring voice.

"You know I don't like it when you press my buttons without permission," the robot said, batting at Boo with its retractable arm.

"Everything presses your buttons."

"Yes, but you shed and the hair gets in my sockets. It's annoying."

"You think everything's annoying."

"But you are especially annoying."

Their bickering was interrupted by the sound of steps along the corridor, a third voice, also already familiar to Leo, calling to them. "Don't you dare say you accidentally reversed the solid waste ventilation pump again. If so, I'm not helping you clean up the cra . . ." The voice trailed off.

Leo saw the black boots first and then the uniform with its gleaming brass buttons, followed by the sharp features and dark eyes of the young woman, the one named Kat, looking down on him. She stared at Leo for a moment as if she were hoping he was a hologram or just a figment of her imagination, then she turned and gave the other two an icy stare. "Please tell me this wasn't either of your ideas."

The robot swiveled its head emphatically.

"We just found him," Boo said. "Guess he snuck aboard at the last stop."

The girl in the black uniform crouched, close enough that Leo could see a scar on her chin, starting low and curving upward, reaching her bottom lip, which was turned downward in a look of minor annoyance.

"What's your name, ship rat?"

"Leo," he managed to cough out.

"Leo. Terrific. Well, Leo, I'm Katarina Corea. This is Boo and the only one smiling because she can't do otherwise is Skits. The ship is called the *Icarus* and you are trespassing on it, which is a crime punishable by death as far as we're concerned. So before we open that compartment and blow you back out into space, you've got one chance to give us one highly convincing reason why we shouldn't."

Leo looked at the floor beneath him, the sheath of metal separating him from oblivion. "I didn't mean to," he protested, speaking quickly, tongue tumbling over his words. "It was my brother's idea. I swear. He made me." Leo couldn't decide what to focus on, the girl's eerily unblinking eyes or the deadly pistol strapped to her side. He kept jumping from one to the other.

"And which compartment is your brother hiding in?" she asked.

"He's not. He left me."

"Jerk move," the robot said.

"Yeah . . . I mean, no," Leo stammered. "He said that we should try to get away. He was afraid the ship, the *Beagle*, that it wasn't going to make it. And our father . . . I swear it wasn't my idea. Please." Leo glanced down at his feet, at the hatch his brother pushed him through. "You have to believe me. I'm not dangerous. I swear. I'm just a kid. I—"

Leo stopped talking when the girl raised her hand, the artificial one with the four cold titanium fingers, each ending in sharp points. "Okay. Got it. Good speech." She looked up at her companions. "You two go scan the other compartments for more Coalition parasites that may or may not be related to this one. Let me know if you find anything."

"You've got it, boss," Boo said, giving the girl a salute before turning to follow the hodgepodge robot down the corridor.

"And you," the girl said, pointing to Leo, "had better crawl out of there before I change my mind and send you floating. Also, I better not find out that you've eaten any of our food while you were down there or, I swear, I will stick my arm down your throat and play the claw game with your stomach."

She opened and closed the metal digits of her bionic hand,

still frowning, and Leo imagined her reaching in and finding the ficken nuggets he'd had earlier, the ones he felt like he was about to lose all over his boots.

"Gareth, what have you done?" Leo whispered to himself.

And what am I supposed to do now?

Leo wished he was back in the storage compartment. It was dark and cramped and uncomfortable and nearly gave him a panic attack, but it was better than being led to see a pirate captain with a bounty on his head by a girl who had just threatened to shove her metal arm down his throat.

At least he wasn't being led at gunpoint. Apparently, the girl named Kat agreed with Leo that he wasn't all that dangerous. In fact, she kept her back to him. He shuffled behind her, careful not to get too close, taking everything in, keeping a sharp eye for possible hiding places in case he could somehow slip away. Not that he could hide for long. The robot—Skits—could easily sniff him out with its scanners. There was nowhere for him to go.

Despite its odd shape and yellow paint job, the *Icarus* was like any other ship in its guts. Any old ship, at least. Tight corridors with metal ladders and overhanging conduits. Blinking lights and hissing jets of steam. Dangling wires that looked like they really should be connected to something. Everything was rusted, bent, or broken. The only things that shone on board were the girl's buttons and boots.

"I like your ship," Leo mumbled.

"This ship is trash," the girl said back. "Black got it from a smuggler who owed him a favor. He sunk most everything he had into repurposing it, and sinks most everything we get into keeping it running. But it flies. Most of the time. That's something, I guess."

Leo didn't know that pirates ever did favors for anyone. "And you call it the *Icarus*?" He had never heard the word before. Could be alien in origin, he thought, even if its captain is human.

"It's a myth. A cautionary tale. Something about a boy who tried to fly where he wasn't supposed to. It got him killed."

Leo swallowed hard. He was pretty sure she was just making that up to scare him. If so, it worked.

"Are you the first mate?" Leo thought back to the alien's salute. She evidently outranked Boo. And probably everyone outranked the robot. In the Coalition everyone had a rank *except* the robots.

"I'm nobody's mate," Kat said. "And I really think it's in your best interest to stop talking."

Leo stopped talking.

He silently studied the girl instead. Black hair still in its braid. Weapon holstered at her side. Her arm—the artificial one—looked to be top-of-the-line tech, though there were no cosmetics, no skin coverings; she made no attempt to hide the fact that it was made of metal. The girl carried herself with a confidence that made her seem older than she probably was. She was lithe, like Gareth. Gareth's leanness, Leo knew, came from running. No doubt this girl had been running for part of her life too. She was a pirate, after all.

As they approached the front of *Icarus*, Leo could hear music playing, could feel it pounding through the metal walls. Rock music. He didn't recognize the song, just the sound of electric guitar chords being crunched and someone scream-singing about love and pain and death. Leo'd never been into music; that was more Gareth's thing. His father only listened to the classics—Ed Sheeran, Taylor Swift, Drake. Whatever Bastian Black was listening to, he obviously liked it loud.

The girl activated the door and the music got even louder.

Leo stepped—pushed was more like it—into the ship's spacious cockpit to find the man from the wanted notice sitting in the pilot's seat with his back to them, drumming his fingers along the console. The music rattled Leo's teeth.

"Captain," the girl said sharply.

The man continued to drum.

"Captain!" she said louder. "Baz! We have company!"

A finger reached out and casually flipped a switch, killing the guitar mid-solo as Bastian Black twisted around in his chair and took Leo in. An initial expression of confusion quickly morphed into a sly smile, as if he knew Leo's entire story already.

"Captain Black," the girl began, "allow me to introduce the latest in a string of mishaps caused by your terrible decision-making. This is Leo. Skits found him hiding in one of the storage compartments."

The captain leaned forward to get a better look, still smiling. Leo didn't like that smile. There was way too much hidden behind it.

"Leo. Like Leonardo?"

"I guess," Leo said.

"The painter or the ninja turtle?"

Leo had at least heard of the painter. "Ninja turtle?" he questioned.

"Heroes in a half shell? Turtle power? Are you serious? You *are* human, aren't you?"

Leo nodded.

"Know what—just forget it." The captain continued to drum his fingers against his leg, the music still playing in his head. He didn't look anything like a ship's commander, though admittedly Leo had gotten used to Captain Saito's straitlaced, tight-cuffed Coalition uniform and stiff-shouldered poise. Black still wore his blue jeans and Dr Pepper T-shirt, but he'd removed his holsters and traded in his sneakers for flip-flops— blue ones with little yellow flowers on the thong. They made him *look* less intimidating, but Leo knew better: this man was wanted. He was an enemy of the Coalition. Nothing he said could be trusted.

"So you're from the ship we just boarded?" Captain Black asked. "The *Basset*?"

"*Beagle*," Leo mumbled. He looked out the cockpit, hoping faintly to catch a glimpse of something familiar, a planet, another ship, anything. But there was only emptiness. He had no idea how far they'd already gone, how much distance was already between him and Gareth. Any amount was too much.

"*Beagle.* And before that, what? Mining colony? Outpost? Military base?"

"Earth," Leo answered.

"Ah. The motherland. No place like home, am I right, Kat?" Bastian Black clicked his heels together three times for no apparent reason. At least, not apparent to Leo.

"If you say so," the girl replied. "I don't really remember."

"Right. Any weapons?"

"No weapons. Just an annoying habit of asking questions," she replied. "And going where he's not wanted, obviously."

"Please, Captain Black," Leo interjected. "It wasn't my idea. My brother . . ." Leo paused, picturing Gareth standing below him, a meter away, just out of reach, closing the door on him. "He put me on here. He told me to wait until the ship landed and then sneak out and go get help. That's all."

"Help. You mean someone from the Coalition?" Kat asked.

"Well . . . yeah," Leo said. *Who else would he possibly go to for help?*

"So you could turn us in?" she pressed.

"No! Nothing like that. Just for a rescue. I swear. It has nothing to do with you. You weren't even supposed to know I was there!"

Leo watched the captain's face. He looked like maybe he believed it.

The girl, clearly, did not. "Or *maybe*," she said, "you thought you'd be a Coalition hero. Sneak on board. Gain our trust. Wait till we were all asleep, then take our weapons and use them to hold us prisoner so you could turn us in yourself."

"What? No!" Leo said, recoiling. "I'm just a kid. I don't even know how to fly a ship. And I've never *shot* anyone."

Kat and Baz exchanged a look. "You were twelve the first time?" he asked her.

"Ten, actually," Kat said. "But it was only in the leg. Just to slow him down enough to pick his pockets. And just for the record, this? This right here?" She waved a titanium hand at Leo. "This just proves my point. It proves *all* my points, actually."

Bastian Black shrugged. "You're the one who said we should take things."

"I meant we should take something of *value*. Besides, we didn't take him. He snuck on. So, what now? You want me to . . . you know?" Kat made a motion with her head. A little backward jerk. Bastian Black raised an eyebrow, clearly not getting it. "You know . . . ," she said, making a lot more motions now, her hands twisting something imaginary, then opening something, like an airlock, then pushing something— or somebody—through that airlock into deep space.

Black got it finally.

So did Leo.

He shook his head, spitting out words as fast as he could. "Please. I'm not dangerous, I swear. Just take me with you. Let me get help. You can drop me somewhere and take off. I won't tell anyone about you, I promise. The Djarik took my father. Gareth is the only family I have left. I need to rescue him. To rescue all of them." Leo could feel the tears forming and blinked them away.

"You say the Djarik took your dad?" Black asked, his eyes narrowing.

Leo nodded.

"And just left the rest of you floating out there on that wreck?"

Leo nodded again. Black rubbed his chin.

"Sounds about right," Kat said, clearly not surprised by the Djarik's cruelty. Then again, three seconds ago she was mimicking pushing Leo out of an airlock into space.

"Please," Leo pleaded again. "I have to help them."

For a moment, Leo saw the captain's eyes soften and he thought *maybe*.

But then the moment passed.

"Sorry, kid. Your have tos and my have tos don't match up. And since I'm the one with the ship and you're the one who snuck *onto* the ship, you get exactly zero say in the matter. So here's what's going to happen. We are going to go to Kaber's Point. We're going to make our delivery and get our money. And when we're finished with that, then maybe, *maybe*, we will try to find somebody who cares. Until then, *you* will sit perfectly still and not say a single word or else you'll find yourself floating back through space to that ship of yours, understood?"

Leo started to protest some more, but thought better of it, nodding instead. He was still alive. And though he had no idea what Kaber's Point was or what the pirates were delivering, at least their captain hadn't completely ruled out the possibility of helping him.

Bastian Black looked up at the girl. "How about you go lock ninja turtle here in the bunks. Let Boo babysit him till we dock. It will still be a while."

"Boo?" Leo repeated. The seven-foot-tall creature with horns and sharp teeth and enough arms to rip all of Leo's limbs from his body at once? "You're going to put me in a *room* with that thing?"

The captain of the *Icarus* put up a finger in warning. "That was ten words."

"Twelve actually," Kat corrected. "I think that's enough to justify shooting him." Leo couldn't tell if she was kidding or not. At least not until Black laughed, and even then he wasn't so sure.

The first mate who was nobody's mate grabbed Leo by the collar, pushing him out of the cockpit as the electric guitars began blasting from the speakers again. Captain Bastian Black of the *Icarus* returned to playing imaginary drums to music that was made on a planet trillions of miles away.

It hadn't taken long for Leo to miss Earth.

The first month aboard the *Beagle* was exciting, he reluctantly came to admit. Meeting the crew, learning the ins and outs of the ship, seeing the planets and the orbital stations, jumping from star to star. And there were things about home he was happy to leave behind. The smog, bad before the Aykari arrived and made worse by their constant drilling. The crowded streets. The constant threat of earthquakes—another unfortunate but unavoidable side effect of extracting precious ventasium from the caches in the planet's crust. He didn't miss the high-pitched whine of those Aykari excavators, as big as skyscrapers, each shaped like the Eifel Tower, burrowing into the ground, nosing their way to stores of V. Or the way the water had started to taste funny, like the metallic aftertaste you get when eating peaches straight out of a can.

But the excitement soon wore off, and Leo began to long for walls that weren't made of steel plates. For toilets that weren't tubes. For the smell of a spring rain and the tickle of a breeze along his neck hairs.

He ached for a sky full of clouds. He sorely missed trees—there were still hordes of them on Earth if you drove far enough out of the city. Tall, thin aspens and blazing red maples, and the sweet stinging scent of an acre of evergreens. Leo missed the smell of pine. He missed the mountains and the rivers and skipping smooth stones to the other bank. He missed hiking through Red Rock. He missed taking the magnet to San Diego to hang out at Coronado beach, chasing seagulls and burying his father up to his neck in sand.

And he missed the food. Oh, how he missed the food. Crisp apples and non-powdered milk and pizza dripping in grease.

He missed licking the drippings from the edges of ice cream cones. He missed the sizzling hiss of fajitas and the smell of roasted peppers from his favorite Mexican restaurant.

And sunsets. Leo might have missed sunsets most of all. You don't think about sunsets until you are on board a ship in deep space with only your watch to tell you when a day supposedly begins and ends.

When he was little he assumed those things would last forever, even as they started to disappear. He took them for granted. He just didn't realize it until they were gone. Fresh air and not-freeze-dried food. Bird chirps and beach sand. Sunsets and greasy pizza.

It was a glorious combination.

Sitting with his mom and dad on the back porch, watching as Earth's nearest star crept slowly toward the horizon, making a canvas of the sky. The sound of his brother's basketball clanging off the rim in the driveway, having already scarfed down his three slices of plain cheese. That's all he and Leo ever ate. One medium cheese for them. Another with everything on it for Mom and Dad.

They sat right next to each other like always, never across from each other like his friends' parents, double-dipping their crusts in the same garlic sauce. The inseparable Fenders.

"Can you imagine not being able to eat pizza?" Leo's father wondered.

"Who can't eat pizza?" Leo asked around a piece of crust. But as soon as he asked he knew the answer. The Aykari couldn't. They couldn't eat any solid food; they had no teeth. They subsisted on a purely liquid diet—some synthetic mixture that human scientists were already trying to adapt for the Earth market, no doubt with the goal of spawning new fad Eat-like-the-Aliens diets. Leo had to admit the Aykari were all skinny.

"Their loss," Leo said. What kind of a superior alien race doesn't even have teeth? Or taste buds? Sure, they'd created a fusion engine the size of a deck of cards and could cure a host of diseases, but what was the point of living if you couldn't taste chocolate? Or bacon? Just the thought of it was horrifying.

"Well, at least that's *one* thing we have that they don't," Leo's mother said.

"Speaking of . . . the university is set to approve my grant tomorrow," Dr. Fender said. "To establish a partnership with the Aykari on the study of the additional applications of ventasium here on Earth. We're going to look at everything. Medicine. Military. Construction. Environmental science. Cosmetics."

"Cosmetics?" Mom asked.

"Philip Ganderson over in the chemistry department thinks it might be reconfigured to stimulate hair regrowth."

"Ganderson. He's the bald one, right?"

"So he's a little biased," Leo's dad said. "I'm sure most of it will lead to dead ends. The important thing is that we'll be working together, Aykari and humans. A two-way street. We need to show them that we have more to offer than what they can dig out from under our crust. We need to be a part of the bigger picture."

"What bigger picture?" Leo asked. Only after his mother groaned did he realize he had walked right into his father's trap. The warning signs flashed in his brain: lecture incoming. He should have gone to play basketball with Gareth.

"*The* bigger picture," Dr. Calvin Fender said, smiling. "The *biggest* picture. The thing we're all striving for. A free and peaceful galaxy. That's what the Aykari are working toward with their Coalition. It's what we *should* be working toward, it's just that humanity hasn't completely gotten on board with it yet—for whatever reason. Governments are dragging their feet. Afraid to commit."

Coalition. Leo had heard his father use that word before.

Dr. Fender took a bite of his pizza, chewed it thoughtfully, then stared at the slice he was holding for a solid minute before pointing at it. "Let's say this pizza is the universe."

"No wonder I'm stuffed," Leo's mother joked.

"I'm trying to illustrate something," Leo's father said. "So this is the universe. Or our galaxy, at least." He began to point to the toppings. "You've got your onions. Your pepperoni. Sausage. Bacon. Green pepper. Mushrooms. Garlic. Spinach. Tomatoes. Olives. They're like planets all mixed together."

"Disgusting," Leo said, taking another bite of his plain cheese.

"Delicious," his mother countered.

"The point is," Leo's dad continued, "all these different planets, these different civilizations, they are separate, unique, independent, but they are all bound by something greater."

"Cheese," Leo said.

His mother laughed. His father didn't.

"Yes. Exactly!" Dr. Fender said. "The Coalition is the cheese holding it all together. Making it one big peaceful, productive, egalitarian piece of pizza."

"And your father calls *me* a dreamer."

"It's not a dream. It's an inevitability. It's going to happen. The Aykari have made it possible. It's up to us humans now to band together as a species and find a way to contribute beyond just giving them access to our ventasium. It's hardly enough, considering how much they've done for us."

It sort of seemed like enough for Leo. After all, without the ventasium, the Aykari wouldn't get anywhere. "So which are we?" Leo wanted to know, still staring at the slice of the universe in his father's hand. "Which one is Earth?"

"We're the mushrooms," his mother said, plucking one out of her cheesy coalition and popping it in her mouth. "Don't you think, Dr. Fender? Humans—the fungus of the galaxy?"

Leo's father smiled, but his eyes were elsewhere already, looking up, not at the resplendent pink glow on the horizon, but higher, at the half-moon already visible, beyond the blockade of Aykari ships forming a defensive perimeter around Earth like a big brother curling his fists, threatening to take on any would-be bullies. Staring deep into the sky, as if his vision could reach the edges of the solar system, to the spiral arms of the Milky Way. Leo stared up there with him, sucking the grease off his fingers. It was a nice idea, this Coalition. Probably something worth being a part of. Even for the mushrooms. Maybe especially for the mushrooms.

There was no way of knowing then just how soon it would happen. No way for eight-year-old Leo to know that before his next birthday, the peoples of Earth would do exactly what Leo's father predicted they would—join forces with the Aykari and start down the path of fulfilling Dr. Calvin Fender's dream.

And the nightmare that would make it happen.

There was no escape.

Even if the door wasn't locked—and Leo couldn't be sure— there was no way past the creature guarding it.

Though, to be fair, the alien wasn't so much guarding it as simply sitting beside it, slumped in his seat, staring at a data-pad, occasionally grunting to itself. Close up, Boo looked no less intimidating. Its face appeared more of a blend of musk ox and mountain lion, with fine, curled whiskers prickling out of its snout; but it was still so massive, its muscular chest peeking out of the V-shaped fold in its robe, the rolling muscles of its arms no doubt capable of snapping Leo's bones like pretzel sticks. Its curly ears occasionally twitched like a dog's, and then one of the creature's four hands would scratch it absently.

For what seemed like an hour, Leo stared silently at the

alien, who didn't seem to even acknowledge that anyone else was in the room. Until, without even looking up from its datapad, it said, "That's it. I can't stand it any longer. Just ask."

The soft voice coming through Leo's translator surprised him all over again. He cleared his throat, mustered the courage to utter two words, even though he was already eleven over his limit. "Ask what?"

The alien set down its pad and turned to Leo. Leo could see now that its eyes weren't all black—there were flecks of orange scattered within them like constellations. "Whatever it is you're wanting to ask me. You've been staring at me for forever. So just go on. Get it out of your system."

"But I'm not supposed to talk," Leo murmured. "That's what Baz . . . what Captain Black said. And Kat—the girl—she threatened to shoot me."

The alien snorted. "Yeah, she says things like that. It's mostly talk. She doesn't normally shoot anyone. . . . Unless they try to shoot her first. . . . Or if she thinks they are going to shoot her first. . . . Or if she thinks they're *thinking* of shooting her."

"Oh."

The alien raised all four of its arms, showing Leo its hairless gray palms. "But I don't even have a gun, as you can see, so go on. Ask."

Leo didn't think a gun was really necessary—the hulking babysitter could probably squeeze the brains from Leo's skull like pulp from an orange. Still, he did have questions. About Captain Black. About the *Icarus*. About the shipment they were supposed to deliver. Questions whose answers might help him think of a way to get help. But in this moment, Leo was more taken with the fur-covered creature looking at him with wide and maybe slightly impatient eyes.

"Um. Okay. So . . . what, uh . . . what *are* you?"

"What do you mean, what am I?"

"I mean, like what species are you?" Leo added. "Like I'm human. And you're . . ."

"Not. Yes, I know. As if I wasn't outnumbered already," Boo mumbled. "I am, in fact, a Queleti. I come from a planet in the Gajen system—far out on the Aykari border. Small planet. Lots of mountains. Cold. At least you would think so, given how hairless you all are."

Leo shook his head. He'd never even heard of the Gajen system. He hadn't learned about it in school, and it was never part of the *Beagle*'s itinerary. Of course the galaxy was a massive place, and he'd seen only a fraction of it, which could explain why he'd never met a Queleti before either.

"Don't feel bad. I'd never heard of your planet either until I met Baz. Sounds lovely, from what he tells me—minus the constantly rising temperatures, rampant social injustice, and the disease-carrying insects and whatnot. My full name is Bo'enmaza Okardo Ryulen Zafar. House Okardo. Tribe Zafar, but the others just call me Boo."

Boo, Baz, Kat, Skits. These didn't sound like the names of pirates. They sounded more like characters out of a children's cartoon. "And your name?" Boo asked.

"Leo Tyson Fender. Um, house Fender. Tribe American, I guess."

"An honor to meet you, Leo of House Fender." The Queleti gave Leo a four-armed salute that Leo couldn't exactly replicate. The courtesy of such an introduction took Leo by surprise. Compared to the robot that wanted to starve him to death, the girl who threatened to shoot him, and the captain who forbade him to speak, this alien suddenly seemed the least scary of the lot.

"You don't act like a pirate."

"And how am I supposed to act?" Boo asked.

"I don't know. Pirates are, you know . . . cruel. And bloodthirsty. And they don't care about anyone but themselves. They just steal whatever they want."

"Maybe you don't have anything I want," Boo remarked.

Leo considered everything he had on him. His watch. His inhaler. His worn-out boots. "Probably not," he said. Still, Leo knew he should be careful. Just because this creature was soft-spoken and more agreeable than his companions didn't mean he wouldn't tear Leo's heart out with his teeth if provoked.

"So let me ask you something, Leo of House Fender. What are you doing aboard this ship?"

"It was my brother's idea," Leo said quickly.

"Of course it was. That's something I've noticed about your species. You're incredibly adept at deflecting blame. Baz does it all the time. So your brother told you to stow away with a

- 94 -

band of wanted pirates. I'm assuming he had a good reason?"

Leo wasn't sure how good it was. "He said we were going to escape, to go get help, but there was only room for me."

The Queleti nodded, his eyes thoughtful. "So he thought he was saving you."

"Well, we see how *that* turned out," Leo muttered.

"You're still breathing, aren't you?" Boo said. "That's something. And the rest of your House? Where are they?"

It took a moment for Leo to register what the Queleti was asking him. "The Djarik took my dad when they attacked our ship. My mother's . . . gone," Leo said softly.

Boo nodded his understanding. "So they took your father and left the rest of you behind? Seems unusual for the Djarik. Do you know why?"

Leo shook his head. He'd been asking himself that same question for five days, ever since the attack. "He was—*is* a scientist," Leo self-corrected. "He knows a lot about ventasium."

Boo snorted.

"What?" Leo asked.

"Nothing," the alien said. "Just that when it comes to people's motives, that stuff tends to come up a lot. Still, I'm sorry to hear about your parents. It is a terrible thing. And your brother was wrong to put you on board this ship. Family should never be separated if they can help it." There was a sudden sadness in the Queleti's voice.

"What about you? What about your House? Where are they?" Leo asked.

"All of the members of tribe Zafar are still back on Quel. I am the only one who left."

"But you just said—"

"I didn't leave by choice," Boo interrupted. "I was exiled."

"Exiled," Leo echoed.

"I did something terrible. Something that shamed my House and my tribe. I had to go. Eventually I crossed paths with Baz and he took me in."

"What was it? Did you hurt someone?"

"It is not worth discussing," Boo said, his voice deepening into a growl.

Leo took the growl to heart and didn't press it. At least he and this alien had something in common: they'd both been forced to leave their planet with little more than the clothes on their backs.

Though Leo had more clothes to show for it.

"Is that what you always wear?" He pointed to the long flowing robe that was snug around the Queleti's shoulders.

Boo looked at his outfit with admiration. "This is a Yunkai. It's the traditional garb of my people. The thick fur makes clothes superfluous on my planet, so it's just for ornamentation. The color of your robe represents your station."

"So what does white mean?"

"It means nothing. It means I have no station. To my people I am nothing. An outcast."

"So then why do you still wear it?"

"Because Baz says I make him self-conscious without it.

Something having to do with what he calls rock-hard abs."
The Queleti paused. "Also because I am still proud of where
I come from, even if they are no longer proud of me. That
symbol on your garb," he said, pointing to the patch on the
breast of Leo's shirt. "The mark of the Coalition?"

Leo nodded. It was a simple design. A large red planet with
at least two dozen other smaller planets forming a ring around
it in blue. The red planet was Aykar, of course. The Bringers
of Light. Preservers of order and peace. Earth could be any
of the two dozen circles surrounding it. Leo traced the ring
with his finger. He'd forgotten all his shirts even had that
insignia—every scrap of clothing he had was provided for him
by the Coalition.

Even in translation, Leo could catch a hint of something in
the alien's voice. A wariness. "What's wrong with the Coalition?"

"Nothing. So long as you are part of it," Boo said. But
before he could elaborate, Bastian Black's voice piped in over
the ship's internal coms.

"This is your captain speaking. We are coming up on Kaber's
Point, so make sure your seats are in their full and upright positions
and that your robes and artificial limbs are securely fastened."

"What's Kaber's Point?" Leo asked.

"It's a place for people like us."

"People like us?"

"The ones who don't belong," Boo replied.

The ventasium was always there, waiting for us to find it, just as we were always here, waiting for the Aykari to find us. Whether these two events transpiring so close together is a matter of chance or fate, I do not know. But I do know that without either one of them—the element or the aliens—our planet, and our species, were surely doomed for extinction.

—Enrico Ventasi, *The Discovery of Our Species*, *2045*

AN UNEVEN EXCHANGE

LEO COULD NAME OVER THREE DOZEN PLANETS, NOT including the eight in his own system. His teachers told him it was part of his responsibility as a galactic citizen to be knowledgeable of worlds and species other than his own. His father wholeheartedly agreed.

In the fourth grade, he had to give a presentation on one of the other known inhabited planets in the Milky Way—a name humans stubbornly stuck to, even after the Aykari informed them of the galaxy's standard numerical designation. The students in Mrs. Dolson's class drew a planet from a hat and were told to describe its general location, nearest star, climate, gravity, composition, life-forms and civilizations, major galactic contributions, and so on. The students showed pictures of their planets on the giant vid screen at the front of the room. Most of them played dramatic classical music in the background. Strauss proved popular.

Leo drew Tildus 4, a little blue marble orbiting a very distant M-class star. Temperate and mostly covered in water, though unlike Earth, Tildus 4 had produced only primitive sea life due to a somewhat inhospitable atmosphere. Thus its major contribution to galactic culture was that its oceanic creatures were considered delicacies among the galaxy's other species, like lobster or caviar to humans. Leo told his class that he hoped one day to own a shell from this planet to add to his collection, though he would have to wear a clunky protective suit and helmet if he wanted to go beachcombing, otherwise he would choke to death on the highly toxic air.

What struck Leo about that particular assignment wasn't the presentations—though Misty Treach's twenty-minute, fully animated vidflip on Cygnus 7 was overdoing it—but how full the hat had been. Mrs. Dolson had restricted them to only "a handful of possibilities," picking only those planets that would provide "ample information available to research" and were in "relatively close proximity" to Earth, yet the list was still a hundred planets long.

Leo knew that only a fraction of the planets in the known galaxy were capable of supporting life, and only a fraction of those had a species intelligent enough to master space travel or at least take advantage of it when it was handed to them. Fractions of fractions. One in a million. Which made humans rare, but not unique.

And certainly not the center of the universe.

Sitting in his antiquated wooden desk in Mrs. Dolson's class, staring at that hat full of planets, Leo was struck by the immensity of it. The universe and its infinite possibilities. Why then, he thought, does it sometimes still seem so small? How is it that with millions of planets circling millions of stars and the vast stretches of nothing in between that you sometimes still couldn't find a space where you felt safe, a place you could go to escape the things that haunted you?

After all the presentations were finished the class was greeted with a surprise—a virtual visit from an Aykari educational ambassador. The class wriggled and buzzed at the chance to talk to an Aykari face-to-face. After an introduction where the ambassador touted the mission of the Coalition—a collection of free peoples forging a bold new path in the galaxy through the sharing of information, technology, and resources while protecting each other from those who would try to undermine those freedoms—a dozen hands shot up with questions for their alien guest, nearly every one starting with *Is it really true*.

Is it really true that Aykari have no tongues? (True, their species never had a need for them.) Is it really true that the planet Aykar was the first place ventasium was discovered? (True, though the Aykari didn't and don't call it that.) Is it true that the Aykari and Djarik have been at war for hundreds of years? (Human years, yes. We all measure time in our own way.) If you really have no tongues, then how do you . . . you know . . . make out with each other and stuff? (The answer this time from Mrs. Dolson over the stifled giggles of half the class: *I don't think that's an appropriate conversation to be having right now.*) With every query answered, three more hands shot up.

Mrs. Dolson never got around to calling on Leo.

A hundred planets in a hat. Thirty-eight presentations. A conversation with an alien who had literally traveled halfway across the galaxy. And yet Leo's question remained: If there was somewhere in the whole wide universe you could go that your nightmares wouldn't follow.

Leo would not have been able to draw Kaber's Point out of Mrs. Dolson's hat. The hat only held planets, and this was definitely not one of those.

What it was was a floating junk pile. At least that's what it looked like from the cockpit of the *Icarus*. A multiship pileup on the interstellar expressway. A collage of freighters and cruisers all mashed together.

"*That's* Kaber's Point?"

He forgot he wasn't supposed to be talking, but no one bothered to remind him. Kat sat in the pilot's seat this time, navigating their approach. The captain sat beside her changing shoes, leaving his flip-flops under the console and slipping back into his high-tops. The robot was nowhere to be seen.

Leo wasn't sure why he expected Kaber's Point to be a planet. There was a planet nearby—Leo could make out the orange and yellow profile of it in the distance—but that wasn't where they were headed. A docking bay of a giant cruiser beckoned them with open jaws, ready to swallow them up.

"Kaber's Point is an outpost. A trading center. Making it out of a few massive ships keeps it mobile," Baz said, lacing up his shoes. He turned to Boo, who barely fit in the chair next to Leo, and pointed at the shoes. "You like these? They're Jordans."

"How did Jordan feel when you took them?" the alien asked.

Baz shook his head. "Don't even know why I try. Turn as you land, K. I want our nose pointing out, just in case we have to make a quick getaway."

"Is there any other kind?" she replied.

Leo studied the conglomeration of ships all glommed together. It reminded him of the first human space stations. He'd learned about them in history, countries sticking big metal boxes and tubes together like Lego bricks. Except those old space stations could only house a dozen or so astronauts. Kaber's Point was more like a city made of ships. He didn't recognize most of the designs.

"Are any of those Coalition ships?"

From the pilot's seat came a snort, Kat shaking her head.

"Let's just say this place works outside Coalition jurisdiction," Baz said. "Or tries to, anyway."

"What he means is, around here anything goes. So watch your back," Kat said.

Watch *his* back? Did she mean him specifically?

"Wait—am I going *with* you?" Leo just assumed he'd be locked back in the bunk by himself. Or even worse, back in the cramped cargo hold where he'd been discovered.

"I want you where I can see you," Bastian Black said. "Besides, it will be easier to pawn you off on some poor freight jockey this way."

"Or to just leave you in the hands of a pack of Snids," Kat offered.

"What's a Snid?" Leo asked.

"A race of sluglike aliens with voracious appetites and a non-discriminating palate."

"Nondiscriminating?"

"Means they eat whatever they can catch," Boo clarified.

"You get hungry enough and you will eat almost anything too," Kat said. "Trust me."

Leo shivered. On second thought, maybe the cargo hold wouldn't be so bad. Leo had never been *anywhere* that wasn't ostensibly under Coalition control. At least until his brother convinced him to stow away aboard this ship. And now he was headed to an outpost full of criminals and pirates and outsiders and human-eating slugs? "Do I have to go?"

"Don't worry, Leo of House Fender. Snids don't move too fast," Boo assured him.

Kat easily maneuvered the *Icarus* into position, setting down in the belly of one of Kaber's Point's larger ships with a soft touch. Leo unbuckled and stood up with the rest. Kat unholstered her pistol, checking its charge.

"You anticipating trouble?" Boo asked her.

She glanced at Baz. "Always," she said.

The captain of the *Icarus* turned to Leo. "Previous rules still apply. Keep your mouth shut and don't do anything stupid. If you decide to run off, know that I won't even wave goodbye. The sooner you're someone else's problem, the better. And *this?* This is gonna have to go." Baz grabbed the Coalition patch stitched onto Leo's shirt and ripped it loose, leaving a noticeable tear to the left of his heart. He handed the patch to Leo. "The less most people around here know about you, the better."

People around here. The kinds of people that pirates tend to mingle with. Leo nodded and stuffed the patch in his pocket, then stuck his finger through the brand-new hole in his shirt.

"Now whose clothes look funny?" Boo asked.

Leo couldn't get the image out of his head. Him crammed into the cargo hold, reaching down for his brother's hand. The look on Gareth's face—sadness, regret, but also resignation. The look he might get before starting a race he knows he is destined to lose.

At least this way I'll know you got out.

Leo had gotten out, all right.

This was the plan: hide in the storage compartment aboard the pirate's ship, wait for it to land somewhere and for the crew to depart, and then make your escape and go find help.

The ship had landed. The crew had departed. The problem

was Leo was departing with them.

At least most of them. As they stood on the ramp of the *Icarus*, Baz gave instructions to the robot who was being left behind. It appeared to be picking little bits of debris out of its treads, looking bored, if such a thing was possible for a robot with an unchanging facial expression. It only looked up when Baz spoke to it.

"Listen, while I'm gone I want you to refuel and then try and fix the cooling system on the second sublight engine. Okay?"

"Fine," the robot moaned.

"I'm serious, Skits. That thing has been running hot for days. And I don't just mean a slapdash job that makes it *look* like you fixed it. I mean actually fix it."

"I said, fine. *God.* What do you *want* from me?"

Leo had never heard a robot speak like that before, with that petulant mix of annoyance and resentment. Most robots were programmed to sound patient and helpful or gruff and intimidating. Skits's voice replicator had a distinctive nasally whine to it.

"I'm just saying, sometimes I ask you to do something and I come back and you haven't even started. You need to take a little responsibility around here."

"Stop lecturing me, all right? I'll fix your stupid engine. Jeez."

The robot spun around and trundled off. Baz sighed. Leo recognized the look on his face—the same shoulder-tensed, tongue-bitten expression his father would sometimes get when he and Gareth broke something horsing around or forgot to finish their homework or tracked mud through the house. Back when they still *had* a house.

Back when he still had his father.

No. He couldn't think like that. His dad was still alive. Leo was sure of it. He was still out there, somewhere, just like Gareth, waiting for rescue. *We'll find each other.* Better yet, he would find them. He would find and rescue both of them.

As soon as he got some help.

Which meant getting away from this lot.

"Okay, crew. Stick close and try not to attract any unwanted attention. You especially," Baz said to Leo, which seemed funny given that he was standing next to a seven-foot, four-armed, barely dressed, ox-faced monkey man. "Just act like you belong."

Act like you belong. With a posse of pirates. On board a movable city full of aliens you've never even seen before.

Leo said he would try.

The ship they were docked in was easily ten times the size of the *Beagle*—nearly as large as an Aykarian frigate. Leo had seen several of those in orbit around Earth, studded with guns all pointing upward, outward, forming a barricade. But those ships were filled with Aykari, Leo knew. This one was filled with all kinds of beings, none of them Aykari.

"Act natural," Leo whispered to himself as he synced his footsteps with Baz's, fully aware of Kat walking close behind him. He was used to the *Beagle* with its mostly human crew.

Here humans were a minority. In the hangar alone, Leo spotted a dozen alien species he couldn't name—beings that clearly hadn't made their way out of Mrs. Dolson's hat. It's hard to look like you belong in a crowd when that crowd includes an amorphous pink blob slithering past you, leaving a sticky slime trail in its wake. Or the stout, three-headed purple creature with the metal spikes for hair looking over three ship manifests at once. Or the hunched and hairy thing looking almost prehistoric save for the overalls and the giant blaster cannon strapped to its back.

One thing they all had in common though: nearly every living thing in here carried some kind of weapon.

"Not polite to stare," Kat said over Leo's shoulder.

Leo fixed his eyes on his shoes. It was true. A three-headed alien has a three times better chance of noticing you being impolite, but it was hard not to look. Kaber's Point was a whirlwind. A giant market sprawling across its hangars, spilling out into its corridors. Makeshift huts, colorful banners hanging from the rafters, vendors with carts standing at the corners, shouting prices, hocking objects of unearthly design. The whole place reminded Leo a little of Chinatown back in San Francisco—if Chinatown was housed inside a spaceship and frequented by slithering pink blobs.

None of the other crew of the *Icarus* seemed at all fazed by the people parading past them, however, Baz leading the way at a determined pace. Leo wondered how much more of the galaxy they'd seen than him, how many other planets and systems they'd been to. Enough to feel comfortable in a place like this.

How long does it take to feel like you belong in the universe?

Leo looked back at Kat. "Don't you wonder about them? I mean, where they come from? What they do? What they're made of?" he said as they passed a creature that looked—or at least smelled—like it was made of cheese. *Old* cheese.

"I'm more interested in what I can do to avoid them," she said. "Curiosity will kill you."

"Like the cat," Leo said, remembering one of his mother's sayings.

"Which cat?" Kat asked.

"Nothing. Never mind." At last he spotted a somewhat familiar face in the crowd, the dark blue skin and three narrow eyes of an Edirin, the same species as Tex, the *Beagle*'s chief engineer. Except this Edirin was decked out in armor with two menacing blades dangling from each side and a look that warned everyone to stay out of his way. Leo turned back to Kat. "None of them are part of the Coalition?"

"I don't see any patches, do you?"

"So then they are all . . . you know . . ."

Leo wanted to say outlaws. He wanted to say enemies. But he guessed Kat wouldn't see it that way. She might take offense. And Leo didn't want to be on her bad side any more than he probably already was.

She answered before he could finish the question. "They are

who they are. Doing what they have to do to get by. Just like us. And didn't Baz tell you not to talk?"

Leo nodded and shut his mouth, but he kept his eyes open wide, partly just taking everything in, but also scanning the crowd of traders and merchants for someone who at least *looked* friendly. Nobody even bothered to look Leo in the eye, though. He was nothing. A nobody. Not their concern.

Maybe because they thought he was a pirate too.

They exited the hangar and traversed several more corridors, passing even more alien species that Leo couldn't name, until finally Baz stopped. The door they stood before looked the same as all the others save for a small engraving etched above its control panel. The symbol looked like an octopus with huge jaws filled with rows of serrated teeth. Leo hoped that wasn't a sign of what was waiting behind the door.

Baz huddled them together. "Okay. Stay frosty," he said, looking back and forth from Kat to Boo, his eyes skipping over Leo, who stood between them. "Grims is bound to be cranked off already because we're late. Plus that bounty on my head isn't getting any smaller, so . . ."

"Wait, you don't think Grimsley?" Kat questioned.

"Doubtful," Baz answered. "I think we're still more useful to him alive than dead, but you never can be sure. He's an opportunist."

Leo didn't like the sound of that. If there was one thing you wanted to be sure about a person, it was probably whether or not they wanted to kill you.

"Just keep your eyes peeled and let me do all the talking."

Baz pressed a button on the control switch. "Bastian Black," he said into the com. The door slid open. The crew of the *Icarus* hesitated, its captain making minor adjustments to his hair of all things.

"I hate this part," Boo mumbled.

"Why do you hate this part? Why does he hate this part?" Leo asked, glancing from Boo to Kat.

"He doesn't trust this guy. Neither do I. Gerrod Grimsley is a snake. But I guess maybe you have to be when you play both sides."

"Both sides of what?"

"You really are naive, stowaway," Kat said, following Baz into the room, her hand resting on the handle of the weapon by her side.

"She means the war," Boo whispered.

"Right," Leo said. *And what side are you on?* Leo almost asked. But then he caught himself. It was a stupid question. They were pirates, after all.

They didn't have a side.

This wasn't Leo's first encounter with traders. Far from it. The *Beagle* would often stop to resupply at Aykarian depots, way stations in space, like orbiting 7-Elevens. While docked, their father would take Leo and Gareth to the open market to get a few things that weren't standard issue. Usually candy—the Krellian kind that felt like paper but melted on your tongue, leaving a treacly aftertaste—but sometimes there were imports all the way from Earth. Snickers bars or stale animal crackers or bags of chips that had passed from hand to hand, cargo ship to cargo ship. But you had to be careful; at one post they purchased what they thought were pineapples a little past their prime. Turns out they were a kind of floating swamp creature that had been harvested from a nearby planet—a truth that became apparent the moment Leo's dad cut it open and its stinking guts spilled out.

The best was six months ago. They'd stopped at a base run by the Aykari but with a heavy human contingent on board, including a woman who had an unopened container of popcorn. Actual Orville Redenbacher. Dr. Calvin Fender, seeing the look on the boys' faces, forked over twelve pentars for it—an extraordinary sum—and that evening they managed to pop it in the *Beagle*'s food warmers, adding a blizzard of salt. The Fenders huddled on Leo's cot and watched vid feeds of old superhero movies, shoveling in the precious puffed kernels by the fistful while the Avengers beat back the alien hordes. Iron Man and friends made it look so easy.

There was no popcorn in the room Leo entered, but thankfully there were no menacing toothy octopuses either. There appeared to be nothing at all for sale. If this Grimsley was a merchant, he kept his wares well hidden. Instead, there was a bar and a viewport of the starscape. Several chairs of a fashion Leo didn't recognize were scattered around the room. Only one of them was occupied.

"Bastian Black. You made it. . . . Finally."

The human Leo guessed to be Grimsley stood up to greet them. He was tall, nearly equal to the Queleti Leo stood beside, and dressed in a style much different from the *Icarus*'s captain. His fine black suit shimmered when he moved, the strange material capturing and rearranging the light. Hoops of gold on his wrists reflected the light as well—as did, Leo noticed, his completely bald crown. Everything seemed straight and narrow on the man, except for his nose, which took a serious curve about half the way down. Leo guessed it had been broken. Probably more than once. It explained the nasal quality of his voice, a kind of steady whine, not unlike Skits's.

"Nice to see you, Grims," Baz said, moving forward, leaving the other three by the door. It was only then that Leo noticed the two bipedal robots in the corners on either side of the room, both of them plated with armor and holding rifles. Security bots. Cheaper than hired thugs in the long run and much less likely to stab you in the back—provided no one programmed them to. If Baz noticed the armed robots standing guard, he didn't show it. Then again, he'd obviously been here before. Leo glanced over his shoulder at the door; at least he could make a quick escape if he needed to.

Is there any other kind?

"You want something to drink?" Grimsley said, motioning to the bar. "I've got some starshine. There's a lady on board who cooks it up. Tastes like elephant piss but what are you gonna do? The nearest brewery's a hundred light-years away."

"I'm good, thanks," Baz answered.

"What about your crew? I see you've added to it since we talked last," Grimsley said, his eyes resting temporarily on Leo. This man really *did* think he was a pirate. Leo started to shake his head.

"What? You mean Leo?" Baz said nonchalantly, pointing with a thumb. "He's temporary. Found him hitching a ride in my cargo hold. Speaking of which, you wouldn't happen to know any mostly honest pilots making a run into Coalition territory, would you?"

Grimsley gave Leo one last hard stare—intense enough that Leo glanced down at his Coalition-issued boots. "I don't know anyone honest," he replied. "But that shouldn't come as a surprise." The trader's eyes gravitated to the large metal case the Queleti held. "Are those?"

Baz nodded and Boo stepped forward, depositing the case at the captain's feet before coming back to the door to stand beside Leo. "I told you I'd get them," Baz said, running a hand through his hair, perhaps to proudly show off that he still had some. "It just took a little longer than expected."

Grimsley knelt down—Leo heard the man's knees pop, that's how quiet it was in the room—and undid the latch on the case, releasing a soft hiss and a trickle of steam. Leo could guess what was inside. The very thing Bastian Black had boarded the *Beagle* for. The most precious substance of all.

"Fifteen cores," Baz said.

In its raw form, ventasium gave off an iridescent, greenish-blue glow, but all Leo could see were cylinders made of a special metal alloy, the cores built to keep the V stable and safe—just waiting to react with the other more common elements and charge up an FTL drive, blasting you from one star to the next.

Grimsley stared at the three rows of canisters. Leo could see the look of disappointment—or was it frustration—pass over the trader's face. He also noticed Kat's eyes darting to the corners of the room, to the two robotic sentries. They hadn't moved. But that didn't mean they wouldn't. Their owner would only need to give the command.

"We said twenty," Grimsley said. His voice sounded calm. Just stating a fact. Pointing out the math.

Baz put one hand up. "Right. I know. And honestly I hoped we'd have them all, but the last ship we boarded had already been cleaned out by the Djarik. There wasn't much I could do."

The last ship. Bastian Black had actually hoped to score five cores of ventasium off a crippled Coalition vessel sitting dead in space. Instead, he got Leo. Raw deal, Leo thought, from both their perspectives.

The trader didn't care much for Baz's offer, or his excuse.

"We agreed on twenty. I paid you up front for ten. When we make an agreement, I expect you to deliver. That's good business. This . . ." Grimsley sighed as he looked over the contents of the case. "This is a disappointment."

Kat's eyes darted to the corners again. Her hand still rested on her pistol. Leo felt Boo inch one step closer to him, near enough that Leo could smell the alien's musk; it reminded Leo of mossy damp earth. Earth earth. He didn't mind being so close, though; Grimsley might be almost as tall as Boo, but the Queleti had twice the arms and probably ten times the muscle.

"I realize that," Baz said, his voice strained, but still calm. "And I tried. But you have to understand, it's getting crazy out there. I can't go to a single system without being spotted by an Aykarian enforcer or running into a Djarik warship. It was fine when they were just picking on each other, but they've made me a target now."

"I know," Grimsley said. "I've seen the notices. Word gets around, Baz. You're getting famous. The Djarik bounty is almost as big as the one the Aykari put on your head."

"So then you see how difficult it is," Baz protested. "I'm lucky I could get this much."

"Save the excuses, Baz. I need those cores. You know how this works. I have customers of my own. A reputation to uphold." The trader bent over and slid one of the cylinders of refined ventasium out of its padded slot in the center of the crate, careful to hold it by the ends. The casing surrounding the V was impenetrable—a special Aykarian design—but some people, humans especially, were still nervous when handling them. Understandable, when you knew the kind of power they contained. When you knew the cost of getting them in the first place. Leo had personally never held one. He never wanted to.

Grimsley moved to the bar and slotted the container into a machine—one Leo had assumed was used to make drinks, but instead must be used to test ventasium. The machine hummed for a moment and then a string of green lights marched across its face. The trader's face lit up as well. The core was at full strength—enough juice to allow a ship to jump halfway across the galaxy and back. And he had fifteen of them. He carefully returned the canister to its nest.

"I'll tell you what," Grimsley said with a sigh of resignation. "You promised me twenty, you brought me fifteen. I already paid you for ten. We'll just call it even."

He went to close the case. Baz stopped it with his foot.

Leo felt Boo's hairs bristle; that couldn't be a good sign. The door was right there. He could bolt. Head back to the hangar. Try to find someone else who could help him. Baz already said he'd let him go. But at the same time, Leo was afraid to move, worried that it might cause those two security bots in the corners to twitch, and even the slightest twitch could set Kat off. He remembered what she'd done to Captain Saito—how quick she could move. She already looked like a rattlesnake coiled in a bush.

Baz, on the other hand, was waving his arms around dramatically. "How is that *even*?" he said, raising his voice. "You at least owe me for five."

"Consider it a promise-breaking fee," Grimsley replied.

"The cost of doing business poorly."

"Poorly? How about *my* fee for letting *you* sit on your butt in your fancy suit and your fancy chair making people like us do your dirty work for you? You and I both know you are going to turn around and sell this stuff for double what you paid me for it. I risked my life to get these. *We* risked our lives," he added, motioning behind him to his crew. "So how about *you* walk over to that little safe you keep behind the counter and pay me for the five cores you still owe me. And *then* we will call it even."

A heavy silence settled over the room, so quiet Leo could hear the whistling exhales making their way through the trader's crooked nose.

Grimsley stood up, straightened his suit, and gave his bald head a rub. He casually walked back to the bar.

His hand vanished under the counter.

Leo had practiced magic for years. He knew about stashing things in secret places. He held his breath, trying to watch the robots and Grimsley and Baz and Kat all at once. *Are you happy now, Gareth?* he thought. *Is this what you had in mind?*

The hand reappeared from under the bar, not with a weapon like Leo feared, but with a stack of ornately engraved metal chips. Aykarian pentars in large denominations. One of the few currencies generally accepted among the various tribes and species in this little dust cloud of the universe.

Leo started to breathe again.

The man crossed the room and handed the money to Baz,

who stuffed the chips into an inside pocket of his jacket.

"You are a difficult man," Grimsley said, which prompted a snort from Kat. "But you're right: it's getting even more dangerous out there. This blasted war is everywhere now and it's only getting worse. Whispers around the Point say the Djarik are working on something. Something big. Something that could tip the balance in their favor permanently." The slick-suited trader glanced at Leo once more, taking him in from head to toe. It made Leo shiver. Grimsley turned his attention back to Black. "You have to understand, it's getting harder and harder to remain neutral. I'm not sure how much longer we'll be able to do business, you and I."

"You gotta do what you gotta do." Baz said. He turned and nodded to Kat, who activated the door. "Nothing lasts forever," he added.

"No. Nothing does," Grimsley agreed. The trader extended his hand. The captain hesitated but finally took it. "Goodbye, Baz. It has been a pleasure."

"Till next time," Black said.

Grimsley just smiled.

Once they were past the door, Bastian Black started to walk quickly. So quickly that Leo nearly broke into a jog to keep up. The captain didn't stop until he turned a corner. He looked around and then removed the pentars from his jacket, counting them more carefully.

"All there?" Boo asked.

Baz nodded, though he didn't look happy.

"Well, that went better than expected," Kat said. "Nobody got shot at least. And we got paid what we deserved."

"Not exactly," Baz said. "This is for fifteen. We only gave him ten." Baz dropped the pentars back into his pocket.

"What are you talking about?" Kat asked. "There were fifteen cores in the case. I counted."

"There were fifteen containers. But five of them were empty. Grimsley always takes one from the middle to test. Never from the ends. Every time. Besides, he's been short-changing us on the price of V for a while now. He deserved it."

So much for honor among thieves. "Wait. So when he does test them all, isn't he going to be angry?" Leo asked.

"He's going to be thoroughly cranked. Which is why we need to move. Besides, I'm pretty sure he wants to kill me anyway," Baz continued. "I saw it in his eyes when we said goodbye. He'll collect the bounty on my head and use me as an example to others who don't make their deliveries in full and on time. *That's* good business, at least as far as he's concerned."

"So how long do we have?" Boo asked.

"Well, knowing Grimsley, he's probably testing the other cores as we speak—so we should probably be on the ship about five minutes ago."

Leo took a second to process what Baz was saying. "Wait, so we're leaving already? But you said—"

"I know what I said, kid. And you are more than welcome to hang out here and try to find some other ship to hitch a ride with. But the *Icarus* and its crew are leaving."

Kat glared at Baz, drilling holes into him like an Aykarian excavator.

"What?"

"Seriously, Baz? We can't just leave him here," she said. "Look at him. He won't last a day in this place."

"I'm not the one who suggested feeding him to Snids," Black countered.

"I was kidding. He's just a kid. What's he supposed to do?"

"Maybe not stowaway aboard my ship for starters."

Leo's eyes danced from Kat to the captain. He didn't disagree with her—he probably *wouldn't* last a day—but he also didn't know why she was sticking up for him all of a sudden. She'd seemed plenty serious about blowing him out of the airlock earlier. A loaded look passed between the two pirates—a conversation somehow transmitted with chin juts and frowns. Finally Baz turned to Leo. "You can do whatever you want. Stay here, come with us. Your choice. But we are getting out of here. Now. End of debate."

The captain continued his quick steps. Kat shook her head and followed, one hand still resting on the butt of her pistol.

Leo looked up at Boo, who shrugged, all four palms turned upward. "Sometimes it's better to sleep out in the rain than to risk going into the cave," the Queleti said.

Leo's finger felt for the hole in his shirt where his patch

had been, touching the bare skin underneath. His hands were cold. This whole place was cold, as if the void of space managed to sneak its way through the hull of the ship somehow and worm its way inside him. Stay here in this unfamiliar place full of unfriendly faces and people like Grimsley or take his chance with the crew of the *Icarus*. It wasn't an easy choice.

The rain sucked, sure. But you didn't know what could be lurking in the cave. At least with Bastian Black, Leo knew what he was getting into. Sort of.

Leo nodded.

"C'mon then," Boo said.

They caught up to Baz and Kat at the end of the corridor where it intersected with the main hall leading to the hangar bay. Kat was peeking around the corner. "We're too late already," she said. "Two sentries. Right by the hangar entrance. Same kind as the ones in Grimsley's chamber."

"So what's the plan? How do we get to the ship?" Boo asked.

"Only two by the entrance," Baz said, "but I'm guessing Grim's got more inside. We start blasting now, they'll close the hangar doors and lock us in before we can even get the ship powered up. Unless . . ." The captain grabbed the communicator from his jacket. "Skits. Are you there? Skits, come in."

No reply.

"Skits. We've got a situation out here. Do you copy?"

Still silence. "She's ignoring you," Kat said.

"She's not ignoring me."

"She's a robot. It's not like she left her communicator on the bridge while she went to the bathroom, it's part of her hardware. I keep telling you that you need to reprogram her. Her protocols are completely whacked. Whatever evolutionary algorithm you've got her programmed with is stuck in pouty teenager mode. Pretty soon she's going to flip a switch, hijack the ship, and crash us into an asteroid just to make a point."

"It's just a phase. She'll get over it."

Kat gave him a dirty look. "Whatever. I'm just saying— a normal robot would answer your calls."

Baz peeked around the corner again. "If one of us could sneak past those guards and get to the *Icarus*, fire up the engines . . ."

"Except we're all wanted. They are probably looking for all of us."

"Maybe all of *you*," Leo said.

The pirates all stared at him, and for a moment he regretted opening his mouth. But then he thought of Kat sticking up for him just now and Boo standing tall beside him in Grimsley's chamber. He thought of his brother's last words before closing the cargo hatch.

Be brave, Leo.

"Grimsley just met me," Leo continued. "Maybe the guards aren't on the lookout for me. I could slip past them into the hangar, get to the ship, find Skits."

"Forget it," Baz said. "Nothing about you is sneaky."

"I managed to get on your ship without you knowing," Leo said, though really that had been mostly Gareth's doing.

Boo snorted. "He has a point."

"And what if those security bots *do* recognize you?" Kat said.

"That's when you guys come charging in," Leo said.

At least he hoped.

Baz was still skeptical. "And how do we know you won't just turn us over to Grimsley, hoping he'll help you as some kind of reward?"

The thought honestly hadn't even crossed Leo's mind. "That sounds like something a pirate would do."

As soon as he said it, Leo regretted it, but Baz surprised him with a laugh.

"Okay, kid. We'll watch your back. Once you're in, go straight to the *Icarus* and tell Skits we've got a code fourteen. She'll take it from there."

"Code fourteen," Leo repeated.

"And whatever happens, once you get aboard that ship, you stay on it. Find somewhere safe and hunker down. Things could get messy, and I don't need you getting in the way."

"Got it," Leo said.

"This is a bad idea," Boo muttered.

"Yes, but it wasn't my bad idea for once," Baz said. "Good luck, ninja turtle."

With another deep breath, Leo turned the corner back into the main corridor facing the hangar and the pair of security bots guarding the entrance. The Aykari seldom used mechanicals for security. One Aykari soldier was equal to five armed robots. But two armed robots were probably equal to a dozen Leos.

They certainly looked menacing enough, their armor plating suggested something like the medieval knights Leo learned about in ancient history. Their faces were more like jack-o'-lanterns—slits for mouths and point-down red triangles for eyes that pulsed each time someone passed, probably scanning faces. Leo hoped his wasn't one of the faces they were looking for, hoped he was right and Grimsley didn't count him as one of the *Icarus*'s crew. As he merged with the crowd, he fitted in behind a pair of Terratrins—a species he had at least seen before—their tall frames dwarfing Leo's own. With their beak-like noses and leathery brown skin they looked a lot more like a mutant turtle than he did. He moved in close, close enough to walk in their shadow and overhear their conversation.

"The Djarik have captured three planets out near Orion's Arm, taken over the refineries, and forced the population into labor camps. I don't think there's a planet left that one of the two haven't touched."

He was only ten meters from the hangar now. Leo could see that the security bots weren't top-of-the-line models—their armor was already dented and warped. Nothing in this place looked new. Even the robots were used goods. But the guns seemed plenty functional.

"If one side doesn't win soon, there won't be a galaxy left to rule over."

Rule over. No doubt that's what the Djarik would do—seek to control every planet still remaining after the war was over—but it was the exact opposite of everything the Coalition stood for. Though the two aliens Leo was trailing obviously didn't see it that way.

"It's all about the resources and who gets to control them. Doesn't matter the cost. It's all about greed, if you ask me. Greed and control."

Eight meters.

Leo froze as a mechanical head swiveled in his direction; he felt those pulsing red eyes taking him in. Any second now he expected a mechanical voice to command him to halt as rifle barrels converged on him. He resisted the urge to look back over his shoulder, to signal for help, to take off running. He hoped Kat could shoot as well as she could kick.

Stay cool. Keep your head down. Just breathe.

Five meters from the door, almost even with the guards, the one still watching him. Scanning him. Processing.

They're not looking for you.

"Sometimes I wish there wasn't even such a thing as EL-four eight six," one of the Terratrins said. "That would fix it all."

"Except how would we get back home?"

"That's the point—we never would have had to leave to begin with."

Two meters. Almost there. What would Gareth say if he knew what his little brother was doing right now? No doubt he wouldn't have cajoled him onto that ship. They would have faced whatever awaited them together instead of him going it alone.

Leo closed his eyes as he stepped over the threshold and into the hangar.

The security bots gave no orders to stop. They hadn't been scanning for him after all.

Because I'm not a pirate, he thought.

No, he was just a kid. A kid who was sneaking around, dodging guards, looking to blast his way out of a hangar in order to avoid the wrath of a black market dealer of V who'd just been swindled.

Leo frowned. No. Nothing unseemly about that at all.

We are all strangers, strangers in a strange land

Crawling through the smoke, starting to choke, spinning out of control

This world, it isn't ours anymore.

It's a strange, strange land, and we want to get out,

But we've got nowhere else to go.

   —Blind Republic, "Strange Land," Firestorm Records, 2053

6

A NARROW ESCAPE

LEO WOULD NEVER FORGET HIS MOTHER'S SMILE.

He could conjure it whenever he wished, even without the memory saved on his watch. He made a point to remember it because it was such a rare thing. You don't remember every brown-feathered bird that lights upon the branch of the tree by your room, but you remember the scarlet tanager that perched on your windowsill one gray Sunday morning, flamboyantly fluttering his wings before flying off. His mother's smile was like that. Bright and elusive and fleeting. Something to be cherished.

It wasn't that she was unhappy, at least he never thought so. But Leo's mother lived in the future, her mind always four hours away, three days down the road, fixated on the years yet to come. Always planning, contemplating, fretting, so concerned about what might happen next that she sometimes lost track of what she was doing. Leo would find her standing motionless, a forgotten thing in her hand—a book, maybe, or a spatula, staring off into space as his grilled cheese started to burn. She would get that look in her eye, and Leo would know that she'd gotten ahead of herself again.

"She always worried too much," Dad said after she'd gone. "Forgetting to open her own presents on Christmas because she was already planning what to buy us for next year."

Unlike his father who often looked on the future with a wide-eyed stare and a boyish grin, Leo's mother met it with frowns and nervously nibbled nails. Dad contemplated the future's rich possibilities. Mom tried to anticipate everything that could go wrong.

Both of his parents thought Leo took more after her.

But she could only fret over the future—she couldn't *see* it. If she could, she wouldn't have gone into town with her sister that day. She would have joined Leo and his brother and father down by the beach instead. She would have kept them all together. If she had known.

Nothing good ever comes from leaving the people you love.

Of course nobody knew what was coming. Not the humans. Not even the Aykari, who had sworn to protect them, who had defenses in place to repel such an attack. Except those defenses weren't strong enough. Not on that day. They were all taken by surprise.

Leo remembered his mother smiling at him that morning, getting somehow stuck in the moment long enough to give him that gift along with a hug goodbye. She asked him to bring her back a shell, the prettiest one he could find. He promised her he would.

She had long brown hair with light red streaks that stood out in the sun. Her name was Grace. And in that moment, and in all the moments before, she was the center of Leo's universe.

Then the missiles struck and the whole world shook.

And that smile was all Leo had left.

Leo finally allowed himself one quick glance over his shoulder—all the way down the corridor to the turn, just catching a glimpse of the top of Baz's head peeking after him—then turned back to the hangar. The *Icarus* was halfway across the bay, its peeling yellow paint standing out against the silvers and grays of the other ships.

There were at least a dozen of them. A couple two-seat fighters, some smaller star-jumpers, a few freighters the same size as the *Icarus*. A dozen different starships heading a dozen different places. They couldn't all be pirates. Some of them had to be traders or merchants. Obviously not honest ones if they had to come here to do business, but maybe not *as* dangerous. Maybe not with a price on their heads.

Maybe he could bribe someone. A smuggler would recognize a potential payout when she sees it; there had to be *some* reward for rescuing a Coalition vessel and its crew. It might be worth trying. Finding another pilot. Or even just sneaking aboard, taking his chances with another ship, another crew. After all, it hadn't been that hard the first time.

At least until he got caught sitting in the storage compartment that had once held two large containers of food.

Containers that had been left behind on the *Beagle* by the worst pirate in the galaxy to ease the conscience that he supposedly didn't have.

As Leo scanned the array of unfamiliar-looking ships docked in the hangar he heard Kat's voice in his head.

We can't just leave him here. He won't last a day.

Could he, though? Could Leo just leave Bastian Black and his crew after saying he'd help them? They were counting on him to get to the *Icarus*, to warn Skits, to power up the ship. This stowaway. This kid they hardly knew. But what reason did he have, really, for keeping his word? Because two of the crew were human? Because the alien talked to him and told him about his bathrobe instead of tearing him limb from limb? What would his father expect him to do? He would say that pirates couldn't be trusted; they were just as dangerous to the Coalition as the Djarik.

And his mother?

She would have told him to trust his gut. And to do whatever he could to get back to his family.

Leo's gut told him that one of these ships was probably piloted by someone who would find it in their heart to help him, but that it was even more likely to be owned by a mercenary who *would* actually feed him to a Snid or sell him off at the next port.

His eyes fell back on the *Icarus*. The only ship in the hangar he recognized. Sometimes it's better to sleep out in the rain. Even Bastian Black with all his talk hadn't made good on any of his threats to leave Leo behind. Yet.

Leo steeled himself, his mind made up.

Except there was a problem: the two additional security bots standing by the *Icarus*'s loading ramp, rifles slung across their metal chests.

"Nerts!" Leo hissed. Even if the security bots weren't looking for him specifically, they were clearly watching the ship. He had to get on the *Icarus* without being seen.

Or maybe just without being *caught*.

Leo looked at his watch. It was the first rule of magic—the first rule his mother had taught him at least: always give the audience something else to look at, something to draw their attention away from the real action.

"Belgips. Ripe belgips. Ten for one pentar."

Off to Leo's right stood a Jorl with its spiky orange head and catfish whiskers holding up some strange-looking purple fruit about the size of a baseball. He had a whole cart full of them. Leo turned his watch dial to four—the same recording he used whenever he and Gareth played tag—then changed course, heading for the cart.

He'd never stolen anything in his life, unless you counted

sweets from his own pantry after midnight, but it was only one piece of fruit. Besides, the peddler could have his belgip back as soon as Leo was done with it. Provided it was still *in* one piece.

He slipped around the back of the carts and pilfered one of the Terratrin's goods while its back was turned, cupping the purple globe in his hand. It was heavier than he expected, its outer rind tough as tree bark. Perfect. His fingers curled around it reflexively, remembering the hours spent tossing baseballs with Gareth in the glow of streetlamps back on Earth, and just as many hours doing the same in the hangar of the *Beagle*. Gareth always had the stronger arm, but Leo's throws were more accurate.

Leo ducked behind a stack of shipping crates within a belgip's toss of the *Icarus*'s ramp. He only had one shot. Leo cocked. Aimed. Fired.

The belgip pegged one of the security bots in the back of the head, the tough skin of the alien fruit resounding with a hollow *gong*. Both robots swiveled to see Leo taking off from behind the crates, running at full speed across the hangar bay.

They called for him to halt—their voices clearly meant to be the authoritative and intimidating kind—and moved to intercept with their rifles raised, but the boy they were chasing didn't heed their warnings. He just kept running.

Straight into the hangar wall.

At which point he vanished. Poof. The security bots looked around, scanning the hangar.

Had they picked that moment to look at the *Icarus*, they would have seen Leo's real boots disappearing up the ramp.

Leo's mother had been the one to teach him how to do magic tricks. It had been a hobby of hers in high school. In fact, it's how she and the future Dr. Calvin Fender had met: he picked a card and she pulled it out of his ear and wrote her number on it. It was, as both of them remembered fondly, the jack of hearts.

Leo and his mother would sometimes spend all evening learning new tricks. While his father worked late in the lab and his brother was at practice, the two of them would sit on the porch and make cards levitate, spoons bend, and coins disappear. She was the master, Leo her struggling apprentice, the thread getting tangled, the coin often slipping from between his fingers and bouncing on the floor, the ace of spades never materializing as it was stuck somewhere up his sleeve. And when he grew frustrated—which was often—Grace Fender would put her hands on his, calming him.

"It takes practice, Leo. Don't worry. You'll get it. You're only seven. I didn't start performing magic until I was twice your age. Besides, it isn't supposed to be easy. That's what makes it so special. If anyone could do it, it wouldn't be magic, would it?"

Along the way she taught him the rules. Like rule number two: never divulge how a trick is done. So when Gareth, who was better than Leo at most things but had no knack for sleight of hand, begged to know how his brother performed each trick, Leo would shrug and say, "Magic, of course," before turning and smiling at his mother, the secret stuck between them.

And rule number three: never perform the same trick for the same audience. Because if they know what's coming, there can be no surprise, and the surprise—the revelation—is what gets you.

Leo and his mother weren't the only ones who knew that rule. The Djarik knew all about the element of surprise.

The day the missiles struck Leo was distracted. By seagulls and darting fish and the feel of wet sand squishing up between his toes. The sky was empty. There was no way of knowing that a fleet of Djarik warships had just come out of their jump in Earth's orbit, arming their ordinance, picking their targets, most of the missiles launching before the Aykari even had a chance to respond.

The devastation was worldwide. So many cities left burning. So many lives lost.

The night before the attack, Leo's mother had introduced him to a new trick, seemingly passing a chain of colored scarves through her skull, in one ear and out the other. "I'm cleaning my brains," she said. "Just getting the dust out." It was marvelous, just like she was. He begged her to teach him, but it was already late.

"Tomorrow," she said. "I promise."

The fourth rule of magic was one he learned the hard way: Always leave your audience wanting more.

* * *

"Skits," Leo said as loud as he dared, not wanting to be heard from below in case Grimsley's mechanical sentries had returned to their post. "Skits, where are you?"

The only response was the muffled sound of music coming from the ship's engine compartment. Piano and strings. Sad and slow. Leo followed the sound but stopped when the robot's high-pitched voice came belting along the corridor.

"'And I need you now tonight. . . .'"

Leo shuddered.

He burst into the *Icarus*'s engine room to find Skits with two mechanical arms extended from its torso, one holding a torch that was welding two pipes together, the other tapping time to the music against her metal torso right above a sticker for Joe's Crab Shack, in perfect imitation of Baz. The music came squeaking out of a speaker somewhere on the robot's midsection, though Leo wondered how in the galaxy she could possibly hear it over her own screeching.

"'And I need you more than ever. . . '"

She certainly didn't seem to notice Leo waving his arms and shouting her name from the entry, afraid to get too close to a temperamental robot with a blowtorch in her hand.

"Skits!"

"'And if you only hold me tight . . .'"

"SKITS!" Leo shouted, jumping and waving his arms.

The robot spun, the music instantly shutting off. "Gaaaah-hhh!" she screamed, her torch flaring, its flaming tongue shooting across the room, nearly singeing Leo's hair.

Leo screamed and leaped backward, banging into the wall. "Hey! Watch it!"

The appendage holding the blowtorch retreated, folding up and back into Skits's metal middle. "What. The actual. Hell," she said. "Why did you sneak up on me like that? I could have burned your whole ugly human face off."

"Skits, please—"

"And where's Baz?" she continued, head spinning. "Did something happen? Did you do something to him?" Skits let out an electronic gasp. "Did you *kill* him? Because if you did, I will have no choice but to annihilate you." The robot advanced a couple of feet.

"What? No. Would you just shut up and listen?" Leo sputtered. "Baz is in trouble. He's been trying to contact you. He says it's a code fourteen!"

Those, apparently, were the magic words. No sooner had Leo finished his sentence than something flashed in the robot's oval eyes and she went tearing down the corridor, knocking Leo into the wall, bouncing on her three uneven treads all the way to the cockpit. Leo recovered his balance and ran after her, catching her hovering over the ship's controls.

"Are you powering up the ship? Because Baz said something about powering up the ship."

As if in answer, two different claws emerged from the bot's body and danced along the console. He could hear the *Icarus*'s systems coming to life. The cockpit lit up in yellows and blues.

In three seconds, the robot whirred around and started back down the length of the freighter, headed toward the boarding ramp, knocking even more things over on her way, including Leo again.

"Wait, where are you going? There are armed security bots down there!"

"I don't care! Bastian's in trouble!" Skits yelled. Leo stared after her. Robots were loyal—they were programmed to be— but he'd never seen any bot act like this before.

Skits careened down the ramp. Leo followed, making it halfway before skidding to a stop.

The situation had gotten worse. The two security bots were now four, and they had Skits surrounded, their lasers trained on her. "Where's Bastian Black?" one of them demanded.

In response, Skits turned her music back on, cranking it up even louder than before.

Then she exploded.

Maybe exploded wasn't the right word, though there was definitely fire and smoke. Skits's ever-smiling head spun wildly as every little hatch and compartment in her body opened at once, revealing at least a dozen arms and extensions of various sizes and types. The blowtorch returned, spouting torrents of flame. Pointy appendages shot out like torpedoes, impaling one of the security bots through its exposed mechanical joints. Thick white plumes of smoke poured from Skits's backside like a never-ending stream of foggy flatulence. One clawed arm gripped a rifle and wrenched it out of the security bot's hands before it had a chance to fire, while flares shot out of Skits's head, bursting against the roof of the hangar in a shower of red sparks that sent the other traders, merchants, and pilots running for cover.

It was instant chaos.

And through all of it, the music continued to blare—something oddly appropriate about living in a powder keg—as Skits bellowed like some wounded animal. "I hate you! I hate you all! Die, you hunks of rusty tin!" Within a matter of seconds she somehow had all four of the security bots disabled. Her head swiveled back to Leo. "See. Now *that's* how it's d—"

The energy blast came out of the smoke, hitting the robot square in the chest.

"Skits!" Leo yelled as another blast followed, tearing into her treads. The music stuttered, flared once, then vanished. A thick black plume billowed from her torso.

Leo peered through the haze to see six more security bots advancing on the *Icarus*, weapons at the ready. Grimsley must have sent everything he had, maybe even borrowed some mechanical muscle from someone else.

One of the sentries raised its rifle, advancing toward Leo, who stood paralyzed on the ramp, his legs refusing to work. *Move*, he told himself, but he couldn't. He found himself back on the beach, staring up at the sky, at another black cloud of smoke. Frozen. Even as the foremost guard trained the muzzle of its weapon on him, ready to pull the trigger.

But not before its own head shattered, bursting into a

thousand little metal shards. Another blast sent a second robot spinning. The remaining four turned just in time to see a giant Queleti emerge from the smoke, hair rippling, robe flapping. With all four hands he grabbed the nearest robot, lifting it clear off the ground before spinning and smashing it into two of its friends. The fourth turned to fire but didn't get a shot off before its head was struck by a mechanical fist attached to a mechanical arm attached to a very determined-looking pirate in a smart black uniform.

And bringing up the rear was Baz, both pistols in hand, running and twisting to fire behind him, back at the hangar doors.

"Definitely outstayed our welcome!" Baz shouted.

More energy bolts filled the hangar, reinforcements firing blindly into the smoke that still continued to pour out of Skits's damaged body.

"What are you doing, Skits? Let's move!"

"She's got a busted tread!" Boo shouted back. The Queleti had come up behind the robot, putting all four gorilla-like hands against Skits's frame, pushing with all of his considerable strength. Her right tread was grinding and sparking, refusing to turn. She started to go in circles.

In a heartbeat, the captain was next to Boo, both of them driving their shoulders into Skits, barely getting her to move forward. Kat dropped in beside them, firing back over her shoulder at the fresh wave of security bots taking cover by the entrance.

Leo looked behind him into the belly of the *Icarus*, then back at the three pirates pushing their broken companion into the waiting yellow ship.

Find somewhere safe and hunker down. Things could get messy.

Things had definitely gotten messy. Laser fire tore through the hangar. The robot was barely budging. Leo knew what he was told to do. He could hear the voices in his head.

He listened to his gut instead.

"Nurtz!" he hissed again, his boots thudding back down the ramp. Leo squeezed in between the captain and the Queleti, ignoring their questioning looks as he put both hands on Skits's heated torso, digging in with his heels as best he could.

Finally, something snapped loose or clicked into place because Skits's right tread started to move again, catapulting her forward and up the ramp. Leo felt a hand on his own back as Baz gave him a push as well. Kat bolted ahead for the cockpit with the captain right behind her, Boo turning and hitting the switch on the ramp just as the posse of robotic guards started to close in.

"Hold on to something," Baz called over the ship's coms. "This is going to be rough."

Leo toppled sideways as the *Icarus* lifted off. He could feel the slight shudder of rifle shots hitting the hull as he stumbled through the ship to the cockpit, finding Baz in the pilot's seat, Kat next to him, both of them cursing under their breaths. Outside the cockpit window Leo caught the slight shimmering blue of the electromagnetic field that maintained the artificial atmosphere while allowing solid objects—such as the *Icarus*—to pass through unharmed.

Just beyond, however, the titanium hangar bay doors were starting to close like a pair of jaws clamping shut. No solid object was getting through those.

"Um," Leo said.

"I know," Baz muttered.

"But—"

"I know!"

Leo felt his stomach clench as Baz leaned on the ship's accelerator, launching the *Icarus* across the hangar bay toward the ever-narrowing gap, rubbing against a couple of other ships along the way, giving off sparks.

We're not going to make it, Leo thought. He closed his eyes. He heard the scrape of metal on metal as his head banged hard against the console beside him. He thought of his brother and father. He thought of seashells and snow-covered mountains and the way the pond behind his house would glitter in the sunlight.

He recalled his mother's smile.

And then he heard Captain Bastian Black holler as the *Icarus* squeezed between the closing metal doors, shooting out into the suddenly beautiful black blanket studded with unknown stars.

And so, in committing this act of terror, the Djarik have left us with no option but to defend ourselves, to defend our planet, and to seek justice for the thousands upon thousands who were lost. So it is that the United Peoples of Earth do hereby join with the Coalition of Planets in declaring war on the Djarik empire and its allies.

—Manan Arya, secretary general of the UPE, 2050

THE ACHE OF MEMORY

LEO HAD CHEATED DEATH BEFORE.

He thought about it every day. How arbitrary it was, how random. How he'd been spared when so many others hadn't. How close he'd been when the world went up in flames.

The image was seared into the memory of every human on the planet at the time, branded by melted metal, ingrained through the haunting peal of emergency sirens wailing through the smoke. Across more than fifty major cities scattered all across the globe: Beijing. Osaka. Chicago. Cairo. Lagos and Calcutta. Bangkok and Toronto. Cities packed with office buildings, bridges and museums; cities packed with innocents. In Sydney, Saint Petersburg, São Paulo. Tokyo. Shanghai.

The attack was massive. Dozens of Djarik cruisers jumping to within striking distance, unleashing their barrage, raining missile after missile into Earth's atmosphere, taking the Aykarian defense forces off guard. The Aykari scrambled their fighters, stopped as many of the incoming warheads as they could, but it wasn't enough. Those that sneaked through found their targets. Some military installations. A few mining facilities. But mostly urban civilian centers. The idea being to render Earth helpless. To disrupt its steady flow of ventasium. And to send its citizens a message:

Humanity had picked the wrong side.

The friend of my enemy is also my enemy. Never mind that the Aykari had gotten to Earth first, that they had shared their seemingly limitless technology, offering humanity an olive branch in exchange for its precious resources. The people of Earth had made a choice. And they paid steeply for it.

But the Djarik obviously hadn't studied human history. They didn't know how resilient humans were as a species. Resilient and with a firm—often bloody—sense of justice. Shock gave way to grief, but it didn't take long for grief to turn to anger; and a planet that was still trying to find its place in the galaxy suddenly found itself readying to defend it. In the weeks after the attack, every country voted unanimously to join the Aykari-led Coalition, vowing to help rid the galaxy of the Djarik menace.

It wasn't the first time the whole world had been at war, just the first time it wasn't fighting with itself.

Leo was standing in the sand when it happened, looking for that perfect shell to bring back to his mother. When the missile struck, there was no sound at first, just the blinding light and the break of the surf against the shore. When the sound did come, its roar drowned out the ocean. It blackened the sky and stole his father's cries.

But it left Leo. Standing there, looking toward the thick coil of smoke rising up and up, reaching to the atmosphere of an Earth that had been turned to ash and would have to be rebuilt.

Leo Fender cheated death that day, he knew. And not a day went by that he didn't feel guilty about it.

The moment they were out of range and Baz was certain no ships were in pursuit, the captain set a course and went to the back to help with Skits. Leo could hear the mechanical screaming from the rear of the ship—the robot hollering at Boo to get his paws off her and the Queleti hollering at Skits to stop fidgeting so much. "Try not to crash into anything," Black said, leaving Leo alone in the cockpit with Kat.

"Close one, huh?" he ventured, not sure if the no-talking rule was still in effect after what had just happened.

"I've seen closer." Kat didn't even look over at Leo; she was busy inspecting her mechanical arm, working the four-pronged claw open and closed, face pinched with concentration. It seemed as if one of the digits was sticking, refusing to bend. He watched her for a moment. She had beyond Gareth-level focus. Leo wasn't sure he'd ever met anyone quite so intense.

"I wanted to thank you," he said. "For sticking up for me

back there. With the captain, I mean."

"I wasn't sticking up for you. I was calling Baz out on his BS. Besides, I wasn't lying. You wouldn't have survived the night on Kaber." She paused, glanced at Leo. "Though I have to admit, you do have some guts, sneaking past those guards, coming to help with Skits. You're not entirely worthless. For a stowaway."

"Thanks," Leo muttered.

"Sure," she said, then she tilted her head back and let out a frustrated growl. Leo wondered if it was because of him.

"Everything okay?"

Kat shot him a dirty look. "Why do people always ask if everything's okay when it's obviously not?"

"I don't know. The same reason people say everything's okay when it's obviously not, I guess," Leo murmured.

Kat grunted. It was close to a laugh. Leo slunk down farther in his chair. Outside the cockpit he could see legions of distant stars but no planets. He had no idea where they were going. He was afraid to ask.

"I think I damaged it when I clotheslined that security bot back there," Kat said gruffly. "The middle finger won't close."

"Want me to look at it?"

"You have experience repairing bionic arms?"

Leo shook his head. "Not really. But I sometimes helped the engineers with repairs on the *Beagle*. Tex—he's the head engineer—he said I had a knack for fixing things." Mostly, Leo knew, he had a knack for handing people the tools they asked for, but you could learn a lot just by watching.

"Funny. I have a knack for breaking them," Kat replied. Then, to Leo's surprise, she shrugged. "Fine. Just don't make it any worse." She held out her claw, resting her arm across her knee. Leo slid out of his chair and knelt down next to her to get a closer look. The girl smelled like smoke and sweat. He peered at the artificial arm, taking in the delicate network of pistons and rods, the little gears and transistors buried underneath. They made robotic limbs with artificial skin, of course—humans had at least perfected *that* technology before the Aykari showed up—but Kat obviously didn't care to hide her mechanical side. It made repairs easier, at least; you didn't have to cut away a layer of fake flesh to get at the inner workings.

Leo inspected the four-fingered claw and the metal forearm it attached to, the whole contraption meeting at Kat's elbow where he could just make out the thin tendrils of pinkish-white scar tissue fused with her brown skin. Above that, he could see a tattoo of a snake's head peeking from under her rolled-up sleeve.

"How'd you get it?" he asked.

"The arm or the tattoo?"

"The arm, I guess," Leo said, though the snake seemed interesting too. His mother had had a tattoo. A flower, just above her ankle. It was blue. She said if he touched it and made a wish it might come true. It never worked.

"I've been a thief since I was your age. A pretty good one.

Right up until the one time I got caught." Kat stared at the arm, at the point of connection between metal and flesh. "I was an orphan living in a colony on Andural, this piece of crap mining world in the Mhyrist system. Though I'm not sure you'd really call it living."

"Never heard of it," Leo said. If Andural had been in Mrs. Dolson's hat, nobody pulled it.

"Not a place you'd care to visit. Trust me," Kat said. "My parents were some of the first colonists to volunteer after the Aykari arrived. They were migrant workers on Earth, farmers, but work was getting harder and harder to come by, so when the recruiters for the mining company came around promising a new life off-world they jumped at the chance to start over."

Leo had heard this before. Stories of the people Earth had no room or no need for. Those who left more by circumstance than by choice. Colonists. Miners. Soldiers who joined the Coalition for the paycheck as much as the chance at getting payback for what the Djarik had done. Not everyone left just because their father made them, though this was at least one thing he and Kat had in common: neither of them had much of a say when it came to leaving home.

"They didn't get to start that new life, though," Kat continued. "My parents died in a fire on board the ship before we even got where we were going. Engine malfunction. I was twelve at the time. Hardly old enough to be on my own. Somehow I ended up on Andural in the hands of some whack job caretaker named Nero. Just like the crazy Roman emperor. You know. The one with the fiddle?"

Leo shook his head. He only knew one Roman emperor. The one who got stabbed by all his friends. Talk about your bad days. He gently prodded one of the rods with his finger and Kat winced.

"Sorry," he said.

The corners of Kat's mouth hinted at a smile. "I'm just playing with you, ship rat. It's all metal. I can't feel a thing."

Leo went back to his prodding. "So Nero . . ."

"Was drunk half the time. Hungover the other half. But he fed me. Clothed me. Protected me. Made sure I had a bed and a roof. And I earned my keep through stealing whatever I could from the other colonists. Money. Weapons. Food. If we couldn't use it ourselves, we turned around and sold it. I learned to pick pockets, locks, easy targets. Nero taught me to fend for myself . . . and where to kick someone to make sure they go down and don't come back up."

"You mean the—" Leo self-consciously looked down.

"Yeah, it's not the same for every species, just so you know," Kat said. "For the Zendaru, for example, it's actually their armpits."

"Armpits? But how does that even . . . I mean, how do they . . ." Leo couldn't remember ever having seen a Zendaru before, but he started to get an image in his head regardless. "Never mind. Don't answer that."

"Suit yourself," Kat continued. "Anyway, Nero knew how to find someone's weakness and exploit it. Eventually,

I realized he was doing the same to me, just using me for his own personal gain. So I decided I'd take back everything I earned for him. Unfortunately, everything I knew, he taught me. He saw me coming and caught me stealing from him. And then I paid for that too."

She flexed the three digits on her arm that worked, making an almost fist and Leo realized what she meant.

"That doesn't seem right," Leo said. "Wasn't there somewhere you could go? Someone you could talk to? Aykari? Coalition? The mining corporation?"

"Right. I'm not sure what all you've been through or what you've seen, Leo, but I can tell you it isn't that easy. There's not a lot of law and order on some of these mining worlds, especially after the ventasium starts to dry up. Doesn't matter who controls them, you dig down deep enough and you find people take matters into their own hands. And sometimes . . ." She held up her artificial arm and flexed her mechanical fingers again, the one still refusing to budge. "After that, I was damaged goods. Nero kicked me out to the street. For the next two years, I did what I had to to survive. And then I met Baz. He joked that no pirate crew was complete without somebody missing an arm or a leg, and since he wasn't willing to part with any of his, he took me on, and I've been floating on this yellow piss bucket ever since, swiping V and making sure Baz doesn't get his head blown off."

Sort of like Boo, Leo thought. Kicked out. Rejected. Ending up here.

"And what happened to Nero?" he asked.

"Funny story," Kat said. "Two weeks after he took my arm, old Nero broke his neck falling off a balcony."

"Wait . . . he just fell?"

"He didn't *just* fall," Kat said. "He landed too. It's the landing that gets you."

Leo could tell by her tone that was the end of the story. He focused harder on Kat's titanium hand, poking around the tiny servos and springs, plates and hinges. "There," he said, pointing to a slightly bent rod half concealed by other pieces. "See right there where it's just a little out of shape? A pair of needle-nose pliers and we can straighten it out."

Kat leaned in to see and her forehead nearly touched Leo's. "You've got good eyes, stowaway," she said.

"My dad says I got my mother's eyes. I don't quite remember."

"Why is that?" Kat asked.

Leo didn't answer. He didn't have to. The silence was enough.

"I'm sorry, Leo," she said. "I'd like to say it stops hurting after a while, but that's not true, is it?"

Leo shook his head.

The girl opened her mouth to say something else, but snapped it shut when she heard the captain coming through the door. Baz's face was streaked with sweat and black grease.

"You two are both still too young to get married," he said.

Leo, realizing he was still on his knees and holding Kat's artificial hand, stood up and took a step back.

"He was helping me with my hand, for your information," Kat explained. "Can't bend my middle finger. It just sticks straight up. See?" She showed him, bringing it right up in his face. Baz raised an eyebrow. Leo wanted to smile but was afraid to. "How's Skits?"

Captain Black shook his head. "We had to shut her down to make the repairs. Her tread's mangled and the shot to her torso damaged her power capacitor so she's getting these surges, fritzing her neural network. Boo's working on her now. I'll go back and help him in a sec."

"You know, while she's out, you should just reprogram her," Kat suggested. "I'm not saying a complete reboot. Just scale it back a bit. Adjust the personality matrix. At least cut down on some of the drama."

Baz shook his head. "She's growing, Kat. It's an adaptive algorithm. I don't want a robot who only does what she's told. I want one who thinks for herself."

Kat rolled her eyes. "How progressive of you. You could have at least fast-forwarded her through the teenage years."

"Yeah—some days I've wished the same thing about you."

Kat showed him the problem she was having with her finger again. This time, Leo did smile. "I'm going to go make my own repairs and try to find something to eat, provided you haven't given it all away."

"Great. You do that," Baz replied. "Ninja turtle and I need to talk anyway."

The captain looked at Leo.

"Don't we?"

Leo's smile disappeared.

It was a Saturday afternoon when Earth shook.

The Fenders were visiting Leo's aunt for the weekend. His mom's sister Rebecca lived near Los Angeles, running a small community theater in Pasadena. It was a gorgeous March day minus the spreading gray haze settling across the sky from the offshore platforms—you could find them everywhere now, sucking out ventasium. In mountains, oceans, rain forests, plunging deeper and deeper into Earth, milking it dry. But the California hills were still studded with trees and the breeze coming off the water was delicious.

Leo remembered the day being unusually balmy for early spring. They were supposed to walk around downtown all afternoon, Leo and his brother, his parents and Aunt Becca, but Leo's father insisted on taking the boys to the beach instead.

"What eight-year-old boy wants to go shopping when it's this gorgeous outside?" he said, kissing Leo's mom on the cheek and saying that the sisters would have more fun without three grumpy guys tagging along. Leo's father loved the ocean and wasn't overly fond of his sister-in-law. And maybe he was right: the ladies would have more fun catching up on their own. His mother wasn't much of a swimmer, though she could have spent hours spotting hermit crabs with Leo, sifting through handfuls of broken shells and turning to see their steps vanishing behind them. There was a kind of magic in the ocean as well, in how it could make your footprints disappear.

Leo could still picture the look on his brother's face that morning, waiting impatiently by the door, so eager to get away that he squirmed out of his mother's hug. Leo didn't have a choice. He was too little to wriggle free. His mom kissed the top of his head and made her request—the prettiest one on the beach, she insisted. He begged her not to get ice cream without him. She smiled and said she would never.

His father drove them to a dark brown stretch of sand studded with rocks and lorded over by seagulls. Leo spent the first hour hurdling waves and the next burying Gareth up to his neck. The plan was to stay half the afternoon and then to meet up with Mom and Aunt Becca for an early dinner, but Dr. Calvin Fender looked to be in no hurry, camped out underneath a rainbow umbrella with his beach hat tipped down to his nose, only his sandy feet sticking out in the sun. All fine by Leo, who didn't feel the pinking of his shoulders or the wrinkling of his fingertips. He could have stayed on that beach forever.

Leo had just finished adding seaweed tapestries to the bucket castle he'd built when the warhead bound for the city pierced the clouds. He didn't see it at first because his head was turned the other way, watching a pelican dip into the water, angling for a catch.

At that very moment somewhere in the city, Grace Fender was thinking about where she would take the boys for dessert.

"Wait, who was Shredder?"

Leo sat in the copilot's seat across from Black, who had changed shoes again, his flip-flopped feet resting on the console. Leo assumed that the thing they had to talk about was Leo himself, but instead, Baz spent the first five minutes trying to explain the concept of *Teenage Mutant Ninja Turtles*. Leo was having a hard time following it.

"Shredder was the villain," Baz repeated. "He was like this evil samurai warlord bent on taking over the world. But then in the thirties' remake he turned out to be a good guy. And Splinter—he's the rat, remember, the sensei who raised the turtles—well, his son Thorn became the new bad guy, taking over the Foot Clan and killing his father. It was a good twist. You didn't see it coming."

The third rule of magic, Leo thought. Leo never watched old cartoons. Or the even older cartoons that the old cartoons were based on. He couldn't understand why the turtles all had Italian names. Or what *cowabunga* meant. "And how did the turtles learn kung fu, again?"

"Ninjutsu," Baz corrected. "And it was radioactivity, obviously. Seriously, I can't believe you haven't at least heard of these guys. You are Earthborn, aren't you?"

Leo nodded. Earth was still what he thought of when he thought of home. He wondered if Kat felt the same. Maybe to her, home was this ship. Or maybe she didn't think of herself as belonging anywhere. "I'm from Denver," Leo said. "Originally."

"Brooklyn," Baz said. "But only for a bit. My father was a pilot. Jets, not starships. We relocated a lot. Never stayed anywhere more than a couple of years. Guess that's why I can't sit still now. Always on the move."

Probably also has something to do with being wanted for piracy, Leo thought, but he didn't say it.

Bastian Black's fingers tapped on the *Icarus*'s console, mashing buttons or maybe just playing out some beat that was stuck in his head. "Boo told me what you said about *your* father. You've had a helluva week, kid. Attacked by the Djarik. Dad taken prisoner. Brother shoved you in the cargo hold and sent you into space with us. Then you meet a black-market V dealer and get caught in a shoot-out with a posse of security bots and barely make it out the back door. Probably not what you imagined when you signed up."

"Signed up for what?"

Black pointed to Leo's shirt. More specifically to the hole where his patch used to be.

"I didn't really sign up," Leo said. "I mean, I did, I guess. But it was mostly my dad."

"Tough call, packing up your kids and sticking 'em on a Coalition vessel during the middle of war."

"He said it was the right thing to do," Leo said, rehashing his father's lines. "He thought he could keep us safe."

"Mm. And how'd that work out for you?"

Leo felt himself shrink, curling up in the chair, arms las-soing his legs, chin buried between his knees. It was as small as he could make himself, but he still couldn't get away from Bastian Black's burrowing blue eyes.

"Forget it. I'm sure he had his reasons. We all have our reasons." The captain turned back to his controls, this time definitely keying something in. "I'm taking you back to your ship," he said.

Leo was sure he'd misheard. "The *Beagle*?"

Black nodded. "I'm pawning you back off on your brother. It's what he gets for trying to pawn you off on me. And I know what you are going to say, so I'll save you the breath: this isn't a death sentence. Once you're back on board, I'll find a way to notify the Coalition and give them your coordinates, then they can come pick you up."

The tone of Baz's voice suggested he wasn't sure about the very last part. But Leo was. The Coalition wouldn't leave one of their own ships with almost a full crew stranded in the void.

"But you said your have tos and my have tos . . ." Leo began. "I mean, I thought you just wanted to get rid of me."

"I *am* getting rid of you," Black said. "You belong with your brother. He should have never left you to begin with. Besides, you helped us out of a scrape back there. And then with Skits. That was a *sijan*."

"A what?" Leo asked.

"It's a Queleti word. It means a selfless act. I'm not a huge proponent of them myself, but I know one when I see one. I told you to stay on the ship. You didn't. I get the impression you're lousy at following orders, which is one thing we have in common at least."

Leo didn't bother to tell him that he almost always followed the rules; only when his orders came from pirates did he feel free to disobey them. Maybe he just didn't want to think that he really had anything in common with the man sitting across from him, outside of the fact that they were from the same planet.

"Thank you," Leo said softly.

"Don't thank me. This isn't a favor, I'm just making us even. And so we are clear: I'm not doing this for your Coalition, your ship, your crew, or your dad. I don't owe them anything. And after this I won't owe you anything either. Understood?"

"Yes, sir," Leo said. He still wasn't sure what had changed Black's mind—if he really was paying Leo back or not—but it didn't matter. Soon he would be back on board the *Beagle*, back with Gareth where he belonged. And hopefully not long after that—if Black was true to his word—they would be rescued. Then the Coalition could set about finding and rescuing their father.

And after that? Leo didn't allow himself to even imagine what "after that" would look like, but deep down he hoped it meant finding somewhere to settle down. To stay put. Somewhere safe. In other words, finding a home.

"It's still going to be a while. That sublight still isn't fixed so we aren't at full speed, so why don't you make yourself useful and go see if Kat found anything worth eating."

Leo nodded and turned to go when Baz's voice stopped him.

"What was your father's name again?"

"Calvin Fender," Leo said. "Dr. Calvin Fender."

"Doctor?"

"He's a scientist," Leo said. "He's sort of an expert on ventasium." *You know, the stuff you steal from other people. The stuff you tried to steal from us,* Leo thought. *The whole reason you had to shoot your way out of that hangar to begin with.*

Leo thought he saw a glint of recognition spark in Bastian Black's eyes at the mention of his father's name, but one second later the captain shrugged and said, "Never heard of him."

Then he pressed a button on the ship's console and the guitar chords began to rip.

Our planet. Our fight. Our duty.
—Coalition Navy Recruitment Center
marketing slogan, 2051

LOST AND FOUND

SOMETIMES THERE IS NO GOING BACK.

In the aftermath of the Djarik attack, Leo's father did what he could to try and make life normal again. The boys went back to school. Gareth started running for his middle school track team, the Westbrook Wildcats, leaving it all on the oval. The hurt and regret, the backward-glancing fear, intensified now by the constant presence of patrol ships—joint forces of human and Aykari both—hovering in the sky. He ran so hard he made himself physically sick. Then he wiped his mouth and got ready for the next event.

Leo didn't even try to outrun the pain. He knew he wasn't fast enough. Instead, he tried to bottle it all, capping it and shelving it indefinitely, hoping to build a wall around it. But everywhere he went, he was reminded of what he'd lost. The war slogans. The news. The discussions in class. The giant vid screens on the sides of the towers replayed footage of that day as part of their military recruitment efforts. *It is up to you. Join the Coalition Expeditionary Force and help put an end to the terror that threatens our galaxy. Together we can unite the free planets, defeat the Djarik, and bring a lasting peace.*

Lasting peace. But everywhere you looked, the world was gearing up for war. Factories that had been producing cars and air conditioners began producing transports and torpedoes. Pilots once trained to fly everything from 747s to F-19s were retrained to fly Aykari starfighters and bombers. The number of excavators churning through Earth's crust seemed to double overnight, extracting the ventasium necessary to power warships across the expanse of space. Leo could look out his bedroom window and see one of those excavators towering in the distance. And when you looked down on Earth from a satellite view, you could zoom in to see the holes they left behind, empty pores in the planet's skin too deep to fill. Leo passed by one on his way to school, though you couldn't see it beyond the titanium wall designed to keep people from falling in. If you did, you would probably feel like you were falling forever.

That's how Leo felt most of the time anyway.

Meanwhile his magic paraphernalia gathered dust in his closet, the top hat getting bent under the weight of dirty clothes, the wand that could produce a puff of colorful smoke. Most days he couldn't even bear to look at it all.

But his father noticed. One night after dinner, two months

after the attack, he asked if Leo would put on a show.

"Why?" Leo asked.

"Because I want you to."

"But what's the point?"

"The point is you're good at it. And I enjoy watching it. And I think if you try it again, you'll enjoy it too."

"But it'll still be the same old tricks," Leo protested. "It's not as if I'm going to learn any new ones."

"And why is that, exactly?"

Leo didn't answer. His father knew exactly what he meant.

Dr. Fender frowned. "I don't think your mother would have wanted you to just give up on what you love. Now that she's gone, there's a lot less magic in the world, which means it's up to us to fill it. We owe it to her to keep going, Leo. To better ourselves. To better each other. Don't you think?"

Leo pictured his mother sitting on the porch, the single blade of grass pressed between her fingers. *I see you, my little lion.* If she were here, she could teach him the scarf trick. She could show him how to make the ace of diamonds stick to the wall. She could teach him all the rules he hadn't yet learned. There were magic books, videos, camps, classes—but the truth was, he didn't *want* to do it without her. The truth was, he needed her to show him the way.

Leo's father sighed. "I know everything seems dark right now. I know you're angry and sad and confused because I'm all of those things too. But we are going to get through this. And I'm not just talking about your mom, I'm talking about all of it, this whole big mess we've been caught up in. We are going to get through it because we are smart, and we are strong, and most important, because we have each other. You, me, and Gareth. We are our own coalition. And you may not feel this way, but I know in my heart that your mother is up there somewhere, watching over us—just like the Aykari watch over us—guiding us, protecting us. But we still have to do our part. And that means using the gifts we've been given. Like your talent for pulling quarters out of my ears. So what do you say? Put on a show?"

Leo shrugged. "Maybe," he said. It was as good as his father was going to get.

That night Leo stood in front of his closet, staring down at the open chest with all his magic stuff inside. His hat, his magnetic wand, his many decks of cards. He spotted the string of scarves all tied together, every color of the rainbow.

He softly closed the trunk and shut the closet door.

Leo stared into the mouth of his tin cup and the bubbling orange goo it contained.

This, apparently, was what the crew of the *Icarus* had to eat. Leo had spent some time in the back helping Boo with the repairs to Skits's tread when the Queleti heard Leo's stomach growl—loud enough to be heard above the welder he was operating.

"What was that? Is there an angry parasite living inside you? If so, I'd like fair warning if it tries to escape."

Leo put a hand over his stomach, embarrassed. "Just hungry, I guess." Boo said he knew just the thing, and moments later, Leo was staring at it, trying not to grimace. It smelled spicy; one whiff tickled his nose hairs and made him sneeze. "What did you say this was called again?"

"Gyurt," the Queleti said, taking a huge spoonful of the stuff from his own cup and swallowing it contentedly.

"Geyurt? Like yogurt?"

It *looked* like yogurt. Sorta. If yogurt had chunks. And bubbles. And made your eyes water.

"No. Gyurt," Boo insisted. "Like . . . gyurt."

"I call it dog vomit," Kat said matter-of-factly. "We had a dog back on Andural when I was young. Named it Hurk because it threw up constantly. Looked just like that." Her cup held water, not gyurt. Leo should have taken that as a sign.

"Gyurt is a traditional Queleti dish made from nerlfing milk and boiled jak tree bark. It's a staple among my people," Boo insisted, happily slurping from his own cup.

"Sounds delicious," Leo lied. Leo had no idea what a nerlfing even looked like. He pushed his gyurt around with the tip of his spoon. "What are the chunks?"

"Magu bean," Boo said.

Leo grimaced again.

"Boo's what we would call a vegetarian," Kat said. "Doesn't eat anything that he can look in the eye. Just try it. It's really not bad, as far as dog vomits go."

Leo's stomach gurgled. He put a little bit on the edge of

his spoon, brought it to his lips.

"The important thing about gyurt is to not let it sit on your tongue too long," Boo warned. "The jak tree bark gives it a nice kick, but it can also cause blisters."

Leo set his spoon gently back in the cup.

Boo snorted dismissively. "Humans. You claim to be so adventurous, but you're afraid of everything." The Queleti caught Kat glaring at him. "With some exceptions," he amended.

"And your people really eat this stuff? Like, all the time?" Leo wanted to know.

"Our people eat bologna," Kat said, coming to the Queleti's defense.

"What's a bologna?" Boo asked.

"Honestly? Nobody really knows," Kat replied. "A mystery in every bite."

Leo would kill for a bologna sandwich right about now. He took one more sniff of his gyurt and then pushed the cup away from him just as Bastian Black's voice called out over the coms.

"Kat, can you get up here? We have a situation."

"What now?" She handed Leo her empty cup and took off in the direction of the bridge.

Leo handed both cups he was holding to Boo, who had the hands to spare, and followed, ignoring the Queleti yelling at him. "You didn't even try it!"

He got to the cockpit but stood just outside the door, listening, to Kat's voice first, followed by Baz's. Both of them were tense.

"You're sure these are the right coordinates?"

"I'm telling you. I checked the log. This is where the kid's ship was when we boarded it."

Leo felt his already gurgling stomach start to ache. There was only one thing this could mean. He stepped into the cockpit to see for himself.

There was nothing *to* see. The ship—*his* ship—was no longer there.

"Where is it?" Leo asked, getting the attention of the other two. "Where's the *Beagle*?"

Where's my brother? is what he almost said, but it amounted to the same question.

"I don't know, kid. According to the nav log, this is where we left it. Something happened. Maybe they found a way to repair the sublight engines. Maybe they're already on their way to r—"

Baz's sentence was cut off by Kat pointing out of the cockpit at something coming toward them. A twisted hunk of metal as big as the *Icarus*, hurtling through space. And then another. And another.

Debris. Wreckage from a ship that had been destroyed.

Leo felt his knees buckle, his chest tighten. He reached out for the back of Kat's seat to hold himself up but missed, collapsing to the cockpit floor. Everything started to blur, but even through his fuzzy vision, Leo caught Baz unbuckling his restraints, coming to kneel beside him. "Leo? What's happening? What's wrong with him?"

"How am I supposed to know?" Kat said.

Gareth. Gareth was on that ship. Leo had left him there. Along with Tex. Captain Saito. Lieutenant Berg. He'd left them all there. He'd abandoned them. His chest tightened further, the panic clawing its way inside, wrapping cold fingers around his windpipe, squeezing mercilessly.

"Baz, we've got a problem."

"Tell me about it—I think the kid's having a heart attack."

"No. Different problem. Djarik fighters. Incoming."

"You've got to be *kidding* me!" Bastian Black hissed. He crawled back into the pilot's seat. "Help him," he shouted, pointing at Leo. "Boo, get your big furry butt up here!" he shouted even louder.

Kat was next to Leo now, leaning close, her eyes only inches from his. "Breathe, Leo. Just breathe," she whispered.

She sounded like his dad.

The pressure on his chest was unbearable now. He fumbled at his pocket, wrapping his fingers around his inhaler, pulling it free just as the Queleti appeared. "What's going on? Is Leo okay?"

"Does he *look* like he's okay?" Kat snapped.

Dark shadows crept into the edges of Leo's vision. He heard Baz's voice: "These guys are closing fast. There's a whole swarm of them. Too many to take on. We've got no choice. We've got to get out of here."

No, Leo wanted to say, but he could barely even breathe, so the cries only echoed in his own head. *No. We can't leave. Not without Gareth. He told me to get help. He told me to come back for him. And I came back.* He fumbled with the cap on his inhaler, but it slipped out of his shaking hands. Baz's voice rang out again. "Boo—get that kid strapped in, we're going to have to make a jump."

"Jump where?" Kat asked.

"You let me figure that out. You just try to keep those fighters off our back."

Leo fumbled around on the floor, one hand brushing up against his inhaler, knocking it even farther away.

"It's like they were just waiting for us," Kat said.

"They were definitely waiting for *someone*," Baz answered.

Leo's eyes fluttered. He could just make out the Queleti holding his inhaler out to him. "Here," Boo said.

Leo took it with both hands, brought it to his lips, took as deep a breath as he could manage. Just enough. He felt himself lifted by four arms and placed into a seat. Heard the click of the buckle snapping home. He still had his inhaler clutched tight in one hand, but with the other he reached out to the seat in front of him.

"Gareth," he rasped.

"Sorry, kid," Bastian Black said. "I tried."

And almost like flipping a switch, Leo's world turned black.

Breathe.

Some days it was as simple and as difficult as that.

Just breathe.

There were nights, not long after the attack, Leo would wake with a monster sitting on his chest, a nebulous black beast crushing him under its weight. He would swing out with his fists to knock the imaginary creature off, screaming, knocking the lamp from his nightstand instead, tangling himself in his comforter, his door opening to reveal his father, or sometimes Gareth, flipping on the overhead light, then beside him, holding the mask from his nebulizer.

Just breathe, they said.

And some days, it seemed, that was all he could do. While the world around him raged—while humans from every nation signed up to board naval cruisers, volunteered to man distant outposts, gave impassioned speeches on the need to bring the Djarik to justice for their crimes against Earth—Leo tried to leave the house as little as possible. He closed himself in his room. He seldom saw his friends outside school. He avoided looking at the pictures on the walls. Every night the Aykari would play its Coalition message of unity, broadcast from the ships that umbrellaed the planet: *Citizens of Earth, we are with you.* And every night Leo would curl up with Amos the cat and Houdini the stuffed rabbit and will himself not to cry.

But as the weeks and months passed, the pain abated. The black beast didn't come to haunt him as often, and the hole inside Leo slowly started to fill as he realized the one consoling truth: that he wasn't alone. His mother was gone, but he had his dad. He had Gareth. He had his cat, his shelf of shells, his view of the mountains, the hammock in his backyard just in reach of the shade of a cherry blossom tree where he and his brother would sit and read, kicking each other to get more room.

And then the cherry blossom tree died—stricken with an unknown fungus that had spread throughout the backyards across the entire neighborhood, causing its bark to bloom white, its leaves to shrivel and fall. As soon as it was taken down, Leo and Gareth convinced their dad to let them plant another.

The tree was little more than a sapling when the Fenders boarded the *Beagle*, waving goodbye to the only home any of them had ever known.

Leo had no idea if it was even still there.

When Leo came to he was lying on a cot, half naked, staring into an eerily smiling face.

"About time," Skits said.

Leo blinked. Everything looked unfamiliar, too bright and smeared around the edges. He tried to sit, to at least pull himself to his elbows, but the strap across his chest made it impossible. "What's going on?" he croaked, finding his voice. His throat felt raw. "Why am I strapped down?"

"You were thrashing about in your sleep. Screaming too. I wanted to stuff a rag in your mouth to shut you up, but Bastian said I couldn't."

Leo fumbled with the buckle, but the way it fell across his

arms, he couldn't quite reach it. "Where's my shirt?"

"You covered it in vomit when we made the jump. It was revolting. Baz told me to wash it but I burned it instead. It was easier. It had a hole in it anyway."

Leo didn't remember being sick. He didn't even remember making a jump. He struggled again to reach the buckle, fumbling with the straps.

Skits watched him. "You look ridiculous," she said. "Be still."

With one of the claws that extended from her torso, she released the buckle and the straps fell free. Leo noticed the robot had been fully repaired. A new titanium plate had been grafted over the hole from the laser blast, and across that a brand-new sticker had been plastered: *Coffee first, then we'll see.* He wondered if Skits had any notion what coffee was supposed to taste like. He looked down at his own bare chest, the sunken cavity of a stomach that hadn't been full in days. He tried to sit up, but regretted the move instantly, a sudden sharp pain ricocheting around his skull. If felt as if someone had struck the back of his head with the flat end of a shovel.

"Right." Skits continued watching him rub the spot. "So, Boo might have accidentally slammed your head into the side of the door carrying you back here. Not that you noticed. You apparently fainted the moment we jumped away from those Djarik fighters."

"What Djarik fi—" Leo started to say.

In a rush it all came back to him. The captain's plan to take

Leo back to his ship. The bits of wreckage floating in space. Pieces of mangled metal scattered to the stars.

Gareth.

For a moment Leo felt like he might pass out again. He put his head between his knees and took a deep but shuddering breath. "What happened?" he asked.

"I already told you. You threw up, then you fainted, then Boo slammed your head against the door, then I burned your shirt and tried to gag you, and then—"

"No. What happened to my ship?" Leo said sharply. "What happened to the *Beagle*?"

"Oh . . . that," Skits said. "Bastian isn't sure. Says it could have been any number of things. Malfunction in the emergency power system triggering an explosion. More pirates. Maybe the Coalition came for a rescue and then scuttled the ship, thinking it unsalvageable. Most likely, though, it was the Djarik again. Come back to finish the job."

Finish the job. Leo remembered Kat yelling at Baz. The squadron of fighters bearing down on them. "What about the crew? My brother?"

"Bastian says we can't be sure of that either, but I have my suspicions. Would you like to hear them?" Before Leo could answer, the robot added, "No, you probably wouldn't."

Leo rubbed his head, tried to stand, swayed by the dizziness and nausea. "Where is Captain Black?"

"With everyone else having a big important meeting in the cockpit. But was I invited? Of course not. Because I'm just a robot, so I was stuck watching over you."

Leo took three steps, the whole room spinning around him. He put a hand out, finding the wall, using it to guide him.

"You should lie back down; you could have a concussion," Skits called after him. "But you know what. Go ahead and ignore me. See if I care. You're as stubborn as the rest of them."

Leo made his way through the *Icarus*, hands on the sides of the ship's narrow corridors to keep from falling down. He could hear voices coming from the front. Boo's. Kat's. The captain's.

"Why would a whole squadron of fighters stick around after the ship was already destroyed?"

"Maybe it was a trap. Maybe they were waiting for the Coalition but caught us instead."

"Or maybe we just got there moments after they blew the blasted thing up."

"That still doesn't quite explain why they came back to the ship, given they were the ones to strand it in the first place. It just doesn't make sense—"

Kat was the first to notice Leo standing there, Skits rolling up behind him.

"I told him to lie down, but he didn't listen to me," the robot complained. "Because nobody listens to me."

"It's all right, Skits," Baz said. "How're you feeling, kid?" he asked Leo, then answered himself. "Stupid question."

Leo stood in the doorway, shivering, arms crossing his bare chest. Seconds later Boo was beside him, taking off his robe, his Yunkai, wrapping it around Leo's shoulders. It draped off him, piled up at his feet, but he could feel the Queleti's residual warmth and the shivering slowed.

"So that was it," Leo said. "That was really the *Beagle* we saw?"

"I guess we can't really say for certain," Kat answered. "It was a big ship. And the coordinates were right."

"And the crew?" Leo pressed.

"We can't be sure of that either," Baz said. "It's possible they weren't on board when the ship was destroyed."

"Possible," Leo repeated.

Possible his brother escaped somehow. Possible his father was still alive. *Possible* was a funny word. Possible was a piece of driftwood floating in the middle of the ocean. Something just big enough to cling to, to keep you afloat. It wasn't hope. Hope was spotting an island on the horizon or hearing a ship's horn in the distance. Possible was something less than that. The potential for hope. And with it, that sickening dread, like a stomach full of wriggling maggots. Leo looked through the cockpit into the seemingly never-ending blackness. He started to falter, but Boo held him up.

"I've got you."

Leo felt his throat ache, his eyes sting. Then he heard his brother's voice again. *Be brave, Leo.* He wanted to, but it felt like it took everything he had just to stay standing. He scanned the blackness for something familiar. "So where are we now?"

"On our way to Vestra Prime," Black said. "It's the planetary equivalent of a dive bar—only regulars ever go there."

Regular *what*? Leo wondered.

"It's a good place to lie low," Kat explained.

In other words, they were on the run.

"We jumped as close as we could, but we ran out of V," Baz explained. "Guess I should have given Grims nine cores instead."

They were running away, and they were taking Leo with them to another place he'd never even heard of. Leo shut his eyes and felt himself move away, his mind slipping out of the ship, through the emptiness, jumping from one point of light to another, searching for something familiar—a turquoise marble with swirls of white, a two-story house with robin's-egg blue shutters, a patch of green overdue for mowing, the sound of a ball slapping into the pocket of a glove. Leo could almost smell the leather. Could almost hear his brother's voice telling him to get underneath it. To not be afraid.

It was Baz's voice that brought him back. "Leo?"

Leo opened his eyes. Remembered where he was. Who he was with.

"What was on that ship, Leo?"

"What?" Leo asked, blinking.

"Your ship. We suspect the Djarik came back for it. Why?"

"I don't know," Leo said, shaking his head. "I don't know why they'd come back. They took what they wanted the first time."

"Your father, we know," Baz said. "But there had to be

something else worth coming back for. Something they must have missed the first time around. What was it?"

"I don't know!" Leo shouted. "I don't know *what* they would be looking for! They crippled the ship and left us for dead!" Leo glared at the captain, his body shaking, even under the heavy robe. "But you know that. You saw it when you boarded us. Then you left us there too."

Leo realized his mistake as soon as he said it, *Us.* Because they hadn't all been left behind. Leo was standing right here. He had gotten out. Just like Gareth promised.

At least this way I'll know.

Warm tears coursed down both cheeks. He knew they were all watching but he didn't care.

"Does he have to do that? It's making me uncomfortable," Skits asked.

The sound of Kat's mechanical hand smacking the robot's steel plating echoed through the cockpit, followed by a heavy silence. Leo kept his head down, afraid to look at them. At least until he heard Baz's voice again.

"We can't be sure what happened to your ship or your brother. But . . . there *might* be a way we can find your dad."

Leo brushed a tear-smeared cheek against one of the Queleti's many sleeves. "What?"

"Your father. If he was taken by the Djarik, then there's probably some record of him in their military database. We could find out where he's being held. We'd have to hack into it, of course."

Leo was confused, unsure why the notorious Bastian Black was helping him again.

"You can do that?"

"*We* can't," Baz said. "But there are a couple of guys on Vestra who can." The captain glanced knowingly at Kat. After a second she threw her hands up in revolt.

"Please, no, Baz. Not them."

"If anyone can worm their way into the Djarik security system, it's those two."

"Yeah, but they're just so . . . And the one with his . . . you know . . . sitting right there . . . in the thing . . ." Kat shuddered. "It creeps me out just thinking about it."

Leo sniffed, pulled his borrowed robe tighter around him. "You think they could do it? You think these guys can really find my dad?"

"I don't know," Baz said. "I imagine Djarik network defenses are pretty strong. And there is also the question of payment."

"How much?" Boo asked.

Leo thought of the pentars probably still sitting in the pocket of the captain's jacket. Leo didn't have a pentar to his name. If he did, he would have tried to bribe Bastian Black the moment they met.

Apparently it didn't matter.

"With these two it's not always about the money. Their forms of acceptable currency are a little more *specific*. But I think I might have something to persuade them."

"And what do you get out of it?" Leo wanted to know.

"I'm still just trying to settle up," Baz said. "I told you I'd try to get you back to your family."

Leo kept his eyes on the captain. It was a trick his father used against him all the time growing up: just keep staring and the truth wriggles its way to the surface.

"Okay, maybe that's not *all* of it," Baz admitted. "Those fighters were waiting for something. Maybe even for us. That complicates things a little. Contrary to what recent events might suggest, I don't enjoy being shot at, but if I'm *going* to be shot at, I'd at least like to know why. This way maybe we can both get some answers."

Except even if Leo got the answer to his question—whether his father was still alive and where he was taken—it would only lead to an even bigger one.

How could Leo possibly get him back?

For where your treasure is, there will your heart be also.
—Matthew 6:21 (King James Version)

ONE MAN'S TRASH

LEO'S DAD TAUGHT HIM ALMOST EVERYTHING HE knew about the universe. The advantage—or disadvantage— of having one of the world's foremost astrophysicists (among other things) as your father. Dr. Calvin Fender informed his son about planetary bodies and black holes and dark matter and interstellar travel, bought him a high-powered telescope with a digital projector, made him memorize the constellations and their major stars. He talked fast when he lectured, like a kid recounting the scenes from his favorite movie, arms flailing to imitate orbits and explosions and comets streaking across the sky.

The only thing he didn't teach Leo was how big the universe was, though he certainly tried. He spoke of superclusters and galactic groups. He showed Leo the numbers. Ninety-three billion light-years across (at least what they could see of it), each light-year approximately six trillion miles. "It's so much bigger than you can even *imagine*," Leo's father told him. And because he said so, and he was the expert, Leo didn't even try.

So it fell to Leo's mother to teach him about the size of the universe. She did so one morning while his father was in the study and his brother was still asleep. She was making pumpkin pancakes—a delicacy given the recent scarcity of pumpkin around the world, another casualty of an environment increasingly thrown out of whack.

Seven-year-old Leo sat on the counter next to her while she cooked, helping to sprinkle the chocolate chips into the batter as it sizzled. They reminded him of the stars decorating the night sky, the ones only his father could name.

"You know, when *I* was born, we had only landed on the Moon," she said to him. "We hadn't even set *foot* on Mars. We weren't even *close*. Now Mars has its own Hyatt." She laughed. Leo's mother had a strange laugh, the kind that suggests a great deal of effort, like it just took too long to surface and came out at half steam. "Of course we had some help."

She meant the Aykari. The ones who made human hotels on distant worlds possible. Not just with their faster-than-light travel, though that was the key, but also gravity stabilization, water and oxygen reclamation, terraforming technology— everything humanity needed to fulfill its dream of planting a Starbucks on every rock it could land on. There was a Starbucks inside the Martian Hyatt lobby, or so the commercials said.

"In the past few years I've seen people go places *my* parents could only dream about. I've seen pics and vids of planets I never even knew existed. Your father says it's just the tip of the iceberg. He tells me all the time how amazing it is, and I'm sure he's right, but you know what? I think it doesn't matter how far you go or how many planets you see—everything that *actually* matters is right here." She pointed to Leo's head. "And right here." She pointed to his heart. "Your universe never needs to be any bigger than that if you don't want it to be. Okay?"

Leo nodded and asked if he could add more chocolate chips. Just as he reached his hand into the bag, he heard an explosion in the distance, felt the house give a little shudder, the glasses in the sink clinking together.

"It's okay," his mother assured him. "Just the excavation teams clearing away the mountain to get at more V. Nothing to worry about."

Yet she stared out the window for a moment, spatula hanging by her side until Leo pointed at the pancakes in need of flipping.

Grace Fender smiled.

"Why don't you go see if it woke up your brother. Tell him breakfast is almost ready."

Leo hopped off the counter, the corners of his mouth smeared from sampling the chocolate chips, thinking about what his mother had said, about his head and his heart, and how they could contain an entire universe between them. But mostly he was thinking about how good those pancakes were going to taste.

Six weeks later, the Fenders drove out to L.A. to visit Leo's aunt.

His shirt had been burned to ashes, and Boo wanted his robe back, so Leo needed a new one. Preferably one with long sleeves.

"It's cold on Vestra," Baz warned him. "It's the wind that gets you." But only one person on board the *Icarus* wore anything close to Leo's size.

Kat led him back to the bunks and rooted around in her storage compartment for something suitable. All her clothes looked roughly the same, Leo noted: rugged pants with extra pockets stitched in and plain, military-style shirts with tears or old stains in various places. She handed him one of these, made out of a thick gray fabric. A rust-colored spot bloomed on the shoulder.

"You don't have one that doesn't have bloodstains, do you?"

"Don't worry," she said. "It's not my blood."

Leo wasn't sure that made him feel any better, but he put it on anyway.

"Here—" Kat handed Leo a leather jacket, cracked and faded but surprisingly bloodstain free. "I wore this back when I was picking pockets. It won't stop an energy blast, but it should break the wind."

Leo slipped into the jacket. The sleeves were a little long, but it would do. "Thanks," he said.

"It looks good on you. Now you don't look like some spoiled, fresh-faced Coalition poster boy who's never taken a punch in his life. Honestly, if I'd seen you walking around Andural when I was growing up, I would have robbed you in a heartbeat."

Leo didn't mind his Coalition clothes, and it was true what she said about never having taken a punch. But he *had* been shot at now, at least—thanks in part to her.

"So you don't like them either?" Leo said.

"Your clothes?"

"The Coalition." Not that that should come as a surprise. But it was different hearing Boo say it. He wasn't human. Maybe the Aykari hadn't saved his planet like they saved Earth.

"You shouldn't take it personally. I don't really like anyone," Kat said. "But if we are being honest, no, the Coalition aren't high on my list."

"But they're the good guys," Leo protested. "They're trying to bring an end to the war. They just want peace and order and unity." He realized he was starting to sound like his father. Or a recruitment commercial.

"Both sides are trying to end the war, Leo. It's called winning. And who's to say the peace and order imposed by the Aykari and the Coalition is going to be any better than what we have now?"

"It will certainly be better than what the Djarik would do!"

"Yeah," Kat muttered. "Not a huge fan of them either."

Leo realized there was no point in arguing. He and Kat were both human, but they were coming from different places. The little bunk room got quiet, Leo staring at the first officer's meager pile of clothes. This was probably everything she owned, right here. A fire had taken her parents. A man named Nero had taken her arm. He was sure she'd probably lost more along the way.

Then again, maybe they weren't that different.

As if she could hear his thoughts, Kat leaned over to catch Leo's eye. "Listen, I'm sorry about your brother," she said, her voice uncharacteristically soft. "If we'd have known . . ."

"Then what?" Leo said, suddenly angry. "He could have saved them, you know. When he had the chance. Maybe not all of them, but a lot." As many as he could fit into the *Icarus*, at least. Including Gareth.

"We're pirates, Leo. In case you haven't noticed, we have our own concerns. We aren't really in the business of saving people."

Of course. Except Leo knew that wasn't exactly true. Kat had once been living in the streets of a run-down former mining colony. No family. No home. Until a man named Bastian Black came around and offered her a place on his crew.

"He saved you," Leo said.

Katarina Corea opened her mouth, then snapped it back shut. She shook her head. "I earn my keep," she said. She held up her hand. "And I've paid my dues."

"Did you find something?"

Leo swiveled to see the captain leaning in the doorway.

"Hey. I remember that jacket," he added. "You were wearing that when you tried to pick my pockets."

"I actually *did* pick your pockets," Kat reminded him. "You just didn't have anything in them worth taking."

Baz grunted, then motioned to Leo. "If you're finished playing dress up, come with me. I've got something I think you might be interested in."

Leo glanced anxiously at Kat. He pictured airlocks. He pictured sluglike Snids. No matter what he imagined, it wasn't good.

"It's okay," she assured him. "He probably just wants to show you his buried treasure."

As Leo followed the captain out of the room, Kat called after him. "And be careful with that jacket. I want it back when this is all over."

Leo wasn't entirely sure what she meant by *this*. But he assured her she could have all of her clothes back. Hopefully without any new bloodstains.

Buried treasure.

Leo thought that was just a myth, something made up in movies and books, along with talking parrots and walking the plank. Real pirates didn't bury their treasure, they spent it as fast as they could. That's what he thought. Then again, it was possible he didn't know everything there was to know about pirates. Before he stowed away aboard the *Icarus*, he didn't know they wore flip-flops and ate gyurt and played antiquated rock music too loud, though maybe he could have guessed the last one.

Moving along the corridor, Leo caught a glimpse of his reflection in the *Icarus*'s narrow viewport. The jacket did look kind of good on him. The rest of him looked like hell.

"I'm showing this to you because I think you'll appreciate it," Baz said as he motioned Leo into his quarters, the smallest room on the ship, barely big enough to hold a bunk and a hook for the pirate's holster.

Tucked underneath the bunk sat a trunk much like the one Kat had pulled clothes from. Baz typed a code into the digital lock—2-6-E-4-U. Make that one more thing Leo knew about Baz: he was the kind of guy who used the same password for everything. The trunk hissed open.

For a moment—less than a second—Leo expected gold. Or jewels. Blood-colored rubies and glittering emeralds. But he quickly realized how stupid that was. Those things had value only on one tiny little rock in the galaxy, as far as he knew, to a species that still got giddy about things just because they sparkled. But there were no doubloons or diamonds in Baz's chest. There was just stuff. Old stuff.

Earth stuff.

"This is everything I managed to bring with me, plus a few things I've managed to scavenge along the way."

Leo flashed back to the image of his father telling him to go and pack. The peculiars and the particulars. This was Baz's version of the backpack from home.

"Kat doesn't get it. She doesn't remember much of her childhood before she left. And Boo—to him Earth is just another dot on the galactic map."

The Earth clearly wasn't *just another dot* to Black, Leo thought, or else he wouldn't have a trunk full of treasures like this. And he wouldn't be showing it to Leo.

Which meant he obviously cared about *something*. Leo wasn't sure what to do with that news.

The captain started riffling through the trunk's contents, looking for something specific or just browsing. Leo could identify most everything in the trunk. There were a few books, actual book books made of paper and glue, their pages yellow and crisp. Leo scanned the titles. *All Quiet on the Western Front. A Wizard of Earthsea. Watchmen.* Leo hadn't heard of any of them, but seeing them in all of their bound glory put a lump in his throat. The last time Leo had journeyed through a book with paper pages had been in his bed years ago—with his mother curled up beside him, reading out loud.

"Here. Check this out." Baz pulled out a clear plastic rectangle with a picture inside—some kind of fiery red dinosaur looking just a little ticked off. "Charizard. First edition holographic. My grandfather used to collect these when he was a kid."

"I used to collect seashells," Leo said.

He didn't mention how he collected them with his mother. How she always managed to find the best ones. How he'd brought his favorites with him when he left Earth, keeping them on a shelf by his bunk on board the *Beagle*.

How those same shells were now just space dust floating in the darkness.

The captain dropped the flaming dinosaur back into the chest. He picked up a baseball.

"Surely you know what *this* is," Black said.

"Yeah. I know what a baseball is," Leo confirmed. He pictured his backyard with its long grass. His father on the deck, reading by the light of the ships overhead, Gareth tossing pop-ups with the glow-in-the-dark ball because the high ones were Leo's favorite to catch. "My dad used to take us to Rockies games sometimes. What does this say?" He pointed to the signature scrawled across the leather.

"Miguel Ramos. 2046. That was the year he hit eighty home runs."

"Wait, so is this . . ."

"No," Baz said. "That's not the one that broke the record. Just a foul I caught. But he still signed it after the game so I held on to it."

Leo twisted the ball over and over in his hands, the hide scuffed, starting to split at the seam. He brought it to his nose and took a deep breath. He could almost smell the popcorn. He placed the baseball gently back in the trunk and watched Baz continue to sift. He caught a cover of *Time* magazine from 2044, famously sporting the iconic photo of an Aykari cruiser hovering over the Manhattan skyline, *THEY'RE HERE* in big white letters. There was a motley-colored cube with a couple of stickers peeling off and a ball cap with the Superman logo stitched into it. Leo recognized Superman at least. He'd seen *Superman Reborn* at least seven times with Gareth.

This was all Baz's stuff, specific to him, and yet everything in here brought memories of home. Leo's home. His own personal universe.

"Ah. Here we go."

Baz brought out a thin cardboard square that had been buried near the bottom. It showed a picture of a man outside an apartment building at night, standing next to a pile of cardboard boxes. Leo had never heard of anyone named David Bowie or Ziggy Stardust. "What is it?"

"It's called vinyl," Baz said, a touch of reverence in his voice. "Back in the dark ages, records like this were the only way you could listen to music. They disappeared for a while, then came back, then disappeared again, which makes this"—he held up the square of cardboard proudly—"an exceptionally rare artifact. Hopefully rare enough to get us some information."

There was that word again. Not *you. Us.*

"You think these guys—the ones you told me about—you think they will help us"—Leo stopped, corrected himself—"help *me* for *that*?"

"Just because it's old doesn't make it worthless," Baz said. "Not everything of value has to have a sleek silver exterior or run on ventasium. It's too easy to forget that things like this existed."

His piece of treasure found, Baz started to close the chest, when Leo spotted a black box that had been pushed to the corner. Normally it wouldn't have caught his eye, except it had a familiar emblem on it, one he hadn't expected to see in the pirate's goody box: one large planet surrounded by a dozen smaller ones.

"What's this?" Leo said, picking it up.

"Nothing. Not important," Baz said, reaching for the box, but Leo had already opened it, its hinges clicking to reveal a medal. A gold sunburst with a silver star at its center. A bright red ribbon snaked out from the top. Leo had seen medals like this before. Captain Saito had one too.

"It's not nothing," Leo said. "It's military." Leo read the inscription. The top half was in Aykari, but the bottom was in English: *For exceptional courage in the line of duty.* He read the name engraved in the center, also in English.

Lt. Sebastian D. Blackwell.

"This is yours?"

"It's trash," Baz said. "Honestly, I'm not even sure why I still have it."

"But this is a Coalition medal. That means you—"

Baz snatched the box from Leo's hands. "Yeah, well . . . my father wasn't the only pilot in the family," he said.

Leo remembered. Jets. Not starships. Except for Baz it must have been the other way around. "Hold on . . . you were part of the Coalition?" And now you're *this*? Leo thought. It didn't make sense. How does one go from Coalition pilot sworn to defend Earth from its enemies to thieving pirate, boarding Coalition ships and leaving their crews stranded and helpless? "What happened?"

"Same thing that happened to all of us," Baz said. "To everyone on Earth that day."

He meant the attack. The day the missiles struck. The day that haunted Leo and replayed itself time and time again in his nightmares, the ones that took his breath away. "You were there," Leo said. While Leo was standing on a beach watching the smoke rise, Bastian Black was only a matter of miles—not light-years—away.

Black nodded. "I was twenty-five when it happened. Like everyone else, I watched the cities burn. And like everyone else, I was mad. I wanted to do something, wanted to fight back."

"So you joined the Coalition."

"I already had some experience in the cockpit, so I joined the navy and they put me through flight school and stuck me in a starfighter." Baz angled the medal in his hands, watching the glow from the overhead light skate across its gleaming surface. "That's where I was when I earned this. We were raiding a munitions factory that the Djarik had seized, some planet I'd never even heard of, but it had a small supply of ventasium, so that made it worth fighting over. My missiles took out the factory and all the buildings around it. Turned out the factory was mostly abandoned, but the other buildings weren't. My Aykari superiors said they didn't know, but that it also didn't matter: the mission was still deemed a success, despite the civilian casualties."

Baz snapped the box closed. The sound made Leo jump.

"Those civilians—the ones in the blast radius—they weren't Djarik sympathizers. They weren't part of the Coalition either. They were just caught in the middle. Collateral damage— that's what it's called, just in case you were wondering."

"I'm sure if they had known . . ." Leo started to say, but the look in Baz's eyes was enough to cut him off.

"Sure," he said. "Except there was collateral damage everywhere I looked. People forced to give up their land to make room for Aykari drills. Orders to abandon the defense of a planet because its ventasium stores were all dried up. Factories people counted on to provide food, clothes, you name it, commandeered and repurposed to make weapons and ships. I've seen things, Leo. Maybe not as bad as what the Djarik did to us, but they were still things I wanted no part of. I told them I wanted to quit, but the Aykari ordered me back in the cockpit. So I folded up my uniform, left it sitting on my cot, and found a different ship to fly."

No wonder the Coalition bounty on his head was so high, Leo thought: Bastian Black wasn't just a pirate.

He was also a traitor.

Baz carelessly tossed the box back into the trunk. "This war—this one we're all caught up in? It's not about us, Leo. You and me? We're just a resource. Our precious planet Earth? Just a fueling station. A pit stop along the way. And once we're all used up, we'll all be tossed on the side of the road and forgotten, so you might as well learn how to survive on your own sooner rather than later."

Baz started to close the trunk but paused, reaching for the black box again. This time he handed it back to Leo, practically shoving it into his hands. "On second thought, here. You take it. Give it to your father, if we find him. I'm sure he's done something to deserve it. Or keep it for yourself. It's got to be worth more to you than it is to me."

Before Leo could think of what to say, the captain pushed his trunk of treasures back under his bunk, reburying it. He left the room with Leo still in it, on his knees, speechless, a pirate's jacket tight around his shoulders, a Coalition medal heavy in his hands.

The Fender study had always been full of accolades. Plaques lined the walls of the house in Denver; medals hung from bookshelf corners. The Andrew Gemant Award. The Tate Medal. The Dannie Heineman Prize for Astrophysics. The Gerhardt Award for Achievements in Geochemistry. Everywhere you looked Dr. Calvin Fender's name was wrought in gold and bronze.

Leo would sometimes take some of the medals down and hold them, just to feel their weight, once draping them all around his neck like an Olympian, leaving him lopsided, leaning over, making it difficult to walk. All those awards told a story. A tale of a scientific genius. An expert in the fields of physics, astronomy, chemistry, you name it. One of the foremost human authorities on ventasium and its possible applications. The kind of human being that even a far superior alien race such as the Aykari could admire.

In short, a tough act for any kid to follow.

Not that he didn't try. Leo would bring home certificates, fresh from the printer, with embossed gold stars and fancy script.

This certifies that Leo Fender *has achieved the rank of Outstanding in the Grade-Wide Reading Challenge*

We hereby recognize Leo Fender, Fourth Grader, *for making High Honor Roll this semester*

Congratulations, LEO FENDER, *for completing the Colorado State Physical Fitness Test*

Leo knew they were nothing like the awards hanging in his father's office, awards that were given to only one or two people in the world. It didn't take a genius to feel the minor heft of a sheet of paper with a gold sticker on it and realize how insignificant it was, how dozens, even hundreds of other kids in your school had the same piece of paper tucked into their folders to give to their parents in the hopes of having them magneted to the fridge.

And he would be lying if he said it didn't cause an inkling of doubt, a moment's hesitation, standing in the space between the study and the kitchen, the certificate held behind his back, looking at his father the famous scientist who says, "What do you have there?" Knowing that there was no way it could possibly compare.

But slowly, reluctantly, Leo would show him. And every time, Dr. Calvin Fender, winner of an actual Nobel Prize, would read over the certificate carefully, once to himself and then again out loud, his voice deep with gravitas, his eyes beaming with pride. And every time he would point to the certificate and say, "*That* is remarkable," before handing it back. "Be sure to show your mother."

And Leo would say, "Yes, sir," even though he'd already shown her, because he always showed her first.

After the attack, Leo stopped showing his father every little slip of paper that came home. The report cards full of Bs. The occasional note informing Dr. Fender that his son had been tardy to class. There didn't seem to be much of a point. Even the medals and plaques hanging in the study didn't seem to carry the same gravity as they used to, their polish faded, their brightness dulled. After all, what good is a bronze plaque against an alien menace that can appear out of nowhere at any time and tear your world apart? An engraved medal, no matter how prestigious, couldn't deflect a Djarik missile. It couldn't bring your mother back.

And what good, really, was a stack of papers celebrating your achievements if you only had the one parent to show it to?

✳ ✳ ✳

Leo found everyone in the cockpit again. Kat was piloting—
she had changed clothes as well, finding a warmer coat with
a fur-lined hood, her holster cinching the coat closed. Bastian had traded in his flip-flops again, but now also sported a
pair of gloves. Only Boo was dressed the same, his robe back
around his muscular frame, though Leo guessed his thick coat
of fur provided all the warmth he needed. Outside, Vestra
Prime loomed before them in all its rugged ugliness.

"I forgot how desolate this place was," Kat said as she wove
the *Icarus* between the crags of brown rock jutting from the
planet's surface.

"Yeah. It's mostly a wasteland," Baz said. "Just a handful of
outposts. Undoubtedly one of the most depressing places in
the universe."

"Then why does anyone bother to come here?" Boo asked.

"Because nobody else wants to," Baz replied. "It's too far
from the more populated systems. There's no V. No precious
metals to be mined. Nothing of value save for a breathable
atmosphere and a couple of halfway decent places to drink. It's
a place tailor-made for outsiders and rejects."

"So we'll fit right in," Kat concluded.

Leo leaned over and whispered to Boo, "You been here
before?"

The Queleti shook his head. He was staring out the cockpit.
"There are no trees," he said. "My planet is covered in trees,
but this place is nothing but rock." It was true. All Leo could

see were the towers of stone erupting from a jagged surface that swirled with red dust. In the distance he could make out what appeared to be buildings of metal fused with the landscape.

"Mine used to be," Leo said. "Covered in trees, I mean."

Boo grunted. "What happened to them?"

"We did, I guess," Leo answered.

As the buildings grew closer Leo could see they were connected by bridges, most of them at least three hundred feet off the ground.

"The dust clouds stay close to the surface, but they're still hard on the lungs, so the first settlers built up, using the outcroppings as anchors," Baz said. "Also the notorious Vestran wind makes it difficult for hovercraft to maneuver, so mostly people just walk wherever they need to go. Not that there's much of anywhere *to* go."

Unless you are trying to track down your father, Leo thought.

"There," Baz said, pointing. "That's the tower we need." Kat nestled the *Icarus* down on a landing platform, fighting with the controls as the aforementioned wind shook the ship. Aside from the *Icarus*, the platform was empty. It really was a place nobody wanted to be. Kat unbuckled and checked the charge on her pistol again. Maybe it was just second nature. Or maybe Leo was just hoping that was the case.

Baz led them all to the back where Skits was waiting for

them, two of her metal appendages crossed. "Let me guess," the robot said. "I'm not coming with."

"Did you finish your repairs?" Baz asked.

"Yeah, mostly."

"Mostly?"

"I mean, I got them, like, *half* done. But then I had to save all of you and then watch over the kid and some other stuff happened—and I don't know how you expect me to do everything all at once, all the freking time."

"She's cursing now? That's new."

"Bite me, Kat," Skits said. It seemed so strange to hear the robot hissing insults from the voice box beneath a painted grin.

Baz nodded to the ramp. "You guys go on. I'll catch up to you in a second."

"Father–robot daughter chat," Boo whispered to Leo. "We probably don't want to be here."

As he made his way off the ship, Leo saw Kat step close to Black.

"Be honest, Captain. Are we really here to get out of trouble? Or are we looking for more of it?"

Leo paused at the top of the ramp, waiting for the response.

"Haven't quite decided yet," Baz replied.

Leo glanced over his shoulder to find them both looking his way. He tucked his head and followed Boo down the ramp.

Baz hadn't been lying about the wind. Leo felt it the moment he stepped off. It didn't feel like one blast of wind but several, a volley of currents whipping at him from all directions, nipping at any part of him that wasn't covered, roughing his cheeks and instantly pulling tears from his eyes. And the sound. Howling at times, but at others just a hiss or a rumble like a crashing wave. And when it died down—which it did only for spells of a second or two—it almost sounded musical, like notes played on a flute. "It's singing," Leo said, but nobody could hear him because the Vestran torrent had already kicked up again, making it hard to have a conversation.

And difficult to walk as well. Twice Leo nearly fell over as a gust threatened to sweep his feet out from under him. Both times Boo caught him and kept him upright. The landing pad was situated on the edge of a collection of steel domes and stalwart towers sprawled across a slate of red rock. Swirls of the dust that supposedly stayed close to the surface still managed to find their way up here, though they were never allowed to settle for long. Leo coughed. Between the cold wind and the red dust, the air was only just breathable; it felt like he was sucking in tiny slivers of glass. Leo couldn't even imagine where the planet's oxygen came from: there wasn't a bush or a patch of grass to be seen.

Nor was there another living being outside of the *Icarus*'s crew. Whoever lived here was clearly content to stay indoors.

Ghost town, Leo thought. And to think, he was here to find

someone. In this place people went to *not* be found.

Baz caught up to them without Skits in tow. They all huddled close to be heard.

"How did that go?" Kat asked.

"About what I expected. She hates everybody and nobody understands her and the whole universe can just go collapse in on itself for all she cares."

"And you still don't think she needs a personality matrix adjustment?"

"I don't know. I feel that way sometimes. Like the world is out to get me. Don't you?" Baz grinned and pointed to one of the towers just across the long, narrow bridge. "That's the one. Let's hope they don't mind us stopping by unannounced."

The bridge was long but looked stable enough with thick cables and support pylons. The railing was high—up nearly to Leo's shoulder—so at least you couldn't blow right over the side. Not unless you were stupid and tried to sit on the edge, then you would plummet to your death for certain. Baz led the way. The tower in question took on an odd shape, actually getting wider and curving at the top. Sort of like a saucer.

Or a radar dish.

Leo leaned into the wind, keeping his hands on the rails. Eventually he noticed a pattern to the wind's blowing: it got louder just *before* it was about to whip up and try and knock you over, which meant he could anticipate it and plant his feet against it. There was no way he could ever live here. The howling alone would drive him insane.

They made their way wordlessly across the bridge to a set of titanium doors on the other side. No control panel, just a small black globe like an eyeball set above the entry. A security camera.

Baz reached into the satchel he'd brought and removed his treasure, holding the vinyl record up to the black eye. Ziggy Stardust and his spiders from Mars were the key to getting in, it seemed.

After a moment, the doors slid quietly open.

And the pirates slipped quickly inside.

CONGRATULATIONS!!!

You may have already won an all-expenses-paid Venusian cruise for two. You and a guest will be transported on a luxury Lockheed-Carnival pleasure yacht to the orbit of hot and sexy Venus, the planet of love. There you can enjoy all the onboard amenities, including the fully enclosed star-gazing pool and our famous exotic alien buffet. Plus choose from a variety of planetary excursions, including lava gliding, volcano watching, or take a rover to the top of Maxwell Montes to see the sun set in the east! Leave Earth behind and experience something new. Some exclusions may apply.

COLONISTS WANTED

For terraforming and mining opportunity in the Lyran system. Three-year commitment. All living expenses paid plus modest monthly stipend. Transport and security provided. Must have level-one interplanetary travel clearance, provide valid work permit, and pass basic health and fitness screening and criminal background check. For more information, click here or contact your local Off-world Opportunities office.

   —Banner advertisements on digital
   newsfeed, 2048

THE PRICE YOU PAY

SLOWLY THE CITIZENS OF EARTH BEGAN TO SLIP away.

When the first colonists set out, the destinations were familiar. Better, after all, to stay in the solar system you grew up in with the sun you were used to. The initial expeditions went to Mars. Some relocated to Coalition space stations already in orbit around Jupiter and Neptune. The more ambitious volunteered to help terraform the least inhospitable planets around Alpha Centauri, essentially a stone's throw away with an Aykarian jump drive and a pocketful of V.

No matter your skill set, the Coalition could use you. There was a place for everyone somewhere out in the universe, provided you had the right permit and security clearance. If you were poor, underpaid, out of work, or just looking for a change, the Coalition would happily put you on one of their transports and send you where you were needed most. Farm-hands and busboys hung up trowels and towels to go build water reclamation facilities on distant settlements. Prisons all over Earth suddenly found themselves with cells to spare as convicts were shipped out to work in off-world mining facilities, reducing their sentences by serving their time chipping precious minerals out of a cave on Cygnus 7 or operating excavators on the Aykari's most recent discovery. The pay wasn't always great, but the views on the journey over could be spectacular.

If you were rich, you didn't colonize—you vacationed. Thousands booked passage on luxury space liners where you could marvel at the surface of Cerberon 7 from the viewport of your spacious cabin, only a short stroll from the spa. Then you came home to your climate-controlled compound on Earth and bragged to the jealous kids in your class how you got to spend your summer.

However, most who left never came back.

What started out as a trickle swelled into a stream, as more and more humans said goodbye to the only home they'd ever known. For some it was the thrill of conquering the final frontier. For others it was a chance to start over.

For Leo it hadn't been a choice; he'd simply been told to pack. The Aykari had given Dr. Fender an opportunity to serve—to assist the Coalition, advance science, and aid humanity all at once. It was everything he ever wanted. Or at least everything he believed in.

But deep down, Leo always suspected that his father was also running away. From a planet that was slowly falling apart and a house that was haunted by the ghost of the only woman he ever loved.

Pack light. That's what his father had said to him, and Leo had tried. But there's no accounting for the weight of memory.

And there are some things you just can't let go of.

The first thing Leo noticed when he entered through a second set of doors was the carpet.

Actual carpet.

How long had it been since Leo had seen—no, since he had *felt* carpet? Three years aboard a ship with ice-cold metal floors that nipped at your toes if you dared walk across them barefoot. But here was a plush and precious shag covering the length of the room. He ached to take his boots off, slip out of his socks, and feel the soft piles of blue-tinted fibers brush against his soles, but he thought it might be rude.

The wonder that is carpeted flooring was soon overshadowed by other discoveries as Leo's eyes swept over the giant room. It was like stepping through a portal, jumping across both space and time, and landing back on Earth, but an Earth that hadn't even seen an Aykarian cruiser yet. The furniture—soft fabric and solid wood, not cold steel and molded plastic. Lights hanging from the ceiling with old-fashioned screw-in bulbs, not embedded strips chemically radiating lumens along the wall. There was even a fireplace, though that might just be for show: there was no fire burning and Leo hadn't noticed a chimney. In front of the fireplace sat a couch, though from where he stood, Leo could only see the back of it. Still, he imagined it would have to be more comfortable than the cot he'd slept on for the last three years.

Leo took slow, measured breaths, slowly spinning, absorbing it all. The walls were painted vivid pinks and greens and purples, at least what you could see of them in between the gild-framed oil paintings and posters for old movies that his grandfather used to talk about, movies like *Jaws* and *Jurassic Park*. Giant oak cases, two stories high, were jammed with books (real ones again) and trinkets—toy models and stuffed animals and mysterious chunks of glittering rock that hopefully weren't radioactive. On one shelf Leo spotted a diamond-crusted tiara sitting on the head of a bald, yellow, one-eyed alien holding a banana—a species he didn't recognize. Another shelf held what looked to be a collection of empty drink bottles—one was Dr Pepper. Plastic action figures lined up to do battle. A cascade of automobile license plates covered one section of wall; a rack full of ancient weapons—Earth weapons, swords and axes—hung on another. A shelf full of tiny glasses. A display of candy bar wrappers. The room was Baz's treasure chest times a thousand.

"What is this place?" Leo asked no one in particular.

"It's our little slice of home," said a voice.

Leo followed the sound to a young man dressed in a blue

mink coat to match the carpet and a pair of yellow-and-red-striped bathing trunks revealing a pair of deep brown, stork-like legs. His shag of black hair shot off like a burst firework. He looked younger than Baz, older than Kat. He was shorter than both.

This, apparently, was one of the jackers. That's what Leo called them. They had other names, he knew: Networms. Moles. Cypirates. There were kids at school who had aspirations of one day dropping out and becoming one of these. The same kids who would access the school database to change their evaluations or steal someone else's identity and go on a shopping spree. His species had been hacking into computer systems for over a hundred years, Leo knew, long before they knew the Aykari or Djarik even existed.

Maybe it was just human nature—to go where you aren't supposed to.

Of course when the network suddenly grew to be galaxy-wide, there were a lot more places you weren't supposed to go, and the jacker's skill set got even more valuable. Especially in certain circles.

Leo knew that jackers weren't to be trusted. They stole valuables and sold them to the highest bidder. They operated outside the law. They looked out for only themselves.

Sort of like pirates.

And yet here *he* was, hoping—praying—that they would help him. What circle did that put him in?

"If it isn't Bastian Black," the man approaching them continued. "Captain Black Sparrow. The Bastian of Badness. Captain Badazz."

"Captain Badazz?" Kat whispered. "He's not serious."

"Yeah. That one's new," Baz whispered back. "Hello, Dev. Nice to see you." Leo wasn't sure he really meant it.

"And is that Katarina Corea hiding behind you? The girl with the titanium arm and the steely-eyed stare. How long has it been, Kat? A year? Two?"

"Not long enough," Kat said curtly.

The jacker put a hand over his chest. "You wound me. Straight to the core. And who are Calvin and Hobbes here? Fearless additions to the crew?"

"This is Bo'enmaza Okardo," Baz said, pointing to Boo. "And this is Leo."

"Leo. Leonardo. Like the painter?" Dev snapped his fingers.

"The ninja turtle," Leo said.

"Even better." Dev grinned, a devious sort of smile that suggested to Leo that he had just unwittingly become part of some secret club. He slid up to Boo, running a finger along the sleeve of the Queleti's robe. "I'm not sure what *you* are, but this robe is nice. What is this? Aykarian microfiber? Egyptian cotton?"

"It's mine," Boo said brusquely, crossing all four of his arms.

"Fair enough," Dev said, taking a step back. "Probably a little big on me anyways. So what's the deal, Cap?" he said to Baz. "What brings you to our lovely hunk of rock in the middle of nowhere? You on the run?"

"Always," Baz replied. "But that's not why I came to see you." He pulled the record back out of the satchel.

"*Ziggy Stardust*," Dev said. "A rare gem indeed."

"Near mint condition." Baz handed it over. Leo still wasn't sure how it worked or why you would need something so big to play music with, but judging by Dev's saucer eyes, the captain had at least been right about its value. "I found it at a garage sale fifteen years ago," he continued. "At the time there were only a hundred or so copies left. Who knows, by now this could be the only one."

Dev licked his lips, flipping the record over and over in his hands. "I know they say ventasium is the most precious thing in the universe, but vintage vinyl's got to be a close second, am I right?" The man slipped a black disk the size of a small pizza from the cardboard sleeve and admired it. "Not a scratch," he added. "This may be the only thing to make it halfway across the galaxy without a mark of some kind."

"It's yours," Baz said. "All I'm asking for in return is a little information."

Dev slid the disc back in its sleeve, eyes narrowing again. "And I'm guessing the kind of information you're looking for isn't easy to come by."

"I wouldn't need someone like you if it was," Baz admitted.

Kat, apparently, figured that was enough flattery. She cut right to it. "We need you to hack into the Djarik security network."

Dev stared at her for a moment, then back at Black, holding it in for three whole seconds before exploding. His laugh grated on Leo's ears—like a squeaky windshield wiper. "The Djarik military mainframe? You're joking right?"

Baz smiled and shrugged. Kat didn't smile at all.

"My stars and garters, you're serious. You want me to infiltrate the Djarik military mainframe for *Ziggy Stardust and the Spiders from Mars*? Have you been licking kerodium crystals? Because something has definitely scrambled your brain."

"So are you saying you can't or you won't?" Kat pressed.

"I'm saying, my beautiful minx, that it would be suicide. Their security is top-notch. Do you have any idea how tight the Djarik firewalls are? They're nearly impossible to bust through. It'd be like trying to squeeze an elephant into a Dixie cup."

"What's an elephant?" Boo whispered to Leo.

"A really big animal with tusks," Leo whispered back, measuring the space with his hands. "Like *really* big. Bigger than you."

"Ah." Boo nodded. He thought for a moment. "What's a Dixie cup?"

The man in the swim trunks couldn't stop laughing at Baz's request. Maybe help wouldn't be so easy to come by after all.

"I mean, you must be out of your mind. You think I want a bounty on my head the size of yours?"

"Come on, Dev. It's not like we're asking you to access weapons specs or anything," Baz said. "I just need you to

- 214 -

locate one person. A prisoner."

"Dr. Calvin Fender," Leo interjected, getting the jacker's attention. "He's my father. He was captured several days ago. When our ship was attacked . . . the first time." The last part slipped out. Or maybe it didn't. Maybe he meant to say it.

Baz shot Leo a sidelong glance, then he turned back to Dev. "We need to know if the kid's dad is still alive and where he's being held. That's all."

"Oh . . . that's all." Dev snorted. "That's *all*. Seriously, Bizzazz, I don't care if you just want directions to the nearest intergalactic porta potty, I'm telling you it's not possible."

"Oh, it's definitely possible," a different voice said.

The voice came from the couch, Leo realized. The one sitting in front of the cold, empty fireplace.

"We've done it before," the couch continued.

Leo stood on his tiptoes. He could just make out a shoulder of someone lying there. Then the shoulder moved and the thing that had talked suddenly sat up, revealing both shoulders. And in between those shoulders . . .

Leo gasped. He couldn't help it.

"Right. Probably should have warned you about that," Baz said.

The human sitting up had no head.

There was a brain, to be sure—just no skull. No face. No hair. No teeth. Only a brain enclosed in a clear cylinder that was affixed to the rest of the body by a metal ring where the neck would be. A football-sized mound of wrinkly gray tissue, a lumpy sponge floating in clear liquid and attached to a tangled stem of nerves, tubes and wires, both organic and artificial, that disappeared into the ring, presumably snaking their way down into the thing's body. As he sat up and turned around, the brain bobbed like a jellyfish.

"Leo, Mac. Mac, Leo."

"Pleased to meet you," the brain said, its voice emanating from the metal ring the jar was connected to, much like the speaker Skits was constantly whining out of.

"Um. Uh. Hey." Leo stammered, staring at the hunk of gray matter he'd just been introduced to. He had seen his fair share of prosthetics. Artificial eyes and ears. Cybernetic limbs like Kat's. One kid back on Earth had her entire lower body replaced after a bad car accident; she was carbon fiber from the waist down. But he'd never seen a brain without a skull before—at least not one that was still attached and functioning. Leo studied the round aquarium-like contraption resting on the man's shoulders. There were tiny sensors that might have acted as his eyes and ears, maybe even his nose as well. That is, if he still smelled things. *Did* he smell things? How did he even *eat*? "Your head . . ." Leo began.

"Is missing. I'm aware," Mac said. "I was there when it happened. The good news for you is that makes me, literally, the brains of this operation. And I'm telling you that what you are asking is possible."

"You are out of your freking mind, as always." Dev turned back to the crew with his hands up. "Don't listen to my partner. The Djarik security systems are brutal. If they track us—and they *will* almost certainly track us—they could infect us, blitz our rig, cause a surge that sabotages our whole setup. Or worse, they could literally, *physically* hunt us down. Home in on our location and send a warship here to bomb this whole place to the ground. No album is worth that. Sorry." He shoved the record back into Baz's hands.

"But you just said you've done it before," Kat pressed.

"Yeah. Once. And we almost got busted for it. Took months to repair our system and get the Djarik off our scent. And the Aykari agents who asked for our help paid a lot more than you guys, I can tell you that."

Leo snorted. That couldn't really be true, could it? The Aykari wouldn't hire people like this, even if it meant undermining their enemy.

Dev gave him a funny glance but continued. "Not to mention the Djarik security protocols have probably only gotten tougher since then. In case you haven't noticed, there *is* a war going on out there."

"We've noticed," Boo said.

"So then you know it's not a good idea to draw extra attention to yourself if you can help it."

"We know that too," Kat said tartly. "At least some of us do," she added, looking at Baz.

"So then why are we even still talking?" Dev asked.

"Because I think we can do it," the floating brain countered. "We just have to be quick about it. If that's the only information we need, then it should be possible to get in and out before they even know we're there."

Dev shut his eyes. Sighed. Opened them. Put up a finger. "Would you excuse me a sec? My partner and I need to talk." He spun around, his robe swirling with him, and stalked over to the couch. His agitated whisper wasn't much of a whisper at all; Leo could hear every word. "What is your deal? You know how dangerous this is. And you don't even *like* David Bowie."

"Doesn't matter," Mac replied. "The kid is looking for his dad."

"So?"

"So, it's the human thing to do."

"I think you mean *humane*."

"Same difference. If it was your dad, wouldn't you want help finding him?"

"Are you kidding?" Dev fired back. "My father was a jerk. And besides, we aren't talking about hacking into some civilian database to steal library card numbers. You're really telling me you want to risk jacking into the Djarik network again? After what happened last time?"

"All the more reason," Mac said. "A little payback. Give those Scalies the middle finger. Besides, if we're going in anyway, you never know what else we might find digging around. Could be some good dirt. A piece of juicy data worth the price of admission."

The two grew silent as if they were both staring straight into each other's brain. After a moment, Dev groaned. "You're going to get us into trouble. You know that."

"We're already in trouble," Mac said. "That's why we are hiding out on this windblown rock in the middle of nowhere. Besides, it beats sitting on our butts playing video games all day."

"Says you. I *like* sitting on my butt playing video games all day. I thought that was the dream."

"The kid lost his dad," Mac pressed. "I think we should at least try. If it gets too hot, we bail."

The man without a shirt clearly wasn't convinced by the man without a face, but Leo could tell the discussion was over. The brains of the operation got the final say, it seemed.

Dev came back to Baz, frowning, and snatched *Ziggy Stardust* back from his hands. "Fine. We'll do it," he said. "But no promises. If it looks like we're being bugged, I'm pulling the plug *and* keeping the record. Got it?"

Baz nodded.

"Also," Dev continued, "I think this incredible act of generosity on our part deserves a little something extra. A bonus." He looked straight at Kat, one eyebrow arched.

She looked back at him. Both eyebrows arched. "Really?"

"Just one kiss. Three seconds. No tongue. What do you say?"

"I say I will break your heart."

"That's a price I am willing to pay," Dev admitted.

"No. You don't understand," Kat continued. "I mean, I will literally dig my way into your chest with this claw and

- 219 -

squeeze the still-beating thing to a bloody pulp in my cold, mechanical fist."

Kat's eyes blazed, her cybernetic fingers already curled, but before she could make a move or Dev could rescind his request, the Queleti stepped close, grabbing the little man with all four giant furry arms. Leo was sure Boo was about to snap him in two, but instead he drew Dev close, sweeping him clear off his feet, their two robes mingling as Boo planted his black lips on the other's thin pink ones.

Boo held the man there, legs kicking, emitting muffled screams, one of the Queleti's horns making a dimple in Dev's cheek, before releasing him with an audibly wet smack.

"Three seconds. No tongue," Boo said.

Dev stumbled backward, gagging, scrubbing his lips with the sleeve of his robe. "What is *wrong* with you? Why'd you do that?"

"You were asking for it," Boo offered.

"You *were* asking for it," Baz concurred. Kat smiled with satisfaction.

Dev did not. His whole face was shocked red. But his partner was clapping.

"That was the best thing I've seen in years. You definitely get our help now." Mac pointed to a door with a poster for the movie called *The Matrix*. "This way to Cerebro."

Leo fell in behind a still-grinning Kat, who thankfully hadn't had to rip out anyone's heart. She certainly seemed like she was about to. Beside him the Queleti snorted. "I don't see what the big deal is," he muttered. "I've been told I'm a very good kisser."

Leo reached up and touched Boo's shoulder. It was the first time he'd actually touched the Queleti's fur, he realized.

It was even softer than it looked.

They had to wait for Dev to go gargle something—like alcohol, he said, or maybe acid—before they could begin. But when he came back into the chamber off the main room he was carrying a can of soda.

Real fizzy soda. Leo could hear it crackling. It made his mouth water.

"Is that . . ." Leo started.

"Coca-Cola, yes. The original. Full-on sugar. You think Bowie's rare, try finding one of these that isn't flat." Dev took an exaggerated gulp, followed by a satisfied if slightly exaggerated "aah." Leo licked his lips. It had been years since he'd had any kind of soda. Beverage choices on board the *Beagle* consisted of reclaimed water, weak coffee, and powdered milk substitute, sometimes flavored with cocoa when he could get it. He raised his eyebrows in what he hoped was an obvious hint.

"Sorry. I'd give you a sip, but I need it all to get the taste of this guy's hairy lips out of my mouth," Dev said, shooting an eye at the Queleti. He took another sip and sighed. "So refreshing."

"Good luck getting Dev to share anything," Mac said. "He's

incredibly possessive of the classics. Coke. Super Mario Bros. Motown. If it was invented before the year 2000, he's all over it. Despite the fact that you were born, what, twenty-six years ago?"

"Twenty-eight," Dev corrected. "And I appreciate things from all ages, from Beethoven to Cardi B. to my Robot Concubine. I am a true connoisseur of human culture."

"Is that why you have all this stuff?" Leo asked.

"We have all that stuff so we don't forget how cool we used to be. Before the Aykari showed up and basically told us we were obsolete. I mean, it's not like everything humans ever did is suddenly crap because some aliens came down and showed us how to make spaceships and laser guns."

"Though laser guns are pretty awesome," Mac said. "Provided that they aren't pointed at you."

Leo felt the same way. More so recently.

"Though if we're being *perfectly* honest," Mac continued, "you have to admit that a lot of what we came up with is junk. . . . Like boy bands."

"What are you talking about?" Dev protested. "Boy bands were a necessary step in human evolution. Without them we would never have Justin Timberlake."

"Exactly," Mac replied. "Back me up here, Black."

"Boy bands were totally uncalled for," Baz said matter-of-factly.

Leo waited for Boo to ask him what a boy band was, but perhaps the name was self-explanatory.

Dev stuck to his guns. "Whatever. You love what you love, and you hang on to it no matter what. Am I right, Leo?"

Leo shrugged. His father wouldn't have appreciated the shrine these two had built in the other room; of all of them Dad'd been the most willing to leave all their Earthly stuff behind. *There's so much out there. So much we haven't even discovered yet,* he told Leo once. *We'll make a new home,* he insisted, though he never explained when or where or how. But it didn't matter. All that mattered is that this new world that was promised would be better than the old one.

Obviously not everybody felt the same.

"Time to plug in," Mac said, settling into the chair in the center of the room. The chamber they stood in was much smaller than the one with the cozy carpet and shelves full of relics. The floor here was metal again, as were the walls, though most of them were lined with vid screens and humming machines. The chair—one of only two places to sit in the room—reminded Leo a little of when he used to visit the dentist as a kid, except it had almost as many buttons and switches as the cockpit of the *Icarus*. Leo never liked going to the dentist. For all the advances in technology the Aykari had brought with them, they had done little to improve dental hygiene. Leo supposed he couldn't blame them: the Aykari didn't even have teeth.

"This is Cerebro," Mac's voice box said. "The best network infiltration system money can buy. Please don't touch a single thing." Mac undid the top two buttons of his shirt, revealing

the intersection where metal met flesh, where the contraption that held his brain and kept it steady on his shoulders
narrowed to a V between his collarbones, ending in a round
circle just above where his heart would be, a hole the size of
a marble in its center. Leo tried not to stare at the scars where
the steel had been grafted to skin, but Kat, it seemed, couldn't
help herself, reaching with her right hand and rubbing her left
arm above the elbow.

The crew of the *Icarus* circled around as Dev attached a thick
yellow cord with a metal adapter directly into the jack in his
partner's chest. Mac was now literally plugged in.

The giant center screen in front of them flashed to life.

"My partner here was actually named after a computer, don't
you know," Dev said. "Maybe that's why he thinks like one."

"Self-fulfilling prophecy," Mac said.

Leo had never hacked into anything before. Computers
weren't his thing. He was pretty good with his hands—he
could help fix a gas leak or steer the hydraulic forklift that his
brother and he used to do doughnuts in the *Beagle*'s hangar—
but anything more complicated than his watch or his datapad
eluded him. "How does this whole thing even work?"

"It's basically a big game of leapfrog," Dev said. "We use
the high-powered transmitter stationed in this tower to get
access to any com systems it can reach. Then we pirate those
coms to jump out to others until we find one with a Djarik
signature. The Djarik don't have a huge presence in this part
of the galaxy, thank god, so that could take a while, but we

will get there. And that's when the fun begins."

"What's the fun part?" Boo asked.

"The best part of stealing any treasure," Mac said. "Not waking up the dragon."

Leo watched as a stream of code marched across the giant screen in front of them, all in symbols he couldn't decipher. His implant was terrific at translating alien speech, but it was no help when it came to reading another language—especially not an encrypted one.

"Once you're inside the Djarik network, how long will it take you to find what they've done with Leo's father?" Baz asked.

"Hopefully not more than a couple of minutes," Dev said. "Anything longer than that and we will be toast."

In the chair, Mac's fingers danced wildly along the controls. Leo half expected to see blossoms of color exploding on the surface of his brain, like when doctors used to do those scans that showed neural activity, but Mac's cerebral cortex just floated there peacefully. Dev caught Leo staring.

"Fascinating, isn't it? The way it just bobs around. It's just so strangely beautiful and hideous at the same time. I mean seriously, sometimes I can just sit and watch it for hours."

"You're making me self-conscious," Mac admitted.

Leo looked away.

"In case you're wondering, and I'm sure you are—it happened a long time ago," Dev said. "When he was just a kid. Tragic ceiling fan accident. Too much elevation while jumping on the bed. Isn't that right, Mac?"

"Don't listen to him," Mac said. "I got sucked into a turbine on board a cruiser. Took it clean off. Thankfully there was an Aykarian surgeon on board. Saved my noodle, just not my pretty face."

That was the Aykari for you: no advances in dentistry, but they could reattach your brain to your body.

"Trust me," Dev said. "It's for the better. I've seen pictures of this guy as a kid. He was no JT, I'll tell you that."

Suddenly the code disappeared. The center screen above went black, then flashed green briefly before it showed an image of a pixelated figure running down a corridor filled with hundreds of branching hallways. "We're in," Mac said.

"In? In where?" Leo asked.

"The Djarik data cluster," Dev answered, tapping on another screen beside him. "That didn't take long. They must have a ship not too far from here."

"Hope it's not a warship," Kat said. Though Leo had never seen a single Djarik ship that *wasn't* built for waging war.

"This is a low-level entry point," Mac said, his fingers tapping even more frenetically. "The Aykari have much stronger frontline security protocols and are harder to hack into initially, but the Djarik aren't pushovers. The security will increase exponentially the deeper we get. They keep the good stuff locked up tight."

On the screen Mac's avatar darted down one corner and then another, making turns seemingly at random. It reminded Leo of one of those retro video games—the kind that you had to use an actual handheld controller to play. "Is that what it really looks like inside?"

"Hardly," Dev said. "Mac and Cerebro are basically churning through strings of data, sifting through code. We just translate it into an image so he doesn't have to tell me what's happening every second. Besides, it's more fun this way."

"For you," Mac said. On-screen, the figure encountered a series of doors that opened the moment Mac's fingers typed a sequence into the console on his chair. "Easy as the square root of pi . . . hold up . . . security spikes. *Now* we're getting somewhere." Leo looked back at the screen to see that the corridors had narrowed and the walls, ceiling, and floor were covered in pointy barbs.

"Like running through a cactus farm in your underwear," Dev said, taking another giant slurp of his soda, though Leo was too entranced by what was happening to feel thirsty.

"What do the spikes do?" Kat asked.

"They're like little code land mines. Mac touches one and it echoes back and destroys our own security walls, allowing the Djarik to trace our signal, find our location, hack back into our system. From there they can shoot a virus back across the galaxy, straight into Cerebro, and through it into the processor in Mac's chest, causing it to overload and explode. Pretty amazing, actually."

Into his *chest*?

"Wait, you mean they actually can *blow him up*?" Leo shouted.

"It's all right. Mac's an expert. This is pretty much all he does in his free time. That and watch *Lost* over and over again."

"Hurley's the bomb," Mac decreed.

Leo felt like *he* was about to hurl. He knew this would be risky—Dev had been abundantly clear about it—but it hadn't really sunk in until now. He'd been too absorbed with the possibility of finding his father to think about what it might cost. Now, seeing Mac plugged in, risking his life for some kid that he'd just met, Leo felt his stomach sour.

The on-screen avatar continued to leap and dodge as the tunnels grew narrower, the spikes more plentiful.

"Speaking of *Lost*," Mac continued, his voice strangely serene given that he was one spike away from possibly exploding in his chair, "did you know that of the hundreds of free-thinking, sentient life-forms we've encountered in the universe, human beings are the only ones to have invented scripted television? It's true. I mean, most alien races have some form of storytelling, naturally, but they don't have, like, soap operas and *NCIS*. We invented those. Those are *ours*."

"And fast-food restaurants," Dev added. "A uniquely human invention. Oh the glory of it all."

"Soap opera?" Boo repeated, no doubt trying to figure out how his own translations of those two words could possibly go together. Leo was no help; he had no idea what they were either.

"Bingo," Mac said, his body suddenly stiffening as his digital projection came to the end of a corridor. On the screen

Leo could see a podium with a massive book sitting on top, an old-fashioned lamp illuminating the pages. "This is it. The Djarik military network."

"It's a book?" Baz asked.

"No. That's just the graphic we use to represent it," Dev explained. "It's actually a giant data mine, near endless strings of information. But if your father *is* a Djarik prisoner, he'll probably be in there somewhere."

On-screen, the book opened, revealing more alien code, the pages flipping fast as a hummingbird's wings. There had been a hummingbird feeder in the front garden when Leo was little. His mother used to let him fill it with nectar, and then the two of them would sit on the porch and wait for the birds to arrive. One year they just didn't show up—something in Earth's rapidly changing ecosystem caused them to slowly die out, like the sea lions and spider monkeys before them. Too much change, all too fast—even the hummingbirds couldn't keep up.

"Scanning files," Mac said. "Naval logs. Military communications. Prisoner data files. What did you say the name was again?"

"Fender," Leo said. "Calvin Fender." *And Gareth*, Leo thought, clinging to the possibility that he'd been taken as well, but one step at a time.

"Fender," Mac repeated. For the first time the room was silent, everyone watching the screen above them, the pages flipping. "Fender. Fender. Hang on. I think I've got something."

Leo jumped. Kat put her flesh-and-blood hand on his shoulder.

"Calvin Fender. Human. Coalition scientist. Captured during a boarding of the research vessel *Beagle*."

Leo tasted blood on his bottom lip and realized he'd bit down hard enough to split it. "That's him! What does it say? Where is he? Is he alive?"

Mac paused for a moment—long enough that Leo's own heart, already beating a thousand times per minute it seemed, threatened to explode.

"Yeah. He's alive," Mac continued at last. "Says he was taken to a top secret mining and research base somewhere in the Quar sector where he is currently being held prisoner."

Leo felt his legs quiver, about to fold underneath him. His father was alive. In Djarik hands, but alive. Mac's fingers dashed across the console even faster. "I'm accessing the exact coordinates of the facility now. These security walls are really hard to crack. They do *not* want this place to be found."

"What about my brother?" Leo asked. "Gareth. Gareth Fender. Does it say anything about him?"

"Wait? We need to find your brother too?" Dev said. "Did they take your whole freking family?"

Leo didn't answer. He held his breath. The hand resting on his shoulder squeezed gently.

The pages of the book started to ruffle again, Mac frantically scanning the Djarik database. "Give me a sec," he said. "There are some files here attached, substreams, but they're way more heavily encrypted. I've never seen security like this before."

Leo shut his eyes. *Please let it be Gareth. Please let him be there too. Please let him be okay.*

"Wow. This isn't just prisoner details. Your father must be important because this is some serious *Mission Impossible* stuff. Just let me try one thing . . . see if I can unlock this portal . . ."

Mac's fingers danced.

Kat's finger pointed. "What is *that*?"

Dev dropped his can of Coke, the last of the precious soda splashing his feet. "Oh crap," he said. The screen suddenly started flashing red. A jarring series of beeps emanated from the banks of computers.

"What's going on?" Leo looked to the screen to see what appeared to be a giant white spider skittering toward Mac's avatar. It came out of nowhere. And it was moving fast.

"Time's up," Dev said. "Big nasty bug headed straight for you."

"Yeah. I see it," Mac fired back, his voice sounding panicked for the first time.

"If you see it, then what the hell are you still doing there?"

"Just give me three more seconds!" Mac's fingers continued to fly over the controls of Cerebro as the spider scrambled closer. Leo felt as if a hundred little white spiders were crawling over his own bare skin, digging underneath, burrowing inside him.

"You don't have three more seconds," Dev said.

"Hang on!"

"Mac . . ."

"I think I've got it!"

"Mac, get out of there! Now!"

On-screen, the spider lunged, driving its fangs into the avatar's chest, wrapping its long legs around the digital projection. Mac's real body suddenly began to convulse, his arms and legs jerking violently, hands flying off the controls, his brain knocking against the side of its container. He yelled. Sparks flew.

Dev dove for the cord snaking out of his partner's chest, pulling hard.

Leo screamed as the screen above them turned black.

The Aykari notion of love, as we humans have come to define it, doesn't exist, at least not in the romantic sense. Marriage as an institution does not exist. There are no core family units. Procreation is simply a matter of survival and necessity and is handled with an almost clinical aspect. Their society, their entire civilization, is based upon a communal ideal wherein every Aykarian is essentially your life partner—a bond that is expected, immutable, and lifelong, and which serves as the foundation for their social contract. In this sense, the Aykari's sense of devotion is much stronger than that of humans, who are often fickle and self-serving in forming relationships, making and breaking bonds based on individual whim rather than the needs of the collective. A single Aykari will always refer to itself in the first person plural; with them it is always *we* and never *I*. Perhaps that is one reason why they are the more advanced civilization, and we are the toddlers just now learning to walk.

—*Hans Zupter*, The Aykari Way, *2047*

THE BATTLE AT
THE BRIDGE

LEO'S FATHER WAS ALIVE.

It wasn't all that mattered, but it was all Leo could think.

He'd never allowed himself to truly believe otherwise, but the doubt had been there, lurking, all the same. Now finally he could see the island in the distance. Possibility had turned to hope, and he clung to it just as desperately. His father was out there, and Leo knew where. He was being held prisoner, but he was alive.

Thankfully, so was the human lying on the couch, his clear canister of a head resting on a pillow.

Leo had feared the worst when the socket in Mac's chest popped and sizzled, an electric-blue arc dancing around it, followed by a thin tendril of white smoke. The spider, the virus—whatever it was the Djarik had unleashed to defend its data mine—had somehow worked its way across a seemingly endless stretch of space, attacking Cerebro and the man connected to it, causing him to slump out of the dentist's chair and collapse to the floor.

"Is he dead?" Leo asked, panicked. Mac had no eyelids to flutter or lips to move. But then his chest rose and fell, his perfectly normal lungs taking in air from the vents near his voice emitter.

"Not dead yet," came the crackling response.

Boo had carried Mac out to the couch and Leo followed, kneeling down beside him. The headless hacker's optical sensors focused on Leo. "I'm sorry. I tried. I couldn't find anything about your brother. But that doesn't mean he's not alive. The Djarik may have him, too. And even if they don't, you still can't be sure. Anything is possible."

Says the man who once had his head chopped off and then reattached. Leo blinked away a tear. This man had done him a favor, and the Djarik had nearly killed him from halfway across the galaxy for it, yet he still felt the need to apologize.

"Don't be sorry," Leo said. "You were fantastic. You found my dad."

He'd done more than find him, in fact—he managed to download the coordinates of where Dr. Fender was being held. But that was all the information Leo was getting; the Djarik made sure of it. The bug they'd sent had completely infiltrated Cerebro's mainframe, poisoning it, sabotaging it so that Dev had no choice but to shut the whole thing down.

"It's completely infected," he said, reentering the room with Captain Black in tow. "It's going to take days, maybe weeks to fix. We won't be plugging in again anytime soon."

Not that it mattered. Even if their system was working, Leo could tell by the tone of his voice that Dev had reached the limits of his charity. Baz was out of records and Leo didn't think another kiss from the Queleti would get them very far. The jacker in the swim trunks was clearly unhappy. With the Djarik for crippling their rig and almost frying his friend. With Baz for showing up at his door. Even with Mac for agreeing to do it in the first place, though underneath the scowl, Leo could sense relief that his partner was okay.

"Got my excitement for the day, at least," Mac said. "I thought my brain was going to boil."

Leo definitely would not have wanted to see that. He whispered a thank-you close to where he guessed Mac's hearing sensors were located.

"It's a dangerous universe," Mac said. "Our kind have to stick together."

Our kind. Maybe he really thought Leo was a pirate. Someone outside the Coalition. Or maybe he just meant as human beings. That last part he could agree with.

With Mac back on the couch, it was up to Dev to see them out, which he did promptly, insisting they'd caused enough trouble. "You got what you came for. Here are the coordinates for your nav system," he said, handing Baz a datachip. "And these are for the road." He held up a box. Leo stared at it—the red bubble letters set against the blue and white background.

"Are those—?" Baz began.

"Twinkies, yeah," Dev said. "Don't ask me how I got them or how old they are. The package says best by March 2052, but I'm pretty sure that's just a suggestion. I'm only giving them to you because I don't like them, and Mac . . . Let's just say that Twinkies are hard to squeeze through a feeding tube."

That was one question answered, at least.

Dev handed the box to Baz and then glanced over at Kat. "There's still time for a kiss goodbye," he said. "Considering everything you just put us through."

In answer Kat made a gesture with her cybernetic fist: heart goes squish. Dev took the hint and a wise step back, then addressed the captain. "Do me a favor, Baz: don't come back here for a while."

"And good luck finding your father," Mac called out from the couch, waving one hand over his cylindrical head.

Leo looked over at Baz to gauge his reaction, wondering what the captain of the *Icarus* intended to do with the information he'd paid for, but Bastian Black didn't meet Leo's eyes. "Enjoy your Bowie," he said, before turning and walking through the door into the bracing Vestran wind, followed by a still-glaring Kat and a lumbering Boo.

Leo was the last to leave. As he stepped through the doorway he felt Dev's hand on his arm, staying him just long enough to lean in.

"Be careful out there, Leo Fender."

The door shut behind him.

The day they left, Leo's father took the sign off the door. It was a smooth wooden plaque, walnut stained, scrolled at the corners. The name Fender had been burned into it in fancy roman lettering. It had been a housewarming gift so many years ago. He told the boys to go get in the car while he made sure everything else was in order—the enviro-stat set, the air filters running. The people who had bought their house were moving in the very next day and he wanted it to be comfortable for them. Always thinking of others.

The doors on the *Beagle* weren't like the doors on their house. They were all metal and activated electronically, sliding smoothly into a crevasse in the wall. It would be impossible to hang a sign on one: it would get knocked off every time the door opened. Instead, there was a little silver plaque above the entry controls that said 74A. Their new permanent address, Leo thought: *74A, Main Deck, the* Beagle, *God Knows Where.* That's what he would put on letters to Amos and Mrs. Tinsley—if there were such a thing as letters anymore.

They were given a day to adjust. One day to unpack and get used to their new surroundings before those surroundings launched into space. There were orientations and tutorials scheduled throughout the day—how to use the showers, how to access the network, how to avoid potential radiation exposure—but before they started, Leo's father took them on a tour.

He showed them the labs where he would work, the three separate mess halls where they could eat. The exercise bay. The entertainment lounges. The observation deck where, just a day from now, they would be able to stand and watch their marble of a planet spinning on its invisible axis. He lectured them on the wonders of artificial gravity (in his opinion, only the fourth greatest Aykarian invention), and explained where their water would come from—thankfully not from their own urine like Gareth had been teasing.

They toured the engine room and the life-support systems. He took them to the hangar where he promised they would have plenty of room to play catch and let them sit at the controls of the shuttle and pretend to fly it. He showed them where the ventasium was stored. "We have plenty. There's nowhere we can't go."

Nowhere, Leo thought, except for back home.

Eventually they made it to the bridge where they met the captain, one Arisu Saito. She greeted them with both a bow and a salute. "Welcome aboard the *Beagle*," she said. "I'm honored to have you among my crew." Leo was impressed by her many medals. Gareth, of course, was impressed by the energy pistol slung at her side.

"Hope I never have to use it," Captain Saito said. "This is a science vessel. Our mission is research. After all, we have one of the sharpest scientific minds on the planet standing right here." Dr. Fender shook his head. Leo thought maybe he was turning pink, though he should be well used to flattery by now. "Seriously. Your father is an asset to the Coalition. It is my duty to see that he has what he needs. So as his children, you boys feel free to come to me for anything. Understood?" Captain Saito bowed to them again and Leo and his brother bowed back.

Leo liked her well enough. But he knew she was lying. She couldn't get him *any* of the things he wanted. He wanted his cat. He wanted his old bed and his lumpy pillow. He wanted to ride his bike through his neighborhood and lie in the hammock with his brother in the sunshine. Captain Saito couldn't give him any of those things, but he said thank you anyways and told her he was excited to be on board. No doubt she could tell he was lying too. He didn't really care.

After circling the entire ship they finished at their bunk room again. Leo took in the steel-framed beds, the empty shelves, the blank walls.

"So," his father began, rubbing his hands together—a habit of his whenever he got excited. "What do you think?"

"It's pretty cool," Gareth said. "I like the workout stations. And the game room. And everybody seems friendly. It's got pretty much everything. Except, you know, grass."

"Lucky for you. You were just getting old enough to mow it. What about you, Leo? What do you think of our new home?"

Leo knew what he should say—what his father *wanted* him

to say, and it wouldn't even be a complete lie if he did. The ship was remarkable, just like his father promised. But it wasn't the same as home.

"I hate it," Leo muttered under his breath.

"You can't *hate* it," Dr. Fender countered.

"Well, I do," Leo insisted. "It's cold. And the hallways are narrow. Everything's made of metal and the whole place smells weird, not like our house, more like antiseptic. And we aren't allowed to have pets. And there are no other kids my age besides Gareth. And it just sucks."

He knew he was being a brat, but he couldn't help it. His father could force him to be here, but he couldn't force him to like it.

Dr. Fender sat on the bunk between his two sons. "I know what you're going through," he said. "It's a big change. *Another* big change. Sometimes things are uncomfortable just because they're different," he said. "But then, sometimes, different is exactly what you need."

"I don't need this," Leo muttered. "I don't *want* this."

"Maybe not now. It's going to take some time. But *I* need *you* to try, Leo. You know, when the Aykari first made contact even I was scared. Me. A scientist who had studied space travel, who firmly believed that alien life was out there somewhere. But when they first showed up, I didn't know what to make of them. Were they good? Would they hurt us? Had they come to teach us or to conquer us? It took time. Time for them to prove themselves. And thankfully we gave them the chance. Think of what would have happened if we had attacked them at first sight? If we had greeted them with tanks and fighter jets instead of an offering of peace? They would have had no choice but to defend themselves. And they would have wiped us out.

"You have to give it a chance, Leo. I know there's no one on board your age, but the people on this ship—you will get to know them and you will learn to like them if you try. They might even become like a new family to you."

"I don't want a new family," Leo said. "I already have a family." They were all sitting in this room.

Leo's father nodded. "True. But it might not hurt to make some new friends."

Dr. Fender seemed to get lost in his own thoughts for a moment, then he slapped his hands on his knees. "Here. Maybe this will help." He stood up and scanned the pile of bags they hadn't bothered to unpack yet, finding the one he wanted. He unzipped it and pulled something from the top. The walls were metal too, of course, so without a magnet there was no way to hang it yet, so his dad set it on the desk across from the bunks, leaning it so that it wouldn't fall over.

"Everything will be all right as long as we have each other," he said.

Leo stared at the wooden plaque with his name burned into it. He wanted it to be enough. He wanted to nod and let his father know that he trusted him—and if he said it would get better, then it could only get better. But all he could do was stare at the wooden sign that used to hang on his front door and think that it had once been a living thing. It had once been a tree.

And he might never see one of those again.

Leo's body shook. His teeth chattered. Kat's jacket put up a good fight, but the wind was too strong, its teeth too sharp. It somehow wormed inside.

Like Dev's last warning, which continued to wriggle and writhe in Leo's head.

Be careful out there, Leo Fender.

That's all Dev had said, leaving it to Leo to fill in the blanks. Careful with what? With whom? With Black and his crew? With the Djarik? Be careful with the information he was given? How are you supposed to be careful when your life is basically in the hands of a pirate? Especially when you don't know what his intentions are.

Thankfully, Leo wasn't the only one wondering what Black was thinking.

"So what's next, boss?" Boo asked, shouting to be heard above the roar. "What's the plan?"

"The plan," Baz yelled back, "is to have a drink."

The captain led them across another suspension bridge to a much larger tower with a promenade sporting a dozen different establishments: repair shops, an infirmary, a handful of markets—all stationed behind thick metal walls. No one dared peddle their wares outside for fear that the wind would steal them and send them plummeting to the rocks below. Baz stopped outside what looked to literally be a hole in the wall. The glowing orange sign hanging over the hole was written in a language Leo couldn't read. The smell coming out of said hole was less than appealing. Leo's nose and forehead wrinkled.

"Don't worry," Baz said. "It's not one of those kinds of places."

"What kinds of places?" Leo asked.

"You know. Your wretched hives of scum and villainy. Not everyone without a Coalition patch is a criminal or a terrorist. Most everyone in here just wants to be left alone." The captain peeked inside, got a good whiff himself. "Okay. Maybe it's a little on the wretched side. But the drinks are cheap."

He disappeared through the hole and Kat followed. Boo had to duck. "Come on, Leo," he said. "You don't want to stay out here. You'll blow away."

And even if I did, Leo thought, *where would I go?*

Once inside, the place reminded Leo a lot of Kaber's Point. Strange, discordant music trickled out from a back room. Leo's boots stuck to the floor, but he was afraid to look down and see what he was stepping in. He followed Baz to an empty table in the corner, taking in the other patrons, none of whom were human. None of whom gave Leo a second glance. Baz was right: everyone here looked like they just wanted to be left alone. Leo was happy to oblige.

"I think I've been here before," Kat said as they took a seat.

"This is where I broke that fool's wrist and you cheated him out of all his money."

"I didn't cheat him," Baz said. "I asked him if he wanted to arm wrestle you. His fault for not asking which arm."

The server—a five-legged alien with translucent eyes and crystalline blue skin that Leo wanted to touch (he imagined it would be cold, like holding an icicle)—skittered up to take their order. Baz asked for something called a Malvantian mindblast. Boo asked if they had any distilled amber of the Siruvean sun tree. They did not. Kat ordered a water and Leo followed her lead. No matter where you went in the universe, it seemed, the combination of two hydrogen and one oxygen atom was on tap. Even the evolutionarily superior Aykari needed water to survive, though they somehow absorbed it through their skin. Like sweating in reverse.

"Chow time." Baz reached into his satchel and dug out the bent white box with its bright red letters, tossing Leo a pack and taking one for himself. Kat snapped her fingers, insisting on her share. Divvying up the booty—that was one thing pirate movies got right, at least.

"Is it plant-based?" Boo asked. "It doesn't look plant-based. It looks like something extruded from a Terrifalid's anus."

"What an appetizing thought," Kat said, though it didn't stop her from digging in.

Leo broke the crinkly wrapper, putting the open package to his nose. It smelled like birthday cake. Leo hadn't had birthday cake in years—birthdays aboard the *Beagle* were usually celebrated with freeze-dried ice cream—but he couldn't bring himself to take a bite. Not with the thought of his father sitting in a Djarik cell somewhere all alone. The gnawing ache in his stomach wasn't hunger. Leo needed to be doing something, not just sitting here. He needed to get those coordinates to the Coalition somehow. He needed to find out what happened to his brother.

He also needed a drink. He realized just how thirsty he was, how rough his throat felt, when their server set murky cups of water in front of three of them and a larger tankard in front of Baz. Whatever was in the tankard was potent; Leo could smell it from across the table. The captain took a swallow and coughed. "That will wake you up in the morning," he said.

"So will a sunrise," Kat countered. "And it won't give you a headache afterward."

"I already have a headache," Baz said, glancing at Leo. He took another swallow. This one seemed to go down easier.

Baz removed the circular datachip from his jacket, flipping it between his fingers, much like Leo did with a playing card before he made it disappear. The datachip was more like the size of a coin. Easy to palm. Easy to pocket. Easily misplaced.

"Can I see it?" Leo asked.

Baz rolled it between his fingers one more time before it vanished, secreted away back in his jacket. "I think I'll hold on to it for now," he said. "Just to keep it safe."

As if anything within twenty feet of Bastian Black could ever be considered safe. Leo took a drink of water. It tasted better than it looked. Or maybe he was too thirsty to care. "So what now?"

"I'm working on it, ninja turtle."

"But we have the coordinates. We know where he is," Leo pushed.

"I said I was working on it."

"What does that mean?" Leo said, his voice rising, forgetting, for the moment, just who he was talking to.

"It *means* let me finish my drink," Baz said coolly, giving Leo a long, hard stare. Leo could tell that Boo and Kat were feeling the same as him, trying to anticipate the captain's next move. But even they couldn't predict what would come out of his mouth.

Bastian Black glanced around the room, taking in the tarnished tables and cracking walls, the overlapping stains on the floor. He set down his drink but kept both hands on it, as if he was afraid someone might take it, and leaned back in his chair. "How much do you think it would cost to buy this place?"

"This dump?" Kat asked. Baz nodded. "You want to buy a run-down drinking hole on a windswept backwater dust-covered planet in the middle of absolutely freking nowhere? And do what with it, exactly?"

"Run it," Baz said. "Own it. Settle down and grow old with it. You could handle the bar. Boo could be the bouncer. We turn Skits into a jukebox, let her play all those my-life-is-horrible-and-you're-the-reason-why songs she's always screeching to.

We spend our days with our feet on solid ground rather than our heads in the stars. How does that sound?"

"It sounds terrible," Kat said. "And not just because of Skits's screeching. Besides, there's no way in a million years you'd ever do it. You'd probably have to sell the ship, for one."

Baz shrugged.

"Don't shrug at me, Bastian Black. You adore that ship. Plus there's no way you could ever stay still for that long. Even *if* nobody came looking for the bounty on your head, you couldn't do it. It's not in your nature."

"One's nature can change," Baz said, taking another sip.

"Not yours," Kat said. "I know you. The stars are in your blood. Maybe you don't have to be a pirate, but you're certainly no barkeep. You have to be out there, looking for something. Always."

"Not if I've found the thing I'm looking for," Baz mused.

"Except I don't think you even know what that is."

"You underestimate me."

"No. I wouldn't make the mistake," Kat countered. "I'm just saying that whatever it is, I don't think you're going to find it here. And certainly not at the bottom of that cup." Kat nodded at the tankard in the captain's hand.

"Only one way to know for sure," he said, taking another long swallow.

"What about Leo?" Boo asked.

Yes, Leo thought. *What about me?*

"What about Leo?" Baz asked.

"If we bought this place, and I was the bouncer and Kat ran the bar, what would Leo do?"

"I don't know. What *would* you do?" Baz's eyes narrowed, pinning Leo to his seat.

"Are you finished with your drink?"

Baz examined his tankard. "Just about. One more swallow."

"In that case," Leo said, "I would wait for you to take one more swallow. Then I would go and get my father back."

The two of them studied each other, the pirate and the stowaway. After a beat, Baz finished his drink, setting the tankard softly on the table. "I'm going to go use the facilities," he said, reaching into his pocket and setting a five pentar piece on the table. "Don't go anywhere without me."

"Aye, aye, captain," Kat called after him. Leo kept his mouth shut.

After a while Boo gave one of his tusks a thoughtful tug. "What's a bouncer again?"

"He's the guy who picks up unruly customers and tosses them out of the bar," Kat answered.

Boo nodded. "I think I'd be good at that."

Before either Leo or Kat could agree, Bastian Black appeared from around the corner, moving much quicker than before.

"That was fast. You must have really had to go," Kat said.

"We all have to go," he shot back. The captain had that look on his face, the one Leo recognized from Kaber's Point: pressed lips, creased forehead, worried eyes: the look of the chased.

Kat grabbed the box of Twinkies and shoved it in Baz's bag as everyone stood. "What is it this time?"

"An old friend."

"You don't have any friends."

"Not anymore I don't," Baz said. "That's why we're leaving."

As they wove their way through the somewhat wretched hole-in-the-wall, Kat fired more questions at the back of Baz's head in a hissing whisper. He ignored her, moving quickly, eyes alert. Leo looked around, trying to spot someone who looked dangerous, but to Leo everyone looked dangerous. Instead, he looked around for someone who might have once been friends with a pirate. That didn't narrow the possibilities.

They made it to the exit and back into the blasting cold, Baz leading the way, Boo bringing up the rear. Leo glanced behind him. There were a few creatures huddled on the walkways, heavy cloaks or hooded coats cocooned around them. It wasn't the best place for an ambush—right out in the open with so many witnesses. Then again, like Kaber's Point, this planet was outside Coalition authority, so it really didn't matter; there was no local law enforcement to run to. Leo had no idea what Baz's former friend looked like. He probably wouldn't know until the gun was pointed their way.

It didn't take long.

They were halfway across the long metal bridge heading toward Dev and Mac's tower when an energy bolt scorched past Leo's head, burning a hole in the railing less than a yard away.

"That's far enough, Baz," a voice rang, somehow clear and powerful against the howling wind.

Leo turned with the rest of the crew to see a figure clad in brown body armor, her green hair cut severely short, a pair of tinted goggles masking her eyes. She looked at least six feet tall. The huge, deadly-looking rifle in her hands was pointed at Bastian Black's head.

"Hands where I can see them," she called. "The Queleti's too. All of them."

"Frag it," Kat muttered, slowly raising her hands. "You didn't tell me it was *her*."

"Because I knew what you would say."

"Her? Her who?" Leo asked, his own hands up as high as he could get them.

"Zennia. Baz's girlfriend."

"*Ex*-girlfriend," Baz corrected.

"Who also happens to be a freking bounty hunter," Kat added.

Baz shrugged. "We were really only together for, like, a month."

"Right. Because it's hard dating a bounty hunter when you constantly have a price on your head."

"Little bit, yeah," the captain admitted. "You let me handle this. If things go south, you get everyone to the ship. I'll be right behind you."

"Wait, you're not actually going to try and *talk* your way out of this, are you?" Kat asked.

"It's gotta work one of these times," Baz replied. The wind faltered for a moment, though it didn't slow Leo's shiver. The captain of the *Icarus* took a step forward and then another, his palms up in surrender. "Hey, Zen," he called out. "Been a while. What are you doing on Vestra? Just here for some fresh air?"

"It's a business trip," the bounty hunter called back. "I don't normally shoot at people when I'm on vacation. Turns out, a certain already-wanted pirate decided to con a certain wealthy businessman out of five cores worth of V. Then he turned around and trounced a dozen security bots to boot before skipping town."

"Sounds like a real jerk," Baz said.

"Oh, he is. Thankfully said businessman had the foresight to put a tracker on that pirate's ugly little yellow ship. Really, Baz, you're getting sloppy."

"I've always been a little rough around the edges." Baz gave Kat an accusatory, how-come-nobody-bothered-to-scan-the-ship-for-tracking-devices stare, then turned back to his ex-girlfriend with the rifle pointed at his head. "You look good, though," he added, at least *sounding* sincere. "I like your hair."

"You've put on weight," she fired back.

"Twinkies," Baz said, inching closer with shuffling steps. "I've still got some if you're interested."

"Your head's worth more, I think. In fact, Grimsley wants the whole lot of you and promised to pay handsomely. He's especially interested in the kid."

Leo shook his head, certain the howling wind had distorted her words. *Did she say* kid?

Baz, apparently, was just as confused. "You mean *Leo*?"

"He's worth almost as many pentars as you are," Zennia said. "Except he has to be brought in alive. With the rest of you, that last bit's optional."

Leo took in the questioning looks from Boo and Kat. Baz, on the other hand, kept his eyes on the barrel of the gun pointed his way. He took another calculated step. "What on earth does Grimsley want Leo for?"

"I didn't ask. It's none of my business. The only thing I need to know right now is if you are going to come quietly or if it's going to be like old times?"

Baz took a moment to think about it. He scratched his head. It was clearly a sign. Kat and Boo exchanged looks. The pitch of the wind's whine started to rise, the flutelike whistle that portended a stronger blast.

"Get ready," Kat whispered to Leo.

Ready for what? he thought.

Bastian Black shrugged. "You're the one who always said I'd never change."

A giant gust suddenly kicked up, roaring across the bridge, nearly lifting Leo off his feet. It was just enough force to cause the bounty hunter's rifle to lose its bead on Baz's head.

Which was just the moment Baz had been waiting for. He crouched and drew both of his pistols, firing in the direction of his ex-girlfriend, but the wind altered his aim as well, causing both shots to go wide. "Go! Get to the ship!" he shouted over his shoulder. The bridge was suddenly a battlefield.

Leo felt Kat's hands on his back, pushing him toward the other end of the bridge. He looked back to see Baz and Zennia trading shots, missing each other but managing to put a half dozen holes in the bridge's siding. "Step on it, stowaway!" Kat shouted in his ear. "Can't you go any faster?"

Leo thought of his brother, the middle school track star. Of the races that seemed like they were twenty laps long, and how Gareth seemed to hold back sometimes, conserving his energy until the very last lap, when he exploded, his legs a blur, passing the kids in front of him who were already gassed. Leo had never been near as fast as his brother. But then he'd never been chased by a bounty hunter before either. He could see the end of the bridge and beyond that the tower and then the platform where the *Icarus* waited for them. He gritted his teeth, legs pistoning.

Until he felt himself unexpectedly jerked backward by Kat's claw, skidding to a sudden stop as three black floating disks dropped out of the sky in formation in front of him, small turrets protruding from their bellies. The disks hovered, struggling to stay stable against the wind, sensors flashing, choosing their targets.

"Get down!" Kat screamed in Leo's ear.

Leo dropped, his belly hitting the cold steel of the walkway as the drones unleashed a barrage, blasting the metal all around them. Beside him Kat drew her pistol and returned fire, hitting one of the drones, causing it to spin wildly, trailing black smoke as it dropped out of the sky, spiraling to the red rocks below.

Another wind gust howled past, accompanied by a growl and a blur of brown and gray fur, two giant feet stepping past Leo, four straining arms grabbing hold of the top metal rail of the bridge, already twisted and scorched from laser fire. The Queleti managed to wrench a length of railing free, a makeshift metal club almost twice his height, and with all four arms he swung it like a baseball bat—like Miguel Ramos himself—smashing it into the side of another drone, sending it careening off course, its scatter of blasts ineffectually fanning the sky. Boo's second swing missed, however, the final drone it was aiming for swiveling and firing back.

One of its shots hit home, burying itself in Boo's shoulder, spinning him around. The furry alien lost his balance, stumbling toward the already broken rail, his growl of pain and fury mixing with the rage of the wind that struck him in the chest like a fist, sending him tumbling over the side.

"Boo!"

Leo scrambled across the grated floor of the bridge, frantic, finding the alien holding to what was left of the railing by only one hand, the wounded arm above it hanging limp and useless beside him. Leo braced himself against what remained of the railing as best he could and reached out, not thinking about how much Boo weighed or the shots Kat was trading with the remaining drone, finally taking it down, or the bounty hunter in a duel with the captain or the killer Vestran wind that threatened to brush them all over the side of the bridge.

"Grab hold!"

He could see the panic in Boo's eyes as his robe whipped around him. Boo reached with one of his free hands, but another gust rocked him sideways, just out of Leo's grasp. He could see Boo's other hand slipping, losing purchase on its bit of railing. Another shock of wind would knock him loose, send him plummeting to the rocks below.

Leo stretched as far as he could without pitching himself over the edge, reached as far as he dared.

The wind suddenly changed directions, lashing back the way it came, sending the Queleti swinging the other way. He lunged again, this time one rough-padded hand locking on. Leo felt his muscles strain, certain the alien was going to pull him off, send them both into a free fall. *Don't let go*, Leo thought. *Just don't let go.*

It was no use. He was too heavy. Leo couldn't hang on. But as he felt the furry paw slipping free, another arm appeared next to Leo's, its metal grip finding Boo's last free hand.

"Pull!" Kat screamed.

Leo pulled.

With a growl, Boo heaved himself onto the smoking, laser-blasted bridge, huge hairy chest heaving, afraid or unwilling to let go of the hands that held his.

"Leo Fender!"

Leo squinted through the stinging wind and smoke to see Zennia staggering toward him, less than ten feet away. She raised her rifle to her shoulder and Leo stared down the muzzle of the gun.

A porch. A blade of grass. A breaking wave. A column of smoke.

Leo stopped breathing.

He wondered if he would see his mother again.

Then suddenly the bounty hunter's body crumpled, knees buckling beneath her, slumping to the deck of the bridge. Behind her stood her ex-boyfriend, in his jeans and Jordans, holding the pistol he'd just used to knock her unconscious, doubled over, trying to catch his breath.

"Now you see . . . why we . . . broke up," Baz said.

The most significant difference between pirate and other ships was the manner in which the pirate company was organized, and the code by which the pirates operated. . . . A hundred years before the French Revolution, the pirate companies were run on lines in which liberty, equality, and brotherhood were the rule rather than the exception. . . . The crew, and not the captain, decided the destination of each voyage.

—*David Cordingly, Under the Black Flag, 1996*

A UNANIMOUS DECISION

WITH KAT'S HELP, BAZ DRAGGED THE BOUNTY HUNTER to the end of the bridge, propping her unconscious body against the tower's wall and out of the wind.

"We shouldn't just leave her here. She wants to kill you, you know," Kat said, taking Zennia's rifle for herself. "When she wakes up, she won't be happy."

"I realize that," Baz said. "But it's complicated. We have a history. Besides, by the time she does wake up, we will be long gone."

He didn't say where they would be gone to. There was the more pressing matter of the hole in Boo's shoulder to attend to. "Clean shot," the captain said, giving it a cursory examination. "We'll get you patched up when we get back to the *Icarus*. Think you can make it?"

The Queleti shrugged the non-blasted shoulder. "It's just

one arm. More where that came from."

Leo hoped if he ever got shot with a laser blast he'd have a sense of humor about it. Though he *really* hoped it never came to that.

The bridge was easier to cross with no bounty hunters trying to stop them, though the crosswind still proved a worthy adversary. As they passed the second of the two drones Kat shot down, Boo kicked it through the still smoldering gap in the railing. "Next time," he said, "we fight on solid ground."

"Since when do we get to pick our fights?" Kat asked.

As they made their way around the tower to the landing platform, Leo couldn't help but glance behind him every third step, though he wasn't sure what he expected to see. More of Zennia's drones? Gerrod Grimsley with a posse of refurbished security bots? A band of Djarik soldiers? Three weeks ago the idea that he had enemies, that there were people out there set against him, Leo Fender, seemed absurd. Yes, there was a war. Leo knew it as well as anyone, and he had lost more than most, but it hadn't really been his war to fight.

This felt different. He felt cornered. Haunted. Hunted. Father taken. Brother gone. And now people were looking for him specifically.

He's especially interested in the kid.

This is what it was like to live your life looking over your shoulder, he thought, always wondering if those standing behind you were really on your side or not. Living with this constant slush of dread churning in your stomach. But every glance behind him only showed Kat, hunched over in the wind, her new rifle slung over her shoulder.

"Keep going, Leo," she said. "It's okay. I've got your back."

Finally they made it to the landing platform, though the *Icarus* no longer had the place to herself. "Well, kiss my grits," Baz said.

"I've done enough kissing today," Boo replied.

Leo studied the star-shaped fighter sharing the landing platform with the pirate's ship, gleaming silver and studded with cannons and missiles, looking small and sleek beside Bastian's busted yellow pear. It was obviously Zennia's, guessing by Baz's reaction, and it looked even faster than the *Icarus*. It was definitely prettier. Newer. And probably worth a lot more.

"Are we going to steal it?" Leo asked.

All three pirates looked at him.

Kat grinned. "Leo Fender. Did you honestly just suggest taking something that doesn't belong to you? A ship no less?"

Leo shook his head, realizing his mistake. "No. No. I meant you. Are *you* going to steal it?"

"It *would* keep her off our tail," Kat suggested.

"It would," Baz replied. "But I wouldn't be caught dead flying that thing. It looks like a toy, plus it's not my color. I do like the idea of her not being able to follow us though, and we are out of V. . . ." He flashed Kat a look.

"I'll take care of Boo. And find that tracking device."

"Good. Take the kid with you," Baz said, nodding toward

Leo. "And do me a favor and send Skits out here. I'm sure she wouldn't turn down a chance to vent a little."

Back in the *Icarus*, Boo sat on the edge of the table in the mess area, now serving as a temporary sick bay, gently prodding the edges of his wound. "It's not that bad," he said. "Mostly cauterized already. I'll be fine."

It looked pretty bad to Leo. He was surprised to see the Queleti's blood was red. Not all aliens had red blood. Aykarian blood was silver, like mercury. Some aliens didn't even bleed at all. But beyond the charred and blackened hole in Boo's robe, past the burned fur and flesh, Leo could see traces of deep crimson blooming.

"It's getting treated whether you like it or not," Kat said as she dug around cabinets and crates, gathering supplies. She helped Boo remove his robe and examined the wound, looking not at all squeamish herself. Leo guessed she had seen worse. In fact, he knew she had. "Too bad your hair will cover it," she said. "This is going to leave a cool scar."

"I've got scars."

"Yeah, but what good are they if you can't see them?" Kat said, brandishing her bionic arm. "How will people know not to mess with you?"

Boo shrugged his massive, muscular frame. "Somehow they just know." He turned and winked at Leo.

"Since you're just standing there, ship rat, come give me a hand." Kat gave Leo a plastic tube, the same medicine they had on board the *Beagle*, designed to prevent infection, numb pain, and stimulate the regrowth of tissue all at once. Another marvel the Aykari gave to a planet that had been relying on Band-Aids and fiberglass casts. "Squeeze a big dollop of that stuff right on the wound," she said. "Then rub it in a little."

Boo looked at Leo and slowly shook his head.

"Yeah. I don't know if that's such a good idea," Leo said.

Kat's hands went to her hips. She glared at the Queleti. "You're seriously going to be a baby about this?"

"That stuff smells terrible," Boo protested. "And it makes me itch."

"That's how you know it's working, you lug. Now, are you going to let Leo put that stuff on you or am I going to have to hold you down?"

Kat gave Boo a hard stare and a tense silence settled between them. He had twenty inches, an extra functional arm, and at least two hundred pounds on the first mate. He could probably pick her up by one hand and toss her off the ship if he wanted to, in true bouncer fashion. But she had that look on her face and that tone in her voice and that was enough.

"Fine. But make it quick."

Leo dabbed the odoriferous ointment on the wound, trying not to look Boo in the eyes and ignoring his low, rumbling growl. Kat followed with a bandage, wrapping it clear around the hairy shoulder. Leo didn't want to think about how much it would hurt when somebody pulled it off. He hoped that somebody wasn't him.

"I'm going to go find that tracker. You make sure he keeps that on and doesn't pick at it," Kat ordered.

"Right," Leo said. As if there was a single thing he could do to stop him.

But Leo didn't need to worry. Boo didn't fidget with his bandage or scratch at its edges. He simply leaned back on two hands and closed his eyes.

After a moment he whispered, "*Sijan*."

"I know that word," Leo said. "Baz said it came from your people. He said it was like doing a good deed."

"So he *does* listen to me sometimes," Boo said with a snort. "Back on my planet, *sijan* is not just a word, it's a way of life. A path that the Queleti strive to follow. It's a part of everything we do. Unfortunately it is not the path I've chosen. But I still know it when I see it. And I recognize when a debt is owed."

Leo shook his head. "Oh. No. Listen, if this is about what happened at the bridge, it's no big deal. Honestly, I don't even know what I was thinking. And really it was Kat who pulled you up."

"It was Kat who pulled me up," Boo agreed. "But yours was the first hand I saw. And that is *sijan*."

Boo reached out with one of his own hands—the one with the bandaged arm, though it clearly hurt to move, and placed it flat against Leo's chest. A day ago Leo would have flinched, fearing that the Queleti was about to crush his ribs, but now he stood still, felt the weight of Boo's hand. It was comforting, in its way. "You have a strong heart, Leo Fender," he said. "It has a beautiful rhythm."

"Um . . . thanks?"

"No. Thank you." Boo removed his giant hand from Leo's chest, then examined the hole in his Yunkai from the laser blast. "This will be impossible to mend properly, I'm afraid. The wound will heal, but the fabric used for these robes can only be found on my planet. I suppose I will have to live with it."

Leo thought about the hole in his now-burned-to-ashes shirt, the one where his patch had been—one large planet surrounded by a dozen smaller ones. The patch was still in his pocket. Many planets. One mission. One enemy. One cause.

"Maybe you could go back," he said. "To your planet. To Quel. Go back and get it fixed. Or get a new one."

"I cannot go back there," Boo replied. "My people would not accept me. I did a terrible thing. Committed an act of violence against my own kind. It was unforgivable."

"My mother taught me that almost anything is forgivable, as long as you try to make amends for it," Leo said.

Boo shook his head. "Not where I'm from. On Quel, any act of violence against one's own is cause for banishment. We are a mostly peaceful people. We have no soldiers. No warships. We fashion no weapons save the tools we use to farm with. There are no precious resources hiding within our planet's crust as there are with yours. I think that is why we were not invited into your Coalition. Why the Aykari did not share their gifts with us as they did with you."

That *can't* be right, Leo thought, still thinking of his patch. "No. The Coalition is for everyone," he said.

"Not for everyone. Only for those with something to give in return. Which is fine, but it is not *sijan*." The Queleti wove one finger through the hole in his robe. "Perhaps it is better this way," he said. "Now people will definitely know not to mess with me."

Leo studied the bloodstain on his borrowed shirt. He wondered if his patch would cover it.

They both turned at the sound of Baz's boots tromping up the ramp. Skits rolled up behind him, holding a crate similar to the one Boo had toted around Kaber's Point.

"She was loaded. Four whole cores," the captain said triumphantly. "We drained her dry."

"*And* we trashed the cockpit," Skits said, sounding uncharacteristically cheerful.

"*You* trashed the cockpit," Baz corrected.

"*I* trashed the cockpit. And it was *so* much fun." Skits's head swiveled, showing off her menacing smile. Leo decided the robot wasn't just temperamental. She was also a little insane.

Baz pointed to the bandage on Boo's arm. "All good here?"

Boo grumbled.

"It itches, apparently," Leo translated for him. "And the medicine stinks."

"Well, next time maybe don't get shot," Baz suggested.

"Easy for you to say. You're a smaller target."

"I don't know about that," Baz said. "I'm going to go help

Kat locate that tracker. Skits, you make sure those cores get locked into the jump drive. Liftoff in five. Ship meeting in ten. All crew are required to attend."

He looked directly at Leo when he said the last part.

Leo had scars. Most of them were plain to see.

The one on his chin shaped like a comma, earned from slipping off his hoverboard and planting his face on the curb. The pink and white patches on his knees from more of the same. The zigzag of white across his shin from looking behind him while running from his brother and catching the corner of a table, the wood sinking in like a shark's tooth, tearing a gash two inches long that had to be glued together.

And the one below his elbow from falling off the top of the car. He and Gareth had been playing space explorers using the car as their ship. An asteroid had struck the hull and Leo had been sent out into the cold grip of space to make the necessary repairs. Seven-year-old Leo crawled out the airlock—their parents *told* them to roll the windows down—and pulled himself to the roof, his tree branch pistol now acting as a blowtorch as he sealed the hull shut. But he slipped on his way back into the ship. Gravity was still a force to be reckoned with, it seemed. As was the cement driveway.

He must have landed just right—or just wrong. Leo's forearm broke in three places, the pain searing and sudden. It was the kind of break that, had it happened twenty years ago, would have meant a graft, plus a cast for months with added months of physical therapy. But Leo was born in a different age. The Aykari had perfected bone regeneration—an outpatient surgical procedure involving a chemical compound of their own design and an incision no bigger than Leo's fingernail. In four days he was tossing the baseball with Gareth in the backyard again.

The Fenders thanked their human doctor, of course, but she said the same thing: such treatment wouldn't have been possible before the Aykari arrived. They were the ones who deserved thanks.

It was that way with everything, it seemed. So many gifts bestowed upon humanity, handed down literally from on high. And all it cost them was the earth beneath their feet.

Leo's arm was as good as new, the scar barely noticeable. You had to look closely, find the spot where the skin was slightly paler, thicker, like a well-worn trail. Most of the time Leo discovered it by absentmindedly scratching at it.

He had quite a few scars, but the one on his arm was the only one that itched, a reminder of the time he and his brother went into space and Leo saved their lives.

The tracker was finally located, detached, and left on the landing platform. If anyone else was using its transmission to locate the *Icarus*, it would bring them all the way to Vestra. There they could find a cheap drink at a local watering hole, a ticked-off bounty hunter, and plenty of red dust, but they wouldn't find the *Icarus*, its captain, or its crew.

A crew that was currently huddled in the cockpit of the ship, already putting some distance between itself and the wind-weary planet. Baz sat in the pilot's seat as usual, flip-flopped feet resting on the console, Kat sitting beside him. Leo stood next to Boo, who was back in his damaged robe, savoring a second cup of gyurt. Leo's cup was still waiting for him; Boo insisted on saving it for later.

The *Icarus* still sat in orbit around Vestra. It hadn't made a jump yet. To make a jump you need a destination, Leo knew. You needed coordinates.

Of course, coordinates they had. They just hadn't decided what to do with them.

Bastian Black was uncharacteristically quiet. He wasn't even drumming on the controls. It was the first time Leo had seen him sitting there without a song in his head, which meant, as far as Leo could judge by the straight faces of the crew (minus Skits, of course), that there was something particularly heavy weighing on their captain's mind.

Leo guessed that something heavy was him.

"Something's not right here," he said finally. Baz seemed to be talking to himself, forgetting that everyone could hear him in the *Icarus*'s cockpit. "I don't get it," he said, louder this time, fixing his eyes on Leo. "Help me out here. Why would Gerrod Grimsley put a bounty on *you*?"

Leo shook his head, the one that had a price on it, though he had no idea why.

"I don't think it's because you've been tagging along with

us. And it's not just because you helped us escape. There's something else going on. Zen called you out. Said she had to bring you in alive."

Leo didn't need to be reminded. He could still hear Baz's bounty hunter ex-girlfriend calling his name. Could still picture her rifle pointed in his direction.

"Why was she after you?" Baz asked.

"I don't know."

Black's voice turned icy. "Don't lie to me, Leo. What does Grimsley want with you?"

"I'm not lying," Leo insisted.

"Ease up, Baz. The kid doesn't know. Besides, maybe it's not Grimsley who wants him," Kat suggested. "Maybe the Aykari are looking for him and they're going outside the Coalition for help. Grimsley doesn't care who he works for as long as he gets paid."

Leo could believe that, though he doubted the Coalition would stoop to working with the likes of Gerrod Grimsley just to find one kid. Then again, Leo never thought the Coalition would stoop to working with two criminal network jackers either, but Dev and Mac had claimed otherwise.

He could feel Black's stare pressing on him. "I don't know why he would be after me unless it has something to do with you. Maybe we could go back down and wake up your girlfriend and ask her."

"That sounds like a bad idea," Boo said.

"Yeah, especially when she sees what I did to her ship," Skits added.

Baz shook his head, eyes still focused on Leo. "Let's go back to the beginning. A Djarik raiding party attacks your ship, a research vessel, crippling it. They take your V, your weapons—standard practice—but only one prisoner: your father. Why?"

"I already told you I don't know that either."

"But there must be a reason, Leo. You said he was a scientist. What was he working on?"

"Something with ventasium," Leo sputtered. "Finding alternatives to it. Or ways to make it stronger. He didn't talk about it much. Said most of it was classified. He joked that it was above our pay grade." That is, when his father talked about his work. Most of the time he kept it to himself, and Leo hardly ever bothered to ask.

Maybe he should have.

"Classified. Now *that* sounds interesting," Skits chimed in.

"Which might explain why the Djarik wanted *him*, but it doesn't explain why someone's looking for *you*," Boo said.

"Unless they think Leo can somehow point them *to* his father," Kat said. "Which, now, of course, he can. At least *we* can . . . if that's the play."

Leo could feel all their eyes on him now, even the robot's unblinking sensors.

"Believe me, I'm just as lost as you are," he said. "All I know is that my dad's out there. And he needs help. He needs *my* help." *And I need yours,* Leo thought. *Or at least I need somebody's. Because I can't do this alone.*

"Tell me something, Leo," Baz said. "Your father—is he a good man?"

Leo blinked. A good man? What does Bastian Black—a wanted pirate, a thief, a deserter from the Coalition—what would he consider good?

"He cares about people," Leo said. He thought about it for a moment, then added, "And not just me and Gareth. Everyone. He really wants to make the universe a better place."

"Good luck with that," Skits said, earning her looks from everyone this time. "What? I'm just saying. The universe kinda *sucks*."

No one bothered to disagree with her. "He's a good dad, too, if that's what you're asking," Leo added. "I just want him back."

Leo watched the captain's eyes. The Aykari's eyes changed color depending on their mood. Humans weren't so easy to read. Bastian Black was almost impossible. But Leo thought he caught *something* there. A flash of sympathy. Or regret. Or resignation. He'd seen it before, when he first agreed to take Leo back to the ship, and then again when he took back the case holding his medal. It was the look of someone who has lost something. Something essential. Leo knew that look well.

"All right, Leo. If that's the case, then I think we have two options. Option one—we find a way to smuggle you and the datachip into Coalition hands without getting caught, hoping that if we do get caught, they will repay our generosity by not executing us right there on the spot."

"Sounds like an iffy plan," Kat said.

"You haven't heard option two yet," Baz said.

"What's option two?" Boo asked.

"We go in there and get Leo's father ourselves."

Baz's second suggestion was met with silence all around. Leo wasn't sure he'd heard the captain correctly. A rescue mission? From a Djarik base? That was a little more than iffy. It was insane. Why would Baz even suggest it? Would he really risk his life, his ship, his crew, just to help some stowaway?

Skits was the first to speak up. "You forgot option three," she said. "Dump the kid back on the rock below us and conveniently forget we ever met him."

"That's not an option," Boo said shortly.

"Says who? You're not the captain. This isn't your ship."

"This *kid* saved my life."

"And we saved his. Even stephen."

"We're not marooning him," Kat seconded.

But the robot was adamant. "Why not? He's not our problem. He's the Coalition's problem. So is his father. Why should we do their dirty work?"

"Because we wouldn't be doing it for the Coalition," Kat said. "We'd be doing it for Leo."

"Who *is* part of the Coalition."

"Who *is* a person who has lost his entire family. And *we* have a chance to do something about it. To at least bring two of them back together," Kat said. "Besides, I think I remember him helping to push *your* crippled metal butt back into the ship at Kaber's Point. I'm pretty sure you weren't his problem then either."

That shut the robot up, at least for the moment.

"The question is, do *we* trust the Aykari and the Coalition to go in and get him?" Boo asked. "They certainly have more resources than we do."

Baz shook his head. "I don't trust the Aykari to save anyone. But that's just me. Still, we're talking about an awfully big risk here." He looked at Leo. "Not sure it's worth it."

Leo looked down at his Coalition boots, the soles worn, the laces untied as they almost always were. He thought of his father finding him in the driveway after his fall that one day, curled up and crying and clutching his broken arm, scooping Leo up and setting him gently in the car, his panicked brother sitting in the back seat, desperate to explain—*We were just playing spaceship, he was on the roof, I don't know what happened*—his father's soothing voice, telling them he wasn't mad, that everything would be okay. *You'll be all right. Nothing that can't be fixed.*

Leo glanced back up at the captain. Worth it? For Black and his crew? Leo didn't see how it could be. But for him it wasn't even a question.

"He's all that I have left," Leo said

The cockpit grew quiet again. Finally Kat turned to Baz. "You're the captain. You give the orders."

"No. Not this time. This time we all have to agree. So what's it going to be, Kat? You up for a jailbreak?"

Leo caught the suggestion of a smile on the girl's face. "I've never broken anyone out of a Djarik prison before," she said. "Could be fun . . . you know, provided we don't die."

"Bo'enmaza Okardo?"

Leo felt one of the alien's weighty paws rest on his shoulder. "I have seen too many families torn apart. Too many children without their parents. I would see House Fender restored if possible. And, like you, I'm not sure I trust anyone else to do it."

Bastian Black nodded. Then he turned to face Skits. "What about you?"

"Seriously, you're giving the robot a vote?" Kat said.

"She's just as much a part of this crew as the rest of us."

Leo knew what Skits was going to say. They were pirates, after all. Their only responsibility was to each other. Deep down in her electrodes, Skits understood that. Deep down Leo understood it too.

But even a temperamental robot can surprise you.

Skits swiveled her head from Leo to Baz, back and forth. Her speaker emitted something like an electronic sigh. "Will you at least let me off the ship this time?"

"Yes," Baz said. "If we do this, it's going to be all hands on deck."

If the robot had eyeballs, Leo was sure she would be rolling them. "Fine," she said. "We can go rescue the stowaway's father, I *guess*."

Leo was struck with a shiver. He could hardly believe it. Kat looked at him with raised eyebrows as if to say, *Here we go.* Boo gave his shoulder a squeeze.

Bastian Black shrugged. "Guess that settles it then." He removed the datachip from his jacket and fed the coordinates into the ship.

"Let's rock and roll."

Once they made the jump—and Leo nearly lost it all over Boo's robes again—Baz insisted that everyone try to get some rest. It had been nearly two Earth days since most of them had slept, at least it had been for Leo, and the captain wanted his crew to be sharp.

There was no way Leo could be expected to sleep—not knowing where they were headed, what they were about to do—but even as his befuddled brain insisted it was fruitless he felt his body argue otherwise. Just the thought of lying down in a bed—soft or not—made his muscles groan. The moment he started climbing to the top bunk, Leo realized that he was spent.

He lay there for a moment, eyes fixed on the metal ceiling. He'd never had the top bunk before. During summer camp some other kid always beat him to it. And on board the *Beagle* the upper bunk was claimed by Gareth, the elder and heir to the bed of his choice. Leo assumed there was something he was missing. Something mystical, something enchanting, about the top bunk.

There wasn't. It was actually worse, with hardly any room to move or even breathe.

Or maybe he just wasn't used to it. Leo remembered going on vacation with his family, staying at nice hotels with queen-sized beds and mountains of pillows, but it didn't matter, they were never as cozy as his old mattress at home. There's comfort in familiarity.

But not always.

Dr. Fender spent his nights on the couch after Leo's mother died. He never said why, but Leo guessed he just couldn't bring himself to sleep in the bed that they'd shared anymore. Leo would wake up and wander downstairs to find his father curled fetal, a blanket covering him only from the knees down or maybe just kicked into a ball on the floor. He would see his dad shivering and he would unfold the blanket and pull it up to his father's chin. And each time he pulled the blanket up, Leo remembered something his father said to him, not long after his mother was gone.

I can't take care of you, Leo. Not by myself. But we can take care of each other.

Even greater than his faith in the Coalition was his faith in their family. In their ability to hold it together. The three of them. Inseparable. Some nights Leo would grab his own pillow and blanket and lie down on the floor beside him, just so he could fall asleep to the sound of his father's breathing—a steady reassurance that he was there and always would be.

Leo was remembering this when the door hissed and Boo

entered, throwing himself on the bottom bunk, causing the whole metal frame to shake. Leo looked over the side to see a pair of hairy feet hanging well over the edge. There was no blanket on board the *Icarus* long enough to cover him, it seemed.

He must have sensed Leo was still awake because he spoke with his gentle purr.

"We're going to get him, Leo," he said.

Leo sniffed. Suddenly he felt cold up there, all by himself. Cold and alone.

He knew there was hardly any room, and he had no idea how Boo would react, but he crawled off the top bunk anyway and silently squeezed himself next to the alien on the bottom.

Leo felt two big arms coil around him, warmer than any blanket could ever be.

Allegiance to the Coalition and its ideals is unconditional. Any desertion or attempt to desert shall be met, if the offense is committed in time of war, by such punishment as a court-martial may direct. Deserters found assisting the enemy will be tried for treason, and if found guilty, shall always be punished by death.
—*Coalition Military Statute 588, Article 15, last revised, Earth year 2053*

13

CAPTAIN COREA'S
MEAN LEFT HOOK

LEO DREAMED OFTEN OF BEACHES. BEACHES AND bombs.

But mostly beaches.

The silky silt sifting between his fingers. The perfect holes mysteriously bored into the shells littering the water's edge. The sting of salt spray in his eyes. The seaweed underfoot and the gentle rocking as he knelt next to his brother to see who could stay upright in the waves the longest, who could not be moved by the ocean's push and pull.

Leo could always be moved.

Sometimes they would all be there. His mother and father, him and Gareth. Sometimes it would only be Leo.

Those dreams, the ones where he was suddenly all by himself—those were the worst.

He would run along the lapping line of the ocean, staring

out across the water, looking for their bobbing heads, his family, afraid they'd gone under, that something had grabbed hold of their ankles and pulled, causing them to slip, farther and farther, into the deep. He would hold his breath, waiting for them to emerge from the sea or to suddenly appear behind him instead, wrapping a towel around his shivering shoulders, telling him it was all right, not to worry, everyone was safe.

And then, sometimes, Leo's eardrums would split as the whole world lit up in a flash, as if it was having its picture taken, one moment preserved for eternity, and Leo turned to see the curls of smoke rising into the gray-fogged sky, like gnarled fingers reaching upward before billowing into a black fist. And he would be trapped there, between the ocean that stretched on for eternity and threatened to swallow you whole, and the raging fire that would eat you alive if you got too close.

And Leo, still alone, dropped to his knees in the wet sand, rocking himself back and forth, waiting to wake up as the water crept closer and closer.

Somehow, Leo slept. On orders from the captain.

Constantly running from bounty hunters and security bots can be exhausting, but how he had fallen asleep among the earthquake rumble from the creature next to him was a mystery. Boo's snore was louder than an Aykarian excavator. It was like a thousand chain saws cutting down a thousand trees.

How long had he slept? Minutes? Hours? Were they almost

there? Had they finished the jump? No. Leo would have felt that. However much sleep it was, it must have done him some good, because Leo felt instantly awake, hyperaware of everything around him, his brain in overdrive.

Behind him a thousand snare drums rolled. He couldn't stay in this room any longer.

Leo carefully extricated himself from the Queleti's arms, marveling, for a moment, at how peaceful Boo looked in his sleep. Leo passed his scuffed boots and borrowed jacket in a heap, decided he didn't need either, and made his way through the door and up the corridor, wondering if Baz was awake, and, more importantly, if he'd come up with a plan for rescuing Leo's father yet. After all, they'd agreed they were going in, but they hadn't decided on how.

He was nearly to the cockpit when the sound of voices stopped him. Coming from the captain's tiny quarters, the closed door not so thick that Leo couldn't make out their muffled conversation.

Kat was speaking. "So that's your angle, then," she said. "I knew there had to be something."

"It's not an angle," Baz told her. "It's the only thing that makes sense. Something's going on here. My gut tells me Leo's father is worth a lot more than a hundred cores of V. More than even Leo realizes."

"So we're going to be kidnappers now?"

"We're survivors, Kat. We do what it takes. And this could be big. We sneak in there, get Dr. Fender, then ransom him to the Aykari for a small fortune. Leo gets his father back, we get the money. They both go back to the Coalition, and we ride off into the sunset. Everybody wins. At least everyone that matters."

"Not sure Leo will see it that way."

"Then he'll get over it," Baz shot back. "We're pirates, Kat, last I checked. I want to do right by the kid, but the crew comes first."

There was a pause. Leo pressed his ear against the cold metal door. If one of them opened it, they would catch him eavesdropping for sure.

"Fine. I get it. But what if we're too late?" Kat asked. "What happens to Leo then?"

It took a moment for Leo to realize what she meant by *too late*. It was something he wouldn't let himself imagine. Not now. Not when he was so close. But it was possible. Possible that his father was no longer there waiting for him. Possible that the Djarik had already gotten whatever they wanted out of him and didn't need him any longer.

"Kat, I know what you're thinking—" Baz started.

"Yeah. I'm thinking that I was sixteen when you found me. You took me in. You could have left me to fend for myself, but you didn't. You took in Boo when his entire planet kicked him out. You look after Skits. You brought us all together. You made us a family. And Leo—"

"Is a scrapper," Baz said, cutting her off. "Just like you. But he's not one of us. He's Coalition. He's the reason people like us are stuck floating around the galaxy, dodging laser blasts, stealing V, and scraping together our livelihood. There's no room for him in our world, just like there's no room for us in his."

Leo felt something in his chest, working its way up into his throat. Not the python squeeze of an oncoming asthma attack, but a pang of disappointment, a strange and sudden sadness. He swallowed hard but it was stuck there. In the silence that followed, Leo tried to imagine the look Kat was giving her captain. It must have been serious because when Baz spoke again his voice was softer, apologetic.

"Look, I get it. I do. If for some reason we can't find Leo's father, we will find a way to make sure he gets back to the Coalition where he belongs, all right? Now if there's nothing else?"

"No. That's all, Captain," Kat replied evenly.

"In that case you should probably go make sure everyone's up. We'll be coming out of the jump soon."

"Oh no. I'm not waking Boo. You know how he gets."

"So don't. Make the kid do it. He owes us one."

Leo quickly pulled away from the door and tiptoed across the grated floor, hoping to slink away, but Kat caught him halfway down the corridor. "Great, you're awake," she said, her voice back to business as usual. "Go get your boots on. It's almost time. And wake up Boo while you're at it."

"Me?" Leo repeated, trying not to sound too concerned, afraid Kat would figure out he'd been listening.

"Yeah, you may want to use the wake-up stick. We keep it by the door."

Leo nodded and walked slowly back to the bunks, that lump still stuck in his throat. Boo's rumbling grew more noticeable with every step, sounding like an explosion when Leo opened the door. Sure enough, there, leaning against the wall, stood a meter-long piece of pipe.

Make the kid do it. He owes us one.

Leo shouldn't have been surprised. Bastian Black was good at keeping score—and finding a way to stay ahead. Everything could be traded or exchanged. Everything had value. Everything had a price. Even Leo's father.

But what if we're too late?

Then, apparently, Leo would be handed back to the Coalition—or maybe ransomed to them, if Baz thought he could get something for him—right back where he belonged.

Except Leo wasn't sure where he belonged anymore. No ship. No family. What did that leave him with, really? At least here, on the *Icarus*, he wasn't alone. But Baz was right: these weren't his people. And this certainly wasn't his home.

It doesn't matter, Leo told himself. His dad was alive. He would know what to do. He and Leo could find Gareth and they would all be together again. Then they could go somewhere safe. Somewhere where Leo wouldn't have to deal with pirates ever again. He held fast to that hope. He had to. But first he had to get his father back.

Which meant he also had to wake up Boo.

Leo took the stick in both hands. Wasn't there some old saying about sleeping dogs? The Queleti had a few doglike features. The snout. The dark leathery skin on the palms of his hands. The thick pelt of fur. From the lower bunk, Boo continued to drone. Leo took the thin metal pipe, careful to stand the full distance away. "Boo," he said, followed by a little jab in his shoulder.

The pile of fur didn't stir.

"Boo," Leo said louder, poking a little bit harder this time. Nothing. Then,

"Boo!"

Leo didn't know what startled him more—the growl escaping from the Queleti's lips or the speed with which he tore the pipe out of Leo's hands, bending it almost in half, teeth bared as he looked wildly around the room.

"Boo, it's just me! Leo! You were asleep!" Leo said quickly, then added, "Kat made me do it."

Boo looked down at the twisted pipe in his hand, then back up at Leo, recognition dawning. He pawed at the ear Leo had poked him in, then sat up and set the bent pipe gently on the floor by his feet. He stretched all four arms and used the three unbandaged ones to scratch his chest, "Oh, hey, Leo. Are we there?"

"Almost," Leo said, swallowing hard, heart thumping.

"Good. Sorry if I scared you. I was having this strange dream. I was back on my planet. They let me return. Except it was all different. Nobody recognized me. And I didn't recognize them. My house, my clan, they were all strangers. Do you ever have dreams like that? Where everything seems sort of familiar but you still feel like you don't belong?"

"All the time," Leo admitted.

Boo nodded, then he looked at the bent pipe at his feet. He picked it up and tried to wrench it back into shape. Instead, he managed to snap it in two. "Time for a new waking stick," he said, staring at the broken pieces in his hand.

The *Icarus* finished its jump just as Leo was slipping into his second boot. He shut his eyes tight and squeezed himself into a ball, determined not to lose it all over Kat's borrowed jacket, afraid of what she might do to him. Finally the moment passed and he made his way to the cockpit where the crew of the *Icarus* was already gathered. Leo stood in the corner, careful not to bump into Skits, who seemed to be humming, as if her battery had been overcharged.

"Exciting, isn't it?" she asked.

Leo nodded. That was one word for it. He had several others. But the hope of seeing his father again beat back the unease, or maybe just mixed with it into one giant cauldron of anxiety bubbling through his insides, making him feel queasy.

"That's it," Baz said. "Halidrin Five."

The planet did not look welcoming. Nothing like Earth looked from space. It was entirely brown, like a dried leaf that crumbles at the touch. You get used to thinking only of your own world, with its swirling white cotton clouds hovering over a bed of ocean blue. Anything else seems strange, alien, inhospitable.

Of course this planet was under the control of the Djarik, which automatically made it inhospitable.

"My father's really down there somewhere?" Leo asked.

"Provided the information we got from Mac is accurate. The Djarik mining facility's on the planet's far side," Baz continued. "Can't get a reading on the surface with this dense atmosphere, but there don't appear to be any ships in orbit. Could mean security is lax."

"*That's* some serious wishful thinking," Kat said.

"I'm nothing if not an optimist."

"So what's the plan?" Boo asked. "Go in guns blazing?"

"Since when do you carry a gun?" the robot asked.

"Queletis don't need one," Baz answered for him. "They have other hidden talents. But, no. A headlong assault would be suicide."

"So we sneak in?" Leo asked, realizing he was using that word again. *We.*

"Even better," Kat said. "We mutiny."

Mutiny. Leo knew the word. Pirate crews weren't always even loyal among themselves, whether it was the storied ones who sailed the seven seas back on Earth or the bandits who raided spaceships for V out here in the void. Sometimes, if they felt they were being treated unfairly, they would band together and turn on their captain, taking over the ship.

There was never any talk of mutiny aboard the *Beagle*. Captain Saito was well respected, and the punishment if you got caught was severe. Leo had never met anyone willing to turn their back on the Coalition, anyway.

Until a few days ago, at least.

"Wait, so you're going to turn Bastian in to the Djarik?" Skits asked. The robot sounded concerned.

"That's the plan. First officer learns about the steadily rising bounty on her captain's head and coordinates an uprising of the crew. She captures him and takes control of the ship and steers toward the nearest Djarik outpost she can find with the hopes of turning him in for a reward. We all know how much Baz prizes his notoriety," Kat said. "Time to see if all that hard work has paid off."

"It was her idea," Baz said, though Leo couldn't tell if he was praising her for her genius or assigning blame ahead of time. Maybe both.

"Okay. That's how we get in—but what about once we're there?" Boo wanted to know.

"That's where it gets froggier," Baz said. "While Kat's collecting the reward for my head, you and Skits will sneak off the *Icarus*, find the nearest computer terminal, and feed it this." He reached down by his seat and pulled an empty cardboard box from his satchel.

"You want me to feed the computer a Twinkie?" Boo asked.

Baz turned the box upside down and another datachip slid out. "One more little gift from Mac and Dev. It's a worm, a nasty one that should temporarily cripple the Djarik security systems base-wide. Locks. Alarms. Cameras. Defense grids. All you two have to do is find a terminal and plug it in."

"That is, *after* Skits locates Dr. Fender," Kat amended.

"Yeah. Let's not forget that part," Leo added softly.

"So we disable base security and tell you and Kat where to get the stowaway's father, and then you what? Just go break him out?" Skits asked.

"That's the plan," Baz said. "More or less."

"Bastian Black, that is a terrible plan," Skits said. "There are at least three hundred and forty-nine things that could go wrong with that plan."

"Tell her that," Baz said, pointing at Kat, definitely pre-assigning blame this time.

Leo shook his head. For once he agreed with Skits. "You expect a robot plastered with bumper stickers and a hairy four-armed giant to sneak around a Djarik base without getting noticed?"

"Actually, I'm about average height for my people," Boo noted.

"And I can be stealthy when I need to be," Skits whirred. Though the last time Leo had seen her in action she had music blaring out of her speaker, flames shooting out her belly, and smoke pouring out of her rear.

"Skits is right," Baz said. "There are hundreds of ways this can go wrong. Once we are down there, we will probably have to improvise. But unless anyone has a better idea?" The captain gave it a full ten seconds, looking at each of them in turn, just to make his point. When his eyes landed on Leo, Leo stared back, unblinking, until the captain turned away.

"Mutiny, it is," Boo said.

"What about me?" Leo asked. "What do I do?"

"For right now you just stand there and look like you belong," Baz said.

Because you've made it pretty clear I don't, Leo thought. "How do I do that?"

"You know. Try to look more like a pirate," Kat suggested. "Poke out an eyeball or something."

"I can help with that," Skits offered.

Leo was sure Kat was joking. Skits not so much. He settled for fixing his face in what he hoped was a vicious-looking sneer.

"Speaking of which, we will need this mutiny to look convincing as well," Baz said, looking directly at Kat. It took a moment for Leo to figure out what he was hinting at, but *she* seemed to catch on immediately.

"You're serious?"

"They'll never believe I surrendered without a fight," he said. "Besides, you can't tell me that you've never thought about it."

"Two or three times a day, minimum," Kat said. "But that doesn't mean I was ever going to *do* it."

"Well, now's your chance," the captain said. "And make it good. They will need to see the bruise."

Kat shrugged. "Okay. Just remember, you asked for it."

Kat clenched her fingers into fists. Baz closed his eyes. Leo didn't dare.

He definitely wanted to watch this.

Katarina Corea was naturally right-handed. But her left packed more of a punch. The benefits of having a fist made of titanium.

Baz instantly crumpled to his knees, both his hands flying to his jaw. He spat a colorful pink glob onto the cockpit floor. Leo was a little surprised no teeth came with it.

"The left? Really?"

"You said to make it look good. And I didn't want to bruise my knuckles," Kat explained. She knelt down, put her softer hand on Baz's shoulder. "Sorry, Captain."

"You're the captain now, southpaw," he said, working his jaw slowly back and forth. He showed his profile to Leo—the lip split, cheek cut, a purple bloom already starting to work its way to the surface. "How does it look?"

Leo winced. That was answer enough.

"It better look good," Boo said, pointing to the main console and the screens flashing red. "We already have company. Djarik patrol craft. Two of them. Headed this way. So much for optimism."

"No time for the blood to dry," Baz said, letting Kat help him to his feet. "Leo, reach into that trunk beside you and pull out a set of cuffs. Might as well complete the look."

Leo found the trunk in question containing mostly greasy tools, but buried near the bottom was a pair of metal handcuffs.

Not near as fancy as the energy binders the Aykari used to transport their prisoners, but they would do. He handed them to Baz, who slipped them on, tight enough to be convincing, but not tight enough he couldn't squeeze out of them if he had to.

Leo had once owned a set of trick cuffs used in his magic shows with his mom. He'd left them in his own trunk in his room, light-years away. Now he was about to help pull off some sleight of hand that was way higher stakes than any magic he'd ever done.

As Baz clicked the cuffs closed, and Kat took the pilot's seat, a new set of lights began to blink. "They're hailing us," she said. She pointed to Boo and Skits. "You two go in the back and get ready. We don't want them to know you're on board."

Leo still wasn't sure what he should do, so he just kept scowling. He could see two ships closing in. One of them spat a laser blast across the *Icarus*'s nose. Warning shots were an unusual courtesy for a Djarik. There had been no warning shots when they attacked the *Beagle*. There certainly hadn't been any warning the day Leo's world went up in flames—though maybe that *had* been the warning, for the people of Earth to stay out of the war.

It didn't work.

"Get down on your knees," Kat commanded.

Leo got to his knees.

"She means me," Baz said.

With a grunt, Baz knelt down. Kat flipped a switch and the

center screen crackled and fuzzed before revealing two Djarik soldiers in uniform. Seeing them again, their scaled hides, their black eyes, Leo felt a wave of revulsion and anger surge through him. He thought of him and his brother huddled in that dark room, their backs pressed against the wall, Gareth smoothing his hair. Thought of the pieces of the *Beagle* scattered to the stars. The flocks of seagulls taking flight away from the blinding flash and rising smoke.

His mother sitting on the porch with her lonely blade of grass.

"Unknown craft, you are trespassing in Djarik-controlled territory. Identify yourself immediately or be destroyed."

"Not much for pleasantries, are they?" Kat touched a button below the screen. "This is Katarina Corea, captain of the *Icarus*. This man beside me is Bastian Daedalus Black, a known criminal wanted by the Djarik empire for acts of piracy." Baz grimaced menacingly, licking the blood from the crack in his lip, playing it up for the audience. Leo stood just behind him, trying to look cool and composed when inside he was all nerves. "I've come to collect whatever his stinking, cowardly hide is worth."

On the vid screen, the two Djarik soldiers leaned together, conferring. Finally the first alien faced them again. "Hold your current course and await further instructions." The screen went black, the communication ended.

"They've jammed our long-range coms and those fighters are locked on. I don't think they're buying it," Kat said. "I should have punched you harder."

"I really don't think that's possible," Baz told her.

"Oh, it's possible."

The console flashed, the vid screen coming to life again.

"Captain Corea, you are to disable your ship's weapons and then proceed to landing bay three under fighter escort. Any deviation will result in your immediate termination."

"Understood," Kat said, cutting off the coms. She nodded at Baz. "Guess it was hard enough after all. We're in."

Leo allowed himself a breath. They had gone right up to the front door and knocked, and now they were being ushered inside.

Right into a house full of monsters.

Kat turned back to the controls, keeping the *Icarus* in line with the two Djarik fighters as they descended into the planet's atmosphere, breaking through a gunmetal-gray cloud to reveal a sprawling outpost with multiple towers and platforms tethered together by tunnels and bridges built of the same black alloy that the Djarik used to build all their ships. Dotted across the surface, as far as Leo could see, sat dozens of giant smoke-belching machines with their feet anchored in the planet's crust. The shape and construction were different from the ones the Aykari had brought to Earth, but Leo immediately understood their purpose.

"Ventasium," he whispered.

"The planet must be full of it," Baz marveled.

"We aren't here to steal V," Kat reminded him. "We are

here to get Leo's father back."

"I know. But it makes you wonder, doesn't it? Just how many planets like this are even left? And what happens when all of them run out?"

"Then I guess we're out of a job," Kat said.

"Or maybe the war would end," Leo murmured. After all, if there was no V, maybe there would be nothing to fight over. Or at least no way for anyone to go too far from home to do the fighting. For those who still had a home, that is.

"The escorts are peeling off."

Leo squinted through the screen at the giant hangar they were headed toward, currently occupied by a cargo freighter twice the size of the *Icarus*, no doubt designed to transport ventasium cores to the places where the fighting was fiercest. It was the kind of ship that would make a tempting target for a pirate, Leo guessed. "I have to hand it to you, Baz," Kat said as she settled the *Icarus* next to the freighter. "I mean, we've done some crazy stuff before, but only the worst pirate in the world would be dumb enough to try and pull off a stunt like this."

Baz winked at her and wiped the blood from his lip on his sleeve.

The *Icarus* docked, and Leo followed the new captain and her loosely cuffed captive to the back of the ship where Skits and Boo were waiting.

"There's probably a security checkpoint with a control terminal next to the landing bay," Baz instructed. "Hopefully you two can sneak in and access it without attracting any attention. Kat's got the earcom, so you can talk to her, but obviously we can't talk directly to you without giving ourselves away. As soon as you have Dr. Fender's location, you plant that worm and shut down security, then get back to the ship. Kat and I will meet you there."

Leo cleared his throat emphatically. "Wait. What about me? Aren't I coming with?"

"Sorry," Baz said. "You're staying on the ship."

Skits snorted. Leo didn't know robots could snort but she did, a huff of air through her speaker. "Sucks to be you," she added.

Leo opened his mouth to protest, but Baz cut him off. "Listen, Leo. I get it, he's your dad. And I know you want to help, but I'm not going to risk your life trying to save his. This is a Djarik base. This whole operation could go south in a heartbeat."

"Yeah? And then what?" Leo asked. "Somebody starts shooting at me? We have to make a quick getaway? Maybe I almost fall off a bridge?" He stared at the captain, refusing to look down at his feet this time. *Besides, what do you care?* he thought. *Or are you worried that your ransom will be less if I don't make it?* "He's my father. And I'm coming," Leo insisted.

"And as the captain of this ship, I'm telling you you're not," Baz returned.

"Except *you* aren't the captain."

Leo looked at Kat.

"The kid's got a point," she said. "It's not as if we've done a stellar job keeping him out of harm's way up to now."

"And he's come in handy before," Boo added, holding up his injured arm.

Bastian Black shook his head. "Fine. But if anyone asks, you're just a cabin boy. Also, you're mute."

"Wait, why do I have to—"

"Mute," Baz insisted, putting up a finger. Leo shut his mouth. "I don't want you saying anything to blow our cover."

"At least *I'm* allowed to talk," Skits said, swiveling her head so Leo could see her smile.

"Not once you're off this ship, you're not. Stealthy, remember?" Kat reminded her.

"As a ninja turtle," the robot said.

Baz looked over his crew—the handful of misfits and exiles he'd taken in. Plus one Coalition stowaway.

"All right. Hands in."

He placed his two cuffed hands in the center of the circle, followed by the one Kat was born with and one of Boo's furry mitts. Skits extended one of her own metal claws.

They all looked at Leo.

"Well? You coming or not?" Baz said.

Leo took a deep breath.

And added his hand to the pile.

One, two, three, four,
The aliens are at the door.
Five, six, seven, eight,
Better go and lock the gate.
Eight, seven, six, five,
The aliens will soon arrive.
Four, three, two, one,
And when they do, you better run.
        —*Twenty-first-century jump rope rhyme*

14

BEHIND CLOSED DOORS

CAPTAIN KATARINA COREA EMERGED FROM THE RAMP
of the *Icarus* with her prisoner stumbling behind her, cuffed
hands dangling in front, right cheek imitating a sunset. Leo
trailed after him, armed with a metal rod too short to be a
proper wake-up stick but heavy enough to make the right
impression. He was told to whack Baz with it whenever he
tried to speak or made a sudden move—orders from the
captain herself. Leo had to admit Kat looked much more
like a pirate captain than Baz. She strode down the *Icarus*'s
ramp with her jaw in full jut, one hand on the butt of her
pistol, the other dragging Black by a cuff of his shirt, this
one advertising a band Leo had never even heard of—as if
anyone could make jam out of pearls. If she seemed at all
intimidated by the armed Djarik guards approaching them,
she didn't show it.

Leo, on the other hand, held his arms tight against his sides to keep them from shaking.

The hangar was huge. The view from the *Icarus* had shown a massive complex sprawling across the landscape, his father somewhere inside. *We will find him*, Leo kept telling himself. *We will find him, and then together, we will go find Gareth. And then . . .*

Leo didn't even bother with the *and then*. His hope didn't reach that far yet.

Kat dragged her bounty ten more steps and then forced him to his knees. Of the three approaching Djarik, two wore black armor that covered nearly every inch of their scaly bodies. The third one in the lead was dressed differently—in a loosely draped red robe not too different from Boo's. Leo could tell she was female by the lack of quills lining her jaw. On her wrist she wore a device much like Leo's watch, which she appeared to speak into as they approached.

Leo took a step back reflexively as the Djarik closed in. Every thing about them caused his stomach to knot. The way they breathed, their necks pulsing, scales quivering. The thin reptilian crescent of their deep-set eyes. The slight hunch of their backs, the dagger-sharp points of their claws. But when he closed his own eyes and tried to keep the image of them in his head, he saw only fire and smoke. Bright light and crackling sky. The sand grains slinking between his fingers.

And his mother on the porch. *I see you, my little lion.*

The eyes of the robed Djarik settled on Leo for a moment before turning to Kat, making him shudder all over again.

"Captain Corea," the Djarik began, acknowledging Kat with a nod that she subtly returned. "Your presence is unexpected but not unwelcome." Leo had heard the Djarik speak before—vids of soldiers barking commands, prisoners making confessions to Aykari authorities—but this one had a more formal tone. She sounded intelligent, almost respectful, but no less dangerous. "I am Tadrik, an official of the Djarik government. And this human kneeling before us is the infamous Captain Black?"

Baz clearly couldn't help it: he had to grin at the word *infamous*. Kat motioned to Leo and he took the hint, giving Baz a whack across the back with the rod. He tried to make it look a lot harder than it was.

"Bastian Daedalus Black," Kat confirmed. "Responsible for numerous attacks on Djarik vessels and the theft of untold resources. I'm here to negotiate the terms of his bounty."

Eight thousand pentars. That's what Baz had been worth when he'd boarded the *Beagle*. To the Coalition, at least. Leo wondered what he was worth to the Djarik. Or if the price had gone up the last two days. He wondered how big the number would have to be for Kat to turn him in for real, cutting Leo and the rest of the crew loose and taking the *Icarus* for herself. He didn't think there was a bounty high enough. For all her talk about not owing him anything, Leo knew

Katarina Corea was loyal to the captain just the same.

"Certainly," the robed Djarik said. "However, we cannot permit you to enter our facility armed." Tadrik snapped her long, clawed fingers and the two guards came closer. There was a second where Leo thought this might be it, that so many years of scrabbling to stay alive might trigger Kat's instincts, cause her to revert to the go-in-with-guns-blazing plan, but she reached for her pistol slowly, unholstering it and presenting it to one of the guards.

"That as well," the official said, pointing to the rod in Leo's hand.

Leo handed it over and Baz smiled. He stopped when Kat kicked him in the knee.

"I hope you understand—the governing bodies of your species are allied with our enemy. We have to take precautions."

"I understand," Kat said. "But you needn't worry about me. I'm not allied with anyone."

"Everyone is allied with someone, Captain," Tadrik countered. "Come." She tapped something into the device on her wrist as she turned and led the way.

Flanked by the two guards whose fingers rested on the triggers of their rifles, Leo followed Kat and the stumbling Bastian Black through the hangar, not daring to look back at the *Icarus* again for fear of one of the guards noticing, giving away the two crew members who were hiding on board. Waiting until the coast was clear so they could prove just how stealthy they were.

So far, at least, everything was going according to the very terrible plan.

Leo had always known who his allies were. His enemies too. The lines had been drawn all too clearly while Leo stood in the sand and watched. Though in actual fact, they had been drawn long before he was born.

On the one hand, the alien species that arrived with promises of peace, backed by technological gifts miraculous enough to rival Prometheus bringing the fire down from Mount Olympus. A species that could have declared itself an omnipotent overlord but didn't, instead offering to be a partner, a mentor, a protector. On the other hand, a merciless horde of insurgents determined to rid the galaxy of the first species, starting a war that raged from planet to planet, system to system. There was never any question which side humanity would take in the war; it was only a question of when.

The Djarik made that decision easy too.

There was never any doubt for Leo. His loyalties were confirmed with every headline on his news feed. *Aykarian Scientists Provide Possible Solution to World Hunger. Aykari Treatment Proven Effective in Fight Against New Virus. Aykarian Forces Repel Djarik Invaders in Nearby Relgar System.* It was written into the daily pledge at school. *I swear to uphold the shared values of the people of the planet Earth, and to defend it and its allies in the Coalition against any threats to life and liberty, security and stability, prosperity and peace.* Like a chessboard, the pieces belonging to each side were color coded—the silver Aykari ships lined up on one side, the black-hulled Djarik on the other. There was no in between.

Leo and his brother played chess sometimes. Captain Saito had a set made of marble that she'd let them borrow. Their father taught them how to play one afternoon, frustrated at the sight of them staring at their datapads for hours on end. "This is one of humanity's signature accomplishments," he told them. "Even the Aykari are impressed with chess." He taught them how all the pieces moved and showed them some opening plays. He warned them not to underestimate the power of a pawn. "Even a lowly pawn can become a queen if the circumstances are right," he said, leaving his two sons to duke it out, which they did, over and over again.

Gareth always let Leo be white so that he could make the first move—an older brother's lone concession. And because he was white, Leo always pretended he was the Aykari beating back the ruthless Djarik horde.

Which only made it more painful when he lost.

"Good game," Gareth said whether he won or not, and Leo would shake his hand, though they both knew better.

The game was always better when you were on the winning side.

The doors opened up instead of sideways.

That's the thing Leo noticed as he moved through the Djarik outpost—that their doors opened and closed differently from what he was used to. They didn't just slide into the wall the way they had on the *Beagle*—these doors seemed to collapse in on themselves, folding upward as they opened and then cascading back down as they closed, though the door itself appeared seamless.

This is what struck him—not because it was all that strange, but because everything else seemed oddly familiar. The Djarik base had walls and floors, made of a metal that the planet Earth had never seen, but that didn't change their shape or purpose. The lights that illuminated their path hummed the same soft note as the lights aboard the *Beagle*, even if the glow they cast had a slightly orangish tinge. He wasn't sure what he expected, having never been aboard a Djarik vessel, having never visited a planet under their control. Slime dripping from the ceiling, perhaps. Human and Aykari slaves being dragged about in chains. Mucus-covered eggs lurking in the corners, ready to hatch new Djarik spawn. At the very least he expected it to be darker, though he couldn't say why.

He looked up at the vents in the ceiling and the oddest thought struck him.

We are breathing the same air.

There were species that couldn't, of course. In school he'd learned of a race of alien creatures known as the Kithril for whom oxygen was poisonous. But that wasn't the case with the Djarik. Leo could breathe freely here.

- 306 -

If he could only catch his breath.

Leo tried to focus, to make a note of every turn they made, one windowless corridor after another, passing dozens of doors with alien markings. The Aykari chip in his head could translate the Djarik tongue but not its text, so he felt the urge to open every door he passed, not knowing what was behind it, only that any one of them could lead to his father. How long would it be before Boo and Skits managed to sneak their way to a terminal and tell them where to go? Every step they took farther from the *Icarus* stretched Leo's nerves even thinner.

If Kat shared Leo's apprehension, she didn't show it. Not that that surprised him. Her nerves, like her arm, seemed to be made of titanium.

"So this is a mining facility?" she asked, no longer dragging Baz, who was now uncomfortably sandwiched between the two armed guards.

"Primarily," Tadrik said. "The planet is rich with EL-four eight six, what you humans call ventasium. It's one of the few worlds we got to before the Aykari, perhaps because it is so remote. We've tried to keep its location secret, at least while we finished with our extraction. In fact, it's somewhat surprising that you happened to find us at all."

Leo couldn't be sure—his translator wasn't always good at distinguishing shifts in tone—but the Djarik in the gray robe suddenly sounded suspicious.

"A fortunate occurrence for you and me both," Kat said, not

missing a beat. "Bastian Black is a prize. Though if you don't want him, I'm happy to go collect my reward elsewhere. Your sworn enemies have an equally sizable bounty on his head and would be eager to get their hands on him."

"Indeed," Tadrik replied. "The Aykari will stop at nothing to ensure the destruction of their enemies." Leo felt his cheeks burn, picturing his mother hugging him for the last time, asking him to bring her back the prettiest shell on the beach. As if she could read his mind, Tadrik added, "Which requires those enemies to be just as merciless, I'm afraid."

"What you and the Aykari do to each other is your business," Kat said. "Just so long as I get paid, that's all that matters."

"Captain Corea, we both know that's not true," Tadrik said. "War is everyone's business, yours especially."

His head hung, Baz grunted, earning him a look from Kat but not another kick, at least. They passed through another entry—this one flanked by two more armed guards.

"Of course this facility isn't simply used for the extraction and refinement of EL-four eight six," Tadrik continued. "Because of its remote location and its abundant energy supply, we also use it for research and development. Some of the greatest Djarik minds are hard at work on advancements that could turn the tide of this war."

"Advancements. You mean weapons," Kat prodded.

"That is generally how wars are fought, Captain."

Leo flashed back to Kaber's Point. To Gerrod Grimsley

saying goodbye. *Whispers around the Point say the Djarik are working on something. Something big.*

They turned another corner and were led past several more doors, all of them sealed tight save one. "Are we almost there?" Kat asked, talking louder, drawing out her words, unnaturally so. "I was *really hoping* this wouldn't take too long. I'm anxious to get back to my ship and be on my way."

Leo realized she wasn't actually asking the Djarik who was leading them. The communication device buried in her ear was connected to Skits, who was picking up everything she said. He couldn't hear the robot's response of course, if she even gave one, but he didn't miss the frustrated look on Kat's face. He could interpret it easily enough: they hadn't found his father yet. Maybe that meant Boo and Skits were being extra cautious.

Or maybe it meant they'd been caught already.

In response to Kat's question, their escort stopped in front of a closed door just as obscurely marked as the others.

"Captain Corea, you wouldn't want to leave without getting what you came for, would you?" she said. She pressed her clawed hand against the sensor and the door slid open.

Kat's hand instinctively dropped to her waist, to the handle of the pistol that wasn't there anymore, ready to shoot whatever was waiting to ambush them on the other side.

Leo felt all the air suddenly kicked out of his lungs. There, standing beside a long table stood another Djarik in flowing red robes. "Hello, Leo Fender," he said. "We've been looking for you."

And standing beside him, the very thing they came for.

Leo stared at the man in the clean khaki uniform and long gray coat, eyes rimmed red, glasses perched dangerously close to the end of his nose. Everything about him seemed to be frazzled, worn down, on edge, but there was no denying it was his dad.

"Leo," he said.

It sounded almost like a question, like he couldn't believe what he was seeing either. But in the next moment Dr. Calvin Fender was across the room, the two guards behind Leo making no move to stop him. He felt his father's arms swallow him up, squeezing him so hard Leo's ribs ached. Out of the corner of his eye, he caught the sudden look of alarm on Baz's face, Kat's too, as they both watched the reunion, staring at the man they'd come to rescue, not in a cell like they expected, but standing right in front of them, no restraints to be seen.

Leo took a long look at his father, several days' worth of silvery-black beard, looking haggard and exhausted but unharmed. It had only been a matter of days, but it felt like ages. Eons.

"Leo, thank God," Dr. Fender said, stroking his son's hair, chin digging hard into Leo's shoulder. "I was so worried. I thought I'd lost you."

Leo couldn't speak. He could barely even breathe, his face pressed into the folds of his father's coat, locked on, soaking him in. He felt six years old again. Like his father was superhuman and his arms could hold up the world. Instead, they had to hold up his son, whose legs nearly gave out.

"I can hardly believe it," he continued. "There was no record of you aboard the *Beagle* when the Djarik came back for you. I didn't know what happened. I thought you were gone."

Leo wormed his way out of his father's embrace. "Back for me?"

"Yes. Yes," Dr. Fender said quickly. "That was the agreement. I promised I would help them and in return they would go back for the crew of the *Beagle*. Then they would bring you and your brother back here. To me."

His brother? Was it possible?

"Gareth's here? Where is he?" Leo looked behind him, seeing only Baz and Kat, the two armed guards standing behind them.

The look on his father's face was answer enough. Dr. Fender glanced over his shoulder at the Djarik standing behind the table, now joined by Tadrik. His scales had a reddish tinge to them, giving them a slightly rusted look. One of his black eyes was clouded with a white film, from injury or age. Leo guessed he was the one in charge.

"The whereabouts of your brother and the rest of your ship's crew are currently unknown, I'm afraid. They were transferred to one of our transports before your ship was destroyed, but soon after, something happened, and we lost all contact."

"We don't know where he is, Leo," his father said.

The word struck Leo. The one he'd used by mistake when he suggested stealing a ship.

We.

As in his father and the *Djarik*?

"We are doing our best to locate the missing transport and its passengers, including your brother," Tadrik added. "After all, a promise is a promise."

Leo's head spun. Another look at the pirates' pinched faces confirmed they were just as confused as he was.

"Somebody want to tell me what the hell is going on here?" Kat asked.

His father shook his head. "Leo, I'm so sorry," he said, glancing at the Djarik and then back at his son. "I was wrong."

"What are you talking about?" Leo had never known his father to be wrong about much. You don't get a room full of medals for posing theories that never pan out. Dr. Leo Fender had always been exact, meticulous, assured. Any mistakes he might have made were quickly analyzed, dissected, and then corrected.

"Wrong about what?" Leo pressed.

"I'm not sure," his father said. "Maybe everything."

They came from a world called Aykar,
And promised to show us the stars.
They asked for our planet.
We said, You can have it.
And now look at how happy we are.
—*Author unknown*

SAME STORY,
DIFFERENT SIDE

WITH A SIGNAL FROM THE ROBED DJARIK STANDING in the middle of the room, the already fragile plan to free Leo's father collapsed, as the rifles that the two guards had kept by their sides were suddenly leveled at Kat and Baz both.

"You can dispense with the act, Captain Black. Please, have a seat," the Djarik with the cloudy eye said. "And feel free to take off those bindings. We will find you a better-fitting pair later."

The soldiers pushed the two pirates past Leo and his father, leading them to the table with the muzzles of their guns, forcing them into chairs.

"Don't bother trying to contact your two companions. They can't help you."

There was no point in pretending anymore. Kat's voice, so confident up till now, faltered as she ignored the Djarik's command. "Skits? Skits, do you read me? Are you there? Answer!" She and Baz traded worried looks.

"Your robot's communications systems have been temporarily disabled," the lead Djarik continued. "We caught it and the Queleti attempting to hack into one of our terminals. They are unharmed, though I haven't yet decided what to do with them, or with you. On the one hand, you are pirates guilty of stealing countless cores of EL-four eight six from the Djarik empire. On the other, you delivered something valuable. Something we've been looking for." He nodded toward Leo still huddled against his father.

"What's he talking about, Leo?" Baz said. "You told us your father was taken prisoner."

"Oh no. Dr. Fender is not our prisoner," the rust-scaled Djarik said. "Not anymore. We are partners. He is going to help us finally win this war."

Leo shook his head. This couldn't be right. He'd never known his father to be much of a fighter, but he was still a man of principle. He wouldn't help these monsters. He wouldn't turn his back on the Coalition, his planet, his family. Leo searched his father's haggard face for answers.

"Leo, sit down," he said.

Leo refused at first, fists clenched, standing his ground. The Djarik had obviously done something to his dad. Drugged him. Brainwashed him. Threatened him. Something. This wasn't his father.

"Leo, please," Dr. Fender pleaded, and, begrudgingly, Leo

sat. "Director Chellis is right," he continued, glancing at the Djarik standing next to Tadrik. "I *have* agreed to help them."

Leo shook his head. "Help them? How? *Why?*"

Leo's dad started talking quickly. "For you, Leo. You and your brother. I had to find you. I had to find a way to keep you safe. But not just that. Things have changed. The Aykari and the Djarik, what happened to Earth, what happened to us, it's not quite what you think. It didn't . . ." Dr. Fender's voice faltered. He knelt down and took Leo's hands. Leo flinched; his father's fingers were ice-cold. "What I'm about to tell you will be hard to hear and even harder to believe, but I need you to try."

Leo kept his eyes on his father, not wanting to look at the pirates currently being held at gunpoint because of him, or at any of the Djarik who still caused his body to shake with anger and fear.

He nodded. "Yeah, okay. I'll try," he said.

Then he listened as his father told him how the whole war really started.

And how his mother really died.

"They've shown me things, Leo. I've seen evidence," Leo's father began. "What is happening with us, with Earth . . . it has happened before."

Then he told Leo a story.

It was one Leo had heard before, about an advanced alien species, the most advanced the galaxy has ever seen, capable of traveling from star to star with the aid of one precious element, the four hundred and eighty-sixth one they'd discovered.

How they located a planet where that element was stored in abundance, a planet densely populated by a species not as technologically advanced, but still proud. Freethinking and free-spirited. How an agreement was made between the visitors and the planet's inhabitants, an even exchange: Knowledge and technology in exchange for access to the planet's resources.

Then came the Aykari excavators. Thousands of them. Digging deep into the planet's crust. Slowly but inexorably sapping the planet of its strength, slowly and silently poisoning its water, its land, its skies, the more-advanced species taking what they wanted while limply justifying the costs, costs they themselves would not have to pay. The planet began to wither, to blight and burn. And the creatures that lived there began to suffer and starve, their land dying before their eyes, forcing them to abandon the only home they'd ever known using the new technology they were given or else face a slow but unavoidable extinction. This was the price of progress, the intruders said. This was the price of bringing enlightenment to the entire galaxy. They were given two options: stay and watch their world be drained or leave to find a better one.

But there was a third. One the Aykari had not anticipated.

Revolt.

The planet Djar was not quite like Earth, its atmosphere thinner, its water scarcer, its people hardier than humans. But just like Earth, the layers deep within the planet's crust held riches, and the Djar people had only just begun to realize their own world's potential by the time the Aykari arrived.

The Aykari did not expect the Djarik to resist. So many other planets had simply bowed in awe, thankful that the Aykari had come in peace. But the Djarik refused to bow, to accept the sacrifice of their world. Instead, they rose up, expelling the Aykari from their planet. And then from their system and the systems surrounding it.

And what started as a revolution became a war. One that stretched across the galaxy.

A war that found its way to a much smaller rock orbiting a yellow dwarf star and hiding its own cache of resources. An unassuming planet lorded over by a nearsighted species that hadn't even colonized its one and only moon.

Except this time the Aykari had learned from their mistakes. They had studied humans. Their warlike nature. Their capacity for revenge. They needed the planet's stores of ventasium, yes, but they needed allies as well, a way to unite the often conflicting peoples of Earth under a common cause. To give them a reason to fight.

And the Djarik provided it. On one fateful day. Dozens of cities nearly decimated by incoming warheads. Buildings reduced to rubble. An entire species incensed, demanding justice, clamoring for war. A day Leo could never forget.

But that wasn't the whole story, his father told him. Yes, the Djarik attacked, carefully choosing their targets. But the

Aykari decided which of those targets to defend . . . and which to let be destroyed.

The attack was a failure in the Djarik's eyes. Not only did it fail to cripple the planet's supply of ventasium, it drove that same planet to gather arms against them. Which was what the Aykari wanted all along.

"They let it happen," Leo's father said. "They could have stopped it. They could have saved her. They could have saved so many more."

Leo shook his head. It didn't make sense. The Aykari were their allies. They protected them. Supported them. They would never let such a terrible thing happen.

They wouldn't just let his mother die.

Baz slapped his hands on the table. "No. You're lying. *They're* lying," he said, pointing at the two robed Djarik. "I was there. I saw it. I watched the city of Chicago go up in smoke. Those were Djarik ships. Djarik warheads."

"It's true," the Djarik named Chellis said. "We were well aware of the vast resources the planet provided our enemy and we leveled an all-out assault. We hoped by targeting hundreds of sites on Earth we might overwhelm the Aykari's considerable defenses. As expected, they managed to intercept and destroy the majority of our missiles. What we didn't anticipate was how they chose which targets to save . . . and which to sacrifice." Chellis looked at Leo with those contrasting eyes—one a cold and glossy black, the other veiled in white, like opposing squares on a chess board. "They made certain to save most of their mining facilities, of course. The rest were . . . expendable."

The words *collateral damage* flashed through Leo's brain. His head spun as he tried to sift through what all of this meant. He looked at his father. "You mean they let some of those missiles through *on purpose?*"

Dr. Fender frowned. It was a look Leo knew well. The same look everyone gave him at his mother's funeral. That look of helplessness and resignation. The look that said, *I wish it wasn't so.*

"The Aykari were given a choice and they made it," Chellis said. "Our hope was to cripple one of their largest supplies of EL-four eight six. They saw an opportunity to secure an ally in the war. Hundreds of thousands of human lives in exchange for the allegiance of billions. To ensure that your species would not rise up against them the same as mine did, even while your planet was slowly dying beneath your feet. They weren't about to make the same mistake with you that they did with us."

Leo gripped the side of his chair, steadying himself, images of digital billboards touting the great Aykari-Human alliance buzzing around his brain. The recruitment drives with lines of young men and women signing up to join the Coalition forces. Posters of an Aykarian foot soldier standing back-to-back with a human pilot: *Two Worlds. One Purpose.* He thought of all those days sitting in the grass with his father, staring up at the sky, catching glimpses of passing Aykari ships. *They are there to protect us*, his father had told him. *Watching over us. Keeping us safe.*

He thought of his mother on the porch, catching him as he tried to sneak up on her. Her little lion.

"I'm sorry, Leo," Dr. Fender said. "Since they brought me here I've seen things. It's not just what happened that day. I've seen what the Aykari did to their planet. To the Djar people. I've seen what happens when the ventasium runs out, the shells of worlds they leave behind. I'm afraid Earth will be no different. I ignored the signs before; I truly believed the Aykari were our friends. Until now."

There seemed to be little doubt in his father's voice, but Leo could see a question in his bloodshot eyes. There was something else, something his father wasn't saying.

"Listen to him. The Aykari are parasites," Chellis said, his voice laden with scorn and disgust. "Spreading from world to world, system to system, sucking the lifeblood from planets, forcing their inhabitants to flee or to watch their worlds crumble. We never wanted war with your species. You were not the ones who invaded our home. But we also cannot let you stand in our way."

"Yeah, you made that pretty clear when you attacked us," Baz said.

"And when you torpedoed Leo's ship," Kat added.

"We needed Dr. Fender. His knowledge of and research into EL-four eight six and its properties is essential to our efforts. Understand the Djarik empire will do whatever it must in order to end this war."

"*Win* this war, you mean," Baz said.

"That is the only way it *will* end," Chellis said defiantly. "We will not rest until the Aykari are no more. What happens afterward—to your species, to your planet—is up to you."

Baz laughed, a surprising sound coming from a man being held at gunpoint. But Leo knew this wasn't Black's first time focused in a rifle's sights.

"Right. Like you give a crap what happens to us. You or those two-faced, blue-eyed bastards you're at war with. If you ask me, you and the Aykari deserve to wipe each other out. Frankly I wish you'd hurry up and get it over with so the rest of us can get on with our lives."

Director Chellis smiled, revealing rows of sharp teeth. "Good news for you then, Captain. With Dr. Fender's help, it should not take long."

Leo turned back to his father, a question in his eyes.

"I'm sorry, Leo. If it means keeping you safe, does it really matter what side we're on?"

Before Leo could answer, a sound like a thunderclap stilled the room. The lights embedded in the walls flickered as the ground trembled, knocking Leo off-balance.

"Skits?" Kat said, echoing Leo's own thoughts: that she and Boo had somehow managed to get free and disable the Djarik security system after all. The first explosion was followed by a second. Chellis looked at the device on his wrist and shook his head.

"It's not your companions," he hissed, his eyes narrowing to crescents. "It's the Aykari.

"The base is under attack."

Alarms pealed from unseen speakers. A Djarik voice emanated from the walls. "Soldiers, to your stations. Aykarian forces incoming."

Director Chellis sneered, pointing a finger across the table at Black. "You! You led them here!"

"*Me?*" Baz protested. "Are you out of your blitzen alien brain? The Aykari want me dead almost as much as you!"

Chellis ignored him, madly tapping on the device attached to his wrist. "We don't have the resources to fend off a full-scale assault. We will need to evacuate." He looked at Tadrik. "Get Dr. Fender and his son to my ship. I will gather our research and destroy any remaining records. We can't leave anything behind for the Aykari to find."

Leo reached out for his dad's hand. "What's going on?"

"We are getting out of here."

"All of us?"

Leo's father didn't answer. A door behind the Djarik director opened and two more soldiers entered, doubling the number of armed guards. Chellis pointed to the pirates. "Take these two and the ones you caught earlier to a prisoner transport and have them branded and secured. They are potential Aykarian spies and will need to be interrogated once we've escaped."

Leo looked from the two pirates to the four soldiers

surrounding them. "Wait!" he yelled. "You can't do that. They brought me here." He turned to his father. "They risked their lives for me . . . to come get *you*. Can't you do something?"

For a moment there was nothing, no response but a blank stare, so remote, reminding Leo of all those times he caught his father staring up at the stars. Then Leo saw something click, a spark of recognition in his father's eyes, the final step in the equation when the last variable is solved.

"Chellis, please," Dr. Fender pressed. "Just let them go. They aren't important. You have me. What difference could a handful of outlaws make?"

"The agreement was for your sons, Dr. Fender, not for these pirates. They are wanted criminals and will be treated as such." Chellis made a clicking sound and Leo watched as the four soldiers circled around the captain and his first officer. Baz had shed his shackles as requested, but there was still little he and Kat could do, unarmed and outnumbered. Kat glanced at Leo—*Now what, ship rat?*—but what could he do?

What would a pirate do? The kind of person who would rescue someone just to hold them for ransom. Who could use another person as leverage to get what they want.

Leo patted his pocket. He hadn't had much with him when he stowed away aboard the *Icarus*: his watch, still snug on his wrist; the clothes on his back, including the Coalition shirt of which only the patch remained; and the hope of seeing his father and brother again.

Those, plus the thing that—every once in a while, at least—kept him alive.

In three steps Leo was right beside Chellis, his fast-acting inhaler in hand, his finger on the trigger.

"Don't take another step," he commanded, "or I'll shoot!"

The four soldiers paused.

Chellis took an uncertain cross-eyed look at the strange device pointed at his reptilian nose. He waved a leathery hand and the guards took a step back. "You were supposed to have been disarmed," he hissed.

Leo's own hand shook and he took a deep breath to steady it. "This is a high-velocity biotoxin dispersalizer," he continued, stringing dangerous-sounding words together, hoping that the Djarik's translators found equally dangerous-sounding equivalents for them, hoping they had never seen an actual human inhaler before. "It releases a poisonous gas that is fatal to your kind. All I have to do is press this button and this guy's face melts clean off."

Leo hoped he sounded convincing. A jack of hearts can appear to vanish into thin air so long as you don't look up the magician's sleeve, and a Zylar-brand, Coalition-issued fast-acting inhaler can be a deadly biotoxin dispersalizer as long as those who know otherwise keep their mouths shut. Leo glanced at his father, but Dr. Fender gave away nothing, playing along.

"Tell them to put down their weapons," Leo said.

"You are making a mistake." Chellis spoke to Leo but kept

his eyes on the biotoxin dispersalizer pointed at his face. "We do not have to be enemies. And these pirates are certainly not your allies. They do not care what happens to you any more than the Aykari."

Leo hesitated, his resolve wavering. Maybe he *was* making a mistake. All the wires in his brain were crossed and tangled. He wasn't sure who to trust or who to blame—for the start of the war, for the death of his mother, for everything that had happened since. Everything he thought he knew a few days ago had been scrambled. He didn't know anything for sure, anymore.

But there were two things that he *believed* at least.

That his universe didn't need to be any bigger than what was in his head and his heart.

And that if it came down to it, the crew of the *Icarus* wouldn't leave him stranded. Not even its cutthroat captain.

Leo pressed the mouthpiece of his inhaler right up against the Djarik's cheek and spoke through clenched teeth. "Order them to drop their weapons. Now!"

"Do as he says," Chellis commanded, his neck gills fluttering.

To Leo's surprise, the four guards' rifles clattered to the floor. In a blink, Kat had one in her grip, giving another to Baz and kicking the rest out of reach. The alarms continued to screech. The table in the center of the room shuddered again. The voice from out of nowhere crackled back to life, this time accompanied by background bursts of laser fire. "Aykari troops have breached our outer defenses. All nonmilitary personnel should begin evacuation immediately."

"Nice work, Leo," Baz said, keeping his stolen rifle aimed at the four Djarik soldiers. "I knew there was a reason I insisted you come along. Okay, crew, we got what we came for. Let's find Skits and Boo and get out of here before the cavalry arrives."

Kat stuck her head out the door, checking their escape. Leo stepped back toward his father, keeping his inhaler pointed at Chellis. With his other hand he tugged on his father's sleeve. "Come on."

But his father didn't move.

"I can't," he said.

"Like hell you can't!" Kat shouted from the door. "Do you have any idea what we've gone through—what Leo has been through—just to get to you? You're coming with us even if I have to knock you unconscious and drag you out of here."

"I'm sorry," Dr. Fender said. "But you don't understand. There's more at stake than I was able to tell you, more than you know. I have to see this through."

Standing next to his father, Leo felt the tide pulling him under again, taking his breath away, sinking deeper and deeper as he realized what was happening, what his father was saying. He couldn't lose him. Not again. "In that case I'm coming with you," he said. "Whatever it is, we'll do it together."

His father smiled, but it was his mother's smile. The fleeting kind. He took in the two pirates standing anxiously by the door. "They brought you here just to rescue me?"

Leo nodded. *More or less*, he thought.

"Do you trust them?"

That question was harder. Leo wasn't sure *who* to trust anymore, and they were still pirates. But then he thought of the hands stacked one upon the other—human skin and Queleti fur and robot claw. Everybody in.

He nodded again.

His father's voice dropped to a whisper.

"In that case I need you to do something for me, Leo. I need you to go find your brother. He's out there somewhere and I'm not sure I can trust anyone else to do it." His eyes darted momentarily to the two robed Djarik and then back to Leo. "Go and find him and you two stay together, understand? Keep each other safe." He reached for Leo's hand, grasping it tight.

Leo felt something small and cold slip into his palm.

"Do this for me, Leo. It could mean the world."

Leo's fingers curled around whatever it was his father had given him as he was pulled close, arms that held him so many times wrapping around him once more. "I love you," he whispered. "And next time *I* will come and find *you*. I promise."

Dr. Fender stepped away, hands on Leo's shoulders. He looked at Baz standing by the door. "You can get him out of here?"

The captain of the *Icarus* looked confused, but he nodded.

The voice cut in over the alarm again. "All personnel abandon posts. Transports prepare for immediate evacuation."

"We are out of time," Chellis hissed. "Do whatever you wish, but if we do not leave now, there will be no chance for any of us."

Kat cast a worried glance at the door. Leo could hear the footfalls of Djarik soldiers echoing along the corridors.

Dr. Fender pressed his forehead to his son's.

"Be brave, little lion," he said.

And pushed him toward the door.

We cannot allow these foreign invaders to exploit us any longer. We will not stand aside while they strip our planet of resources they have no claim to. We will not let them silence our protests, curtail our freedoms, and force us from our homes. We will not let them use us for their own selfish purposes, to spread, unchecked, throughout the galaxy. We will rise up. We will take up arms. We will repel the invaders and drive them from our world. We will be free again. And then we will continue to fight, no matter the cost, until we are certain that the Aykari menace has come to an end.

—Declaration of the Djarik War Council, 56.4072

THE WAIL OF THE QUELETI

THERE HAD BEEN A MOMENT, THAT DAY AT THE BEACH, before Leo saw death rain down from miles away, when he saw it up close. Right at his feet.

It was a thing he never told anyone about. A secret. Because, compared to everything else that happened that day, it seemed insignificant. And yet Leo kept coming back to it afterward, the image haunting him almost as much as the smoke-filled sky.

He had wandered off on his own, looking for that shell— the one he promised to bring back. He would know it when he saw it. Pearlescent and perfectly round, no chips or holes, a mixture of pinks and blues and lavenders. The size didn't matter—it could be as small as a locket or as big as a sand dollar—so long as it was beautiful. Because if he thought so, she would think so too.

He was so focused on finding that shell that he almost stepped on it—the jellyfish inches from his toes, its gelatinous body splayed across the wet dark sand, looking like a blister on the beach, its tentacles shriveled underneath it.

Such an alien thing, Leo thought. Even more alien looking than the actual aliens that had come to Earth from millions of light-years away. They, at least, had arms and ears and eyeballs. Leo couldn't tell if the jelly was still alive or not. He was afraid to touch it, afraid that it could sting him, even dead.

But what if it wasn't?

Was there a chance he could save it? If he could get it back into the water, would it suddenly blob back to life and float away? Had it come onto shore to die, or was that just a mistake, the work of an indifferent tide? Did jellyfish have a *time*, the way that humans supposedly did—*it was just her time*—or was that too just a lie people told themselves?

For a second Leo considered walking away, pretending he hadn't seen anything at all. But then he heard his father's voice in his head. *We have a choice, Leo. Each and every day gives us an opportunity to do something. To leave our mark. To make things better. So that when we fall asleep at night we can do it knowing that our day made a difference for someone else, no matter how slight. We owe that to each other, don't you think?*

Leo knew he didn't just mean the Fenders, or humans in general, or even the inhabitants of Earth. He meant every living thing. We owe it to the universe to help each other.

Or at least to try.

Scattered among the shells and the seaweed and the tiny scuttling crabs, Leo found a stick, and with it he carefully dug beneath the quivering blob, afraid of hurting it, and yet growing more and more certain that it no longer felt anything, that his effort was a waste, even as he dragged its body out to sea, letting the retreating waves bear it back with them.

For a moment Leo watched the jellyfish bob at the surface, slowly working its way back to shore with the current. He was afraid of what would happen if he stayed, that the creature would simply wash right back up onto the sand to rot. Only if he stopped watching could he entertain the possibility—the hope—that it was still alive. That what he had done mattered.

He glanced across the blue-black expanse, feathered with whitecaps crashing, and far off in the distance, the thimble of an Aykari excavation tower anchored to the earth. Then he turned and ran back to his father and his brother, his quest for the perfect shell temporarily forgotten, toes pressed into the sand, a similar sinking in his stomach, a sense of powerlessness in the face of forces so much greater than him.

It was 2:35 on a Saturday afternoon, and the Djarik warships had just come out of their jump, missiles armed and ready.

"All personnel evacuate immediately."

The alarms continued to sound as Leo trailed Baz through the corridors, back in the direction they came. Getting farther and farther from the man they had come to rescue.

Leaving Leo's father behind.

Leo had waited at the door for a moment, heartbroken, head swamped with doubt, seeing his father, the man he'd come to save, standing next to the two robed Djarik only feet away. An insignificant amount of space, easily crossed in a few strides, not like the light-years traveled to get here. And in that moment Leo felt an overwhelming urge to run back into the room, back into his father's arms, holding on no matter what.

But then his fingers brushed along the edge of the datachip nestled in his pocket, the one that had been handed to him in secret. *Do this for me, Leo. It could mean the world.* He thought of Gareth. Probably—no, definitely still alive. Out there somewhere. And he saw the grimace on Kat's face, knowing that every second he spent standing in that doorway, deciding on what path to take, was one second less the crew of the *Icarus* had to escape. So much seemed to hang in the balance.

But then Chellis grabbed Dr. Fender by his shirt, pulling him through the door on the opposite side of the room, away from Leo. He caught one last glance of his father—caught the silent but still desperate *Go* on his lips.

So he turned his back on his family and threw in with a band of pirates.

Pirates who were now running for their lives. Again.

"That way!" Leo pointed at a turn ahead.

"You sure?"

"I'm sort of sure."

Except he wasn't. His brain was all static and swirl. He

couldn't recall all the turns they took to get here.

How *had* he gotten here? Not just here, but *here*. Allied with a pirate crew trapped in a Djarik base under attack by forces that, less than a day ago, Leo would have run to for protection. If the Aykari really did what his father said, then they were just as responsible for what happened as the ones pressing the buttons, weren't they? Which is worse? Doing the unthinkable or standing back and letting the unthinkable happen so that you could use it to your advantage?

And if Leo was no longer on the Coalition's side, then whose side *was* he on?

"Skits? Are you there? Answer me for Earth's sake!" Kat's annoyed voice brought Leo back into focus. "She's still not responding."

"We'll find them," Baz said.

"All personnel must evacuate immediately," the mechanical voice droned above them. "All personnel must eva—"

The warning shut off in a burst of static.

"That can't be good," Kat quipped.

From other corridors, Leo could hear the blasts of gunfire. The Aykari were inside the base. The allies of humanity. Five days ago—five *hours* ago—Leo would have been on-his-knees-grateful to see Aykarian soldiers. He would have shown them the patch that he still had in his pocket, the one planet so much bigger than the rest, encircled by the smaller ones like bees swarming a hive with its queen at the center.

"This place is a war zone, Baz," Kat said. "And look at us.

Right in the middle like always."

"You voted to come here," he reminded her. "Leo, any idea how far we are from the hangar?"

Leo spun around, trying to get his bearings. None of these doors looked familiar. Or they all did. "We're close, I think," Leo said uncertainly. "Left here maybe."

They made a left and nearly walked straight into a firefight, the hallway exploding with deadly energy, the silver Aykarian forces pitched against the black-armored Djarik.

"Maybe not!" Baz said, pushing everyone back.

They took a different turn instead, Kat still calling out for Skits, Leo still armed with his inhaler, which he'd already taken a hit of, trying to stave off an attack that seemed all but certain. They made it ten more feet before two Aykari soldiers appeared in the corridor, blocking their way, their tall, elongated frames clad in plates of silver armor, covering most of their hairless, pale blue skin. Their eyes shown a fiery orange. Their rifles were raised, spindly fingers on the triggers.

"Don't shoot," Baz said, dropping his own weapon to his side and raising his other hand in surrender. "Please. We're human. We're with you guys."

The gangly-limbed Aykari didn't fire.

They also didn't lower their weapons.

Sometimes what you don't do matters even more than what you do, and in that moment, Leo saw them differently. Rather he saw himself through their eyes. And what he saw wasn't a human being; it was a resource, just like Baz said. A means to an end.

"Man, are we so glad to see you," Baz continued. "The Scalies were going to execute us. Seriously, if you hadn't come along . . ."

As Baz continued to try and talk his way past them, one of the Aykari soldiers removed a scanning device from its belt, a bright blue beam projecting outward, tracing Baz from scalp to heel. The soldier held the scanner up to his partner. Leo guessed the results weren't good by the way they both retrained their rifles on the captain.

Taking their burning orange eyes off Kat for an instant, which, Leo knew, was all she needed.

Two blasts, one right after the other, and the two Aykari guards fell, incapacitated.

Before Leo could even process what had happened, Baz was already dragging him back down a different corridor, cursing and muttering to himself.

"Come out to the coast, we'll get together, have a few laughs. . . ." He pulled both Leo and Kat to a stop. "Hold up. Do you hear that?"

"Hear what?" All Leo could hear was alarms.

"That music," Baz said.

Leo concentrated. He *could* hear something, awfully faint but steadily growing in volume. Harmonizing voices over crunchy guitar chords. Definitely music. And distinctively human.

"'I gotta get outta here. I'm stuck inside this rut that I fell into by mistake.'"

Kat and Baz looked at each other and smiled. "Skits."

They followed the sound down through the labyrinthine hallways until it was enough to drown out the alarms and the explosions, the electric guitar slashing through the thunder of war. Leo turned the corner to a wild sight: Boo, his robe torn and singed, three hands gripping a hunk of metal that might once have been a door of some kind but now served as a shield, feet straddling Skits's treads as if he were sitting on the front of a miniature tank barreling down the corridor.

Leo had to admit, he was happy to see them.

The robot's speakers were blasting at full volume but switched off the instant she spotted Baz. "Finally," she moaned. "I swear, it's not like we've been looking all over for you or anything."

"Found you first," Kat said. She inspected the new burns in Boo's robes. "You okay?"

"Nothing that will leave a scar," Boo said, dropping his makeshift shield. "Sorry about the plan. They caught us before we could even make it to the terminal. Guess we weren't as stealthy as we thought."

"Not your fault," Baz said. "It was a terrible plan."

Boo looked at Leo. "Your dad?"

Leo wasn't sure what to say—how to explain why his father wasn't with them. He didn't really have an answer himself.

Just a whisper, a promise, and a datachip. All the rest was questions and doubts.

"Dr. Fender is getting a ride with someone else," Baz said for him. "The kid's coming with us. I'll try to explain once we get somewhere where nobody's shooting at us."

"That could be a while," Kat said.

"Either of you have any idea how to get to the *Icarus*?" Baz asked. "Because I can't remember where we parked."

Where we parked.

Why didn't he think of this sooner?

Leo glanced at his watch, the gift from his parents on his eighth birthday. Cutting-edge technology. Holographic projector. Health-monitoring system. Database enabled. It could even tell time.

Plus it automatically remembered where you parked your car. Or, he supposed, your ship.

Leo pressed a button on the side, pulling up the app. A minuscule red dot began to pulse on the tiny screen along with a number indicating how close they were. A hundred and eighty meters. "This way," he said.

They darted down two more corridors with Leo now at the lead, avoiding the sounds of gunfire at all costs and finally making it to the door that opened up to the hangar. There sat the *Icarus* less than a football field away, the freighter it had docked beside already gone, escaped with its cargo before the attack—or perhaps confiscated by the Aykari when they arrived.

The ship looked like it was still in one piece.

Unfortunately it was also surrounded by Aykari soldiers.

"Never easy, is it?" Baz said, breathless.

"Not with you around," Kat admitted.

The captain turned to Boo, whose fur stood up on end. "I think we're going to need you to wail on these guys, if you're up for it."

"That's another terrible idea," Boo replied. "You know what it will do to you."

"Yeah. But it will do the same to them. Do you think you can carry Kat? The kid too?"

The Queleti shrugged. "Manageable. What about you?"

Baz knocked softly on the side of the robot. "Skits's got me, don't you Skits?"

The robot extended one of her claws to rest on the captain's shoulder. "Always," she said.

Leo had no idea what was going on. "What are you talking about? What do you mean, what it will do to us? What is *it*?"

"In your time on Earth did you ever hear the Irish legend about the banshee?" Baz asked.

Leo shook his head. He'd heard his father use the phrase "screaming like banshees" before. It always just meant he and Gareth were being too loud while he was trying to work.

"You're going to want to plug your ears for as long as you can," Kat said, slinging her stolen Djarik rifle over her shoulder. "Unless you feel like having your head explode."

"Wait, what?"

Leo watched as Kat stuck a fleshy finger in one ear and a

metal one in the other. Baz stood on the front of Skits's treads, back pressed against her torso, two of her extendable arms locked around his waist.

"Boo, what's going on?"

In answer the Queleti wrapped two arms around Leo, much the same as he had when they were snuggled back on the *Icarus*.

"Kat's right. Plug your ears tight as you can. And don't worry—I won't drop you," he said before sweeping Leo off his feet.

In Irish folklore, the banshee's wail was a harbinger of death. Her keening could drive one to madness or despair.

Boo's wail wasn't too far off.

Leo pressed both hands against his ears but it was like trying to cover Boo with a blanket. The sound emanating from the Queleti's mouth could not be completely buffered or blocked out. It seeped through Leo's fingers, through bone and skin, reverberating straight to his brain where it drove home a spike, a blinding shaft of pain that caused nearly every muscle in Leo's body to seize. He was paralyzed, at least that's how it seemed. His arms and legs were unresponsive, though he could still turn his head to see Kat, her own eyes shut, fingers still jammed in her ears, riding on Boo's opposite hip. He was strong enough to carry them both, even with his one wounded arm. Out of the corner of his eye Leo saw the captain lashed to Skits, clutching both sides of his head and gritting through the pain as she barreled ahead, unfazed. Whatever Boo was doing—whatever head-splitting sound was coming out of his mouth—it had no effect on robots.

The agony on Baz's face was nothing compared to the look on the Queleti himself, though, the anguish in his roar reflected also in his eyes. This sound came from somewhere deep inside him, some shattered place, a wound that had never healed, and it broke Leo's heart even as it blasted his brain.

The sound echoed out across the hangar, rolling like a wave, striking the Aykari soldiers standing guard over the ship. The moment Boo's wailing reached them, they dropped their weapons, collapsing to their spindly knees. Some, like Leo, seemed paralyzed. Others trembled, heads cupped in their hands, adding their own screams to the mix. Boo's yell had rendered them immobile. He had practically frozen time.

He could only wail for so long, however. Long enough to make it halfway to the ship. And in the moment that followed, Boo's wailing faded to nothing and everything that had slowed down suddenly sped back up. The Aykari that had been driven to their knees shook their heads and staggered to their feet. Those that been paralyzed by the sound found their wits and scrambled for their dropped rifles.

But they weren't the only ones who had recovered. His mouth shut, Boo's arms opened—two of them anyway—and Kat dropped free, unslinging her own weapon and firing in the direction of the soldiers beside the ramp, causing them to scatter. Boo refused to let go of Leo, though, just like he promised, running full speed and plowing through one Aykari who was still reeling from the roar, sending it flying.

They hit the ramp and Leo finally felt his feet hit the ground, Boo collapsing beside him. Bursts of deadly energy filled the hangar. Skits zoomed up the ramp next, her treads smoking again, and Kat followed, taking errant shots at the Aykari soldiers behind her without even looking.

And then there was Baz, bringing up the rear this time, making sure every member of his crew was on board. He was less than a meter away when an energy bolt hit him, causing him to stumble toward the ramp. Leo reached out with one hand, Boo with another, pulling the captain on board.

"Kat, get this thing moving!" the captain shouted, holding the side of his head with one hand so that Leo barely got a look at the wound as he staggered past. "Kat?"

"I know! We're going, we're going!" she shouted back.

The ramp was barely closed before the *Icarus* lurched sideways and then up, knocking Leo into the walls as he followed Baz to the cockpit, the captain still clutching his head. He could hear Kat's voice, exasperated, shouting all the way down the corridor from the pilot's seat.

"Just once, just *once* you might take a girl somewhere quiet. Somewhere peaceful. Somewhere where there aren't bounty hunters or security bots or whole platoons of Aykari soldiers all trying to gun her down."

Leo lurched forward and then stumbled backward as the *Icarus* turned and then burst out of the hangar, a parting barrage of laser blasts from the soldiers attempting in vain to stop it.

"Somewhere with a lake," Kat continued to rant as she steered the *Icarus* up and away from the base. "And some trees. Real ones, Baz, not artificial. And a freking duck. Is that really too much to ask? To see some stupid freking ducks again before I die?"

The ship tore through the gray clouds, leaving the Djarik base behind, pulling free of the planet's grip and breaking back into the empty black void of space.

Except the void wasn't empty at all. It was filled with ships. Aykari naval cruisers and frigates attempting to ensnare the Djarik freighters and transports fleeing the planet, swarms of fighters from both sides weaving through the constant bar-rage. The whole view from the cockpit exploded with arcs of energy and bright bursts of flame.

Leo stared. Here, at last, was the war. The one that had been raging long before Leo was even born, the one his father had tried to shield him from, happening right in front of him. Leo wondered if his father was on one of the arrow-like Djarik transports emerging from the planet's atmosphere alongside the *Icarus*, desperate to make their escape. As he watched, one of those same freighters slipped through the wall of incoming Aykari laser fire and jumped safely away.

That one, Leo thought. *Let's just assume he was on that one.*

He had no idea where his father was going, where Chellis was taking him. Wasn't even sure why. *I have to see this through.* Leo only knew that whatever it was, it had to be important.

Even more important than staying with your own son.

A sudden jolt caused Leo to stumble, almost slamming his head, as Kat banked hard, attempting to put as much distance as possible between the *Icarus* and the slowly advancing Aykari blockade, which fortunately seemed more interested in the fleeing Djarik ships than the lone pirate transport.

"Um, we've got an incoming message here," Kat said, punching a button as a holovid lit up above the ship's console. Leo looked to see a brain floating in a glass tube.

"Hello, Baz," Mac's recorded voice said. *"I hope this reaches you in time. If you are still planning on rescuing Dr. Fender, I suggest you do it quickly. It seems my impetuous partner found another party interested in the same information we gave you, and they were willing to pay a princely sum. If I had to guess, I'd venture that said other party is already on their way. I realize it's a bit underhanded, but you of all people know what it takes to survive out here. So if you do make it out alive, please try not to take it personally."*

The transmission ended and Mac's image vanished, leaving Kat with dagger eyes and bared teeth. "They sold us out!" she snarled. "Those double-crossing Herflax humpers sold us out! I swear, when I see those two again they're going to need glass jars for every part of their bodies. And I mean *every* part."

"Maybe we should concentrate on the more immediate problem," Boo suggested, pointing to the array of familiar red lights blaring on the console. Leo recognized the warning by now: incoming starfighters locking on to their ship. Leo couldn't tell if they were Djarik or Aykari. At this point, he wasn't sure it even mattered.

There were no warning shots this time. The fighters came in from all sides. The *Icarus* staggered under a volley of hits, its shields barely absorbing the damage, their pursuers closing in for the kill.

Why when you're on nobody's side are you suddenly everybody's enemy?

"We're taking a beating here," Kat said. "I don't care where we jump to, but we'd better do it now!"

"I know," Baz fired back.

The *Icarus* shook again as another alarm blared. Behind Leo a column of steam hissed out of a pipe.

"I'm serious!"

"I know!"

A new set of lights started to flash, warning the ship's shields were already depleted.

"Baz . . ."

"Just two more seconds."

Leo felt the familiar cold hand gripping his throat. He struggled for a breath. He thought of the jellyfish floating in the waves. The one he'd tried to save.

"Now?"

"Now!"

Two fists slammed down on the console at once.

In the engine compartment of the *Icarus*, inside an insulated FTL drive designed by the brightest Aykari engineers, an electrical spark triggered the release of a very precious substance known to most of the galaxy as EL-486. The element instantly fused with four other much-less-precious substances, creating a chain reaction that Leo—despite his father's teaching and many diagrams and drawings—couldn't even begin to follow. The power it released was immense, but also highly channeled, so that instead of blowing the *Icarus* to smithereens, it served to activate the FTL drive system, creating a minor tear in the fabric of the universe and launching the ship and its five passengers into hyperspace.

It was a beautiful piece of tech, a godly marvel, perfected over centuries of space travel. The kind of technology that allows you to explore the unknown, to expand the boundaries of your empire, to cement your place as the most advanced beings in the galaxy.

Its only failing—and it wasn't a small one—was its dependence on something that could only be found on one planet out of a thousand. And even then, the means of its mass extraction often resulted in the planet's slow decline, disrupting its ecosystems, polluting its rivers, its oceans, its skies; sapping the life out of it and, eventually—inevitably—those who once called the planet home.

There were some who called that progress.

There were others who disagreed.

The rest were caught somewhere in between.

It is far better to grasp the Universe as it really is than to persist in delusion, however satisfying and reassuring.

—*Carl Sagan*, The Demon-Haunted World: Science as a Candle in the Dark, *1996*

PROMISES

THERE WERE DAYS LEO REMEMBERED BECAUSE HE had no choice. Because they were branded on his brain, body, and soul, carved roughly into him by the blunt edge of grief.

But there were also days he remembered because he wanted to. Because he willed himself to. Because if he could accumulate enough of them, they might bury the others under their weight or push them to the corners where they could be ignored.

Memories of him and Gareth sledding down the hill behind his school and of the mugs of marshmallow-laden hot chocolate that followed. Of him and his brother teaming up against their dad, pulling him away from his desk, from his "really important" work, and wrestling him to the ground, piling all the pillows from every sofa and bed on top of him to make a mountain, and then belly flopping onto the pile, reveling in their father's laughing groans coming from underneath.

Memories of his mother stretched out across a blanket in the grass, growing right where it belonged this time—her head resting on his father's leg, blinking against the sun as the boys abandoned their half-eaten sandwiches to find a tree to climb. And Sundays spent hiking through the woods, Leo's father carrying an extra bag to pick up the trash they found littered along the way. *It may not be our trash*, he said, *but that doesn't mean it's not our responsibility to clean it up. It's for the greater good.*

Leo's father often spoke of the greater good—some force that impelled a person to do what was best, not for himself but for everyone else. He said it extended beyond family, beyond home and school, even beyond country and planet, that all species of a higher intellectual order assumed this responsibility—to look out for each other, to care for each other, to clean up after each other's messes. *But it only works if we all believe in it*, he said.

If we *all* believed in it, Leo thought, then there wouldn't be any trash to pick up to begin with. Which meant whoever left this soda can sitting on the side of the trail was either not of a higher intellectual order or they just didn't care. What happens when someone—a person, a species, a planet—decides *not* to believe?

What do you do when the whole galaxy becomes a mess for someone else to clean up?

His father would say that you don't give up. That you keep trying. That no dreams are easy to achieve. But Leo knew better. He knew that most people only looked out for their own. Sometimes, it seemed, that was all you *could* do.

But was it enough?

Leo sat at the table, head in his hands. He was alone, everyone else in some other part of the ship. Leo assumed they were leaving him be on purpose.

He was starting to get used to it—being left to fend for himself.

It seemed like his whole universe was falling apart.

He'd felt that way before too.

What I'm about to tell you will be hard to hear and even harder to believe.

Leo didn't know what to believe. Everything was so knotted in his head that anytime he tried to follow one line of thought it crashed into another and splintered off into a dozen contradictory directions. *What ifs* and *could bes* and *how comes.* His father was right—it was hard to believe that the Aykari would do such a thing—allowing the Djarik to decimate cities, to slaughter civilians just so his planet, his people, would fully commit to their war.

Hard to believe, but not impossible.

Not when you think of hummingbirds and cherry blossoms long gone. Not when you think of the earthquakes and the disappearing beaches. Not when you see what the war has reduced people to. The ones stuck in between. The planets and people used up and discarded or simply pushed away and ignored. Then it wasn't so hard at all.

Harder for Leo to believe that his father was gone again, after being this close to getting him back. That after everything, Leo was right back where he started—on board a pirate ship with his family scattered to the stars.

He leaned across the table, turned his watch dial to twelve, and the projection shot across the cramped dining area of the *Icarus*, revealing the familiar porch and the blade of grass, the puzzled look followed by the fleeting smile. The one he'd never see again, not for real. Leo put his head against the cool metal table. The anger swelled within him as it had so many times before, but he no longer knew where to direct it. Yes, it was a Djarik missile that took her, but it was the Aykari's cold and calculated decision to let it.

And Leo's fault for not insisting that she come with them that day. Nothing good ever comes from leaving the ones you love behind.

I see you.

"You okay there, ninja turtle?"

Leo startled, switching off the projection and tucking his hands under the table as if he'd been doing something wrong.

Baz stood in the doorway, hands shoved into his pockets. He had changed back into his flip-flops and wore a new T-shirt with an obscene set of ruby-red lips and a giant tongue lolling out. A gauzy white bandage was stuck to the side of his head, a rust-colored spot at its center. The captain had lost most of his left ear to that blast back in the Djarik hangar. Of course the Aykari could probably grow and graft on a new one easily enough—except they were the ones who had shot it off.

Leo wiped at his eyes. "All good," he said with a sigh.

"If you ever think about becoming an outlaw, you'll definitely need to work on your lying." Baz took the opposite seat and pointed to the bowl still sitting on the table from last time. "You going to eat that?"

Leo looked at the leftover gyurt, shook his head, and slid it toward the captain. Unlike Gareth, Baz didn't slide it back. He choked down one bite and then torpedoed the spoon back into the bowl. "The only thing worse than gyurt? Cold gyurt," he said, making a face, but following it with a smile. "Though strangely, it kind of reminds me of chili dogs. You remember chili dogs?"

Leo nodded. His father would buy them for him and Gareth when they went to watch the Rockies play. Chili dogs and popcorn and giant sodas—enough to make even Dev-the-double-crossing-jacker jealous.

"I miss chili dogs," Baz mused. "And salsa. With a big bag of crisp, salty tortilla chips."

"Double bacon cheeseburgers," Leo said, his mouth starting to water. "With french fries. And ketchup."

"Loads of ketchup," Baz agreed. "And watermelon. Thick slices, juice dripping off your chin. Oranges too. Not so much eating them, but the smell."

Leo nodded. For some things the smell was really all he

remembered. "Fresh baked cookies," Leo said. "Right out of the oven."

"Mown grass."

"Campfires."

Baz took a long, steady breath through his nose, eyes shut, perhaps going back to the last time he'd sat around a fire. When he opened them again, he still looked far away, but then he found his focus. "We could go on like this forever, you know. Won't change anything. Still just gonna be looking at a bowl of cold gyurt."

Leo tucked his chin into his folded arms. "Yeah. But I can't help it sometimes."

"Me neither."

The captain reached up and touched his bandage, gently tracing the arc of the bloodstain with one finger.

"Does it hurt?"

Baz shrugged. "No more than other things. There's really only like a third of an ear left. Kat says I'll finally look like a real pirate." He laughed at his own joke. "I should say thanks, by the way. For what you did back there. If it weren't for you, we'd all be on a Djarik prison ship right now and there's no telling what body parts I'd be missing."

Leo shrugged. "You would have done the same for me."

"You so sure about that?" Baz asked, but the look in the pirate's eyes told Leo that he was right.

Probably.

Baz took up his spoon again, slowly stirring it along the rim of the bowl like a planet orbiting its sun. Billions of planets. Billions of suns. How much did any of them really matter? Only the ones with ventasium in them? And when that was all gone, then what?

Do this for me, Leo. It could mean the world.

"We tried, Leo. You tried. There was no way you could have known."

"Do you think it's true?" Leo asked. "What my father said? About what happened that day? About the attack?"

Baz had been there, after all. He had seen it. Days later he had signed up to avenge it, like thousands of others. He once wore the same patch as the one in Leo's pocket. The medal—the one Leo had furtively returned to Baz's trunk rather than keeping it—was proof.

Though it was also proof that the captain had his doubts long before today.

"Are you asking me if I believe the Aykari lied to us, letting those missiles hit so that they could use us? Because you already know my answer. The Aykari have been using us from the moment they showed up. You, me, your dad, all of us—fueling their ships and fighting their war, and all for some promise they don't intend to keep. They're really no better than their enemies. And we're all fools for joining their Coalition." Baz tugged on his unbandaged ear, almost as if to verify that it was still there. That he was still half right. "At least with

- 355 -

the Djarik you know what you're up against. Though I wish I knew what it is they needed your father for. Whatever it is, I'm not sure I want to be around to see it."

Leo reached into his pocket—technically Kat's pocket—removing what he'd hidden there and setting it on the table.

"Maybe this will tell us," he said.

"Okay, let's see what this is all about."

They were back in the cockpit, the whole crew gathered to see what Leo's father had given him. Baz clicked the datachip into place. For a moment there was nothing, and then Dr. Calvin Fender appeared from the waist up. Leo shivered looking at the image on the screen; his father looked more like a ghost, a flickering apparition of himself. Leo could tell by the clothes and the beard that it had been recorded in the last day or two—while he was being held prisoner by the Djarik.

No, not prisoner. Partner.

Leo stared at his father's image, waiting for some explanation or apology, something directed at him, but what followed wasn't even meant for Leo.

"This message is for Zirkus Crayt," the recording began. "My name is Dr. Calvin Fender. For the past three years I have been stationed aboard the Coalition research vessel *Beagle*, ostensibly searching for potential sources of EL-four eight six, though in reality I have been working on ways to refine it in order to increase its power. Five days ago I was taken prisoner by the Djarik empire and coerced into helping them instead. As a result, I have learned that the Djarik are on the verge of weaponizing EL-four eight six on a scale never seen before, developing a way to destabilize the element within planets themselves, resulting in a massive release of uncontrolled energy. With such a weapon at their disposal, the Djarik could destroy any planet where the element is found, including my own home of Earth. The Djarik intend to use this weapon to try and end the war, but I fear the cost in lives galaxy-wide would be too great. I believe there is—that there has to be—another way.

"Included on this datachip is all the research I have been able to gather. I believe you are my best chance—our best chance—of countering this new threat. I'm afraid of what might happen if this information falls into anyone else's hands, including the Aykari. I'm also afraid we don't have much time. Though I may be able to stall them, I believe the Djarik's development of this weapon is inevitable. My only hope is that you will find a way to stop it, to succeed where I cannot. Please—for the sake of Earth and for every planet that has been unwittingly drawn into this terrible war—I am begging for your help."

With a buzz of static, the ghost of Calvin Fender disappeared. The crew of the *Icarus* stared into the empty space left behind.

Skits whistled. "Well *that's* a kick in the treads."

"Taking out entire planets, entire populations?" Boo said. "That's monstrous, even for the Djarik."

"Is it really that hard to believe?"

The crew all turned to their captain, bandaged and bruised, the purple bloom on his cheek outlined with a corona of yellow. "I mean, what's the difference? How is this anything new? Djarik. Aykari. Bombs. Drills. It all comes out the same in the end, doesn't it?"

"Maybe *this* is the difference," Leo said, pointing to the datachip. "You heard what my father said. Maybe this Zirkus Crayt knows how to stop it."

"Right," Skits said. "One guy is going to find a way to stop the entire Djarik empire from blowing up the galaxy. We don't know who this Crayt person is or where to find him."

"Maybe not the first part," Kat said. She tapped on the screen, scrolling through data files, images, blueprints. "Most of this is technical—diagrams, specs, all beyond me—but this last part here"—she tapped on a file and a map appeared, alongside a set of coordinates. "It's pretty far. We might not have enough juice to jump there and back. Not that we can't get more if we need to."

Leo knew what she meant. They were pirates, after all.

"So we go there and deliver this chip to this Zirkus Crayt? What about Leo's brother?" Boo asked. "Aren't we going to try and find him too?"

"And let's not forget all the people who want us dead," Skits added helpfully. "The Djarik. The Aykari. Grimsley. Your ex-girlfriend. Wherever we go, somebody's bound to catch up to us."

"And the *Icarus* isn't in the best shape," Kat said. "If we don't patch her up soon, there might not be an us to catch up to."

Leo watched the captain's fingers. *Tap tap tap.*

"You know what a good pirate would do," he mused, talking to no one in particular. "He'd sell this datachip directly to the Coalition. Something like this, top secret intel, the Aykari would pay a fortune. More than enough to buy a little hole-in-the-wall somewhere far off everybody's radar. Hang up our guns. Change our robes. Spend the rest of our days serving drinks and mopping vomit off the floor."

"That's something a good pirate would do," Kat echoed. "The question is what are *we* going to do? We're kind of caught up in this now, Baz." She glanced at Leo. "And I mean all of us."

Do this for me, Leo. It could mean the world.

His father didn't just mean any world. He meant *their* world. He meant Earth. Home of chili dogs and Charizards and Miguel Ramos. Home to scripted television and fast-food restaurants and ponds with ducks and real life trees. Home to families with wooden signs on their doors. Bastian Black drummed on his knee, lost in the rhythm of his own thoughts. "You want to know how you can get away with being the worst pirate in the universe?"

Leo had a guess. Probably something about making it up as you go along or knowing how to make a quick getaway or somehow leaving with even less than you started with. But it turned out Leo didn't know everything there was to know about pirates yet.

"The key is having the best crew," Baz said.

Then he called for a vote.

Leo stood in the cockpit and looked out at the stars.

After their unanimous decision, the crew of the *Icarus* scattered to other parts of the ship. Boo was already rattling the bunks with his snoring, recovering from the banshee-like scream that had clearly taken too much out of him. Kat was in the cargo hold, eating the last of the Twinkies and taking inventory—an easy job given how low the *Icarus* was on supplies. Skits was finally finishing her repairs to the engine's cooling system, some terrible song Leo just barely recognized belting through her speaker.

And Baz . . . when Leo passed his quarters, he was sitting on his bed, open treasure trunk at his feet, a shiny silver medal in his hand. Leo considered interrupting, asking him if *he* was okay, but thought better of it and left Bastian Black alone with his memories. Sometimes you can't help but think about how things used to be.

Instead, he wandered to the front of the ship, still using Kat's jacket to keep out the chill. He stood and stared into the never-ending darkness, stippled with a thousand stars that he didn't even know the names of, forming constellations his father never taught him because the night sky seen from Earth is just one of an infinite number of patterns the universe can take.

Leo really detested space. Too much uncertainty. Too easy to lose your way. And so much distance between the things that mattered. He had no idea how far he was. From Gareth. From his father. From Earth. The space that separated them might as well be infinite.

But then Leo thought of his mother. An early morning making pancakes. He pictured her, pointing first to his head, then to his heart.

"I'll find you," Leo whispered into the canvas of stars. Somehow they would find each other. And then maybe, finally, they would find a home.

TO BE CONTINUED . . .

EPILOGUE

TAKING SIDES

LIEUTENANT GRIGGSON TAPPED THE SCREEN IN another half-hearted attempt to get it to cooperate. Aykarian technology, he thought with a huff. The datapad was supposedly top-of-the-line, but the blasted thing froze up at least thirty times a day.

It was like that more and more with their stuff, he noticed. When it worked it was genius. Time-saving. Lifesaving, even. But it worked less than half the time, it seemed. It was because of the blasted war. Everything was deteriorating, breaking down. Supplies were scarce. He still carried an eight-year-old sidearm that barely held a charge and wore a uniform that looked like it might have been through seven wars already. No doubt the Aykari kept the best stuff for themselves—for their own soldiers and pilots and officers. *But if you are going to come and drag us into this mess,* Griggson thought, *the least you could do is give us equipment that worked.*

The screen finally glitched back to life and Lieutenant Griggson looked over the line of refugees waiting to be processed. He only dealt with humans. It was in his contract. It wasn't that he was speciest, exactly. He had nothing against the Aykari per se, or any of the other races who had joined the Coalition. He would just rather spend his days helping out his own kind. And, lord, how they needed the help.

Half of today's lot was from a transport that had been heading to a colony near Alpha Centauri when Djarik marauders slammed a torpedo in its side. The rest were stragglers, picked up from all over. Most of them would be hungry. Filthy. Some would be injured. Many would be looking for someone. Friends or family, fellow soldiers. And he would often have to deliver the bad news. *I'm sorry, but we have no current record of that individual in our database.*

All of them would have to be relocated.

It was sad, seeing their pale and hollow cheeks, knowing what they'd been through. Griggson hated his job some days, trudging through other people's misery, reading their files, processing their requests. It was a small comfort whenever he could lift them up, put them in contact with a sister or an uncle, maybe even find a way to get them back home. But a lot of them no longer had a home, and they weren't always interested in going back to Earth. Who could blame them? *He* certainly wasn't going back there if he could help it. Not until the Aykari were finished extracting every last shard of ventasium they could find, and by then, what would be left? He tried not to think about it. Better to be here on this outpost several systems away, where at least you could breathe—provided the atmospheric generators didn't break.

"Next."

A young man stepped up and presented his datacard. He looked like he'd been through seven wars as well. Griggson almost didn't want to know his story, but it flashed on-screen regardless.

"How's it going, kid?" he said, making small talk while he quickly scanned the file. It was a stupid question, he knew. If you were standing here, it meant that things were about as bad as they could be. Griggson read the highlighted bits, piecing together the essentials. This kid had seen some action recently.

All he said, though, was "I'm all right."

"Looks here like you were attacked by the Djarik and taken prisoner?"

"Twice," the kid said softly, then louder, as if he remembered that he still had a voice, "We were attacked by them twice. The first time they left us stranded. Most of us anyways. The second time they came and took us all prisoner."

"But you and several other members of your crew managed to overcome the guards and take control of the Djarik ship that was transporting you?"

"Yes, sir. There were thirty of us and only ten guards. Captain Saito was in charge. She—" The boy's voice softened again. "She didn't make it."

"I'm sorry to hear that, son," Griggson said. He didn't know Saito from any of the other officers whose names came up KIA, but you always felt the need to apologize. Good human lives lost in this alien war. "You escaped and made it here safe, though. That's pretty remarkable. No telling what those Djarik scumbags would have done with you. You're lucky to be alive, you know that?"

The boy nodded. Griggson knew he was waiting for something. A question he was afraid to ask. But he'd asked it already. It was right there in his file. "Says here you have a father and brother?"

"Yes, sir," the boy said, leaning so close it looked like he might fall over, his eyes suddenly hopeful.

Griggson hated that look. The expectant look. Like watching a dying fire coughing up its one last spark.

"I'm sorry, son. Unfortunately I've got nothing on their current whereabouts. The last known record of either of them was aboard your ship, the *Beagle*, right before it was attacked."

"The first time," the boy said.

"Right. The first time. Your father's name is Calvin? Calvin Fender?"

"Dr. Calvin Fender," the boy said.

Griggson thought maybe he'd heard *that* name before, at least. Maybe seen it in the newsfeeds somewhere, but he couldn't quite recall. Who could even keep up with the news anymore? "I'd love to help you get back to them, son. And I will do my best to keep digging around, but in the meantime we need to find somewhere you can go. Somewhere safe." He was about to pull up a list of all the nearby Coalition outposts and holding facilities when the boy cleared his throat.

"Actually, sir. I'd like to join up."

"Excuse me?"

"Coalition forces. I want to join. I want to fight. I'm still a little young, I know, but I've got three years' experience on a Coalition vessel and I know my way around a ship. Besides, I think my recent actions should count for something."

Recent actions. Thirty unarmed humans—most of them support staff and engineers—overwhelming their Djarik captors and seizing control of the ship? Yes. It certainly counted for something. That wasn't the problem. The kid's age wasn't a problem either. The Coalition would take him at seventeen. They'd recruited younger. The problem was Griggson—everything he'd seen, everything he knew—and what this kid knew as well. Especially as the lieutenant passed his eyes over the entry about the kid's mother, the date deceased. Griggson still remembered exactly where he'd been the day Earth was set on fire—the moment humanity's hand was forced. Sitting in a bar in Ottawa with his brother, both of them staring dumbly at the screens hanging in every corner, showing the carnage from downtown Toronto.

He massaged his temples with the knuckles of his thumbs.

"Son, you know better than most what the Djarik are like. What they're capable of. Don't get me wrong. The Coalition will take all the volunteers they can get right now. But if you ask me—and this is just between us," Griggson whispered, leaning in closer, "I say let the Aykari win their own freking war. I think you've suffered enough, don't you?"

"Excuse me, sir," the young man said. "But I can't. For all I know, my brother and father are still out there somewhere. And if they aren't, it's all because of the Djarik. I've lost everything because of them."

Griggson looked over the others still waiting in line. He could see there was no point in arguing. Besides, it wasn't his decision to make. Just pass him off to the next official and maybe when he saw what was involved, this kid would get some sense and reconsider. The lieutenant sighed.

"I don't do recruiting. But I can point you in the right direction." Maybe he would get lucky and they would sit him behind a desk where he'd never have to squeeze a trigger or pilot a starfighter. Lieutenant Griggson made a few notes on the young man's file and then handed his datacard back. "There you go, son. Take this to building five—the big dome near the center of the outpost. They can help you there."

"Thank you, sir."

The young man turned to go, and in that moment Lieutenant Griggson was sure he would never see him again.

"Mr. Fender," Griggson called out.

"Gareth, sir," the young man said.

"Right. Gareth. I hope you find your family."

The boy nodded. "Thanks," he said. "Me too."

He turned and walked away. Lieutenant Griggson pointed to the next poor soul in line.

ACKNOWLEDGMENTS

You can get away with being the worst pirate in the universe so long as you have the best crew. You can get away with publishing your first sprawling space opera if you are similarly blessed. Leo and the rest of the scoundrels of the *Icarus* would never have made it out of the hangar if it weren't for the dedication, inspiration, creativity, and hard work of many.

Thanks to the team at Adam's Literary who somehow keep the ship that is my writing career flying even when I seem to have no clear destination in mind. To the stalwart crew at Harper Collins—David DeWitt, Amy Ryan, Kathryn Silsand, Martha Schwartz, and Tiara Kittrell—thank you for helping me turn this rusted junk pile of words into something space-worthy. To Aveline Stokart for creating a cover that perfectly captures the feeling of the book and to Vaishali Nayak and Sam Benson for launching that book out into the universe. To Deb Kovacs and Donna Bray for making such swashbuckling, planet-spanning adventures possible. Finally to Jordan Brown, the best copilot a space pirate could ask for. Thanks for always having my back.

When I was a boy between the ages of six and eight, I lived for every other Friday. That's when my mother would cash her paycheck and take me to Target, where I could pick out one two-dollar Kenner Star Wars action figure—a splurge, given my family's rocky finances. I would make my selection, stowing away copies of the ones I couldn't buy yet in secret places throughout the store, hoping they would still be there two weeks down the road (they never were, and I'm sure the Target employees weren't happy to find Greedo leering from behind a stack of pantyhose). Then I would take my new jedi, bounty hunter, or droid home and engage in living-room-wide warfare, reenacting some familiar scenes but mostly inventing new ones, crafting epic adventures in my head. Of course that Friday's purchase—tight jointed and armed with accessories that I would probably soon lose—would be central to the story line, a new hero or villain to plot with.

My mother would check on me once in a while, standing in the hallway, listening to my pew-pews and spit-laden explosions, and I would look up only briefly and smile so that she would go away and let me get back to the alternative universe I was lost in.

I realize now that the two dollars she spent every other Friday on a piece of molded plastic was as much for her as it was for me—so that she could give me something she never had, given her tough childhood: a chance to play, to escape, to explore, to live out my fantasies. Money well spent so that she could see that smile on my face as I blasted my way through the galaxy.

My mother passed away in the spring of 2020, making this the first book of mine that she never got a chance to read. But there is no doubt that she helped create it—with the stories she read to me and the songs that she sang and the movies she took me to. She helped create it every other Friday, at two precious dollars a pop. She helped create it in the forty years that followed by pushing me to follow my passion and put my fantasies on paper. She was my muse.

This book is for her.

TURN THE PAGE TO
START READING THE SEQUEL
TO *STOWAWAY:*

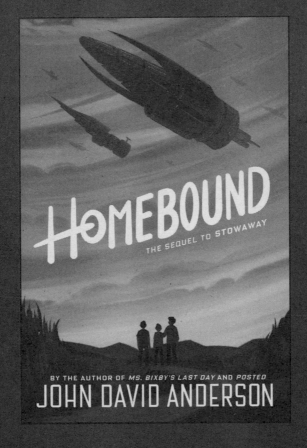

HOMEBOUND

THE SEQUEL TO STOWAWAY

BY THE AUTHOR OF *MS. BIXBY'S LAST DAY* AND *POSTED*

JOHN DAVID ANDERSON

FIRE AWAY

LEO FENDER COULDN'T CRY.

He tried. He stepped on his own foot, grinding the heel of one polished loafer into the toe of another, wincing at the pain, but wincing wasn't the same as crying, and even if it was, they would still be the wrong kind of tears. Physical pain wasn't anything like what he was feeling now.

This was so much worse.

It didn't make sense. He'd cried a hundred times since that day. He'd cried himself to sleep almost every night. He'd teared up at the most random times: clearing the plates at dinner, putting his clean socks back in the dresser, watering the daylilies—the ones they'd planted together—along the front porch. But now, when it was called for, when everyone was surely expecting him to, he couldn't, and it made him angry at himself.

Gareth was crying. His brother's eyes had been swollen for hours, a slow but steady procession like the drip of a melting icicle, earning him no end of sympathetic pats and pouting frowns, not to mention a piece of chocolate from their neighbor, Mrs. Tinsley, who insisted it would make him feel better. Not that Leo wanted anyone's sympathy or their chocolate. He just couldn't stomach the thought that someone else was hurting worse than him—or that he wasn't hurting enough. Cousins and nieces and colleagues and friends were all shedding tears. The tissue box sitting by the guest book was nearly empty. Even the sky itself was in mourning, the rain battering the stained glass windows. But Leo, dressed in his scratchy suit and clip-on tie, couldn't summon a drop. He dug his nails into his arm until they nearly broke skin. Nothing.

Even staring at the picture of her that had been placed on the altar didn't prompt the tears to come. The photo, taken the year before while they were on vacation, long hair and a wistful smile, her searching gold eyes staring across the Grand Canyon, which she was seeing for the first time. The picture, enlarged and placed on a stand, took the place of a coffin or an urn. Grace Fender had been too close to ground zero when the missile struck, practically vaporizing everything nearby. No physical remains—just a million reminders.

Leo fiddled with his watch, tempted to press the button that would summon her. That would play the video of her sitting on the porch. Bring her back to him, if only for a moment. He longed to hear her voice. *I see you there, my little lion.*

"How are you holding up?"

Leo glanced up to see his father standing in front of him, dressed in an almost identical suit to Leo's, save for the fact that his tie required a knot. His father owned a million ties. A new one every Christmas, mostly from the kids because they didn't know what else to get him. Leo shrugged. "People keep asking me that," he said.

Dr. Calvin Fender, renowned scientist, Nobel Prize winner, recent widower, and single father, settled into the pew next to his son. "Strange, isn't it? We can travel to Neptune with the snap of a finger. We can mend broken bones almost overnight. We can unlock the very secrets of the universe itself. But we can't seem to think of the right thing to say at a funeral."

"I can't cry," Leo admitted.

This time it was his dad who shrugged. "It's not a requirement."

"But don't you think I should? People will think I'm not sad."

His father shook his head. "I don't think anyone believes that. Besides, we all experience grief differently. Half of these people aren't even crying about your mother. They are crying about someone else they've lost. Or someone they are afraid to lose. Do *you* feel like you need to cry?"

"I don't know," Leo said, making shapes with his fingers, interlacing them, remembering a rhyming game she showed him once, a long time ago. *Here is the church. Here is the steeple.* "I don't want her to think I don't miss her."

His dad reached out and took both of Leo's hands in one of his own. "Well, *I* know. Believe me. I miss her just as much as you do. And *you* know. And that's really all that matters, right?"

Leo nodded, though he still wasn't so sure.

They sat for a minute more in silence, just the two of them sitting in the front row listening to the steady drum of rain on the roof.

"I want to go home," Leo said.

"I know you do. This will be over soon. I promise."

Leo leaned into his father, eyes falling upon her picture again, staring across the giant fissure gouged deep into the earth, like an open wound that would never heal.

"Hey, Leo."

His brother's voice caused Leo to sit up. He turned but couldn't spot Gareth in the crowd.

"Leo? You with us?"

He scanned the faces before him, all of them suddenly alien and unfamiliar.

"Earth to Leo?"

A finger snap.

Leo Fender shook his head and focused on the man staring back at him, the memory quickly receding. This wasn't his dad or his brother. It was a haggard face with a ragged beard and a sharp, hooked nose, so different from his father's knobby one. Scars arced above the eyebrow, along the chin.

This was the face of a pirate.

The man's hair was cropped short enough to reveal a left ear half-missing, the curved remainder an angry pink whirl of newly scabbed flesh. Leo had watched that ear get blown off by an energy bolt. Fired from the rifle of an Aykarian soldier, no less.

Because that's what you do to pirates. You shoot them. You arrest them. You hang them for treason. At least that's what Leo had always thought. But he'd been forced to rethink a lot of things lately. Especially when the Aykari started shooting at him too.

"Sorry. Got a little lost there."

"Yeah . . . well don't freak out on me, kid. We've got work to do," Bastian Black said.

Leo's eyes readjusted to their surroundings. He'd been deep inside his own head again, somewhere far away. But now he was back. Back inside this hulking, metal, pear-shaped ship hurtling through space, staring at a man with a ratty black T-shirt asking if anyone's Got Milk.

"Seriously, ninja turtle, you okay? You look like you've just had your mind wiped by a Darvatulan brain leech."

Leo had no idea what that was, but it sounded not too far off from what he was feeling. His brain felt scrambled, like someone had scooped it out and dropped it in a blender before pouring it back in. "I'm all right," he said.

Baz put a hand on Leo's shoulder. "Definitely need to work on your lying. Go get strapped in, then. We're coming out of our jump."

Leo nodded and followed the captain of the *Icarus* into the cockpit where the other members of the crew were already assembled. Katarina Corea sat in the pilot's seat, dressed in her customary black uniform, her titanium hand operating the controls while the one she'd been born with fiddled with an ugly fuzzy-blue-haired doll that Baz kept hanging from the ship's console. Skits was busy at another control panel messing with some wiring—whether making it better or worse, Leo couldn't be sure; it probably depended on her mood. She swiveled along her bucket-like torso and smiled at Leo because she had no choice—it was her only available expression. Next to the tank-treaded robot, the four-armed Queleti was busy attacking his toe claws with some kind of industrial bolt cutter.

"Trimming your nails?" Leo asked.

"Baz told me I had to," Boo said gruffly.

"That's because when they get that long I can hear them clicking on the metal floor when you walk," Baz said. "Do you know how annoying that is? All the time. Click-click-click-click-click."

"No more annoying than you banging on the console, playing your imaginary drums constantly," Kat countered. "Besides, why would anyone take hygiene advice from you? When's the last time you cleaned your teeth?"

"I gargled some warm beer an hour ago," Baz informed her. She made a face.

Boo squeezed the handles of the bolt cutter and the tip of one claw went flying. "Incoming," he warned as the clipped nail pinged off the wall.

A week ago, if Leo had been this close to the lumbering hulk of hair and muscle that was Bo'enmaza Okardo, he would probably have peed his standard-issue Coalition khakis. But since then he'd saved the alien's life and vice versa. They'd even slept in the same bed. Not exactly what he'd envisioned three years ago when his father informed him they'd be journeying into outer space—using an alien's fur as a makeshift blanket in the bottom bunk of a pirate transport—but that's what it had come to.

The same went for all of the crew of the *Icarus*. Not long ago, Leo would have looked at them—*did* look at them—with skin-prickling apprehension and distrust, seeing them as outlaws and traitors, the kind of people you would only be caught dead with, mostly likely because they would have killed you. But a lot had happened since then. A lot that Leo still didn't understand. But he at least knew he wasn't afraid of pirates anymore.

Not these pirates, at least.

"Scootch," the captain said, forcing Kat into the copilot's seat. The first mate knew her way around the *Icarus*'s controls—she could fly just about anything—but Bastian Black had been a pilot of one kind or another since he was Leo's age. Before being captain of the *Icarus*, he'd piloted starfighters for the Coalition. And even before that he used to fly old-fashioned airplanes.

Back on Earth. That gorgeous blue-green marble, third parking spot from the sun. Leo's home. At least the only place he ever called home.

A planet that, like many others rich in V, was in serious danger.

Leo conjured his father's voice in his head. *Do this for me, Leo. It could mean the world.* Those were the last words Calvin Fender said to Leo before he was taken away. The second time.

No. Not taken, Leo reminded himself. He made a choice. He could have gone with Leo or taken Leo with him, but instead he left his son in the hands of these pirates. *And now he's gone*, Leo thought. *Again.* All of them were. Mother. Father. Brother. It was just Leo. All alone.

But not exactly.

Kat spun around in her copilot's chair and fixed the captain with a hard stare. "You know, if you're wrong about this, we could be in even bigger trouble. We're already down to our last core, and the sublight engines are barely clanking along as it is. We're leaking coolant out of the starboard tank and I'm pretty sure we took some significant hull damage high-tailing it out of Halidrin. So if there are no good targets out here . . ."

"Kat, Kat, Kat," Baz muttered. "Why don't you trust me? After everything we've been through. Name one—no thr—name *five* times that I've let you down."

The first mate turned to the robot, still futzing with an electrical circuit. "Skits, access the file labeled History of Bastian Black's Blunders and Miscalculations, Volume One."

"History of Bastian Black's Blunders and Miscalculations, Volume One by Katarina Corea," the bot repeated.

Baz frowned. "Volume *one?*"

"I'm leaving it open for the inevitable sequel," Kat whispered as Skits started reciting from the top.

"'Number one: the time he tried to double-cross that Arzuran arms dealer by selling him a crate full of welding torches instead of actual military grade flamethrowers.'"

"Yeah, I remember that," Baz said with a smirk. "That guy was so ticked. Never seen anyone turn *that* purple before, though he *was* sort of blue to start with."

"'Number two, the time he insisted on bringing a Zarbeast on board and it chewed through the wiring in the weapons systems and short-circuited the entire ship, leaving us all temporarily without life support.'"

"Okay . . . that wasn't smart. But you have to admit that little guy was pretty cute. With those ears? And that pudgy little snout? And that spiky tail? You know I'm a sucker for strays."

"'Blunder number three, the time he accidentally detonated a stun grenade that had been left in his pants pocket, paralyzing him for three—'"

"Okay, Skits, we get the point," Baz interrupted. "So . . . I'm human. Shoot me."

"I can name at least five entire *civilizations* that would like to," Kat countered. "Some of them have even tried."

"And failed."

Kat pointed to the captain's mangled ear.

"Hardly counts. You know what? I don't need this from you. I'm still your captain. Just bring us out of the jump at the coordinates I gave you. You'll see I'm right."

"First time for everything," Kat quipped, but Leo knew she was just giving him a hard time like she always did. There was no one Kat trusted more than Bastian Black. When she was at her lowest point, scrabbling and scraping for her very existence, a one-armed pickpocket trapped in a mining colony, Black had been the one to come along and rescue her. To take her in. To give her a family.

Leo knew a little bit about Black's history too. He'd gotten a glimpse of it secured in a box stowed beneath the captain's cot. The man who had defected from the Coalition. Turned his back on the Aykari. Stolen from his own kind. Though maybe *he* wouldn't see these as missteps. Just decisions with consequences. Or maybe just the only way to get by.

His latest adventure, though—busting into a Djarik research facility to rescue a high-profile prisoner—*that* had turned out to be a failure, though Leo couldn't blame Black for not saving his father. Not when he had the man himself to blame.

At least his father had apologized. *I'm sorry. I have to see this through.* This. Whatever the Djarik had captured him for. Whatever was on the chip Leo's father had slipped him. A way to end the war, Leo was told.

At the cost of whole planets.

"All right, ship rat. Time to strap in," Kat said.

"And try not to blow chunks all over the cockpit again," Skits scolded.

Leo found the seat beside Boo and buckled up, closing his eyes and willing himself not to throw up this time. He couldn't imagine how it could even be possible: the last thing he could remember eating was a crème-filled sponge cake that was somewhere between three and thirty years old. That, and some fake chicken he'd split with his brother, Gareth, the last time the two of them were together. What felt like eons ago, though it was only a matter of days.

"Here we go," Kat said.

A flick of a few switches and the *Icarus* shuddered. The whole ship seemed to shrink and then expand like an accordion, and Leo felt his body doing the same, every cell seemingly turned upside down and inside out before recombobulating itself, all in less than a second. A sharp pain stabbed at the backs of his eyeballs and he felt his stomach lurch, but there really was nothing inside worth getting out. He heard his father's voice inside his head. *It's normal, Leo. No living being was meant to hurtle through space and time like this. Ventasium-based space travel breaks just about every law of physics known to humankind. It's bound to give anyone a tummy ache.*

The first time Leo ever made a jump he'd been holding his father's hand. All three of them threw up. Leo. Dad. Gareth. A Fender family chuck-a-thon. Eventually his father and brother got used to it—the side effects of hyperspace travel. Leo, not so much.

With the jolt and lurch, the *Icarus* reentered the void of space, and Leo found himself staring at the red disk of an unfamiliar planet.